What readers say about BURNT RECORDS:

"I just finished your great mystery book and loved it! I feel I have lost two friends, Colby and Diane. I hated to get to the end of the book."

LISE S. - Tucson, Arizona

"This is to let you know how very, very much I enjoyed reading BURNT RECORDS....You have captured the culture from which we came, fleshed out our history and kept me up late a night captivated in suspense. You creatively crafted the plot...."

DENNIS B. - Waukesha, Wisconsin
(formerly of Atlanta, Michigan)

"During my ninety plus years I have read hundreds of novels. BURNT RECORDS is in the top tier of all of them....A great read."

JON S. - Tallahassee, Florida

"Just a note to tell you how much my wife and I enjoyed your book. It must have been as much fun to research and write as it was to read."

LAWRENCE S. - Glasgow, Kentucky

"A great story well told"

DARRELL B. - Seattle, Washington

"What a wonderful Book! I couldn't put it down. It would make a great movie. Oprah should read it."

VAWN G. - Rogers City, Michigan

"BURNT RECORDS is a great read. It keeps the reader in suspense at every turn. Whenever I put it down I couldn't wait to start reading again. It also gives the reader a sense of how things used to be in northern Michigan."

JOHN Z. - Atlanta, Michigan

BURNT RECORDS

a novel

by: E. Dan Stevens

Advocatus Books

Publishers and Distributers of Quality Books

2804 Walter Scott Road
Tallahassee, Florida 32312
www.advocatusbooks.com
Email: advocatusbooks@cs.com

Email: eharbor@cs.com

Cover design by Tom Young

ISBN-10: 1-59975-893-8
ISBN-13: 978-1-59975-893-0

Printed in The United States of America

This book is dedicated to the memory of
LAWRENCE "TUFFY" MARLATT (1941–1993)
He taught me how to trout-fish
and lots more about growing
up in northern Michigan.

EDS

INTRODUCTION

Tragic coincidence or a well-executed plot? At the time, few residents or officials in Montmorency County, Michigan, suspected foul-play when the County Courthouse, its only newspaper office, and finally the school community building (where the previously undestroyed official county records were taken) were all destroyed by fire within a few months during 1942 and 1943. It was only later, when the effects of the three fires on the ability to do business, own and sell land, and know the County's history became painfully apparent to its citizens, that gossip about the origins of the fires began to surface in Montmorency County.

Most of the early rumors as to who might have set the fires, and why, were based on improbable scenarios.

By the time this writer began practicing law in Montmorency County some thirty years later, the effects of the fires on land titles and other legal issues were still very much a part of the real world. No documentation existed for divorces and other court proceedings, recorded deeds and liens, taxes and other official county instruments filed or kept prior to April 15, 1943, the date of the last fire. Lawyers, bankers, landowners and many others doing business in Montmorency County were affected by the absence of official records in the years following the fires.

The newspaper office fire only compounded the problems. The newspaper archives, dating back to the early years of Montmorency County, had been another source for many of the events documented in the official county records. Too, the newspaper had been the chronicler of most nonofficial happenings of note during the county's first sixty years.

All went up in smoke.

By the 1960's many county residents believed that the fires had been intentionally set; the only questions were by whom and for what purpose. No one had a clue.

BURNT RECORDS is a rendering of this writer's imagination. It features similar fires and events in fictional Montgomery County. It is intended to entertain the reader and does not profess in any manner to suggest a cause or solution to the mystery of the real Montmorency County Courthouse fires.

EDS

PROLOGUE

August 2, 1919, near a lumber camp in northern Michigan

The freight wagon careened and slid blindly along the muddy, rain-soaked lumber camp road, missing cedar trees lining the narrow passageway by mere inches. The young teamster struggling to keep control of the two large dray horses at near-gallop had known fear and panic before, mostly in the Great War. But this was worse. Then it had been worry about his own life as he heard the scream of German artillery streaking above his wagon. Now it was fear for Donna and their unborn child.

A flash of lightning abruptly lit the road ahead. He jumped up and with all his strength pulled hard on the reins, leaning his six-foot, one-inch frame backward to add his full weight to the effort. "Woah!" he yelled at the top of his lungs. His left foot pushed the brake lever down until he was sure it would break, all the while knowing that the steel-rimmed rear wheels were already locked by the wooden brake shoes, sliding through the rain-soaked mud almost as easily as they would roll.

The two big horses were more sure-footed. In less distance than he believed possible, they had managed to stop, in part because they veered to the right, causing the wagon to skid around to the left. Another flash of lightning showed that both horses and wagon had come to rest just inches from the trunk of a fallen tamarack tree which was blocking the full width of the trail.

The doctor he so desperately needed was still a mile away and the tree was more than he could move off the road by himself. Another lightning flash made his decision easy. He saw two more trees across the road ahead; one was huge and lying high on its limbs, too high for a horse, even without a wagon, to step over. He jumped to the ground and quickly lashed the reins to the tamarack. He climbed over the fallen trunks and started running through the mud and rain toward Sparr where the doctor lived.

The pains were more frequent now and lasted longer. She was sure something was wrong, had been since earlier in the day. That's why she sent her husband for help. But now she felt alone and helpless. The wind driven rain pelting the cabin and the frequent flashes of lightning added to her sense of despair. The gusting wind pushed through cracks in the walls of the old trapper's cabin, making the two kerosene lamps flicker. She feared they might blow out.

She heard something outside the cabin, a voice. Had her husband returned already? It seemed too soon. Maybe she was dreaming. Her next pain would start within seconds, she knew. Was the door really opening? Yes, she could see a man, but it wasn't her husband. The pain started, she had to scream, she had to scream. The man came closer. She cried out.

"Donna." The man was standing by the bed, reaching for her. She could also see a woman, a girl really, standing beside the man. The pain started to ebb. She began to hear the man talking to her. She knew him. He was their friend, Walter Kincade.

"Donna, this is Miss Scott. She works in the kitchen over at the lumber camp. We're here to help you."

"Where is my husband? Is he with you? Did he get the doctor?" As a nurse she knew that her time was short unless someone helped.

"He went on to get one, the doctor in Sparr." Jacob sounded calm, but Donna could see he was frightened. "He asked me to stay with you until he gets back. I brought Miss Scott to help. She's the only woman in the camp."

She felt the pain starting again. She had to scream. This time it seemed like it wouldn't end.

When she could finally speak again, she knew that they had to act quickly. "Miss Scott, the baby is breached, I'm sure. I can tell you how to turn it around, but it will be hard. Will you do it? The baby will die if you don't."

Miss Scott moved closer to the bed and looked down at Donna. She nodded.

"Jacob," Donna said, "you'll have to hold me down. When she reaches in and turns the baby, the pain will make me want to quit. You've got to keep me down until she finishes, no matter how much I cry for relief. It's the baby's only chance."

The teamster put the whip to the tall, reddish-brown mare pulling Dr. Lister's carriage back along the lumber camp road toward the downed trees. A flash of lightning illuminated Dr. Lister, his eyes wide, hanging on to his seat with one hand and his bag with the other. The carriage bumped and jumped over the narrow road, often sliding when its wheels hit pockets of the ever-deepening mud. But each time it seemed on the verge of sliding out of control, the driven horse pulled it back on course.

Neither man had talked, except for the teamster's admonishments to the horse, since they left Sparr. Now they were slowing and the teamster said, "The trees are across the road just ahead."

"Can't say I'm sorry to see us slackening," Dr. Lister replied. "I thought we were going over a couple of times back there."

The teamster did not reply, instead concentrating on his search ahead for the downed trees. The night was pitch dark, but the frequent lightning allowed him to see the road ahead well enough to keep going.

Finally, he recognized the dark image of the first of the trunks and branches blocking their way. He pulled the reins and slowly guided the horse and carriage to a complete halt. "My team and wagon is just on the other side of these three trees," he said to Dr. Lister. "I'll tie your horse to this first one so she'll be here when I bring you back. Sorry she'll be in the rain all that time."

"Can't be helped," Dr. Lister answered as he climbed out of the carriage, still clutching his satchel. "These things always seem to happen during the worst weather. Haven't seen a summer storm like this one in some long time."

"Let me walk ahead, doctor. I'll stop and help you cross each tree. The first one is a dandy."

The lightning flashes were becoming less frequent, making the darkness of the night more of an obstacle as they made their way over the blown-down trees. A whinny from one of the dray horses told them they were almost there.

After helping the doctor over the final tree and then up to the wagon seat, the teamster walked around the horses, checking and adjusting their harnesses by feel. He then backed the team, standing between the horses with a hand on each bridle, until the rear of the wagon rested against one of the cedar trees crowding the south side of the narrow road. After handing the reins to Dr. Lister to hold, he pulled himself up on the seat.

"It's gonna be close," he said to the doctor, taking back the reins. With a little flip along the leather straps leading to the bridles, the horses started to move. "Gee, Gee, easy now, girls." He pulled strongly on the right reins to both animals. They walked in unison in that direction, pulling the single wagon tongue running between them around and slowly forward as the harness tightened and began to pull the wagon. For one frightening second it seemed that the tongue might snap as the horses forced the front of the wagon almost sideways, but in the next second they were rolling down the road toward the lumber camp and the nearby trapper's cabin where he had left Donna. He hoped Walter had arrived in time with that cook-lady to help.

"Hang on, doctor. This thing is rough compared to your carriage." With that he snapped the reins again, this time hard. "Get-up, Nell; get-up, Sas!" The dray horses increased their pace to a trot. He snapped the reins again. "Hagh, Hagh!" he yelled. The horses moved quickly to a near-gallop, as fast as he dared take them without upsetting their unity.

The doctor was nearly thrown from his seat at the first bump, but adjusted by placing the bag between his feet and holding on to the seat with both hands.

By the time they had traveled the three miles to the lumber camp the rain had stopped. They could see the cook shack's kerosene lamp for the last quarter mile to the camp, and it provided a guide for the teamster as he turned left before the banking grounds onto the two-rut trail leading to the old trapper's cabin. Reluctantly, he slowed the team as even he began to fear that they might miss one of its narrow turns.

The half-mile to the cabin seemed like it would never end, but finally a faint light became visible among the trees ahead, the reflection of one of the kerosene lamps through the cabin's open front door. The teamster pulled back on the reins, completely stopping the horses before guiding them at a walk across the bridge to the cabin.

He could wait no longer. "Walter, Donna!" he yelled as he jumped from the wagon and ran toward the open door, momentarily forgetting the doctor he was leaving behind.

Walter appeared in the doorway. "Where's the doctor? Did you get the doctor?" he asked.

"Is everything okay? Is Donna okay? I got the doctor. He's on the wagon. I'll get him."

The teamster turned and nearly ran into Dr. Lister who had managed to climb off the wagon and was also hurrying toward the cabin door, bag in hand. At that moment the unmistakable noise of a baby crying came from the doorway, loud and sounding angry.

Walter said, "The baby, it's a boy. I think he's all right. But Donna's not so well. She's breathing hard. You better hurry, Doc."

BOOK ONE

September 3, 1939–April 15, 1943

"O what a tangled web we weave,
When first we practise to deceive!"

SIR WALTER SCOTT (1771–1832)

CHAPTER 1

The nephew carried his coffee, yesterday's Detroit newspaper, and the three letters which had just been delivered by the Ashford mail carrier to the screened porch overlooking the lake. There was no hint yet of the impending northern Michigan fall which would soon turn the lakeshore into a many-colored landscape of autumn leaves on the maples, oaks and elms crowding the water's edge—except where the creek entered. On both sides of the creek's mouth, a scattering of evergreen cedar, balsam fir and spruce trees delineated swampy lowlands. Today, the third of September, everything was still summer green.

The nephew read the headline, "Hitler's Army Invades Poland," with the detachment of someone who expected to be unaffected by it all. After skimming through the rest of the paper, he set it aside, intending to read the war details later in the day. He then turned to the three letters, all addressed to his uncle. He had been his uncle's accountant, personal secretary and overall chief assistant for most of the dozen years since he had been orphaned as a teenager and had come to live with his mother's only sibling. Since his uncle's stroke last winter, he had become his personal valet as well.

Not that he was complaining. His future was far more promising than for most his age in Ashford, he thought. Ashford, the county seat of Montgomery County, was located some 250 miles north of Detroit. Montgomery County had been the center of the vast white pine lumbering industry that had fueled a significant part of Michigan's economy during the last half of the 19th Century. But its once thriving lumber camps and related activities and businesses had mostly disappeared as first the white pine and then the hardwood and swamp timber vanished before the lumberjacks' saws.

In 1939, only a few small operations harvesting second-growth timber, several dozen barely productive family farms and a scattering of fishing and hunting resorts kept the county residents going, not counting those families which had previously amassed fortunes during the timber booms. Many of its sons and daughters, and in fact whole families, had left Montgomery County during the depression to find work in the factories of Flint and Detroit and other areas. The county's population in the summer of 1939 was barely 4,000 souls. His uncle was one of the few who could be described as prosperous.

The first two letters he recognized to be from customers of his uncle's timber business, so he put them, unopened, in his briefcase. He would address the timber orders, which he was sure each contained, when Jack arrived for their daily meeting. Jack would later fill the orders from stock at the log banking grounds on the Detroit and Mackinaw Railroad (D & M) spur north of Ashford, supervising the loading of railroad cars to be shipped to the customers' mills. The nephew would write back to the customers, confirming the shipments and also providing them with an updated list of the log inventory. His uncle had developed this mode of doing business after the large lumbering operations over the last half of the nineteenth century and first thirty years of the present one had depleted most of the sizable timber tracts in the area. He had made a fortune buying tracts of land at depression foreclosures and tax sales, and then finding saw mills around the state to buy the different types of timber salvaged from those lands.

The third envelope had a San Francisco postmark. It did not show a return address. The nephew would not have enjoyed his sip of coffee before opening the envelope had he known its contents. He looked again at the envelope with its bold, almost familiar handwriting, addressed simply with his uncle's name and "Ashford, Michigan." He tore open the flap and began to read.

San Francisco, California
United States of America
August 23, 1939

Dear Father,

I have only learned of you this past year after my mother died and I examined her private papers. I came upon her divorce decree which was issued by the Montgomery County Chancery Court, and also papers by which my stepfather adopted me in Australia and gave me his name. I did not know I was not his real son until after his death. I also came across the two letters which you sent to my mother in 1924 and 1926. Only you know whether she ever answered your questions in them about me.

I have come to America to find you. I don't know if you are still in Ashford, or for that matter if you are still alive, but this is the only address I have. If this letter reaches you, I ask that you meet me when I arrive in Gaylord on the morning train, 11:10 a.m., September 8. If you are not there to meet me, I will make my way to Ashford as best I can and learn what I might of your whereabouts.

If you can be at the train station, I will be wearing a tan colored hat with a feather stuck in the band. The hat is curled on both ends as is common in Australia. I have not seen any like it in America. Also, I have red hair, which must have come from you.

Your son,
David Alexander Baxter

As he read and reread the letter, the nephew felt as if he couldn't breathe; he was actually gasping for air. A cold terror crept over his being. He felt on the verge of complete panic. He wanted to scream. His uncle had never told him about a son or any other relative. He had always believed that he was the only living kin.

The sound of a truck climbing the driveway hill afforded temporary relief from his anxiety. He realized Jack would be coming for their daily meeting. Jack was probably hauling a load of logs cut from the old Fournier property which had been recently acquired for his uncle at a tax sale. He got up and folded the envelope and letter to fit in his vest pocket. He needed time to think.

He went to the door and opened it before Jack could knock. He tried to remain calm as he said, "Jack, I'm not feeling well today."

Jack, a broad shouldered man with a ready smile, seemed taken back at being met in the doorway. "You don't look so good, at that."

"I don't know what's wrong, but it might be a something you could catch. Maybe you'd better not come in. Let's skip our meeting today; come back tomorrow."

"You're right about me not wanting to catch anything. Too nice a day to get sick. See you tomorrow." Jack turned and walked back toward the logging truck. The nephew closed the door, wishing that he had not been so abrupt with Jack.

The old Model B truck didn't always start when it was hot, and he was relieved when after several tries he heard it fire and rumble to life. It eased around the circle driveway and headed back down the hill to the county road.

It wasn't until after the truck's sound had nearly vanished that he remembered the two customer letters. They can wait till tomorrow, he thought.

The nephew found Mrs. Simmons in the kitchen slicing onions for a vegetable soup already simmering on the old wood range. The heat from the wood fire combined with the warm sun coming through the window to produce a hot, stifling kitchen. He could see that her round, full face was flush.

"Mrs. Simmons, why don't you use the new electric range I bought for you, especially on these warm days?" the nephew asked for the umpteenth time that summer.

"I've told you before, the electric stove don't make good soup." Mrs. Simmons, a middle-aged widow, was both cook for the household and Uncle's private nurse. She lived in the apartment over the garage. She didn't clean, except for dishes. Mrs. Irwin came in on Mondays and Thursdays to clean. In addition to the main house, she cleaned Mrs. Simmons' apartment every other week.

Usually the nephew chuckled at the thought of Mrs. Simmons using the wood range on hot days, but he didn't find anything very humorous this morning. "I see Uncle is sleeping," he said. "Tell him I've gone to town when he wakes up." He turned and walked toward the garage before Mrs.

Simmons could finish chastising him for missing lunch and the soup she had slaved over.

The nephew walked woodenly, hardly aware of placing one foot in front of the other. He opened the left-hand garage door, then the driver's door on the big Lincoln Zephyr his uncle had purchased two years earlier. He paused, suddenly aware again. He needed to think, and he needed to start now. He didn't know exactly what he was going to do in town, but he might not want to draw attention to himself. The Zephyr was always noticed. It was one of a kind in Ashford.

The Model A next to the Zephyr wasn't nearly as fancy or comfortable, but it was one of a hundred or so still on the roads every day in Montgomery County and would not stand out. The old coupe started on the first push of the starter pedal. The nephew let it run for a minute, pushed in the choke, adjusted the spark and backed out of the garage.

By 3:00 p.m., when he reached the County Clerk's office in the old wood-frame county courthouse in Ashford, the nephew felt more in control of his emotions. A deep gnawing remained in the pit of his stomach, but he could overcome its effects, he knew, by concentrating on his actions and the purpose at hand.

And his goal was to get information. After all, the letter could be a hoax, maybe even a practical joke by one of his friends who knew that he was someday going to inherit his uncle's business and lands and fortune. His old high school chums, David Green and Bud Jakes, both knew how much he was counting on the inheritance.

But the gnawing in his stomach was real. He didn't believe the letter was a joke.

The assistant Clerk, Joan Farrier, nodded as he walked around the counter and past her desk into the circuit court records vault. His presence here and in the deed records' vault next door was not unusual. Since his uncle's stroke, he had done the land title research necessary for foreclosures and tax land purchases and was often in and out of both vaults.

He heard Joan say into the telephone that Clerk Meston was out of town until Monday next. Good, he thought, I'll have the vault to myself. Joan will stay at her desk to watch the counter.

In the vault, he pulled the folded letter from his vest pocket and reread: "... came across the two letters which you sent to my mother in 1924 and 1926 ..." His uncle had written to his ex-wife as early as 1924. The court indexes were by filing date, one for chancery and one for the other kinds of cases. He was pretty sure that divorces were in chancery, so he picked the 1923 chancery index and worked backward. He felt better after finding listings for several divorce cases in that index. He also found a file in which his uncle was a defendant, but it was a land title case. It looked as if Uncle had a second mortgage on the property which was the subject of that action. The case was settled before trial, but the disposition of his uncle's mortgage was not apparent from the index notes.

None of the 1923, 1922, 1921 or 1920 indexes showed any other actions involving his uncle. He began to feel better. He almost laughed out loud. Whoever had played the joke with the letter was in for it. He would find out and make the jokester pay. Then his heart stopped. It was the last case filed in 1919. He saw it when he flipped open the back cover of the index. Uncle had been the petitioner.

The nephew considered it lucky that the 1918–1920 case files were stored in the fourth drawer from the bottom in the archive file cabinets. It was necessary for the Clerk to have the courthouse janitor retrieve files from drawers six through twelve with the help of a ladder. The nephew pulled out the file drawer and quickly found the file. The top edge was dusty and it appeared to have been untouched since being placed in the drawer. He removed it.

The first document in the file was the petition signed by his uncle. He made himself read the entire document. It confirmed that his uncle had a son named David. Curiously, the petition asked that custody of the son be given to the mother.

He fought the growing panic which made him want to run from the courthouse with the file hidden under his vest. No, he had to think. He heard Joan coming toward the vault and quickly returned the file to its drawer and pushed the drawer closed.

"Do you need any help?" Joan asked as she peered into the vault. "Say, are you feeling all right? You look like you've just seen a ghost."

"No," he mumbled, "or … ah … I mean yes, I'm okay. It's hot in here. I'm going out to get some air. I'm through for today anyway. Thanks."

For two days the nephew did nothing more about David Baxter's letter. He didn't tell anyone, including his uncle, about the letter or his new knowledge regarding the son; his cousin, as he finally admitted to himself. On the first day, he met with Jack and took care of the customer letters from the day before and spent the rest of the morning and afternoon making the August entries in his uncle's account ledger. The next day he drove to the log banking grounds with Jack to get a new inventory. But he couldn't keep his mind away from David Baxter for very long.

On the third day he resolved to address the issues raised by the letter. He had always believed that he was his uncle's sole heir. He was not aware of a will and he had not encouraged his uncle to make one. His uncle was as likely as not to give a substantial part of his property to Jack and others who had loyally worked in the business over the years, he had rationalized. With no will, the sole heir would take all. My god, he suddenly thought, a son would be the sole heir.

As the day wore on, the nephew's mood began to brighten as he resolved to take action regarding the letter. The day itself had started with an early morning rain shower, but by 10:00 a.m. the sun was beginning to shine through the breaking cloud cover. Jack stopped by for a brief meeting, driving his 1937 Chevrolet. Afterwards, the nephew focused again on the problems attendant on the letter, now safely hidden in his locked desk drawer. The desk was actually his uncle's, but since Uncle's stroke he had moved from his small corner desk to the large one overlooking the lake.

Maybe it's not too late for a will, he reasoned. Uncle can still communicate and is usually coherent, especially as to matters from the past. He doesn't always remember what happened last week, but he might be competent enough to make a will—at least he would seem that way to strangers.

That afternoon the nephew sat in the waiting room of Sam Gassel's law office, trying hard to hide his impatience. For many years Sam had been the only attorney in Montgomery County. Sam, his brother David, and his wife Pearl had come to Ashford a few years after the Great War. David operated a clothing store in Ashford and Sam conducted a law practice. Most of the local businessmen retained Sam for their legal work, although they didn't have that much. There was an occasional deed or contract, the latter only when they were involved in a deal with a company from out of the county. Usually the people of Montgomery County dealt with each other by handshake. Most often for litigation, attorneys from Alpena, the county seat of the much larger county to the east, were used. This was partly because Sam probably had represented both parties in the lawsuit at one time or another, and partly because the judges were from Alpena and the Alpena attorneys were considered to be more politically connected.

By the time he was called into Sam's office, the nephew had decided to be cautious. After all, Sam had been his uncle's lawyer for nearly two decades and maybe knew things about his uncle's affairs which he didn't. His caution was wise. Even though Sam was not the attorney listed in the divorce file, it soon became clear that he was aware of the prior wife and son, even though he didn't actually say so.

Rather than pretend that his uncle had sent him to have a will drafted as he had originally planned, after pleasantries and the usual conversation about his uncle's health, he began, "Sam, Uncle said something last night about a will. He seemed to be half asleep, but I think he wanted me to come see you about a will."

He was startled by Sam's immediate response, "I'm not going to talk with you about your uncle's will unless he himself directs me to. He was very emphatic to me that it was to remain confidential, especially from you."

"I-I can't believe …"

"Well, believe it," Sam interrupted. "There are things in your uncle's past that only he and I know about. Ben Willard knew before he died, but now only your uncle and me, and I'm not going against his instructions regarding his secrets."

The nephew recognized the name, Ben Willard, as his uncle's lawyer on the divorce petition. After a pause, Sam continued, "I've probably said too much already. This war over in Europe has me worried. I've got relatives in Warsaw, first cousins. I don't much like Hitler's group. I don't know if I'm thinking straight right now. You need to ask your uncle about the will, not me. And I'd appreciate your not mentioning that I said he had secrets in his past."

"Of course," the nephew replied.

After a pause, Sam went on, "Of course, if I visited and got your uncle's okay I could tell you everything. But as I recall his instructions, he didn't want me to tell you anything about his will until after his death, even if he was to become disabled. Not much more I can say."

The nephew hardly noticed that the rain had started again as he walked back to the Zephyr parked on the main street of Ashford, a half block west of Sam's office. He was stunned by Sam's disclosures. He had believed that he knew everything about his uncle's business and personal affairs. He would have bet no will existed. Of course, only two days earlier, he was absolutely positive that he was his uncle's only living relative.

The rain continued to come down as he drove toward the lake. It was much cooler than only two days before, but the steady rain and heavy cloud cover would likely prevent a frost during the night. The newly paved state road appeared to be slippery, but he hardly noticed. The weather matched his mood. He felt that his world had crumbled. But unlike the weather, he was not at all sure that his personal situation would improve. On the other hand, his own actions could, perhaps, cause some change in his personal situation. He decided to confront his uncle.

CHAPTER 2

The rain continued after the nephew arrived at the lake and into the night. It was more than a drizzle, not falling hard, but not letting up. He forced himself to make a fire in the dining room fireplace and steeled himself to show none of his despondency during the dinner hour. He ate alone as usual, served by Mrs. Simmons. The fire in the fireplace was not necessary for heating purposes, since his uncle had installed a central oil-fired steam heating system just before his stroke, but it did brighten the room in the face of the continuing rainfall.

"Mrs. Simmons," he said as she cleared the table, "don't bother with the dishes this evening. They can wait until tomorrow. It's awful outside. After Uncle has eaten, you go on to bed. I'll sit up with him tonight until he goes to sleep."

Mrs. Simmons didn't argue.

The uncle had spent most of the past eight months in his bed, his body steadily shriveling from its former six-foot, one-inch robust frame. The stroke had paralyzed his right side, which together with his chronic arthritis, made movement away from the security of his down-filled mattress uncomfortable. He had twice allowed Mrs. Simmons and his nephew to maneuver him to the large over-stuffed sofa in the living room, but even the view of the lake from there had not outweighed the pain and difficulty he had experienced in getting to the sofa, and then back to his bed. After the second sofa trip, he had declined all further suggestions by Mrs. Simmons and his nephew to try a third. He had become quite proficient at rolling onto his left side, which not only made the use of a bed pan easier, but also allowed him some comfort as well as relief from the soreness associated from lying for hours in the same position.

He had not made much of an effort to learn to write with his still functioning left hand, but his speech, though slowed and slurred by the stroke, was understandable. He usually slept through most of the daylight hours and seemed most alert and communicative during the evening hours after being fed by Mrs. Simmons. He often urged her to stay or asked to see his nephew as she cleaned up after the meal, usually mashed potatoes and some kind of ground meat. He also liked the tomatoes which Mrs. Simmons canned each summer.

On this evening the nephew wanted very much to inquire about the divorce and the will, but dreaded what he expected would be the answers. He had not yet decided whether to tell his uncle about the letter from David Baxter. He sat in the high backed chair beside his uncle's bed, waiting to speak until he heard Mrs. Simmons leave for her garage apartment. Finally a faint click sounded from the hallway as the back door closed.

"Uncle," he said gently, "are you awake?" The old man's eyes opened.

"I happened on your old divorce decree in the Clerk's office yesterday. I didn't know you'd been married."

His uncle's head turned quickly to face him and the watery eyes narrowed. The bedside lamp was directly behind his uncle's head and cast a shadow which masked his uncle's. The sound of rain falling on the cellar door outside the window became suddenly loud in the prolonged silence.

The old man's voice was soft and slightly slurred when he spoke. "How did you know about that?"

"I was searching the title for the Kincade foreclosure. I had heard he'd been divorced and couldn't find a decree in the land records, so I was looking through the chancery indexes," he lied. "I saw your name and looked up the file."

Again there was a long pause. Finally the uncle began, "Guess you got a right to know. You'd a found out when I died anyway." Another pause. "I didn't want you to quit me, and I know'd you've been expecting to get it all when I go." A look, almost sadness, touched the man's face. "You'll most likely get it all anyways. I doubt they'll ever find him."

"Uncle," the nephew began, but fell silent at the rise of his uncle's left hand.

"I can't tell you if you break my thoughts … it's hard for me to think and talk." More minutes passed. "It started when I was in France … in the Great War." He smiled faintly. "Donna was a nurse, for the Brits. She was from Australia."

The uncle then slowly and haltingly told the story of his marriage and divorce. Surprisingly, his voice seemed to get stronger as the evening wore on. He had met Donna at a social sponsored by some local women's group in the French town near his Army camp. They were both left sitting when a barrel of beer being uncorked drew nearly everyone else outside the hall. Maybe it was because they were both older than most of the other soldiers and nurses that they stayed behind. They began to talk and soon learned that they came from different backgrounds—he, raised since age nine in a Milwaukee orphanage, she, the daughter of a wealthy sheep farmer in New South Wales. But they both had had enough of the war—and France.

After that night, they began to seek each other out whenever they could. A lull in the fighting on the front gave them both plenty of free time. His work as an ordinance supply teamster was not needed when the artillery was quiet, and her work as a scrub nurse in surgery lessened as well. Each became a salve for the other's loneliness. Only three weeks after they met, the announcement came. The war was over!

The giddiness of the following days as the armies and their supporting institutions demobilized probably prompted his proposal—and her acceptance. They were married in a Catholic church in the same small French village where they met, although neither was Catholic. Not being conversant in French, they answered all of the priest's questions in the affirmative during their premarriage conference.

Only eight days after their wedding, he boarded a ship with his unit bound for home. She was scheduled on a ship for soldiers' wives to leave in three weeks. It didn't sail for three months. He arrived in New York on Christmas Eve and waited there for her, foregoing his U. S. Army paid trip home to muster out. He watched every day for her ship. When he learned of its delay, he got a job at a lumberyard stacking lumber. He was lucky; thousands of soldiers were mustered out in New York and soon were living on the streets, with no work or hope of finding work. His foreman at the lumberyard let him sleep on the shavings behind the big planer in exchange for his promise to shovel the shavings into the boiler and start the fire each morning before daylight. His pay was ten dollars for each sixty-hour week.

He checked every few days at the Hudson River wharfs for news of her ship. Finally he learned that it was due on March 22nd.

After starting the boiler fire at the lumberyard as usual on the morning of her scheduled arrival, he hoisted his army bag which he had packed the night before onto his shoulder, checked to make sure the forty-four dollars which he had saved from his final soldier's pay and the lumberyard was secure in the watch pocket of his pants, and left for the docks. When he arrived, the ship was already secured at the landing and passengers were in the process of unloading. He witnessed dozens of joyful reunions along the wharf.

He scanned the crowd already on the wooden pier while trying to closely watch the unloading ramp. Beginning to fear that he might not recognize her, he moved to an area where she would see him while coming down the walkway. Hours passed. Finally the only people left on the pier were a few persons still trying to get their baggage loaded at the loading area at which horse-drawn wagons and gasoline-powered trucks were jockeying to park.

He was frantic. Had she missed the ship? Had she disembarked before he arrived and wandered off to become lost in Manhattan? What if she had decided not to come and had gone back to Australia? How would he find her? He saw a ship's officer walking down the ramp. He asked if any of the passengers were still aboard. The officer said that he thought not. He walked on, but then turned and said that there might be a few passengers still in the ship's sick bay on the second deck.

"I left my bag sitting on the pier and ran up the ramp. On the main deck, a crewman directed me down to the infirmary." The uncle's eyes closed and a frown appeared as he seemed to relive the experience. After several minutes he continued the story.

Donna was in the first berth as he entered the infirmary. He didn't recognize her as he walked in and was almost past when he heard his name called. He whirled around and still did not immediately see that it was she. Only when she spoke again did he recognize her eyes. She was almost chalk white and seemed to be half the size she was when he left her in France. He sat on her bed and took her outstretched hand. She told him that she was going to have a baby. The combination of morning sickness and seasickness had almost done her in. She hadn't eaten since the ship left port in France ten days before.

After talking to the ship's nurse, he left the ship to book a room at a hotel. The first three he came to were full. The fourth had a small room usually used by the hotel janitor. He rented it for a week. Outside, he hailed the first taxi he saw. It was the first time he'd ever ridden in one. He had it wait at the pier while he went to get Donna. He first carried her three bags to the taxi. He then went back on board and carried her off to the waiting car, blanket and all. He put her in the back seat and started to get in beside the driver. Then he remembered his army bag which he had left on the dock when he first went aboard the ship. He went to where he had left it. The bag was gone.

After vainly searching the pier along the entire length of the ship, he returned to the taxi. Donna was visibly shivering from the cold and dampness of the early evening in the unheated automobile. He directed the taxi to the hotel. He carried her up the four flights of stairs to their small room.

Fortunately, the room was warm. It had the same size steam radiator as the regular hotel rooms, but was smaller and in the middle of the building. There was a skylight but no windows. After showing Donna the bathroom down the hall and helping her into bed, he went back outside to find some food. He bought a loaf of bread and some butter from the bakery across the street, and some soup from a cart vendor. The soup was in a glass quart jar.

Donna ate a thick slice of buttered bread and a cup of soup before falling into a deep sleep. He sat and watched her for most of the night. He was afraid to fully face his situation. He was in New York City with a sick and pregnant wife, with only forty-two dollars and the clothes on his back, and with no work. He was sure that one of the thousands of veterans in the city had already taken the job he had abandoned at the lumberyard.

And things got worse. It took four weeks for Donna to regain enough strength to travel. By then he was down to eighteen dollars.

"I went out every day of those four weeks to look for work, except Sundays, but there was a hundred men ahead of me for each job in the city." He paused again for so long the nephew thought he had dozed off. The hall clock had long since chimed twelve times for midnight. Then he asked, "Would you fetch me a glass of that cold milk? I surely like the way that new electric icebox works."

The nephew obliged and also poured a glass for himself. He went back to his uncle's room and helped him sit up enough to drink. He drank half the glass and then lay back down. The nephew was entranced by the story his uncle was telling, even while the knot in his stomach was growing as he began to realize the effect the disclosures were likely to have on his future.

"Then one day I spotted a posting in the paper for loggers in

Michigan," the uncle began again. "There was a New York address promising train fare for able-bodied men. I went to the place first thing the next day. There was a line there, too. I waited for over an hour. As I got closer, I noticed that most of the men were leaving a mite upset. When I got to the desk I found out why. The company was requiring payment for the tickets, and promising to refund the twelve-dollar price when the men got to the lumber camp in Michigan. Most of the soldiers didn't have the money and they'd already been cheated enough times to be plenty skeptical.

"I didn't have twelve dollars with me either, and I started to walk away after I learnt what was up. Then I had an idea. I decided to take a chance. I took the gold watch my father had given me before he died. It had his initials, DOH, engraved on the back, you've seen it. It's in my top drawer. Hasn't worked for years, but it still kept pretty good time then. I offered it as security for my ticket. The agent looked it over and agreed. I think now after the trouble it took me to get it back that he planned to keep the watch, probably expected me to never show up in Michigan. I got the ticket and a receipt for my watch and then high-tailed it back to the hotel to tell Donna."

They used twelve of their last sixteen dollars to buy Donna's ticket. She was still weak, but was able to carry her smallest bag as they made their way to Grand Central Station. The trip to Detroit was scheduled for eighteen hours, but took twenty-two because of a freight derailment near Albany. They had to wait another fourteen hours in Detroit for the next Michigan Central train to Gaylord. That leg made its seven-hour run on schedule. A motor car shuttle took them up to the B.C.G.& A. station on the south edge of Gaylord to the waiting eastbound daily milk train. Forty-five minutes later it let them off at the Sparr crossing. As promised, a K & P Lumber Company wagon was waiting to meet the train.

Two other men got off the train with them and loaded their gear on the wagon. The driver looked skeptical about Donna, but helped her to the front seat beside him. At the lumber camp, three miles east of Sparr, the foreman was more than skeptical; he was emphatic. No woman was staying at his camp!

"The foreman didn't see or didn't care that Donna was with child. It was starting to show pretty plain by then. She was almost as pale and weak looking as she had been on the ship. That was about as bad a moment as I'd ever had. I could see the driver leading the unharnessed team to the shed. I was sure we'd be walking back to Sparr. I had seen a rooming house there when we got off the train. I only had a dollar twenty-five to my name.

"After the foreman left, an old lumber jack, his name was Walter Kincade, came up to us and said that he'd found an old trapper's shack over by the river. He'd been staying there, but he still had a bed at the camp. We could stay there 'till the missus was better, he'd offered. We didn't have any other choices." It seemed as if he chuckled as he thought back. He paused again for several minutes.

The nephew finally broke the silence. "Was Walter related to Jacob Kincade? We're planning to buy his place at the foreclosure sale next Monday."

The uncle raised his left hand to get his nephew's attention, and said, "You buy that place, okay. Then you deed it back to Jacob. No strings attached."

"But, Uncle—"

"No buts about it," his voice seemed as strong as before the stroke. "Jacob is Walter's only son. I owed Walter. Not only did he give us his shack on that dark day of my life, he brought us food every night from the camp mess, until I got some stake to buy supplies. He even gave me some hooks and line and showed me how to catch trout out of the river. You might say he saved our lives." After a pause, he said softly, "He probably did save my son's life. I don't think Donna would have made it without that shack. It was our only house together. She had it looking pretty by the summer. She liked to get flowers and replant them by the door.

"No, you get that place and give it back to Jacob, free and clear."

"Yes, sir," the nephew said, trying to hide the bitterness he felt after all his work in preparing to buy the Kincade place at the foreclosure sale. It had nearly forty acres of good cedar and he had a ready market for cedar. Then he thought, it looks like it would never be mine anyway.

The uncle continued the story, but his voice was noticeably weaker and the pauses longer. He told how he had worked at the lumber camp, although he intensely disliked the foreman, and years later was able to get even, in a sense, although he didn't say how.

K & P moved the camp about five miles further east in mid-July. He asked for and received the job of hauling supplies and mail from Sparr and Heatherton to the new campsite so he and Donna could stay in the old trapper's cabin. He had met K & P's area superintendent while getting his gold watch back from the agent in New York, which not only helped him get the hauling job, but also assisted in his efforts to buy the 80 acres of swamp on which the old cabin sat. They gave him a one-year option to buy it for one hundred twenty dollars.

The baby was born on August 2, 1919. Donna had complications and he went to Sparr for help. The baby was born before he returned, but the doctor he brought saved Donna's life. Donna was weak and sick for almost a month afterwards. He had to bring milk home from Sparr because she was having trouble feeding the baby. It was a boy. They named him David Alexander, the middle name being Donna's family name.

"Jacob was there," he started, "and Mrs...." He stopped in mid sentence and seemed preoccupied with a thought that he didn't share.

After several minutes he continued, "About two weeks after David was born, Donna gave me a letter to mail to her family in Australia. Nearly ten weeks later she received a reply. The next morning she told me she was going home.

"We talked almost all night by candlelight in that old cabin. It wasn't that she didn't love me, she said; it was just that she couldn't stand northern Michigan, at least the part she had seen, the lumber camps and swamp cabins. Even Gaylord didn't please her, although she had seen it only one time, when she was sick following the long train ride from New York. She had taken the train once into Ashford for church, and the ladies there were nice, but she longed for her home in Australia and her familiar family sheep ranch. She asked me to go back with her; her father had sent a draft for four hundred U.S. dollars, more than enough for two tickets. But I let my male pride dictate my response."

He seemed to reflect back with disapproval, a frown dominating his face as he continued to tell the story. He didn't want her to take their son, but he really had no other choice. He could not care for a baby and work too. He would barely have a chance to earn and save enough to exercise the option to get the land he so desperately wanted by working seven days a week for the next year, even without taking the time to be an only parent.

Two days later they caught the eastbound train again. This time they got on at Sparr and rode all the way to Alpena, the end of the line. He held David all the way, hoping that Donna would see how attached he was to his son. She did seem to notice. He thought she wiped away a tear once or twice, but he could tell she had her mind made up. That night they stayed in the Alpena Hotel and made love for the last time. He was surprised at her passion and at his own.

The next morning she presented the draft at the Fletcher Bank for collection and was promised the money by 1:00. The bank needed to wire for confirmation by the draft's guarantor. He and Donna then went to the office of Ben Willard, supposedly one of the best lawyers in Alpena. Ben took them right into his office even though they had no appointment. They explained their situation. Since Donna was leaving for Australia, he would need to be the petitioner so he could testify as to the grounds when the judge made his next monthly trip to Montgomery County. They agreed that mental cruelty would be the closest to a legitimate cause. Mr. Willard promised to have the petition ready for him to sign, and the acceptance of service ready for her to sign, by 1:30. They explained about the draft and promised to have his fifty-dollar fee upon their return.

The baby must have sensed the urgency of the day for he didn't cry once, even though he had ample reason to. They got the money at 1:00 as promised, signed the papers at Attorney Willard's office at 1:30, and caught the westbound train at 2:45. They were at Sparr by 5:30. It was already dark. He had left the K&P wagon and team in the fenced area behind the store. He knew he was in trouble with the company for not making his delivery for two days, but he didn't care at the moment and knew he would probably be fired when he didn't make tomorrow's delivery either.

Donna stayed up all night, first packing and then cleaning the cabin. At first light they headed by wagon for Gaylord. If she had waited to catch the westbound train from Sparr, she would have had to stay overnight in Gaylord to be in time for the next day's Michigan Central southbound train. Instead, he got her there in plenty of time for the southbound that day, the noon train to Bay City. There she would transfer to the overnight Grand Trunk and Western express to Chicago.

They arrived at Gaylord in time to have an early midday meal at the Sugar Bowl Restaurant. Strangely, they didn't talk much. She did make him promise to move one of her potted plants inside for the winter that day when he returned to the cabin. He promised.

In spite of their early start and arrival in Gaylord, they were almost late for the train because of slow service at the Sugar Bowl. At the train they hugged and he kissed his son for the last time. She was visibly crying when she stepped on the departing car. His tears didn't start until he had the team and wagon a block away from the train station. They didn't stop until he reached the cabin.

It was after dark when he remembered his promise about the plant. He took a kerosene lamp and went out to where she had told him to look. He found it easily and set down the lamp to pick it up. He carried it to the cabin and then went back for the lamp. It was then that he noticed the tobacco tin under where the plant pot had been placed. He took it back to the cabin and opened it on the table. It contained a hundred dollar bill and a twenty dollar bill.

He heard from her only once more. She sent a letter about three months later saying that she and David had arrived safely and asking him to send a copy of the divorce papers when everything was final. He wrote to her three times, once the next June to thank her for the money and send the divorce decree, and twice more over the next few years to ask about David. He never heard from or about either of them again.

He used the money to pay off the option for the 80 acres. Harvesting its cedar, tamarack and other swamp timber was his first business venture.

"It's been a rare day since that I haven't thought about Donna and David, wondering what became of them." He then fell silent.

CHAPTER 3

The uncle had finally fallen asleep without ever mentioning his will. The nephew must have dozed off, too. He was awakened by the sounds of Mrs. Simmons in the kitchen making breakfast and washing dishes from the previous evening. He noticed the rain had stopped. After watching his uncle sleep for a few minutes, he went quietly to his own room. He had not told of David's letter even though he had been tempted to at the end.

He lay down on top of his bed and thought of the things which his uncle had disclosed during the long night. He felt totally empty. His previously perceived position in his uncle's life was destroyed by the revelations of last night. The security he had enjoyed when he believed he was his uncle's only family and the principal object of his uncle's love and attachment was gone. Surely, when David arrives, he thought, he'll replace me as Uncle's right hand. It'll be the same as happened to Jack when I came here, only it will happen all at once. And not only in the business; he'll be Uncle's family. I'll only be the nephew—and cousin.

As he was trying to stem the tide of panic which was washing over his exhausted body and mind, he began to think about the loneliness which his uncle must have felt over the past twenty years. Surely, seeing his son would be a great tonic for the sick old man. Slowly, he began to imagine the effect David's arrival would have on his uncle. And he, the nephew, would be the one to deliver the prodigal son; well, maybe not exactly the prodigal son, but akin to that situation. His uncle's feelings toward him would be warmed by his role in producing David. And time was getting short. Tomorrow would be the eighth. His thoughts were interrupted by Mrs. Simmons' announcement that breakfast was ready.

After breakfast he went back to his room and fell sound asleep. He slept until late morning when Mrs. Simmons awakened him to announce Jack's arrival for their daily meeting. The meeting didn't last long; Jack didn't have anything new and the nephew was thinking of other things. He did tell Jack that he was planning to go trout fishing on the East Branch the next day so there wouldn't be a meeting.

On the morning of September 8, 1939, the nephew laid out his fly rod, creel and hip boots on the back porch rail next to the garage. The night before, while Mrs. Simmons had been fixing supper, he had quietly put the old single-barrel shot gun, broken down, in the trunk of the Model A, along with a shovel. His earlier despair was replaced by something approaching exuberance for reasons he didn't fully understand.

At breakfast he announced to Mrs. Simmons that he was going trout fishing for the day, and that she should plan on trout for dinner. He also suggested that he might be bringing a guest. He then poked his head into Uncle's room to tell him, but he heard the slow breathing which he associated with Uncle's sleeping. By 7:30 he had loaded the fishing gear and had the Model A headed west on Old State Road that went to Gaylord by way of Sparr. The new state road was much quicker, and was paved, but it missed Sparr by six miles. Only six years earlier, David Baxter could have taken the train all the way to Ashford, but the old B.C.G.& A. was now the B.C.& G.; the tracks had been removed east of Gaylord when the last Stevens camp harvesting swamp timber at Rattlesnake Creek had closed.

He had been to the old cabin on the East Branch of the Black River many times with his uncle over the years and had always known that it was the place where his uncle had first lived when he came to Montgomery County. However, until two nights before, he had not known its complete history, certainly not the part about Donna and David. Now, as he drove up the old trail in the Model A, the cabin held a more remote place in his feelings, as if it were part of a conspiracy in which he had no part.

After he turned off the ignition, he sat in the car for nearly a minute trying to shake the gloomy feeling which had grown since he entered the yard area next to the cabin. Was he experiencing the loneliness which must have dominated his uncle's life for those years after Donna left with David? Or did his gloom foretell yet more tragedy for the old trapper's cabin?

He finally got out and retrieved the shovel from the trunk. He went over to a wet spot near the riverbank and began to dig. Within minutes he had uncovered and gathered nearly a dozen earth worms from the black, loamy soil. He then put together his fly rod, but instead of choosing a streamer from his fly box, he attached a bare hook to the end of his leader. He then went to a spot nearly a hundred feet upstream from where he had dug the worms. From there he could reach out with the rod to drop the line just upstream of an old fallen cedar tree jutting into the river. After baiting his hook with one of the worms, he swung the line so that the hook and worm fell just off the end of the fallen cedar. The river's flow carried it down into the hole made by the current running under the tree. Within seconds the rod bent and he could feel the brook trout heading downstream with the hook in its lip. He applied enough pressure to slowly bring the fish back under the tree without jerking the hook out of its tender mouth.

Once he had netted the eleven-inch trout and removed the hook, he carried it over and released it in the small spring beside the cabin. Soon he had eight more nice brook trout swimming around the spring. It would have taken him most of the day to catch that many trout using an artificial fly, but of course it would have been much more fun. But he had other plans for the day.

He unlocked the cabin with the key he retrieved from its hiding place under a windowsill and placed the shovel inside. He then went back to the car and got the shotgun. After putting its parts back together, he placed it inside the cabin next to the shovel, against the wall beside the door. He also laid the fly rod across the homemade dining table in the center of the one-room cabin.

He closed the door without locking it and walked back toward the car. On the way he glanced in the small spring pool and watched the nine trout. Only the slowly fluttering gills showed they were alive as they lay near the bottom in the cold spring water. As he neared the Model A he pulled his watch from his pocket and noted that it was 9:45. Just enough time to get to Gaylord and park before the train gets in.

It took the Model A almost twenty minutes to travel over the quarter mile of the two-rutted driveway to the old mill site and the next three miles over the slightly better K & P trail to Sparr. From there, the twenty miles to Gaylord took forty-five minutes over the old state road.

By 11:05 he had found an unoccupied bench from which his view of the entire passenger platform stretching in front of the Michigan Central Gaylord train station was unobstructed. He could hear the train whistle as it steamed over the numerous crossings for roads and driveways leading to the vacation cottages along the western shore of Otsego Lake. He could tell that it would be on time this day. That is good, he thought. Too much time to think might cause him to have second thoughts. He marveled, momentarily, at just how calm and detached he felt about meeting the cousin whose existence was unknown to him just five days before. He quickly reread the part of David Baxter's letter describing the hat he would be wearing. It wasn't clear whether it meant the hat or the feather would be curved at both ends.

It didn't take long to determine that it was the hat. David Baxter was the second person off the train, beaten only by a well-dressed lady who made a beeline to the station. The hat was unmistakable. So was the red hair. The nephew waited for nearly a minute to see if anyone joined David or if anyone else he knew was on or meeting the train. During this time he watched David anxiously examine the few persons on the platform, trying in vain to find his father among them.

After perversely watching the torment for another thirty seconds, the nephew slowly walked up to his cousin and quietly said, "David—David Baxter?"

"Yes." The young man whirled around, his relief evident. "That's me."

"I'm your cousin." He put out his hand. The Australian's grip was firm. David was not as tall as the nephew had anticipated, not more than 5'8", he guessed.

"I rather hoped my father would be here. Is he…"

"Your father had a stroke several months ago," the nephew interrupted. "He's too sick to travel, but had he been able he would have been here to meet you. I live with him and take care of him." He waived a hand at the old carpetbag at David's side. "How much luggage do you have? I only brought a Model A coupe."

"I have a trunk and this bag. I hope the trunk has arrived. I checked it from San Francisco to here several days ago." David had an accent which made it difficult for his cousin to understand. He must have realized that because he repeated with gestures, "Trunk," and pointed to the baggage room. A small brown trunk could be seen through the open door. David walked over to it and examined the tags on the handle.

"Ah, this is it," David exclaimed as he turned to get the attention of the station agent. "It made it here."

The trunk just fit on the shelf above the jack and tire tools in the small Model A luggage compartment. David had to place the carpetbag between his legs on the floor in front of the seat. Not much room in the old coupe—the nephew wished that he had brought the Zephyr, although it wouldn't have made it to the old cabin without hitting bottom several times along the way.

They stopped at the Sugar Bowl Restaurant and each had a plate of beef stew and coffee. As they ate, the nephew told David about his long night with Uncle and the part of the story about David's parents having their last meal together at this same restaurant. He also told David about the old cabin where he was born and the plan to stop there on the way back to pick up the fresh trout and possibly bag a few partridge for supper—and the surprise of bringing David home to his father.

The Model A hadn't traveled a mile out of Gaylord before David was sound asleep. His cousin tried to slow down for the biggest bumps so as not to wake him. David had been almost incoherent from exhaustion after he had finished his stew at the restaurant. That and his strange accent made it hard to follow what he was trying to tell, but now with David asleep in the passenger seat, the nephew reflected on what he had so far understood. He knew of Donna's death from David's letter, but hadn't known that she had been killed in a train accident. But the big surprise was that David had a sister only eleven months younger than he. The sister, Elizabeth, had died from fever at age four, three years after Donna had married Donald Baxter. David had come to believe that Elizabeth, too, was Uncle's child. He was unaware of whether or not Donna had ever communicated any of this to Uncle. In fact, David himself had not known about his real father until after his mother died.

Although he had prepared himself to act warmly with David, the nephew was surprised at how close he already felt toward his cousin. For one thing, his small size and strange accent made David seem far less of a threat to step in and take over his father's business affairs anytime soon. For another, the knowledge of his uncle's years of longing caused feelings of affinity which he had never felt before.

Because he drove slowly to avoid waking David, it took nearly an hour and a half to reach the old trapper's cabin. As he turned down the last quarter-mile–long trail to the cabin, the nephew pulled his watch from his pocket. It was 2:20. He reached over and gently shook David awake.

"We're almost there, thought you'd like to see it as we drive up beside the river."

"Where—where are we, mate?" David sleepily replied as he straightened in the seat. "Oh, these are thick trees—and green. Out the train window, most of them were starting to turn yellow."

"These are cedar trees. They stay green year round. Watch out over on your side. We'll be alongside the river just up ahead. See if you see any partridge graveling on the riverbank. Your father really likes baked partridge, as everyone around here calls them. They are more properly called ruffed grouse, but most of the people I know wouldn't know what you were talking about if you referred to them as grouse. Whatever you call them, I told Mrs. Simmons I'd try to bring a couple home for supper—along with some trout. Mrs. Simmons is our cook and..."

"There—there across the water," David interrupted as he pointed to two birds looking up at the Model A.

The nephew stopped the car. "That's two of 'em, all right. Too bad I left the gun at the cabin. But we'll walk back. There's usually a lot of them out in the afternoon this time of year, graveling on the riverbank."

Slowly he eased the Model A back into motion and over the final bit of trail and bridge to the old cabin. "This is where you were born, David," he said as he braked to a stop in the small clearing that served as the cabin's yard, parking area and turnaround. He glanced at David. Seeing his cousin's expression, he added, "I gathered from what Uncle told me that your mother never could feel at home here."

"It's quite different from anything in Australia," David replied. "It gives me a bit of the creeps, how thick the trees are and all. Even the wet areas back home aren't like this. I can understand why Mother might have been ill-at-ease here. But the river, it's fascinating. Are there any fish in it?"

The nephew led David over and showed him the trout in the bottom of the spring and explained that he had caught them that morning and that they were being kept alive and fresh for supper. "Now," he said, "we need to get four of those partridge to go with the trout. Are you any good with a shotgun?"

"I've never used one, though I've had plenty of experience with a rifle. If you don't mind, I'd like to watch you for a while and then maybe try myself."

"Fair enough," answered the nephew as he opened the cabin door and retrieved the shotgun. He also stuffed six shells into his pants pockets and took one more from the box to load in the gun. As he looked at the shell, and then at the box, he said, "Damn it, brought the wrong box of shells. These are number two shot. I normally use number sixes or sevens for birds. We'll be lucky if we get one without blowing it apart with these. Have to shoot from farther away."

"What's the difference?" asked David.

"It's the size of the shot in the shells. The smaller the number, the larger the balls of lead in the shell. Because they are bigger, there are fewer of them in a two than in a six. The two will go farther and one ball will do more damage to the bird, but the pattern will have a lot more empty space in it, a lot more room for the bird to fly without getting hit by one of the BBs."

"Then why would you need to shoot from farther away?"

"Because a hit from close in would have too many of the larger balls hitting the bird. Too much damage. There wouldn't be enough left to eat." The nephew paused, looked at the shell again and stuck it in the gun barrel. He closed the gun, set the hammer in the safe position, and continued, "Oh well, let's give it a try. We might get lucky."

"Good, let's give it a go," echoed David.

The nephew paused, then went back in the cabin and came out carrying another four shotgun shells. "Here," he said as he offered the shells to David, "we might need some more chances. You carry these, my pockets are pretty full."

David accepted the shells and put them in his pants pockets, two on each side. He then followed his cousin across the bridge and back up the trail along the river.

They did not speak as they carefully walked back toward the place where the partridge had been graveling across the river. David was looking down to avoid stepping on twigs, leaves or anything else which could cause noise when he felt his cousin's hand on his arm. He looked up to see his cousin pointing at a large bird in a tree about 60 feet ahead near the trail. He took the gun offered by his cousin and began to aim toward the bird. He was surprised that the shotgun had no sights like the rifles he had hunted with back in Australia. He started to bring the gun back down when he remembered what his cousin had said about the pattern formed by the several round shot contained in the shell. He placed the gun back to his shoulder, sighted along the barrel at the bird, and squeezed the trigger. The partridge fell from the tree, but his immediate sensation was the impact on his shoulder from the gun's recoil. It felt like someone had hit his shoulder with a club.

"You got 'im," the nephew exclaimed. "Good shooting!"

David's answer was a sound in response to the pain in his shoulder.

The nephew had failed to alert David about the kick of a 12-gauge shotgun. "I'm sorry. I should have warned you. You have to hold the gun tight against your shoulder. That way you absorb the kick instead of giving the gun a head start to wallop your shoulder."

"I'm okay," David replied, although he didn't exactly feel okay. His shoulder was still very much affected by the painful aftermath of the blow it had received from the loosely held gun. "Let's go fetch the bird."

They both walked toward the downed partridge, which they could see lying motionless in the right hand tire rut of the road ahead. As they walked, David broke the gun open as he had seen his cousin do while loading it back at the cabin. He removed the still smoking empty shell from the barrel and tossed it alongside the road. He took one of the shells from his pocket, put it in the barrel and closed the gun again until it clicked, unaware that he should have also pushed the safety button back to the locked position.

"Nice shot," the nephew said as he lifted the dead partridge and examined it. "It doesn't look like more than one or two BBs actually hit this thing. Good deal. This bird is going to be good eating."

"I guess I was lucky. How do you say over here, beginner's luck? In any event, it's your turn for the next one." David held out the gun. He didn't want to admit just how sore his shoulder was from his first shot.

"Okay, I'll try for one," the nephew said as he laid the dead partridge on top of a stump beside the trail. "Hold on to the gun for a minute while I cover this one with some boughs. I don't think a fox or bobcat would take it while we're so close, but I don't trust the hawks that might be flying over."

After he had covered their kill with cedar boughs, he took the gun from David and started up the road again. David followed, still trying to make as little noise as possible. They passed the place where they had seen the two partridge on the riverbank from the car, but the birds were no longer there.

After another two hundred yards, the nephew stopped and whispered to David, "There's a little hardwood island in the swamp on the other side of the river. Almost sure to be some birds there this time of the year. I can cross the river on an old beaver dam up ahead, but you don't have to come. Your boots might get a little muddy on the other side of the old dam."

"That's all right. I want to come with you," David said, although his shoulder still hurt and he wasn't sure he wanted another turn with the shotgun.

The nephew led the way down the bank from the old road to the river's edge, and then downstream another hundred yards to the old beaver dam. The dam was quite old and had not been used by beavers for many years. However, it still appeared solid as it stretched from the near bank to nearly the far bank. The dam itself ended about fifteen feet from the far bank. Through that 15-foot-wide opening the entire river flowed, deep and with a rapid current. An old cedar tree had conveniently fallen from the far bank, and its top and most of its trunk had landed on top of the dam. It quite effectively bridged the gap between the end of the beaver dam and the far bank. Several years ago, before his stroke, the uncle had axed away enough of the limbs to make the tree an easy walkway over the river as it swept around the end of the remaining portion of the old beaver dam.

The nephew was just stepping off the tree onto the mound created by its roots and David was about halfway across when a partridge exploded into flight from the riverbank under the tree. It flew back up the river. As the nephew started to swing the gun around to follow the flying bird, he was conscious of David falling toward him, startled by the partridge's sudden and loud flight. David's hand reached out and grabbed at the gun barrel as it was swung by the nephew toward the fleeing partridge. David's hand failed to catch the gun, but it did make contact. The discharge was deafening.

CHAPTER 4

At first the nephew thought David had merely fallen in the river from the shock of the gun being fired so close to his face.

David would be caught by a sandbar only fifty feet below the dam, and they would laugh together about the "near miss". Then he saw the water around David slowly turning red.

Later he remembered only two things that occurred during the next few seconds. He remembered watching the gun fall into the racing river beneath the tree-bridge, and he remembered David asking, "What happened?"

He didn't remember climbing over the tree roots and making his way down the riverbank, half running and half crawling, to the small shoal, and then wading to pull David from the eddy pool in front of the sand bar where he was floating just below the surface. He actually laughed when David spoke.

He stopped laughing when he saw the blood gushing from David's left hip area. He wasn't especially knowledgeable about medicine, but he knew David would bleed to death if he didn't get medical help soon. Old Doc Lister still lived and practiced in Sparr and was their only chance.

The nephew took off his jacket and belt. He balled up his jacket and held it against the torn flesh of David's side while he tightened the belt to hold it in place. "You must remain as still as possible while I go for help. I'm going to slide you back in the water. I think you'll bleed less in the cold water. How do you feel?"

"Rather odd, but no pain just yet," David answered. "And Cousin, if I don't get to myself, tell Father 'Hello—and goodbye' for me. And tell him I fancy the piece of land he gave me just fine."

"Piece of land?"

"Yes," David answered, still not feeling the pain, "didn't he tell you? He told my mother in one of the letters I found that he had put my name on the deed for the cabin when he had purchased it, I think with money my mother left for him."

This was news to the nephew, but it was unimportant at the moment. "Don't worry, David, you'll be able to tell him yourself. But I'd better hurry to get Doc Lister. I'll be back as quick as I can. Try to be still."

It took the nephew a good five minutes to splash across the river from the sandbar and fight through the heavy cedar undergrowth up the riverbank to the old trail. Once on the trail, he ran back to the cabin and the Model A. It started easily, but before leaving he decided to remove David's trunk to lighten the load on the car springs so he could drive faster on the rutted trail. He did so, leaving the trunk in the cabin yard.

As he hurried the Model A as fast as he dared over the old trail toward Sparr, he began to think about his predicament. He didn't think David would last until he could get back with the Doctor, and he couldn't imagine being able to get David moved from the sandbar up to the road without causing him to bleed to death. The image of telling his uncle that David had gotten this close—only to be killed by him—slowly began to dominate his thoughts.

At the old K & P lumber camp site, where the cabin trail came out to the Sparr road, the nephew stopped the Model A. He knew he should be hurrying toward Sparr to get Doc Lister and as many other men as he could to help move David from the sandbar where he lay. In the back of his mind, however, he was sure that David would not survive no matter how much help he brought back.

How would his uncle react to learning that David had been this close? Would the news kill him? It would certainly cause the ultimate heartbreak. Would he believe that the failure to tell him of the letter and his son's impending arrival was done to enhance the surprise—or to hide a furtive scheme that led to David's death? For that matter, would Uncle—and everyone else—believe that the shooting of David was an accident? All of the circumstances would appear suspicious, even down to the number-two load in the shotgun shells.

Then the nephew intuitively knew why he was so concerned. When he had first found out about David, he had in fact been thinking of doing just this.

As the realization of what had happened, and of his personal dilemma, began to sink in, the nephew fought the growing panic which made him want to flee and never look back. He knew that running would be disastrous, so he concentrated on overcoming the desperation boiling in his stomach. He also knew that the right thing to do would be for him to hurry to get help—and pray for a miracle. But he didn't believe in miracles. No miracle had occurred when his own father lay dying after a farm accident when he was six, nor had one prevented his mother's illness from taking her away nine years later.

So he sat in the Model A at the old lumber camp site and forced himself not to think of David laying on the sandbar in the river bleeding to death, if not already dead. Instead he concentrated on his own predicament. Had he told anyone about David's letter or expected arrival in Ashford? He was sure that he hadn't. Would anyone have recognized him in Gaylord with David at the train station or at the Sugar Bowl? He remembered actually watching at the train station, and he was sure that he would have noticed a familiar face in the restaurant. He began to believe that it would be better if his uncle—and everyone else—never learned that David Baxter had come to Northern Michigan. David himself had said while they were eating that he had no family back in Australia and that he didn't plan to return.

So instead of hurrying to get help, which he considered futile anyway, the nephew slowly drove toward Sparr. There he phoned Mrs. Simmons from the public phone in front of the store to say he would be staying overnight at the old cabin and that he had been unable to get the trout and partridge which he had promised for supper. He also told her that the friend he thought might join them for supper could not. He said that he would try to get some trout tomorrow. He was relieved that no one came out of the store who might have wondered why he was all wet. He had left his jacket with David, but there were a few bloody areas on his pants which might have been recognized as such, although daylight was fading.

When he got back to the place on the cabin trail where he had climbed up from the river near the old beaver dam, he stopped the car and got out. It was completely dark now. Rain clouds had formed late in the day, although it had not rained yet. Even though the noise of the river rushing past the beaver dam would have made it impossible for David to hear the car as he had driven in, or for him to have heard David crying out, he listened for a minute. He heard nothing and got back in the Model A and continued on to the old cabin.

At the cabin he left the car lights on while he searched for a kerosene lantern. He found one on the shelf beside the old wood range and lit it with a match from the match jar on the same shelf. He then lit the two kerosene lamps hanging on the wall opposite the cabin door, one on each side of the bunk beds.

For the first time since the accident he realized he was still soaking wet—and cold. He stripped and put on an old wool shirt and some pants that he found hanging next to the bunk beds, probably left there by his uncle during some fishing trip in the past. The dry clothes helped, but he didn't really start to feel warm until he had a good fire going in the old wood range, a less spectacular but quicker way to heat the cabin than the fireplace.

The warm cabin did not, however, dispel the gloom which once again was threatening to immobilize him, or worse, cause him to flee. He had to get control of his emotions if he was to avoid becoming an outcast from his uncle's home—and perhaps a convicted criminal. He allowed himself to wonder if David could possibly still be alive. He admitted to himself that his stopping to listen on his way back to the cabin had not given him a clue because of the noise of the rushing river. But he was pretty sure David could not have lasted this long, even had he promptly found and returned with Doc Lister, even a sober Doc Lister. He convinced himself that he was right on that issue.

Should I go bury him tonight, or wait until early in the morning? He had already decided on his way back from Sparr that it would be easiest and best to bury David's body on the hardwood island in the swamp near the river sandbar, the place they had been heading to when the accident occurred. The island consisted of dry sandy loam which would not only be easier digging than the swamp muck, but would allow the body to decay faster as well. It would also prevent the possibility of the body floating to the surface during the spring melt following a winter of heavy snowfall, which could occur in the wet muck closer to the river.

"I don't need to hurry," he told himself, this time aloud. "It will be a hundred times easier in daylight." The only risks in waiting that he could think of were the possibilities of someone accidentally coming by the cabin in the morning or animals feeding on the body during the night. He decided that the former was not a significant risk, and the latter highly unlikely since most of the scavenger animals would avoid fresh human scent. Even if animals did approach the body, he reasoned, it would not be the end of the world.

David's trunk and carpetbag were another matter. He would burn them in the fireplace tonight, together with their contents.

The process took almost two hours. He first built a roaring fire and then threw the clothes and other burnable items from both the trunk and bag on top. Next, he burned the carpetbag itself, consisting of wool fabric and wooden handles. He chopped up the trunk and placed the pieces in the fire. He would pick out the hinges and locks in the morning. The only things he saved from the fire were a metal brush and comb and two bottles, one of cologne and one of shampoo. He also saved a small leather satchel containing some papers which he had found in the bottom of the carpetbag.

After he watched the last of the trunk debris finally become indistinguishable in the glowing coals of the fire, he turned his attention to the satchel. He soon determined that the lantern alone did not provide enough light to read some of the faded documents he pulled from the satchel, so he removed one of the lamps from its holder on the wall. He had to use potholders to avoid burning his hands on the lighted kerosene lamp.

The largest document he discerned to be his uncle's divorce decree. He also recognized his uncle's writing in the two letters written to David's mother, one dated December 12, 1924, and the other December 8, 1926. In the 1924 letter he told her of putting David's name on the cabin property deed.

He also found a copy of David's birth certificate issued by the Montgomery County Clerk and a partially completed U.S. passport application. The remaining papers consisted of a used steamship ticket and his declarations stamped by U.S. Customs and Immigration Services on August 22, 1939.

Should he burn these, too? He knew the only proof in existence that David Baxter had ever reached Montgomery County was spread before him on the table. Even if they found his body, it would never be identified without these papers or those which might be on his body. He had already planned to go through David's pockets in the morning, of course.

Somehow he was reluctant to destroy these last vestiges of his uncle's son—his cousin—of a life which had begun in this very cabin twenty years before. "It's no time for sentiment," he said aloud, but after staring at the papers spread on the table for several more minutes, he placed them back in the satchel and hid the satchel under the mattress of the top bunk.

It was after midnight when the nephew lay down on the lower of the two bunk beds. His sleep did not come easily or without dreams. Once he awoke with a start after the image of the gun falling into the river from the cedar tree-bridge floated in slow motion through his dream again and again.

He was finally awakened for good by the sound of heavy rain falling on the cabin roof. He could see through the window over the kitchen counter that it was beginning to get light outside. Two of the three kerosene lights were still burning; one of the wall lamps had run out of kerosene. He was grateful to be relieved from the horror of his dreams. But then his mind remembered the real horror of the day before, and he could feel the panic starting to creep back. He realized that his hands were trembling.

Again the nephew was able to force the anxiety to subside by concentrating on his plans from the day before. He also became aware that he was hungry. He hadn't eaten since the Sugar Bowl in Gaylord, an event which now seemed like the distant past. He rekindled the fire in the cook stove and then looked in the old cupboard cabinet for food. He found a can of beans and a can of corned beef. He opened both and mixed them in a frying pan which he placed on the heating stove. Ten minutes later the bean juice was starting to bubble. He sliced the meat and mixed the pieces into the beans. He stirred the concoction every few seconds until he was sure the meat was hot. He then placed the pan on a potholder on the table, sat down and ate the whole thing.

It continued to rain steadily, but somehow the nephew felt strangely pacified by the thought of carrying out his gruesome tasks in the rain. He decided to dress in his clothes from yesterday, even though they had not dried much where he had hung them beside the fireplace. The worst would be putting them on.

The nephew stood on the beaver dam, holding the shovel, and looked down the river at David. His body was no longer partially submerged in the river as he had been when the nephew left for help. David had apparently pulled himself up on the sandbar and then crawled over to the riverbank near the trail. From the blood around where he lay he must have been there for some time.

The nephew stood on the dam for several minutes trying to decide whether to drag David over to the island before he dug, or to dig first and then move David. He finally decided to dig first. There was no chance that anyone would be out in this rain, and he wanted to get the hard work done before he actually dealt with David's body. He looked down once more at David. At first he thought one of David's arms was in a different position than when he had first arrived, but quickly decided that his nerves were playing tricks.

He continued across the cedar tree-bridge and worked his way along a deer trail to the hardwood island, some fifty yards from the river. The rain wasn't as cold as he had expected, although he continued to be chilled from his wet clothes. Forty-five minutes later he had finished a hole some four feet deep which he judged to be large enough for David's body. He climbed out, stuck the shovel in the mound of dirt beside the hole and wiped the rain from his brow. He wished that he had worn a hat. There was no reason to wait. He wanted to get this over with.

On many occasions over many years, the nephew would try to separate reality from nightmare when recreating the events of the next few minutes in his mind. When he reached David on the other side of the river, David's body was still warm, in fact, at or near the temperature of his own body. It was immediately clear to him that David had been alive through the night and at least until the few minutes before he got to the body. He was never sure, however, whether he had imagined because of this realization, or had actually heard, David say, "Father—cousin, why?"

This time panic won. The nephew ran and crawled through the cedar thicket up the river and then back up the bank to the old trail. It was only because he was completely out of breath that he lay where he had fallen on the top of the bank at the edge of the road, his left arm submerged in the muddy rut. This was it, he deserved to die right here. He could have saved David, he realized, had he gone for help yesterday as he should have. He had to go back for David, right now.

But now it was too late. Not only could he find no pulse, but David's body seemed to have noticeably cooled. Still, it was clear that death had occurred this morning rather than the previous afternoon.

Through the remainder of the day and into the evening, the nephew acted with a detachment and efficiency which he would later, upon reflection, find almost unbelievable. He dragged David's body along the deer trail to the island mound and rolled it into the hole. His only remembered mistake of the day was that he thought to remove David's wallet and the few coins in his pockets only after the body was in the hole. It would have been much easier to have done so earlier rather than having to climb down in the grave and turn the body over while he removed the items.

A second mistake he missed at the time, but years later would worry about when he couldn't find his own belt with the initialed buckle, was that he didn't make a final inspection of the grave before covering the body. He also worried many times later about not destroying all of David's papers the previous evening. Instead, after refilling the grave with dirt and placing old limbs to disguise the recent activity, he made his way back to the cabin and quickly examined David's wallet. It contained two American ten dollar bills and another four one dollar bills and a picture of a girl which the nephew judged to be about David's age. He turned the picture over but saw no writing. The wallet also contained a card stamped by the United States Immigration and Naturalization Service showing the he had entered the country on August 22, 1939.

After removing and pocketing the money, he placed the wallet in the satchel with David's other papers. He then placed the satchel in an old cookie tin and fitted the lid on tightly.

Next, he took the cookie tin and the shovel around to the back of the cabin to the place where his uncle had once told him they had buried garbage. There he began to dig. The digging was fairly easy, although his shovel hit a number of cans and bottles along the way. The cans were rusty and most of the bottles broke when struck by the shovel. It wasn't long before he had a hole three feet deep, large enough for the cookie tin. He then went back in the cabin and removed his wet and blood stained clothes and redressed in the dry ones from the previous evening. He went back out and placed the removed clothing on top of the cookie tin in the hole and replaced the dirt, careful to camouflage the digging activity. He then took his landing net and caught eight of the trout from the spring and cleaned them on the spot.

"I had better luck today," the nephew said to Mrs. Simmons as he laid the eight brook trout on the kitchen table. "And I know Uncle still enjoys trout. I bet he'll eat two. That leaves three for you and three for me."

After dinner, he went in and sat with his uncle. He told the uncle about his concocted poor day of fishing the day before and about the condition of the old cabin. He was relieved when the old man dozed off. He then walked to his room and went right to bed, falling asleep immediately.

The next morning the nephew approached his business responsibilities with an intensity that had been lacking over the previous several days. He spent the weekend catching up on the accounting which he had recently let slip. He even insisted that Jack come over on Sunday afternoon to review expenditures he thought to be too high. On Monday he attended the Kincade foreclosure sale and bought the property with the high bid, though less than the bank's claim. He found that he was excited about going back to describe to his uncle the happiness and appreciation shown by Jacob when he delivered the deed to him following the sale.

It would be a long time before the nephew allowed himself to dwell again on thoughts of David Baxter or the events of September 8th and 9th.

It couldn't be. Helen stared at the ceiling of her bedroom wishing that sleep would come; no, wishing that she would wake up and find that it was all a dream. Could it happen the first time? She had been so sure that loving David was the right thing to do. It was going to be such a long time before she would see him again. He said he might never return to Australia and had vowed to bring her to America as soon as he became established there.

But she hadn't counted on this. It had been nearly seven weeks since that night and she had not had a monthly since two weeks before then. If only she could talk to her mother to get advice and support. She was so alone. She would have to talk to her mother—and father—sometime. It would not be pleasant. Oh, if only David would send for her—and soon.

CHAPTER 5

Sam Gassel's law office burned to the ground on Christmas eve, 1939. Almost everyone in Ashford and the surrounding area suspected arson, and more specifically, that it was the work of Hans Kohler and his son, Warren. Hans and Warren were outspoken German sympathizers. During the Great War, Hans had stolen a great quantity of rail from an abandoned railroad spur and thrown it in the bottom of a small pond on his farm to prevent its use in the Allied war effort against Germany. Even before the invasion of Poland, on the other hand, Sam Gassel had been very vocal about his disdain for Germany's Nazi government. He was an early and ardent interventionist. His letters printed in the Montgomery County Gazette were often answered by one of the Kohlers, often with blatantly anti-Semitic arguments.

Most of the people in Ashford had little knowledge of the Jewish religion, Jewish history or of the present situation in Europe. They knew Sam Gassel only as a neighbor and leading citizen of the town. For that reason, at least, most of the area residents were displeased with the letters written by the Kohlers which quite clearly were personal attacks on Sam Gassel and his heritage. Many too were aware of Hans' unpatriotic acts during the last war.

Sheriff Charles Green, generally thought to be a competent law officer, had no arson training and was unwilling to call in the State Police from Alpena on Christmas Day, particularly when his only evidence was based on rumors. So the question of whether or not Sam Gassel's law office fire was the result of arson by Hans and Warren Kohler, or anyone else, was and has remained a matter of conjecture.

During the first week of January, 1940, a hand-written letter from Sam Gassel arrived at the lake house addressed to the uncle. As was usual, it was opened and read by the nephew. It stated that all of the uncle's papers which had been held by Sam Gassel, including the will, had been destroyed by the fire. It stated that Sam was setting up a temporary office in the Ashford Hotel and suggested that the uncle telephone for an appointment to redo his will and talk about any other lost papers that would require some action to replace. Sam volunteered to come to the lake to meet with the uncle to accomplish such matters at the uncle's pleasure.

The nephew reread the letter and then folded it and placed it in one of the slots on his rolltop desk. He would say, if asked, that he had placed it there to discuss with his uncle soon, but had forgotten about it. As it turned out, his uncle never raised the subject of his will and Sam Gassel left Ashford without again contacting the uncle, at least so far as the nephew was aware.

Only two weeks after the letter to the uncle, the Gazette published one final letter from Sam Gassel, a long one which took up most of the editorial page, in which he said his farewell to Ashford. He mentioned the fire but made no accusations. He thanked the community for its support, but argued that much of the rest of the world was a place of intolerance for Jews and many other religious and racial minorities, the most heinous of all such places being Germany under its Nazi rulers. He ended by saying that he had enlisted in the Canadian Royal Air Force, and that he would be going to Europe to help fight the Nazi monster. Pearl, his wife, would be moving to Detroit to live with her sister while Sam was at war. Following the letter was a brief editorial by the Gazette's publisher, Frank West, in which he attempted to thank Sam for his service to the area. However, his effort to pacify Hans Kohler at the same time made the editorial seem insincere.

The uncle read the letter in the Gazette, and even commented that the county would miss Sam, but still said nothing to his nephew about his will.

It wasn't long, however, before Sam Gassel's name was again featured in the weekly Gazette. Late in June of that same year, a prominent front-page story reported that Sam had been killed as a member of a crew whose airplane was shot down over the English Channel as it ferried allied soldiers from the French town of Dunkirk to escape the German invasion of France.

Later that same summer, sometime during the night of August

11–12, the uncle died. Mrs. Simmons tried to wake him for breakfast, but quickly realized he was gone. He looked as if he had been in the middle of a pleasant dream. She summoned the nephew, who looked down at the stroke-emaciated body. A slight smile was frozen on the face, and he wondered if Uncle had been dreaming about his son. The thought was fleeting.

The nephew was truly surprised at the turnout for the funeral. Every seat in the Ashford Congregational Church was filled, including some folding chairs which were placed in a row behind the last pews. Jack asked if he could deliver the eulogy, and did so with unanticipated eloquence. Jacob Kincade rose following Jack and gave another, impromptu, eulogy, awkward but moving as he described the uncle's long relationship with his father and gave a tearful account of the uncle's return of the foreclosed land just the year before.

On the morning following his uncle's funeral, the nephew rose early. He had given Mrs. Simmons a week off to adjust to her loss. She left right after the funeral to go to her sister's home in Alpena for the week. He searched the one place where his uncle had denied him access during his lifetime, in the boxes under his bed. There he found a copy of the old divorce decree, David's birth certificate, with his uncle's surname instead of Baxter, and a copy of the will, with notations that the original had been executed on November 2, 1933 by the uncle and witnessed by Walter Kincade and Sam Gassel. Another notation indicated that the original will was being held by Sam Gassel, counselor-at-law.

He read the will. It provided $2,000 to Mrs. Simmons, $5,000 to Jack, $5,000 to him, and the rest of the estate to David, provided that David could be located within one year following his uncle's death. A provision provided $800 as expenses for the executor to travel to Australia to search for David. Sam Gassel was named to be the executor. In the event David could not be located within the year, the residue would go to the nephew.

It was not cold, but the nephew built a fire in the fireplace. He burned the divorce decree, David's birth certificate, and the copy of the will. He thought briefly about the papers in the tin buried behind the old cabin, but did nothing about them. He could find nothing else in the boxes which mentioned the uncle's marriage or David. He then remembered the letter from Sam Gassel which he had placed in the slot on his own desk. He found it and burned it, too.

After completing these tasks, he made a pot of coffee on the electric range, using the smaller of the two aluminum percolators. As the coffee perked, he thought about his next step. He knew that he had to address all of the factors and risks which existed or might crop up with regard to the inheritance of his uncle's estate. This meant he would have to retrace the details of David Baxter's arrival and death, a subject which he had successfully blanked from his mind since the two tragic days last September. If he made a run for the estate and a copy of the will was discovered, or even the fact that his uncle had a son came to light, the Probate Court would look for David. An investigation might soon discover that David had come looking for his father, and could connect him in some way. It was even possible that a thorough search of the cabin area might turn up David's grave, or the gun, or who knows what. He knew that nobody would now believe that David's death was an accident. He had to be sure he was on safe ground before pursuing the inheritance.

Other than the documents in David Baxter's satchel buried behind the cabin, which he considered to be safe and under his control barring an active search, the nephew knew of only three existing documents which might spoil his plans were they to be discovered. They were David's birth certificate, his uncle's divorce file, and the recorded copy of the deed to the 80 acres on which David was listed as the joint owner with his father. All of those documents were located in the Montgomery County Courthouse. Except in one possible event, the nephew decided that it would be extremely unlikely any of those documents would ever be discovered. That one event would be the preparation of an abstract of title for the sale of the 80 acres. If everything worked as he planned, he would be able to prevent the sale of the 80 acres and thus prevent a title search which might uncover the deed containing David Baxter's name.

The sound of a truck pulling into the circular driveway interrupted his thoughts. He looked at the coffeepot. He could see from the coffee visible through the glass bulb on top that he had let it perk too long. He turned the burner off and placed the pot on a cold burner. The perking stopped. He walked to the front door to greet Jack.

"I didn't know whether you'd be coming today, but I'm glad you did. Let's sit out there," he said, motioning toward the screened porch. "You want some coffee?"

"Sounds good," Jack responded.

"I think it's gonna be pretty strong. Mrs. Simmons is in Alpena with her sister for a week. I'm having to learn all kinds of things just to stay alive. Would you like cream?"

Jack chuckled. "No thanks. I've been drinking camp coffee on and off for thirty-five years, ever since I was fourteen. It got better after I went to work for your uncle, eighteen years ago now. He was pretty good at making coffee on any kind of old wood stove. Taught me, really. And then for the last ten years I've usually had Mrs. Simmons' coffee once a day. But I still remember the old days and what we drank. I'll be able to handle yours."

The nephew poured two cups of coffee from the pot and they walked to the porch. They took side-by-side wicker chairs with cushions.

The nephew began, "Your eulogy was very moving. I know that Uncle would have appreciated your remarks—and your stories about the old days. I'm obliged." He knew he shouldn't ramble and didn't want to appear anxious during this particular conversation with Jack.

"Thanks." Jack took a sip of coffee and grimaced. "You're right about this being strong. I liked what Jacob said. Your uncle was like that; he always remembered his friends. I know he's taken care of me pretty well over the years, made me a comfortable life. And he was easy to work for. I can't remember ever being in an argument with him that got nasty, or where he pulled rank, even though we disagreed a fair amount, especially in the early days till I learned that his ideas usually worked out pretty good."

"Jack, I'm sitting here this morning trying to figure out what to do. It's funny, I never talked to Uncle about what was supposed to happen after he died, even though we both knew that he wasn't going to be around forever after his stroke. Has he ever mentioned a will to you?"

Jack thought for a minute. "Seems like he was going to see Sam Gassel about a will, maybe six or seven years ago. But I just recollect him having the appointment—he came out to ask me some things about the business and mentioned that he had plans to talk to Sam about a will. He never told me afterwards whether he made a will or not." He paused. "I guess you can't find out from poor Sam anymore and I understand that all his papers and customer records were destroyed in the fire." He thought for a few seconds. "You know, I got a letter from Sam after the fire saying that an abstract of mine he was reading was burned and suggesting that I get another one made up by the register of deeds. I wonder if your uncle got a letter about any of his records that got burned up. Have you looked through your uncle's papers for a letter like that—or even a carbon of a will?"

"Oh, I would have seen a letter like that from Sam when it came, and none came for Uncle," the nephew lied. "And I've looked through every paper in this house—this morning—and I can't find a will or anything about one. I'm surprised because I'd have thought he might have left something for you. I know he felt that way."

Jack looked up quickly, but said nothing.

The nephew continued, "As far as I know, I'm his only living kin. I think the law is that I'll get everything he had, that is, after lawyers and taxes. If that's so, I'll give you something. That'd only be right."

"Don't worry about me, son. Your uncle took good care of me over the years. I don't need nothing else."

"We'll see."

They sat in silence for several minutes, most of the coffee still in the cups. It was pretty strong.

"As far as I know, you are his only kin," Jack said, "but old Walter Kincade once told me your uncle had a wife when he first came to these parts. They lived out in that old cabin that he had on the East Branch. I guess she only lasted about a year or so. Walter said she left for home, some foreign country. I think he met her in the first great war. I imagine they must have got a divorce, I think that's what Walter said. Too bad he's dead; he'd remember more details." He paused. "But like I say, as far as I know you're his only kin left."

The nephew tried not to show his elation. Jack had no knowledge of David. They talked some more, mostly about the business and how they would run it for the next few months. Sales and prices were starting to pick up. The war created a demand for many of the hardwoods in their inventory, but it was becoming more difficult to find lands with timber at tax and foreclosure sales.

When Jack left, his coffee cup was still half full.

The nephew's first concern the following week was the will. Did anyone else know about it? His second was David. Did anyone else know that his uncle once had a son? It seemed improbable that anyone would know about his daughter, at least in this country, since Uncle himself had apparently never known. If he satisfied those two concerns, he reasoned, he wouldn't have to worry about what happened last year out at the East Branch. He was worried, of course, but he needed to get beyond that. He had to be able to recall everything David told him that day. He wanted to be able to think about the first part of the day without bringing back the image of his gun falling in the river or of him sitting in the car instead of going for help. He would make himself. What was done was done.

But the will was easier and required attention first. He was pretty sure that there would have been two carbons, but he guessed that Sam would have kept one for his file to use after the original was sent to the Probate Court for administration. That one, plus the original, would have been destroyed in the law office fire. If not, why the letter from Sam suggesting a replacement will? The other copy he himself had burned this morning.

He decided to make a list of the loose ends that he needed to tie up in order to fulfill his plans. He would burn it when he was through. He labeled the first column "Will." He was satisfied that the only person who might interfere by knowing about the will was Mrs. Simmons, so he wrote in her name.

The next column he labeled "David." In that column he wrote "Mrs. Simmons," "Jacob Kincade," and, after some thought, "Australia." He included Jacob's name because his father had known Uncle and Donna and probably would have known of their son. Walter might have said something over the years to Jacob, or for that matter, to anyone. For an instant, the nephew was overwhelmed with the possibilities that might wreck his plans. But he fought back the panic. He had come this far. There would always be some risk.

He forced himself to go back over all of his conversations with David after picking him up at the train station. David had said several times that he had no family back in Australia. Both his mother and stepfather had died, as had his sister. He didn't mention anyone else. In fact, David had specifically said that he hoped to stay here in the States. There was the picture of the girl in his billfold, but for all the nephew knew it could have been a picture of Donna. He again went over his conversation with David at the Sugar Bowl and then crossed "Australia" from the list.

He drove the Zephyr to town late that afternoon. After picking up the groceries he needed from Doty's Store, he drove two blocks west and parked in front of the Ashford Hotel. He might as well get a good meal while he had the chance. Mrs. Simmons wouldn't be back until Monday.

After his supper of roast pork, mashed potatoes and string beans, topped off with bread pudding, he drove toward Jacob Kincade's place. Several people had stopped by his table during supper to express their condolences about his uncle, and the owner had offered to buy him a drink in the hotel bar afterwards, but he declined. He wanted to be sober when he talked to Jacob.

The long northern Michigan summer days were starting to get shorter, but plenty of sunlight remained when he pulled into the Kincade place. Jacob was just coming out of the barn carrying a pail of milk toward the house. He greeted the nephew warmly.

"Have you had supper? We just finished, but it's still warm."

"No thanks," the nephew replied. "I just ate at the hotel. Mrs. Simmons is gone for a week and I may starve before she gets back, but not tonight. You know, Mrs. Downing makes the best bread pudding at the hotel. I may sneak into town for some of that even after Mrs. Simmons gets back."

"Come on in," Jacob invited. "The young'ens have to get this milk strained and bottled and I know the Mrs. would want to say 'hello.'"

"Okay, just for a minute. Then I'd like to talk with you for a minute, about Uncle, if you've the time."

Inside, the greetings were also warm. Apparently the whole family knew about the uncle's role in saving their home. They were equally grateful to the nephew. Jacob sent their oldest son down to the spring to bring back a bottle of cold milk. After pouring two tall glasses full, Jacob led the way to the back porch and the two hewn benches facing west. It wasn't a lake, but the nephew had to admire the view of the sunset over the valley created by the meandering Hay Meadow Creek, and said so. He could see why Jacob and his family liked it here. He could also see why Jacob had a hard time making a living from the sandy soils of the glacial hill on which his farm was situated.

"I wanted to thank you for your kind words at Uncle's funeral. They meant a lot to me and I know Uncle would have been pleased."

"I meant every word," Jacob answered. "Daddy always said what a good person your uncle was, but I never really knowed it till he, and you, got our farm back for us."

"Jacob, I've wondered a lot about Uncle in the olden days, about when he first came here. I know that he and Walter were friends back then, but I don't know much else about it. Did your daddy ever talk much about Uncle?"

"Well, I knowed they worked together at the old K & P camps and were friends." Jacob paused while he thought for several seconds. "And I knowed something bad happened to your uncle back in those days. Daddy always said that he got a raw deal out of life, but I don't recollect ever hearing why. In fact, I remember once after he'd had too much to drink, Daddy said your uncle's secrets were his secrets. He said it three, four times, but I never knowed what he was talking about."

That night when he got back home, the nephew poured himself a rare drink, rye whiskey from a bottle which his uncle had kept for years and water, and sat down at the big desk. He got out the list and crossed off "Jacob Kincade."

He spent most of Wednesday and Thursday with Jack inventorying the various accounts and properties of the business. All of the accounts and contracts were still in Uncle's name, and the power of attorney under which he had operated the business became invalid when Uncle died. He did have a fair amount of cash at the house and would manage with that for another week or so, but he and Jack agreed that something would need to be done fast to keep the business going.

He left early Friday morning in the Zephyr for Gaylord. Most people would have advised that he get an attorney from Alpena since it was also the home town of the circuit judge, but he wanted someone who would be less likely to know anyone who knew anything about his uncle's old divorce and other history. Besides, the probate judge was local from Montgomery County. Judge Sharpe was not a lawyer, but each county had its own probate judge. About half of them, statewide, were laymen.

His first stop in Gaylord was the County Courthouse. He followed the signs to the Clerk's office. There he inquired about the lawyers in town, especially those who did probate work. They gave him a list of attorneys who practiced in the local courts, but declined to recommend anyone. On his way out he stopped to look up some of the addresses on the large city map attached to the wall in the entrance foyer. He at first failed to see the woman walking toward him from the stairway.

"Sir," she said to him when she got close. "I couldn't help but overhear you in the Clerk's office. I know they don't recommend attorneys, but I can."

"Oh, thank you," he interrupted, "Miss?"

"Mrs. Adams. My father died a couple of years ago and left his affairs in a heck of a mess. We used Mr. Roy Murray to probate his estate. It wasn't all that easy, but compared to the stories I've heard about such affairs, it really worked out okay. I think he's as good a lawyer for that sort of thing as you'll find in these parts."

He thanked her, got directions to Mr. Murray's office, and, after taking his leave, walked the block and a half as directed to the law office. He was in luck. Mr. Murray was in and could see him as soon as his current client conference concluded. It had been going on for some time and was expected to end soon. It did, in about five minutes.

His conference with Attorney Murray lasted almost an hour. He was asked to come back after lunch to sign some documents. He did so and by 2:30 was driving back toward Ashford carrying a probate petition and several other documents to file with the Montgomery County Probate Court. One of the documents was a petition for his expedited appointment as administrator of his uncle's estate and business affairs and setting a hearing for the following Wednesday.

The only name left on the list he had made was Mrs. Simmons. She would be back Monday.

Mrs. Simmons actually returned late Sunday night. From his bed the nephew heard an automobile drive around the circular drive and then stop by the garage. He got up and looked out his window in time to see Mrs. Simmons standing by the door to the stairway for her apartment above the garage. She was using the light from the car to illuminate the door while she used her key in its lock. After opening it and turning on the stairway light, she disappeared around the car and then reemerged in the light from the headlights carrying two carpetbags. She waved once at the car and then went up the stairs, closing the door behind her. He watched until he saw a light go on in her apartment. At that point the car backed away from the door and headed back down the driveway.

The nephew was greeted the next morning by the smell of coffee coming from the kitchen. When he investigated, he found the percolator sitting on the back of the wood stove along with a pan of warm oatmeal. On the kitchen table was a bowl of fresh strawberries, apparently brought back by Mrs. Simmons from Alpena.

He poured a cup of coffee and half-filled another bowl with oatmeal. After putting sugar on the oatmeal, he added strawberries and then poured milk until the bowl was full. It was so full that he had to abandon his plan to take it to the porch to eat. Instead he sat at the kitchen table. He did take his second cup of coffee to the porch. He did not, however, see Mrs. Simmons during breakfast, which he thought to be strange.

At 9:30 the telephone rang. He picked it up and was greeted by the operator who announced that he had a long-distance call from Gaylord. The caller was Attorney Murray, who explained that Judge Sharpe had called to say that a hearing wouldn't be necessary for appointment of the nephew as temporary administrator. He was instructed by Roy Murray to go to the Probate office at the courthouse to pick up his letters of appointment. Those letters would allow him to carry on the affairs of his uncle's business until a permanent administrator was appointed by Judge Sharpe in two or three months.

After hanging up from Roy Murray's call, the nephew finished his coffee and waited for Jack to come by for their daily meeting. He explained the situation to Jack and then left for town, driving the Zephyr. He still hadn't talked with Mrs. Simmons, but he was confident now that everything was falling into place.

Nothing happened in Ashford to dampen his mood. He had taken the documents from Judge Sharpe's office directly to the bank. There the bank president, E. J. Briley, had personally made the notations on his uncle's accounts that would allow the nephew to make necessary transactions during the time of his appointment as temporary administrator. He also stopped at the hardware store and Drew's store to assure them that he had the ability to make payments for charges incurred by Jack in running the business. At lunchtime he went to the hotel for a sandwich and, of course, a dish of Mrs. Downing's bread pudding.

It was early afternoon when he arrived back at the lake and found Mrs. Simmons at work in the kitchen. She was packing her recipes and some other items, which the nephew guessed were hers, into a box.

"What's this?" he exclaimed.

"My sister has asked me to come live with her in Alpena. I've just decided to go," she answered. "I stayed here for all these years because I adored your uncle and I enjoyed being around him. But I didn't sleep none last night, and this morning I realized that I didn't want to be here without him. I'm sorry."

"Is it more money you want or anything like that?"

"No. Like I said, I just don't want to be here anymore. I've called my sister and she'll be here tonight after supper to pick me up. I'll make supper for you and clean up. I've already packed my things in the apartment. I'll probably have to come back to get all of it."

Trying to hide his surprise, and annoyance, the nephew finally said, "Well, of course I'm disappointed, but whatever you want to do is fine with me." After a pause, he continued, "I'm sure that Uncle would have wanted you to have something for your years of service to him. After I get his affairs in order I'll try to make things as he would have wanted, a bonus, so to speak."

She didn't answer, but he sensed that her feelings toward him were somewhat cool. She was starting to put some more items in the box when he asked, "Do you know anything about Uncle having a will?"

"He did have a will, I'm sure," she replied, staring hard at him. "He kept it in the box under his bed. I see you've already gone through the box. It's the one beside your uncle's desk. Didn't you find it in there?"

The nephew tried hard to hide the effect her accusatory attitude was having. He answered, "No," hoping that his tone and appearance wouldn't betray the lie and the panic he felt at her revelation.

"Well, I'm sure it was there. He had me get it out for him when he first took sick. I put it back after he was done. He talked to Sam Gassel on the telephone while he had it out, at least I think he did. He had me crank for the operator and I thought I heard him ask Mae to ring Sam's office."

He tried to remain calm as he asked the crucial question, "Do you know what the will provided?"

"Not exactly, but—." She paused as if trying to choose her words, and then simply said, "No." She went back to putting things in the box, indicating, the nephew thought, that the conversation was over.

His confidence was returning, however, and he needed to know if she knew about David. "Jack told me he thought Uncle was married when he first came here. Do you know anything about that?"

She thought for a minute before answering. "There's some things he told me over the years where he swore me to secrecy. I reckon he meant it to be forever." Then she looked at him almost loathingly and said, "Anyways, I think you know what I know." Before he could answer she picked up her box and walked out the back door.

He was surprised by her bitterness. For the first time he wondered if there had been more to the relationship between Uncle and Mrs. Simmons than had met the eye. He felt the panic returning.

True to her word, Mrs. Simmons prepared a delicious meal, frying some pork chops she had canned the fall before when she had arranged to buy a butchered hog. She also made a salad from the garden tomatoes, carrots and celery, and boiled several ears of corn, also from the garden. But she didn't accept his invitation to join him at the dining room table.

By the time she had finished washing the dishes, her sister was waiting in the car. The nephew, trying hard to act as if their earlier conversation had not happened, insisted that he be allowed to carry her things down the stairs from her apartment. He guessed that she must have been up half the night packing. It was all they could do to fit everything in the back seat and trunk of her sister's 1938 four-door Chevrolet.

As she was preparing to get in the front passenger seat, he handed her a check for $500.00 and insisted on a hug. He hoped she would soften her attitude toward him, but he was sure the tears in her eyes as she climbed into the car were not for him.

That night he dreamed again of the shotgun slowly falling toward the river below, but this time he could see Mrs. Simmons watching through the cedar boughs.

On the day Mrs. Simmons returned to Alpena to live with her sister, August 8, 1940, Colby Johnson was celebrating his fourth birthday some 250 miles south of Ashford in Washtenaw County. Some of his earliest and most lasting memories were from that day, both because of its adventure for him and because it provided one of his few memories of his father who was killed in North Africa as a First Lieutenant in the U. S. Army two years later.

As his birthday present, his parents took him on a canoe ride and picnic. They caught the interurban car near their apartment in Ypsilanti and rode it to its last stop near Main Street in Ann Arbor. It was Colby's first ride on the interurban and he was exhilarated by its speed compared with the other trolley cars he had ridden. After its last stop, they walked over the Huron River on the Hill Street Bridge. His father lifted him to sit on the rail to watch a New York Central passenger train pull into the Ann Arbor station. At the same time, a freight train was crossing both the river and the New York Central tracks on the Ann Arbor Railroad trestle. Young Colby was fascinated by the heavy layer of smoke and steam coming from the freight engine as it commenced its climb up the long grade north of the river.

But what he most remembered was the canoe ride. The canoe was borrowed from the Les Voyagers, a forestry fraternity of which one of his father's friends was a member. His mother was in the front and his father was in the back, and he sat on a blanket in the middle of the canoe. He had never had such a wonderful day.

CHAPTER 6

Except for the burning of the courthouse, the uncle's estate was settled uneventfully. That's not to say it happened overnight; in fact, it took nearly two years. But the nephew's fears that Mrs. Simmons, or some other person, would come forward to dispute his right to be the sole heir never materialized. Attorney Murray, as had been predicted by the lady in the Gaylord Courthouse, handled the administration effectively. Furthermore, his attention to detail led the nephew to the discovery of two substantial bank accounts, one in Gaylord and the other in Bay City, of which he had previously been unaware.

Fortunately, it was not necessary for Murray to do title searches on each of the properties his uncle had owned. The real estate inventory was established from the tax records. The taxes for the cabin property had always been paid by the uncle and David's name had never been added to the tax roll.

But many other things changed during the two years following his uncle's death. The nephew slowly came to realize that he would be a wealthy young man when the estate was finally settled, in spite of his qualms about someone discovering the facts about David. At the same time he was becoming restless over the prospect of continuing to operate the uncle's old timber business. For one thing, the economic boom caused by the European war had practically eliminated the tax and foreclosure sales which had been for so long the source of inexpensive timberlands. For another, he had begun to develop other professional goals for himself and was thinking seriously about going to college. At age twenty-nine, he did not consider himself too old.

In the meantime, he had hired Jacob Kincade to help Jack keep up with the wartime demand for hardwood. Jacob turned out to be a perfect fit. He and Jack complemented each other, and by the fall of 1941 they were making most of the business decisions and the nephew had reduced his involvement from daily meetings to once a week; Jack and Jacob still came to the house each Friday, payday.

At their meeting on the last Friday in September, 1941, he proposed to Jack and Jacob that they take over the business. He had already discussed his plan with Attorney Murray. The proposal was simple. They would pay for the value of the equipment used in the business over ten years. In addition, they would get the timber rights for most of his lands for fifteen years in exchange for one-fourth of the profits obtained during that period.

On the following Monday, Jack and Jacob came by to tell the nephew that they would agree to his terms. The Probate Judge issued his approval of the deal on November 15th and they all traveled to Gaylord the following week to sign the various documents in Attorney Murray's office. The nephew executed all of the timber deeds as administrator of his uncle's estate, and he signed the contracts in the same capacity and also in his capacity as the sole beneficiary of the estate.

The timber deeds did not cover the eighty acres with the old cabin. He explained to Jack and Jacob that he wanted to keep that land the same as his uncle had left it for sentimental reasons. In fact, he did not want anyone to have any reason to ever do a title search which might turn up David's name and interest in the old cabin property.

The effective date for the transfer of the business was Monday, December 1, 1941. On that same morning he posted a letter to Ferris Institute in Big Rapids, Michigan, seeking information about its curricula. Ferris was a school which was known for preparing students without an adequate high school foundation for attendance at a four year college or university. By the time he received a reply two weeks later, the United States had declared war on the Axis countries. Like most of his countrymen, the nephew was filled with patriotism. He drove the Zephyr to Big Rapids on December 18th and enrolled in the Ferris Institute Army Officer Training Program. He returned on January 22, 1942, this time by train, to commence his courses.

The Montgomery County Gazette was his only regular contact with Ashford during the year of his training course at Ferris Institute. He usually received it by mail on the Monday following its Thursday publication. He also received an occasional letter from Jack which included the quarterly company records and the deposit receipts for payments made to the estate's bank account. Attorney Murray also corresponded with news of the estate proceedings. A hearing had been scheduled for May 15th to finalize the administration. The nephew should have been elated upon learning that everything would then be his, but he received the letter in late February while he was still in the rigorous physical conditioning portion of the course and he was too tired most of the time to dwell on anything else.

The March 21, 1942, edition of the Montgomery County Gazette, however, elicited a much more excited reaction from the nephew. The headline read, "COURTHOUSE BURNS!" and was followed by a subhead which stated, "County Records Feared Lost; Arson Suspected." Together they took up half of the front page. The article said that few details were available at press-time as the site was still smoldering and too hot for men to look through the debris.

The first thoughts which raced through the nephew's mind as he unfolded the paper were no more divorce file, no more birth record for David, no more deed showing David's name. He was exhilarated. He suddenly realized how anxious he had been over the past two years about the possible discovery of his uncle's divorce file or David's birth certificate, both of which were in the archive records of the Clerk, as he had himself discovered, and were available to anyone who might look. In fact, he began to wonder why Mrs. Simmons had not looked. He was sure that she must have known something about David. He had been relieved that she had not intervened at the probate hearing when the Court had found that he was the sole heir.

Of greater uncertainty was the deed with David's name on it. The land records in the Office of the Register of Deeds were more frequently searched than records in the Clerk's office. However, if he didn't sell the old cabin property, thereby prompting a title search, it was unlikely that anyone would take notice of that particular deed, even if they happened upon it.

As it turned out, his sense of relief over the courthouse fire lasted but a week. The next issue of the Gazette brought news that most of the official records of the county had been saved from destruction by the vaults in which they had been stored. The only records which had been destroyed were the Probate Court files that had been kept in non-fireproof cabinets, and a few of the records in the Clerk's archive vault which had been charred by the fire's heat. The article did point out that the Gazette had back copies of all of its newspapers since 1908 and that it had chronicled all of the births, deaths, marriages and divorces in Montgomery County during that time. The article also said that state police investigators could not say with certainty that the fire had been intentionally set.

The change of news caused a new feeling of near panic to surface, a feeling the nephew had not experienced since those fateful two days at the old East Branch cabin. He placed the paper in his desk and left the dormitory, hoping that no one would ask where he was going. It was nearly dark, and the day, which had earlier been spring-like, was becoming much colder as daylight surrendered to a moonless night. He walked north along the state highway toward the downtown.

As he had been able to do in the past, he fought the panic and by the time he reached Barvario's was back in control of his fear. He realized that his immediate problem was the estate administration. Would it be delayed by the destruction of the records in the Probate Court files? By the time he had finished a plate of mutton stew, a piece of apple pie, and his second bottle of beer, he had decided to post a letter to Attorney Murray inquiring about the estate. He also decided to be optimistic about the potentially damaging records. No one had found them yet and the fire might mean that someone else was actively seeking to destroy the Montgomery County records. Whatever the arsonist's motives, the nephew hoped that he would soon finish the job.

He took a taxi back to his dormitory. After all, he reasoned, it had gotten quite cold and he was indeed going to be a wealthy young man. He would have been far less smug had he foreseen a chance conversation that he would soon overhear in Ashford.

When he received Attorney Murray's reply, he once again realized that his choice of lawyers had been fortunate. Murray had already traveled to Ashford to meet with Judge Sharpe. He had produced a complete set of new file documents and order copies from carbons and the Gazette records, and the judge had re-signed all of the orders which had been previously entered, including the nephew's letters of authority as estate administrator. The May 15th hearing was still on, albeit now in the lobby of the Ashford Hotel which was temporarily serving as the county's courtroom.

Attorney Murray had scheduled the hearing for May 15th because it coincided with the end of the quarter at Ferris and was during the break-week before the next quarter of classes began. Jack had agreed to meet the nephew at the train station in Elmira, a few miles west of Gaylord, but a direct route from Big Rapids on the Pennsylvania Railroad and a half-day less of traveling time. He was glad he did not have to arrive at the same station where he had picked up David nearly three years before.

He arrived on Saturday, the 11th. Jack seemed happy to see him and filled him in on the very successful operations of the business since he and Jacob had taken it over. Jack's pride was obvious. The nephew was, of course, happy to hear that his one-quarter share was producing more money to the estate account, soon to be his, than he had anticipated.

It was well after dark when Jack dropped him at the lake house. Jacob had spent the better part of the day getting the pump going and hauling some wood for the fireplace and the kitchen range. A note explained that he had not started the furnace because of the anticipation of mild weather and the difficulty of draining the system again. The note also said that the Zephyr had been started but the Model A's battery was dead. After Jack left, the nephew was too tired to even start a fire in the fireplace. He just got an extra blanket and went to bed. He did not sleep well, however; he dreamed that David and Uncle were sleeping in the next room and that he was trying to get out of the house without waking them up. Each time he tried to open his bedroom door it creaked, so he would close it and try to wait until he was sure they were asleep.

It was worse when he was awake. He imagined that Mrs. Simmons would be at the hearing tomorrow.

The hearing was uncontested. After brief testimony, the Judge signed an order turning over all of his uncle's money and property to him and ending the estate proceeding. He and Attorney Murray then walked the two blocks to the School Community Building where the Register of Deeds and the County Clerk had set up shop with the records which had survived the fire. There they submitted the six-page final probate order to the Register of Deeds for recording in the land records of Montgomery County.

After saying "hello" to Joan Farrier in the Clerk's office, they left. The nephew noted that neither the land records nor the Clerk's records appeared to be stored now in fireproof vaults. He wondered why.

Before going back to Gaylord, Attorney Murray suggested they have lunch at Gavine's Cafe. They both ordered a bowl of vegetable soup and a roast beef sandwich and talked about the few remaining documents needed to close the estate, one of which was a check to pay the attorney fees.

At the next table were several men who the nephew knew were too old for the war, and Waldo LaBlanc, not too old, but a former polio victim with too many remaining infirmities to be eligible for active service. Waldo had recently been appointed postmaster and the nephew was biding his time to offer congratulations, half listening to that conversation while also hearing Murray's instructions.

"Anyone ever hear of a fella named David Baxter around here?" The nephew looked over in time to see that Waldo was questioning the other men sitting at his table.

He didn't immediately hear any of the responses to Waldo's question. He was too stunned at hearing David Baxter's name. But neither did he walk over to congratulate Waldo as he had planned. He wasn't sure his legs would carry him that far or even that he would be able to stand at all. He hoped that his shock was not visible to others, but it must have been.

"Are you all right?" He was aware of his lawyer leaning over the table and placing a hand on his arm. "You look like you've just seen a ghost. Is something wrong?"

"No, I'm okay," he answered, concentrating on not drawing attention to himself. "Just had some food go down the wrong way. I'll be fine in a minute." He took a sip of water. Murray sat back in his chair.

The nephew glanced back over at the other table. He was relieved to see that no one there had seemed to be aware of his near panic. He noticed that Waldo was talking again and strained to listen. He distinctly heard Waldo finish, "… me neither. Nobody seems to have ever heard of him."

He turned his attention back to Murray who was again talking about the estate paperwork. Later he would be unable to recall any of the instructions he had received and was forced to write Murray asking for a written summary of what he needed to know regarding his uncle's remaining property and accounts.

On Friday he headed back to Big Rapids, this time driving the Zephyr. After all, it was his now and he should be enjoying it, but all he could think of was Waldo LaBlanc asking about David Baxter.

In fact, he had done little else since he left Gavine's Cafe on Wednesday after lunch. After Attorney Murray had driven off toward Gaylord, he had returned to the lake and had gone through the motions of getting the house ready to leave again. But he couldn't get his mind off Waldo LaBlanc and David Baxter.

It was likely, he reasoned, that Waldo had heard the name in connection with post office business, but why now? Waldo had become postmaster within the last month. If someone was trying to track down David Baxter, it should have happened long before Waldo became the postmaster.

He had arisen Thursday morning resolved to confront Waldo regarding David. But by the time he had finished his first cup of coffee he had come to realize that it would be risky to exhibit an interest in David Baxter in any way.

The nephew's officer training program at Ferris ended on November 2, 1942. He had the second highest academic ranking of all those who completed the course, but was not immediately offered a commission. Finally, on November 18th he received orders to report to a materials procurement depot in Ypsilanti, Michigan, with the rank of Second Lieutenant in the United States Army.

On the day those orders arrived, Colby Johnson left his first grade class at Ypsilanti Lincoln Elementary School full of anticipation at his mother's promise to buy a pilgrim costume for his part in the school Thanksgiving program on her way home from work at the Willow Run Armaments Plant. Her shift ended at 2:00 p.m. and she almost always was at home when Colby arrived at 4:20, or so, although she left before he did every morning.

He sensed that something was wrong when he saw the costume in the middle of the walk, half out of the partially opened box, and two letters scattered on the lawn. The door was wide open. He ran inside and saw his mother crying uncontrollably, still standing with her head lying on the back of his father's big chair, an opened letter in her right hand. Upon seeing him she walked over and knelt in front of him, tears streaming down her face. She hugged him to her. He began crying although he was not completely sure why. She finally told him that his father had been killed in the war.

CHAPTER 7

His experience in purchasing and marketing timber products for his uncle's business proved to be invaluable to the nephew's work in the Quartermaster Corps. Within two months he was given the responsibility for negotiating all of the Army's purchases from Willow Run Armaments, a subsidiary of Packard Motor Corporation. The Willow Run Armaments Plant, often called WRAP, was one of two former automobile plants located near the Willow Run Airport just east of Ypsilanti which had been quickly converted to wartime production. The other was a Ford plant which had been making bomber airplanes since the Lend-Lease Act became law in mid-1941.

WRAP, on the other hand, was engaged primarily in the production of weapons and ordinance. Because of its wide variety of products, the nephew was responsible for the purchase of many items used by the Army in the war effort. One day he might be negotiating the purchase of ten thousand land mines, the next arranging delivery of machine gun assemblies for the bombers being assembled on the other side of the airport. Often he would have to be able to provide base material sources and allocations for WRAP management in order to make possible its production of a needed product.

In late January, 1943, he met a woman who seriously turned his head for the first time in his life. She lived in Ypsilanti, but was a recent widow. The extent of their relationship during his time stationed there were several conversations at the coffee socials following the Ypsilanti Congregational Church services. But he vowed to himself that he would pursue a romantic relationship with her at the appropriate time.

On February 1, 1943, after only two months and four days of active duty, he was promoted to First Lieutenant, a rank consistent with the duties he had been given with WRAP. But as his responsibilities grew, so did his fear of discovery. He became more and more convinced that it was only a matter of time before someone would come upon either David's birth record or the file of his uncle's divorce or the joint deed. Again and again he would remember his reaction to hearing Waldo LaBlanc mention David's name. Sometimes he would stay awake the whole night wondering where Waldo had heard the name, fearing that Waldo or someone who had heard his inquiries would run across one of the records now haphazardly stored in the old school building and make the connection.

He also worried about a rumor that the Army was considering a large purchase of land somewhere in northern Michigan to establish an air training base. If such a purchase happened to include the old cabin land, David's name would surely surface during the title search. He found himself imagining tens of circumstances that could lead to the detection of David Baxter's existence. Events which might lead to such discovery, which he formerly and realistically had considered to be so remote in likelihood as to be not worth worrying about, he now began to visualize as possible, sometimes as probable. And, he wondered, was someone now looking for David?

Slowly the chances and consequences of discovery became more and more important elements of his life. The disgrace of being discovered as a perjurer in the estate proceedings would surely result in the loss of his officer's commission. And now the opportunity for a woman in his life existed. He had not even let himself think about the possibility of losing the inheritance. And, of course, if anyone started probing, the discovery of David's arrival in Gaylord would be pretty easy. From there, who knows where it might lead. If the courthouse arsonist did not soon finish the job of destroying the court and deed records, he might have to.

At some point, he began to contemplate ways to destroy any document which might connect David Baxter with his uncle—and with him. He knew about the public courthouse files, now stored in the school community building. More and more he began to worry about old newspapers stored in the Montgomery County Gazette archives. He had seen some of the old newspapers. Births, deaths and land transactions during the week were regularly listed in each weekly edition. It was also likely, he reasoned, that the divorce, a rarity in 1919, would also have been reported.

One morning in early February he found himself preoccupied with his fears. The purchase orders in front of him were blurred and he couldn't concentrate.

"Are you all right, sir?" He looked up to see a young corporal standing before his desk. "Captain Arthur sent me for the Willow Run purchase orders."

"Yes, Corporal, I'm fine. Just thinking for a minute. Here they are," he said as he handed the papers to the young man. He hoped that his secretary had done her usual error free job of preparing the documents because he had not actually reviewed them.

After the corporal left, the nephew reflected on steps he might take to eliminate the fears that were beginning to consume him. Action, he thought. The newspaper archives and the courthouse records must be destroyed. I will burn the Gazette office first. It will be easier. Besides, if someone intentionally started the courthouse fire to get the records, he might well finish the job soon.

He also thought about burning the post office, but couldn't think of any way that Waldo's inquiry could tie David to his uncle, or him, without one of the records from the courthouse or an old newspaper story.

On February 16th the means to carry out his plan was suddenly placed in his hands. On one of his many visits to WRAP, he was introduced to an engineer at the plant who had been working on an a smokeless incendiary time fuse which he proposed for Army purchase. It was made with combustible parts so that it would be undetectable when used in espionage activities. The nephew was given two dozen of the fuses for Army testing. He could hardly contain his excitement during the rest of his plant visit.

The next day he handed over twenty of the new time fuses to his immediate superior to arrange testing, the results of which he never did learn. The other four fuses he hid under the back seat of the Zephyr. He hardly drove the Zephyr anymore, preferring to take the train from his base to WRAP, and using other Army transportation when he could.

The Zephyr was still a luxurious automobile and its V-12 engine was the envy of many a young man who had access to enough gasoline coupons to use it. One such person was a fellow officer in the Quartermaster Corps, Second Lieutenant Hausler, who himself owned a 1937 Chevrolet Coupe. Lieutenant Hausler had often voiced his admiration of the Zephyr. When Hausler approached the nephew about joining him and some friends for a weekend outing to Belle Isle, the nephew countered with an offer to exchange cars for the weekend, suggesting that the group would have much more room in the Zephyr for their weekend excursion. Hausler gleefully accepted.

And so on the last Saturday morning of February, 1943, the nephew left the base early in Hausler's Chevrolet Coupe. He packed two of the four stolen fuses and two empty one-quart milk bottles, buffered by his Army issued bedroll, on the floor of the back seat. He also brought along a two-gallon gasoline can which had been in the trunk of the Zephyr over the years.

By noon he reached the town of Standish, about halfway between Ypsilanti and Ashford. He had the meatloaf special at Wheeler's Restaurant, a popular eatery for travelers. His uncle had introduced him to Wheeler's when they had traveled south from Ashford while he was still a teenager. It seemed like a lifetime ago. After the meatloaf, mashed potatoes, corn and hot rolls had been dispatched, he ordered a piece of apple pie smothered with ice cream. About halfway through the pie he felt full, but he finished it anyway. He suddenly felt warm and secure and realized that he had not experienced those feelings for some time. He thought about being in the kitchen at the lake, of his uncle, and of the pies Mrs. Simmons had made back then.

After leaving Wheeler's Restaurant, he drove the Chevrolet across the street to Fletcher's Sinclair station and had the car filled with gasoline. He also had the two-gallon can in the trunk filled, explaining that he would be traveling through the back country and might not find another station. After deducting for the gas, his ration card had only enough points for one more fill-up. He realized that he would barely be able to get back to Ypsilanti after he reached Ashford. Returning the car with an empty tank would hardly make Lt. Hausler happy, but he couldn't think of an alternative.

At the gas station drive entrance he hesitated. Was his plan really a good idea? Maybe he should just go back to Ypsilanti and forget the whole thing. After all, nobody had come across the damaging records during the previous 20 years; why would they in the future? He almost turned back. But then he thought of the many sleepless nights while his mind raced with fear of discovery. Almost all of those possibilities were based on someone finding David's birth records or the old deed or the divorce file. He put the Chevrolet in gear and turned left, north toward Ashford. The clock on the Standish National Bank sign showed that it was 1:05 p.m.

Because of an unusually early thaw, the trip from Standish to Ashford was slow and perilous. The state highway was unpaved in many places, and he was in danger of becoming mired in the deep ruts which existed where the route traversed pockets of clay soil. He did get stuck once, but was able to back the Chevrolet out safely to higher ground. On his next try, using more speed, he was able to get through to a more passable section of the road. Finally, he detoured onto an upland county road over sandy plains through Lumberton, which would bring him to the paved state road west of Ashford. It was fifteen miles longer, but this route would be free of the tricky mud holes.

He was glad the state road had little other traffic as he approached Ashford. While he didn't expect anyone to be looking for him in a Chevrolet, he might still be recognized if someone looked closely. He took his watch from his pocket and saw that it was almost 4:30. Most of his military peers now used wristwatches issued by the Army, but he still preferred his old pocket watch.

He had originally planned to wait for nightfall at an abandoned sawmill site near the Alpena Road east of Ashford. But now, after his detour, he was approaching Ashford from the west. So he decided to drive directly to the lake house which was easy to access from the state road.

Once at the house, no one would be able to see his car from the road nor would anyone likely be on the lake at this time of the year. And, he reasoned, if he was seen and recognized, he could still cancel his plan and return to Ypsilanti with no harm done. He was glad that he had decided to bring his house and gate keys.

His scare came as he was unlocking the gate to the house driveway. He heard the car coming from the direction of the highway along Rouse Road. He hurried with the lock and then walked with the end of the gate as it swung across the driveway. A bushy blue spruce tree grew beside the driveway where the gate swung, and he crouched behind it. The Chevrolet was in the roadway ready to turn through the gate, but the approaching car had plenty of room to pass. He thought he could hear his heart pounding.

If it was Jack or Jacob, his plan was over. Each would surely stop to investigate the strange car at his driveway. The car slowed, almost stopped and then pulled out to go around the Chevrolet. As it accelerated west along Rouse Road he glanced from behind the tree. It was an old car, but not one he recognized.

He closed and locked the gate behind him. At the house he parked the car between the garage and the back door and unloaded the two milk bottles, the gasoline can and his sleeping bag. After looking at the bottles and can for a moment, he put them back in the trunk and closed it. He unlocked the house and went in with the sleeping bag. The electricity had been disconnected and he did not dare risk a fire in the fireplace or wood stove, at least while it was still daylight. The pocket watch read 5:20. He unrolled the sleeping bag on his bed, got in and fell asleep almost immediately. For once, his mind did not dwell on his fears of discovery.

He awoke with a start, uncertain of his whereabouts. He had a sense of urgency, but at first was unsure why. It was pitch black; as he would see later, the night was overcast, with no moon or stars. Within seconds he realized that he was in his old room at the lake. He untangled himself from the bedroll and reached to the bedpost at the foot of the bed where he always hung his pants. He pulled out his watch from one pocket and a match from the other. He struck the match on the hardwood floor and looked at the watch. It was 3:15, an hour later than he had hoped to awaken.

After dressing and rolling up his bedroll, mostly by feel, he lit another match to see if he had left anything. Nothing that he could see. He made his way to the back door and locked it behind him. By then his eyes were as accustomed to the dark as they would ever be, but he still could not see the car, which he knew was less than fifty feet from where he stood. A moment of doubt—what if someone had taken it while he slept? But he regained control and walked in the direction where he knew it was. He saw a slight reflection from a headlight when he was about ten feet away. He found the front door and got in, throwing the bedroll behind his seat. He had to think about the starting procedures; the Zephyr had a button on the dash, but this Chevrolet had a foot pedal above the accelerator.

After several revolutions with the starter, the engine coughed and then started. He pulled down the drive away from the lake, stopped and set the parking brake. Only then did he turn on the headlights. He got out of the car and carried the gas can and the two milk bottles from the trunk around to the front of the car. In the light of the car's headlights, he poured gasoline from the can into the milk bottles until each was about half full. He then stuffed rags into the openings of both bottles, but not so far that they touched the gasoline. There was just enough room on the floor behind his seat to set the two bottles upright. He put the bedroll ahead of the bottles under his seat so that it pinched against the bottles. He would worry about the gasoline smell later. He then placed the gasoline can, still three-quarters full, back in the trunk and removed the two fuses. He looked at them in the light from the car to reassure himself as to the operating procedure, and then put both on the seat beside him as he reentered the car.

He saw no other vehicle, or for that matter even a house light, during the twenty minutes it took him to drive back to Rouse Road, unlock and open, and then relock the gate behind him, and drive the seven miles to Ashford. Once in town, he turned left onto Main Street and drove to the end of the business district and turned around. He saw no one. No lights could be seen in any of the three houses that were interspersed with the store buildings. On the way back he turned right into the driveway between Doty's General Store and the wood-sided Montgomery County Gazette building. It was a single story frame building that covered the 25-foot width of the lot and extended from the sidewalk along Main Street to the alley, a distance of 80 feet.

He turned out the lights, but left the car's engine running. It seemed awfully loud as he gathered the two fuses under one arm and took the gasoline-filled milk bottles from behind the seat. He could see well enough from the street light on the corner of the block to make out the coal storage shed attached to the Gazette building, about halfway along the length of the building. He knew from having been in the building that the shed had only a wooden door separating it from the furnace area inside.

He carefully set the bottles and fuses on the coal-shed step. He was surprised at just how calm and detached he felt. As he expected, the shed door was unlocked. He took both fuses inside and wedged them along either side of the wooden door leading into the main building. He then brought in the bottles and laid one on each fuse at just enough of an angle so that the gasoline began soaking into the rags stuffed into the bottle openings. He looked around, but could see little in the dim light. He started to light a match, but thought better of it. He felt and found the coal pile, and placed several lumps around and on top of each fuse and bottle.

A noise came from inside the building, a soft rumble followed by a thump. It sounded like an object sliding down an incline and smashing into the bottom, just on the other side of the door. The nephew froze. After a few seconds he realized that the sound was caused by the coal in the building's furnace settling as it burned.

He noticed that his left hand was now slightly trembling. He listened for a nearly a minute, but heard nothing more. Satisfied, he pulled the safety pin and turned the knob one quarter turn on first one fuse, and then the other. He then walked to the dim light of the doorway and closed it behind him. He got into the still-running car and carefully backed onto the main street, heading west. It was only as he started forward that he turned on the headlights.

He judged that the fuses should have ignited at just about the time he was passing the turn-off to Lumberton at Haller's Hill. He had already determined that he was going to avoid all unpaved roads on his way back, even though it meant an extra eighty miles by going west to Gaylord, south on U.S. 27 to Lansing, and then back east to Ypsilanti. He reckoned that he had just enough gas points left on his ration card to make it. He also had a little over a gallon and a half remaining in the can in the Chevrolet's trunk.

He had originally planned to set the fuses a full turn, one hour, to allow him to get further away, but he had slept longer than planned, so he set the fuses for only fifteen minutes. He wanted the fire to get as much of a start as it could before anyone happened along and discovered it.

It worked. Although the nephew did not learn the results of his debut as an arsonist for almost two weeks, it was remarkably successful. No one had noticed the smoke coming from the Gazette building on that Sunday morning until almost eight o'clock. By the time the town's old Model A fire engine was brought to the scene, the building was almost completely in flames. Nothing inside was saved.

Diane had David's red hair and facial structure. Helen sensed that their daughter had inherited her own tall and lanky frame. But Diane's smile was all from David. It was sometimes hard to separate the pleasure it gave from the pain of remembrance it invoked.

Helen had finally admitted to herself, at least rationally, that David would not be coming home to rescue her and Diane from their tribulations. Nevertheless, she couldn't quite extinguish her hope. She was fully determined, however, to do whatever was necessary to shield Diane from the consequences of their situation.

Diane would celebrate her third birthday in less than two months. On this Thursday, Helen's day off from her job at the Wallaby Hotel, they had taken a bus and were having a picnic at one of Sydney's beaches.

"Mummy, look at the little girl with her daddy and mummy. When is my daddy coming home? Do I know my daddy?"

"Your daddy is away at the war." Helen had invented the lie about Diane's father to explain her status as a single mother-to-be when she had first arrived in Sydney just over three years before. She saw no reason to tell her daughter otherwise as Diane grew old enough to wonder about her father. "You don't remember him, but you will when he comes home."

"I will. I will."

"You have a grandmother and grandfather, too."

"I do? Do I know them?"

"They have never seen you, but they know all about you from the letters I write. You know 'teddy bear' that you play with sometimes?"

"Yes." Diane wrinkled her forehead, a frown creasing her smooth skin as she looked up at her mother. A trace of freckles dotted the bridge of her nose. She smiled, a gap-toothed grin. "He's my friend when I stay at home, my best friend."

"Well, your grandmother and grandfather sent him to you last Christmas."

"What did Daddy send me at Christmas, Mummy? I can't remember what he sent me. Tell me, Mummy."

Helen looked away, afraid she might cry if she tried to answer. Finally she looked back at her daughter. "Would you like to go for a long train ride? We are going to go see your grandmother and grandfather for your birthday. We have to ride on the train all day. Won't that be fun?"

"Yes, yes. Can we go now? I want to see my grandpa."

"No, we can't go right now—but soon. In two months, that's when your birthday is. You'll be three years old. Do you know how many years that is?"

Diane proudly held up three fingers. "Mrs. Macaby showed us how to count to ten. I know how many three is."

"Good, very good. You are so smart. Now, do you want a sandwich? I made us each a sandwich. I'm hungry, aren't you?"

"I want some cake. You said we'd have some cake on this pic-a-nic. Can't I have some cake, Mummy?"

CHAPTER 8

Arson was not suspected immediately after the Gazette Building fire. Frank West, the paper's owner and publisher, had been warned several times by friends, and even by the man who delivered his coal, that the building's chimney was badly in need of repair. A truck delivering newsprint had hit and dislodged several of its bricks just below the roof overhang. He had been warned that the damage created a fire danger. The damaged chimney was located on the outside of the building next to the coal bunker room in the area where the fire and smoke had first been observed. So everyone, including Frank West, assumed that sparks from the heavily stoked weekend fire got into the wall and rafters and ultimately led to the building's destruction. Alonzo Kent, who had loaded the furnace with coal when he left late Saturday afternoon after spending the day setting type, could not remember later whether he had closed the damper as he should have, or not.

Also, at the time no one, including Frank West, was very much concerned about the loss of the newspaper's archives. Everyone was concerned about how Frank was going to get the next issue of the paper printed and distributed. In fact, Frank was taking some small solace in the fact that he had taken his subscriber list home for the weekend so his wife could prepare the quarterly bills. As it was, he managed to get out a small edition of the paper on the Thursday following the fire, printed by the presses of The Alpena News. But it was not until the second Thursday that he was able to print an edition that could be mailed to his out-of-town subscribers.

The nephew received his first confirmation of the fire and destruction of the newspaper's records and archives when he received that second edition of the paper in Monday's mail, two weeks and a day after he set the fuses in the coal-shed. Of course, he knew he must have caused some damage when the first edition after the fire didn't arrive the week before. Strangely, even though he had no actual knowledge of the results of his efforts, he felt a great sense of relief after his return from the excursion to Ashford, and for several days was not burdened with the constant fear that someone might discover David's death. He was convinced that his unknown accomplice, the person he believed must have caused the courthouse fire, also wanted the county records destroyed and would soon strike again. The records had been moved to the school community building. It was old, made of tamarack logs, and would burn easily and hot.

He buried himself in his job during March and the first few days of April and waited for the news which he hoped would soon be forthcoming, news of another fire in Ashford. But another kind of news came first. On April 7th he received a transfer order. He was being posted to the Quartermaster Corps European Headquarters in London. He was instructed to finish the transfer of his current responsibilities by April 12th, and after a three-day leave, report at 8:00 p.m. on April 15th at Detroit's Michigan Central Station to catch a troop train to New York. He was berthed on a ship scheduled to leave the Port of New York on April 18, 1943.

The next Sunday he attended church in Ypsilanti, hoping for a chance to talk to his friend. She did not disappoint him. He arrived just before the service was scheduled to begin and was ushered to a pew near the front. During the service he glanced around as best he could, but did not see her. He began to worry that he would be denied the opportunity to say good-bye before he left town for his new posting. However, when the service ended and he stood with the crowd to file out, he saw her, also standing, three rows behind him. From her smile when their eyes met, he was sure that she, too, was anxious to see him. He gestured with his head toward the outside and she nodded.

When he finally worked his way through the crowd, he found her standing at the edge of the church's entrance walkway.

"Hello."

"Hello," she responded.

"I hoped that you would be here today"

"Me too, or—I mean I hoped you would be." They both laughed and then looked at each other for what seemed to him like an eternity.

Finally he asked, "How have you been?"

"I've been quite well, thank you. And how have you been?"

"Fine." He paused for a few seconds, gathering courage. "Are you free this afternoon? I thought we might go for a ride in my automobile, if you'd like. I have something to tell you."

She lowered her head slightly. "I would like. But I can't. My mother and father-in-law are here—at my place. They are watching my son while I came here and I must leave soon. She insisted on cooking a big dinner and I mustn't be late." She looked up and could see his disappointment. "But I did want to invite you—I mean—my son is going to their house for the first two weeks of July." She took a deep breath. "I thought you might want to go with me to my company picnic on the Fourth of July."

"Oh, if only I could," answering as much to his own fear as to her, an emotional fear that was unlike his fear of being discovered for David's death. The anxiety he felt now was of being deprived of her, of forces beyond his control preventing his happiness, his chance to be with her.

"I was afraid you might already have plans for the Fourth."

"It's not that I have plans. It's the Army that has made plans for me." He then told her about his new posting order.

For a few minutes they tried to find a time to get together before he left. But she didn't want her late husband's parents to know that she was interested in another man so soon, and they would be staying with her for another week. His leave began in two days. They talked about the idea of her meeting him in Detroit to see him off on the troop train, but she was unsure of who she might get to watch her son, and he decided that he would not like her traveling back to Ypsilanti alone at night on the interurban. Finally they exchanged addresses and phone numbers, although his telephone up at the lake was disconnected and the number would probably be assigned to someone else before he would use it again. They promised to write each other while he was in England. She suddenly kissed him on the lips, turned and was gone, almost running down the street. He could see she was crying, and he felt strangely empty as he slowly walked down the walk and turned in the opposite direction.

That night as he lay in bed he wondered if he might have been able to respond differently in their search for a time to be together if he was not burdened by his fears regarding David's death and the possibility that he might be found out. He fell asleep after realizing that he had one more task to do before he left for England. He began planning another fire.

On April 14, 1943, a Wednesday, the nephew sat on the porch sipping coffee, enjoying the panorama of the lake and its shores. It was an exceptionally warm day in northern Michigan for April; it was an exceptionally early spring. There were no remnants of ice left on the lake and no remains of snow drifts in the forest.

He remembered how as a teenager he had associated the final melting of the lake's ice cover as confirmation that the winter was finally over, and with the realization that the spring would be erratic and fleeting. Even then he knew that autumn was not that far away, and would follow a usually pleasant, but not long-lasting, summer. And then the winter again. The spring leaves of northern Michigan were still a month away, and even then would be bittersweet; theirs a promise which would last only until the first frost, usually in mid-September.

He remembered another time sipping coffee on this porch, opening the letter from David. It seemed like something that had happened in another life, but it was only four years ago and it had affected every day of his life since. Why hadn't he just taken the letter in to his uncle? Because he had at first thought the letter to be a hoax, or was that just an excuse he had fabricated over time? Had he always planned to kill David? No, he thought, but he really couldn't be sure anymore.

Regardless of his real motives then, he still had one more task. One which would eliminate entirely the chance of someone discovering David's death—and his role in it. He would finally destroy the last records of David's existence, at least on this side of the world, and hence any connection which might possibly be made between his uncle, or himself, and David Baxter.

He finished his coffee and carried the cup to the kitchen sink. Later he would clean up and put everything away. It might be years before he returned from England. He had already put the Zephyr up on blocks to preserve its tires, and would do the same with the Model A that night. Everything else he had prepared and stored as best he could. He had covered all of the furniture with sheets, except for the kitchen table. He would cover that just before he left.

But now he had a task to do and he did not want to be seen around the community building that afternoon. He would have preferred not to be seen there at all this day, but it was necessary. The morning would be better than the afternoon. He climbed in the Model A and headed for town.

"Well, look who the cat dragged in." It was Joan Farrier. "Welcome to the Montgomery County Courthouse, temporary, I hope."

The nephew closed the door and looked around the community building. He'd been in it hundreds of times, played high school basketball in it, but he'd never seen it like this. To his immediate left, from where the greeting had come, he saw a counter and signs which identified it as the office of the County Clerk. He could see other desks and counters spread around the former basketball court and stage. He recognized Ken Chadson behind a counter over by the east fire exit door. That would be the Register of Deeds office area.

"Hi, Joan," he responded. "But you're wrong, I couldn't find a cat. Had to get here by myself." They both chuckled.

They exchanged brief histories of the last several months, and he told her of his transfer to London.

"Well, I'd better keep going," he said, anxious to spend as little time as possible in the building. "I've got to look up a couple of old deeds for a project of Jack's. I'll see you again when the war's over. Soon, I hope."

He walked over to the Register of Deeds counter, nodding to people he knew at the desks he passed along the way. He was delighted to see that the Liber cabinet was next to the exit door.

"Hi, Ken," he greeted the Register of Deeds as they shook hands.

Again, the obligatory exchange about the major events for each during the past year took place. Ken even mentioned the increased use of county records since the newspaper archives were destroyed in the Gazette fire. The nephew tried to appear nonchalant.

"I've got to look up a few deeds, descriptions for Jack," he said. "Looks like the Libers are all in that cabinet over by the back wall."

"The index books, too," Ken added. "Except the current one, I'm working on that one now—up here on the counter. But it only goes back to January one of this year. I imagine what you're looking for is before that. All of your uncle's estate stuff would be at the end of the old index—maybe five pages from the back. It's in there in two places, once under his name, 'the Estate of,' and once under yours."

"Thanks."

"You can spread yourself out on the table on the other side of the door. I wasn't real happy they stuck me here with that door right in the middle of my area, but it seems to work okay. I'll probably be happy come July when it gets hot. By the way, there's an inkwell on top of the bookcase next to the table. Do you need a pen and paper?"

The nephew, chagrined with himself for not being prepared for his invented reason to be in the community building, replied, "Yes, Ken, I'd appreciate the use of a pen. One sheet of paper ought to do. With packing everything up and trying to get all these last minute details done, I forgot to bring something to write with."

He tried to look and act normal as he removed the index book from the cabinet. He could scarcely believe his luck with regard to the location of the table next to the fire door. While he could probably set the building on fire from the outside or by breaking a window, he had hoped to be able to unlock one of the exit doors. He well knew, from the days when he and the other teenage boys had left the doors unlocked over many Friday nights so they could sneak into the building to play basketball on Saturdays, that the door could be unlatched by turning and holding the knob while pushing in the lock button. The door would appear to still be locked, though it could be opened without even turning the latch knob. If he could do it without being observed, later discovery would be unlikely.

He first opened the index book and placed it on the table. As Ken had indicated, the entries regarding his uncle's estate were only a few pages from the back. He chose to look under his own name, feeling some pride at seeing it listed in the "Grantee" column of the official index book. He found the listing for the "Order Assigning Real Property" and made a note of the Liber and page numbers.

He then walked back over toward the Liber cabinet, glancing back toward the counter. Ken and another man were looking at a map unrolled on the far end of the counter. They appeared to be engrossed in viewing the map and discussing whatever it was they were searching for. He stood by the door latch looking straight ahead at the Liber cabinet. The Liber he had noted was at the top of the stack, but he bent down, appearing to search for the number. With his left hand he moved the lock lever up. Then with his right hand he turned the knob clockwise and moved the lock lever back down. The whole maneuver took less than five seconds, but after straightening up he glanced back over toward the counter, half expecting Ken and the other man to be staring at him. But they were still bent over the map and seemed oblivious to his presence. He removed the top Liber and carried it over to the table. He glanced down at the door lock. It appeared to be just as it was when he arrived.

The nephew busied himself at the lake house that afternoon washing dishes, tidying and storing items for his anticipated long absence. He also drained the water system. Fortunately, the furnace had been drained when he left for Ferris and had not been used since. He had been lucky with the warm weather the last two days.

He then went to the garage and opened the trunk of the Zephyr and took the remaining two time fuses from behind the spare tire. He gently placed them on the floor behind the driver's seat of the Model A, with its new battery, and covered them with a bundle of rags, also taken from the Zephyr trunk. The rags had come from a rag bin near his apartment in Ypsilanti where they were being collected to help the war effort. He then opened the door of the garage so that a visitor could see that the car was on blocks. He was considering whether or not to also put the Model A on blocks, even though he would have to take it down later, an awful lot of work with the car jack, when the matter was decided for him. He heard a car coming down the drive from Rouse Road. He quickly closed the door behind the Model A so the caller couldn't see that it had not yet been placed on blocks.

The car pulled to a stop between the garage and the house. He could see that it was driven by Jacob Kincade. "Hello," Jacob said as he got out of the car.

"Hello, Jacob."

"The wife thought that you might appreciate an early supper, seeing as how you will be getting up pretty early to go with Jack."

The nephew had already accepted Jacob's invitation for dinner when it had been extended the weekend before. Not only did he have everything for cooking put away, but it would keep him from being seen in town, his other option for supper that night.

"Sounds good. Just finished putting the cars up on blocks," he lied. "Give me a minute to lock up the garage and change clothes."

"Can I help? I can lock up the garage while you change." Jacob had walked around his car and was approaching the garage door.

"No thanks," he said quickly, feeling his heart start to pound. "I've got everything figured and in place. It'll only take a minute." He let out his breath slowly when Jacob turned to follow him toward the house.

Once in the house, he led Jacob to the porch overlooking the lake, on the opposite side of the house from the garage. "Sit here, Jacob, while I dress." He then went in and put on the Army uniform which he had earlier laid out on his bed.

"I'm ready," he said as he walked back out on the porch. "I thought your children might enjoy seeing my uniform."

It was almost 9:00 when Jacob dropped the nephew back at the lake. After a warm goodbye and handshake with Jacob, and a hug from his wife who had ridden back with them, he went into the house and took off his uniform. He set the wind-up alarm clock beside his bed to midnight and then lay down in his underclothes. Sleep did not come as he went over again and again his plans for the early morning hours. Finally, at 11:30, he pushed in the alarm button and got dressed, putting on denim pants and a dark pull-over shirt.

The drive from the lake to Ashford was mostly uneventful. He was startled by two deer jumping across the road only a few yards in front of the Model A. He also was very aware of the kerosene smell coming from the five-gallon can on the floor in front of the seat beside him. His care in keeping the oil from spilling when he had filled the can from the house kerosene tank the day before had gone for naught when the oil sloshed over as he placed the can in the car. "Well, it shouldn't matter," he said aloud, although he was alone. "Nobody but me will be in this car for a long time, probably not until the war's over."

He drove in behind the school and around its west side to a place where the old Ford would be hidden from the view of anyone passing by. It was only fifteen feet from the door he had unlocked that morning. He got out of the car and tried the door. It opened. His heart raced. So far, so good. There was even a light left on inside the building. It would help him once inside, but he was aware that someone walking behind the school would be able to see it when he was opening and closing the door. He hoped no one would be walking there tonight. It was unlikely, he decided.

He first carried the kerosene can and set it on the ground next to the door. He then went back to the car and bundled the rags under his left arm and picked up the fuses with the other. He didn't bother to close the driver side door. He might have a few mosquitoes on the way home but he didn't expect any more than that, and a few mosquitoes then would be better than a passerby hearing the sound of a slamming car door.

At the building door, the nephew looked slowly around with the rags and fuses still under his arms. He didn't see anyone, or even a place from where someone might accidentally see him while riding by. Satisfied, he quickly opened the door and stepped inside, closing the door behind him. He placed the rags and fuses on the table where only a few hours before he had been pretending to read through legal descriptions of lands which he had inherited from his uncle. He then quickly opened the door partially and pulled the kerosene can inside.

While most of the records he wanted to destroy were in the Clerk's office, he did not want that fact to be evident. He had heard that the original courthouse fire had started outside the Register of Deeds office. If it had been intentionally set, the arsonist was probably after the land records. So the nephew decided to start a fire in each of those two areas. If the arson was discovered, the authorities would assume the two fires were connected. At the time of the first fire, he had been on weekend maneuvers as part of his military training, an airtight alibi since he had, in fact, had nothing to do with it.

He carried half of the rags and one of the fuses over to the Clerk's counter and briefly looked around. He chose an area between the wooden shelves, on which were piled the Chancery Court archive file boxes, and a table against the wall. Under the table were several boxes of papers which would readily burn. It wouldn't take much, he knew, to start the old tamarack logs going, and once on fire they would burn hot and fast.

He pulled out his pocket watch and turned its face toward the single light bulb in the center of the room. It was 12:50; time was slipping by, he thought. He turned the end of the fuse three complete revolutions, setting it to go off in three hours, and then placed it at the juncture of the bookcase and table. He then piled the rags around the fuse, on the floor and bottom shelf of the bookcase and under the table, next to one of the boxes. And finally he walked back across the room to get the can of kerosene. He emptied about half of the can, soaking the rags and table and pouring some on the exposed logs of the wall behind the table. He then walked back to the Register of Deeds counter and repeated the process with the remaining fuse and rags, this time emptying the kerosene can.

He started to the door, but stopped to look around for anything he might have forgotten. The air in the building was already saturated with the strong smell of kerosene. He remembered that he should relock the door as he exited, and was reaching for the knob when he heard the sound. It was unmistakable. He was sure his heart would stop beating. Someone had just slammed the door of the Model A, the door he had intentionally left open.

CHAPTER 9

The sound was unmistakable, a car door slamming. It came from just beyond the exit door. On the inside, standing next to that same door, the nephew tried to calm himself. He had to avoid panic now or all was lost. If he was found in the community building with fuses and oiled rags arranged for a fire, the authorities would more than wonder why. Once they started searching the records, it would be only a matter of time before they discovered his uncle's divorce file and learned of David. He briefly wondered why he had taken this chance.

The sound must have been from the door of the Model A which he had left open. He would have heard another car drive up. And there was no wind; at least there had been no wind when he had arrived. Anyway, he would be able to hear a wind strong enough to close the car door with the force that produced the sound he had heard. He was sure a person had slammed the door.

He waited, half expecting someone to come through the door, or at least knock. After a minute he stepped over behind the Liber cabinet where he would not be immediately seen by someone coming through the door. Nothing happened. After another fifteen minutes he began to doubt whether he had heard anything at all. But he knew better. He couldn't stay here all night. Jack would be coming by the lake in just three hours to take him to the train station in Gaylord. He looked at the single light bulb which cast a pale illumination throughout the building. It had a pull-string switch. He quietly walked over and grabbed the string. Before he pulled, he measured the route to the door in his mind. He would have to go around the Register of Deeds counter, but it was his only obstacle. He pulled the string. It was immediately and completely dark. If any light was coming through the row of windows just below the roof, his eyes were not adjusting quickly enough to see it.

He held out his hand and walked slowly in the direction of the counter. His hand bumped and he followed it around until he felt the table. From the table he was able to feel the wall and then the door. He walked to the wall beyond the door and pulled it open a crack. Nothing. He could make out the Model A, but could not tell for sure if its driver side door was closed. He thought it was. He opened the exit door wide enough to stick his head out and look down each side of the building in the area behind the schoolhouse proper. Again, nothing. He waited another minute and then stepped out. He couldn't see anything moving or that looked out of place. He started toward the car, walking as quietly as he could. Halfway there he heard a sound. He froze. He heard the sound again. It was coming from the Model A. Someone was snoring.

The nephew continued toward the car, now slightly crouched. He approached from the rear and walked slowly around to the passenger door. The window was down and the snoring was loud and steady. As he raised himself up to look, he was nearly overwhelmed by the strong odor of alcohol mixed with urine and other smells of a body long removed from its last bath. He wished he had brought a flashlight, but he had left his only one in the Zephyr. He fumbled in his pocket and brought out a small box of matches. He stood up fully and lit one against the friction strip on the box. He stuck the burning match through the window and immediately recognized Johnny Burger, an old lumberjack who had been the town drunk even when the nephew was in high school.

"Old Man" Burger is what he and his friends had called Johnny even back then. His friends had often bragged of getting "Old Man" Burger to buy beer for them, and that was over ten years ago. The nephew was amazed he was still alive.

The match seemed to rouse the old man and he opened his eyes. When he thought about it later, the nephew realized that he should have immediately doused his match when he recognized Johnny Burger, but he didn't. The old man and he stared at each other in the match light.

"What—who," Burger stammered. "Hey, I know you. You're the rich boy who got all your uncle's money. Hey, why don't you give me some. I need some free jack. How 'bout a dollar?"

The nephew was taken aback by how fast "Old Man" woke up. "Hello, Mr. Burger," he said. "I'll give you a dollar, okay, but you'll have to get out of the car." By then the match had burned down and the nephew had thrown it away. "In fact, I'll give you five dollars if you'll help me over here."

"Sure," the old man said. He almost fell out of the car as the nephew opened the door. "Wondered what somebody was a'doing here this time a'night. What I gotta do?"

"Follow me," the nephew replied. "Here, over here by the door, help me lift this thing."

"What thing?" asked the old man as he followed the nephew over to the back door of the community building.

"Down here." The nephew pointed toward the ground beside the door.

Johnny Burger was bent over trying to see the "thing" when the nephew brought both hands clenched together down on the back of his neck with great force, a disabling blow learned at Officers Training School. It was at OTS where the nephew also learned the deadly "choke lock" which he next applied to the old man. The training took over.

Johnny was dead when the nephew finally let the body fall to the ground. He was shaking and wanted to run, to get away from the nightmare he had started, but he just stood there over Johnny's body. He forced himself to concentrate and to slowly gain control over the tide of hysteria which was threatening to engulf him.

After a few minutes, he reached down and grabbed Johnny by the back of his jacket. He opened the door, grateful that he had extinguished the inside light, and dragged the body through the door and laid it down. After a minute, he pulled the feet around toward the fuse and kerosene bottle he had planted by the Register of Deeds record cabinet. Johnny's head was left lying just a couple of feet from the door. One last time the nephew checked for Johnny's pulse. There was none.

The next evening as he waited at Michigan Central Station in Detroit, he was able to reach Jack by long distance. "I want to thank you again for taking me to Gaylord to catch the train. Only a true friend would get up at that time in the morning, or maybe I should say night."

"Yeah, it was kind of early," Jack replied. "By the way, you missed all the excitement. When I got back to Ashford, Main Street was blocked by fire hoses running from the river to the school. The Community Building burned, burned right to the ground."

"Weren't the county records stored there?" The nephew was trying to sound indifferent. "Were they burnt too?"

"Completely destroyed. Everybody here is running around like a chicken with its head cut off, trying to find their original deeds and things. We're all afraid some charlatans will come in and try to claim our land. You're probably safe, I think. Judge Sharp has all the Probate records since the courthouse burned over at his private office. I checked with him this afternoon."

Again the nephew tried to sound detached. "Thanks for checking that for me—and I guess for you, too."

"That's right," Jack said with a chuckle.

"Do they have any idea how it started?" The big question.

"They sure do," Jack said, and paused. The nephew's heart skipped a beat. "You remember 'Ole Man Burger'?"

"Yes."

"They think he somehow got in the building to sleep it off. Must have dropped a cigarette. The place was full of loose paper. Got burning good before anybody noticed. It was probably going when we were leaving for Gaylord. Anyway, Mr. Burger didn't get out. They found his body by the back door."

The nephew struggled to hide his reaction; he wanted to laugh out loud, to shout, "Hooray." Instead he forced himself to speak calmly. "That's too bad. My three minutes are about up. Got to catch another train. I'm at the station in Detroit. Should be in New York by morning and on my ship by tomorrow night. Can you take care of my records okay with the power of attorney I left?"

"Yes I can," Jack replied. "That's why I went by to see Judge Sharpe. You just have a good trip and get the war won. Don't worry about anything here. I'll see to it all."

"I'm much obliged, Jack, for everything. I'll write when I know my permanent address over there. Good-bye."

"Good-bye."

By the time the train reached Buffalo, he had dozed off without the fears that had plagued him for the past several months. He had gone over in his mind every detail of his actions since David's letter had arrived. The noise and motion of the train had seemed to enhance his memory. He couldn't think of any loophole left—except the can buried behind the old cabin in the swamp—by which he could be exposed. And he was confident no one would ever discover the buried can by accident. Yes, he concluded, he would no longer have to fear discovery. And his new fear—with respect to what kind of person he had actually become—he found easy to put out of his mind.

He didn't think about Mr. Burger at all.

BOOK ONE—EPILOGUE

October, 1944
State Capitol, Lansing, Michigan

The House of Representatives Chamber in the Michigan Capitol Building was only two-thirds full on the October afternoon chosen by Governor Comstock for the commencement of the first special session of the 1944 Legislature. He had called the session at the request of Representative Green and Senator Andrews after meeting with them and a contingent of their constituents, government officials and business leaders from sparsely populated Montgomery County.

George Stevens was one of the businessmen from Montgomery County who had strongly pushed the bill which was to be considered at the special session. He now watched from the west balcony, slightly awed by the giant room decorated with large banners bearing the state seal hung between the two-story high windows and the ornate desks and high-backed chairs in rows, two-abreast, facing the two-tiered dais at the north end of the room.

Try as he might, Stevens could not rid himself of the anxiety which had started to build the night before while he and two others from Ashford had dined at the Roosevelt Hotel, across the street from the Capitol Building, with Bill Green, the State Representative from Montgomery County. Representative Green had expressed concern about whether or not a quorum would be present for the special session. The doubt over a quorum had festered as George attempted to sleep, reminded of his stakes in the outcome of today's session by his view of the Capitol dome that dominated the vista through his hotel room window.

George Stevens had come to Ashford in 1895 with little more than a wife, an infant son and the clothes on their backs. Now, nearly fifty years later, he had amassed a modest fortune, the result of hard work, some luck in escaping the bank holiday with most of his cash in his pocket, and the resulting ability to continue his lumbering operations during the depression years. However, most of his wealth was tied up in nearly 20,000 acres of Montgomery County land, land he had accumulated during the rock-bottom prices and tax sales of the depression.

Scattered throughout the county in parcels ranging from forty to 1,600 acres, the land had found new value as the factory workers and executives from southern Michigan sought hunting, fishing and other recreational lands within driving distance from their homes. The only problem was that George Stevens and nearly every other landowner in Montgomery County could not sell their lands. The destruction of the county records of deeds by the fires of the year before had made it impossible to provide evidence of land ownership. Only the most foolhardy would purchase land from someone unable to prove ownership.

At promptly 2:00 p.m. Speaker Nugent brought his enormous gavel down on the special oak block attached to the raised desk and podium. He faced the 110 smaller desks, one for each of the members, in the huge room which occupied the entire second and third floors of the Capitol's north wing. The members moved to their seats and in a relatively short period of time a surprising stillness materialized in the chamber. With no amplification equipment, almost total silence was necessary for those addressing the body of legislators to be heard. Private conversations while a member was speaking were prohibited. The Sergeant at Arms and his deputies were proficient at quickly removing offending members from the chamber.

"The House will come to order," Speaker Nugent blared in a voice which was almost shrill, but easily heard throughout the giant room. Many members believed that his penetrating voice was the major reason he had been elected speaker for each of the last three sessions. "The first extra meeting of the 1944 Michigan House of Representatives as called by the Governor of the State of Michigan is now in session. The Clerk will call the roll."

The House Clerk from his podium at a lower level, but directly in front of the Speaker, switched on the two-year-old electric voting board on which the members' votes were registered from buttons on each desk, and, at the beginning of each session, their attendance. After two minutes of observing the tabulations on a small tote machine located next to his podium, the Clerk announced, "Mr. Speaker, a quorum is present. Seventy-two members are in attendance, thirty-eight members are absent." Daniel Thatcher's voice was much deeper than the Speaker's, but it was loud enough to be heard throughout the chamber and was also an essential requirement for his position as House Clerk.

"The Clerk will read the message from the Governor," blared Speaker Nugent.

Daniel Thatcher opened the folder before him on the podium, took a deep breath and began to read, "Ladies and Gentlemen of the House of Representatives and Gentlemen of the Senate: In my capacity as Governor of the State of Michigan I hereby call you into special session of your respective bodies for the purpose of considering a proposed act to help the citizens and landowners in one of our smallest counties address a problem which has befallen them as the result of fires which completely destroyed all of the official records of the county. I know that many of you will find hardship, and some impossibility, in attending this special session because of your military and other war-related responsibilities in the current world conflict, but I call you regardless because I am convinced that the people of Montgomery County now need, and any other county which may in the future suffer a similar loss of its records will need, a method of dealing with and reestablishing records which have been lost or destroyed.

"Therefore, I submit to you the attached bill which I ask you to promptly consider as the business of the special session called herewith."

"Representative Green. The Speaker recognizes Representative Green of Hillside."

Representative William Green, known to his friends as Bill, was standing at the floor podium on the right side in the front of the House. He was from Hillside, one of four small towns remaining in Montgomery County, and was the State Representative for the Presque Isle District, which included four other northern Michigan counties as well. "Thank you, Mr. Speaker." His voice was more mellow and did not carry as well in the chamber as either the Clerk's or the Speaker's, so he had to nearly yell to be heard as he addressed the members. "I have introduced the bill prepared by the Governor, and have presented the original to the Clerk. Printed copies have been distributed to each member's desk. I request that the bill be placed on first reading and be assigned to the House Judiciary Committee."

"Without objection we go to the order of the first reading of bills," announced Speaker Nugent. "I hear none. The Clerk will read the bill."

Daniel Thatcher took a deep breath and began, "House Bill 4401 introduced by Representative Green to establish an act of the State of Michigan entitled: An act to establish procedures for the reestablishment of land records and other records in counties where the originals of such records have been destroyed by fire, flood or other natural or man-made disaster.

"Section 1: This act shall be known as 'The Burnt Records Act.' Section 2…"

Speaker Nugent interrupted, "Representative Green, for what reason does the gentleman rise?"

"Mr. Speaker, I move that the bill be considered read, and I ask to speak before referral."

"Without objection the bill shall be considered read. I hear none. Representative Green."

"Thank you, Mr. Speaker. Chairman Bryant has agreed to hold a meeting of the Judiciary Committee to address this matter immediately after referral. If it is the wish of the Speaker, the House could recess while his committee meets to consider the bill. If everyone were to consent, we have enough members here, barely, to suspend the rules and advance to second and third readings yet today after the judiciary committee has made its recommendation. May I proceed, Mr. Speaker?"

"I won't stand in the way of your streaking horse if you have the votes, Representative Green. And I don't imagine most of the members will object too loudly to not having a morning session following the parties planned for tonight," Speaker Nugent answered, referring to the traditional gatherings at the Olds, Porter and Roosevelt Hotels hosted by lobbyists on the opening night of legislative sessions. He waited for the laughter to stop before continuing, "Representative Green, you may continue."

"Thank you, Mr. Speaker. Hopefully I can save everybody, including the committee members, time by explaining the Montgomery County problem here. Their situation is this: the County Courthouse in Ashford burned in 1942, but it wasn't too bad because all of the land records and other official county records were in fireproof vaults, and for the most part were saved. Oh, they were out of business for the better part of a month, but the County officers set up shop in the community building at the Ashford School. But guess what? It burned, too, last spring. It was built of tamarack logs and once it got started, it just burned hot, and this time destroyed all the records. Land records, birth and death records, tax records, even records which were in the few safes, like in the Clerk's office, were destroyed by the immense heat of those tamarack logs burning.

"To make matters worse, the only county-wide newspaper office, the Montgomery County Gazette, burned to the ground last January. There aren't even old newspaper records anymore."

"Point of order, point of order," one of the members was shouting.

"Just a minute, Representative Green," interposed Speaker Nugent. "Representative Montgomery, what is your point of order?"

Representative Montgomery was a freshman representative from Detroit. Even though a member of the minority party, he had quickly become respected for his intelligence and liked for his warmth, and, most notably, his wit. "Mr. Speaker, and through you to my honorable colleague, Representative Green. This may not be exactly a point of order, but I'm wondering whether Montgomery County needs this bill or whether they need an appropriation for an arson squad?"

The members, including Representative Green, roared in laughter. After a minute or so, Speaker Nugent restored order with his gavel. "Are you quite through, Representative Montgomery?" he asked, provoking yet more merriment among the members.

Representative Montgomery, still standing, waited for the laughter to die and then said, "Well, when all of the important records in my namesake county are burned, somebody must know why."

This time no one laughed. Representative Green thought for a moment and then replied, "Mr. Speaker, and through you to Representative Montgomery. After the first fire nobody thought too much about it, but now most people in Montgomery County believe those fires were deliberately set, including the sheriff. But nobody has a clue as to who or why, and nobody's even come up with a good rumor, yet." He noted that Representative Montgomery had taken his seat, and then continued. "In all seriousness, the situation up there has become pretty grim. People can't sell their land or even enforce some of their contracts because the records are gone. This bill will set up a procedure by which the Chancery Court can look at the papers people have and hear their testimony, and then grant decrees which will have the same effect as replacing the records which have been destroyed.

"Representative Bryant has worked with me on this. He's had some concerns about due process. I think he's satisfied with this bill now. I don't think this will solve the mystery of who burned the courthouse, school and newspaper, or why, and I think this will put lawyers into the pockets of almost every citizen of Montgomery County, but I don't see much choice. Please help me with this bill."

The bill was passed by the House later that afternoon and by the Senate two days later. The Governor signed it into law in the Senate chamber after the final vote. It became, and remains, Sections 561.1—561.10 of the Michigan Compiled Laws.

A day later as he maneuvered his four-year old Dodge over the unpaved road east of Grayling, the last stretch of his 200 mile trip from Lansing to Ashford, George Stevens started to whistle. He would be able to sell land in Montgomery County for the first time since the fires.

BOOK TWO

July - October, 1969

“The past is not dead.
It’s not even past.”
WILLIAM FAULKNER
(1897-1962)

CHAPTER 10

He was almost gone before the call came. Usually he tried to sneak out early on Wednesday afternoons to pursue his one true passion, fishing for brook trout. He usually fished the East Branch, but occasionally when he didn't take off the whole afternoon, like today, he fished the closer Thunder Bay River between the Old Ford Bridge and Lake 15.

He tried to avoid the call, telling Rose, his secretary, "Can't she talk to me tomorrow? I'd like to have trout for dinner and they're not going to jump into my frying pan without some help."

"She sounds kinda lost, Mr. Johnson, and she's calling long distance," Rose countered. "She has some sort of accent, like British, but not quite. I think you ought to take a minute and talk to her."

"Okay, okay, you win. I'll get it back at my desk. And Rose, how many times do I have to remind you that you're too formal for northern Michigan. Please call me 'Colby.'" Rose House had moved to Ashford with her husband three years before from Raleigh, North Carolina, and had not yet completely adopted the rural informalities.

Colby picked up the phone without sitting and said, "This is Colby Johnson."

"Mr. Johnson, my name is Diane Askew." Her voice was husky and distinctly foreign. "I'm calling from Alpena, but I've just arrived from Australia," she told him, revealing the accent's source. "You were recommended to me by Joel Willard. In fact, I'm phoning from his office."

He hadn't seen Willard in months, and smiled at the idea of a recommendation. "What can I do for you, Diane?"

"I've come to find my father." The husky voice paused, then continued, "It's rather a long story, but the only thing I really know is that he left Sydney in 1939 to look for his father who he believed lived in Ashford, Michigan. Mr. Willard has suggested that you might help me search through the records in your county for some trace of his name. I would like to retain you to help me if I could." Her last words came in a rush.

"When are you planning to come over?"

"One of Mr. Willard's associates has to go to Ashford tomorrow afternoon and has offered me a lift. I would be delighted if you could see me at one-thirty or as soon after as possible."

Colby breathed a sigh of relief; he'd get to the river yet today.

She continued, "Frankly, I have checked into a hotel here for the night and am about to go there. I was able to have a good sleep in Los Angeles the night before last, and some rest in Detroit last night, but it's midnight now in Sydney and I can feel it. So I hope you will let me tell my whole story tomorrow when I will be more awake."

"Sure, Diane, one-thirty will be fine. By the way, what's your father's name? Maybe I've heard of him."

"David Baxter. I have corresponded with Sheriff Wanika over the past few months. He hasn't found anyone who knew of him. I believe he must not have stayed in Ashford, but I am hoping for some bit of information to show that he was here and where he might have gone."

"You're right. I've never heard of anyone around here by the name of David Baxter. I'll look forward to seeing you tomorrow afternoon."

"Thank you, Mr. Johnson, good-bye."

By the time Colby reached the old ford on the river it was nearly 4:30. He pulled his one-year-old Jeep Wagoneer onto the old roadway leading to the gravel shallows where once wagons and early automobiles had forded the river before the bridge had been constructed at a site just upstream. Even now teenagers occasionally drove their cars through the river at the old ford site.

The day was nearly perfect, a haze dimming slightly the sun's glow, almost no wind. The temperature, now in the high 70's, would fall seven or eight degrees by the time the sun set. The cedars along the rushing water were bright green even in the hazy sunlight, but after the sun set they would darken to deeper shades and finally become black as darkness fell. The river is the one place where I'm alone but not lonely, he thought.

Colby walked parallel with the south bank of the river, heading east, but some 100 yards from the riverbank. Brook trout were easily spooked and he was taking no chances. He would fish back upstream and into the sun. When he could make out Lake 15 through the trees, he turned north toward the river.

At the river's edge he stopped and watched for nearly five minutes. There were no tell-tale ripples to indicate that the trout were feeding on the surface. A caddis fly hatch might occur later, but for now it was either a wet fly or a spinner and worm. He decided on the latter and quickly removed his fly reel and replaced it with a closed-face spinning reel. Deftly he threaded the fly rod with the spinning line and tied on a small gold spinner. He next attached a #10 long-shanked hook to the spinner and removed a lively worm from his bait box. After threading the worm on the hook, he leaned the rod against a cedar branch while he wiped a layer of 6–12 insect repellent on his bare arms, neck and face. He hated its smell, but not as much as he hated mosquito bites. They would thicken as night approached.

His last chore was to pull his wader suspenders up over his shoulders, raising the wader top to cover his chest. He grabbed his fly rod and slowly stepped down into the river. It would get shallower as he made his way upstream, closer to the ford, but here it came to within a foot from the top of his waders.

On his third cast, just above an old tree trunk leaning down into the river along the north bank, Colby got his first strike. But he was slow to set the hook and the fish got away. As he approached the half-way point back toward his car, having missed on seven of his ten strikes along the way, he realized that his heart really wasn't in his fishing tonight. Besides, he had three ten-inchers, plenty for dinner. He sometimes had to remind himself that it was just him now.

He waded through the river over to the south bank and pulled himself up to sit on an old tamarack stump with roots extending down into the water. It was still warmed by the fading sunlight. He lit a Marlboro. He had started smoking again after Janice took the children back down-state and filed for divorce. He only quit before because of her nagging. She was probably right on that one, though.

Colby and Janice had moved to Ashford five years before, Colby then fresh out of law school with the bar exam under his belt. Their son Brent was not quite a year old when they moved, in May of 1964. Traci was born during their second year here.

They had come to Ashford at the urging of Colby's new stepfather, Dennis Mays, then and still president of the Montgomery County State

Bank. He had persuaded Colby of the need and opportunity for a lawyer in Ashford and had promised to provide and outfit a law office, books and all, if Colby would come. Colby came and Dennis made good on his promise.

If Colby had any doubts about his move to Ashford, they were removed by an event which occurred shortly after their arrival. It was on May 30, 1964, Memorial Day. Colby took Brent to watch the parade along Main Street, not much really, the high school band, the town's two fire engines, and the veterans marching, most from World War II, one from World War I, and another from the Korean War. It was the veterans, proudly marching in their old uniforms for all to see, that got to him. He was suddenly very proud to be where he was. There was his stepfather, Dennis Mays, president of the bank, and the others, all but one of whom he had met in just the three weeks since he had come to live here. Jack Sams, owner of the insurance agency; Bud Jakes, the gasoline and fuel oil distributor; Don Baird, superintendent of schools; Joe Kern, high school principal; 'Mick' Vaughan, owner of a truck line that hauled milk for all the farms in the northern part of the state; Dane Jackson, owner of the general store; Eldon Darwin, timber jobber; Edson Drew, owner of the lumber yard; all three real estate brokers in town, Claude Murphy, Bernie Valley and Eldon Bird; and several others who he was acquainted with, more or less, but whose names he didn't know or couldn't remember.

The sight of those middle-aged men, the community and business leaders of Ashford, trying, and in most cases succeeding, to fit into their old service uniforms, marching along the street was a moving experience for Colby. It might have been because his father had been killed in World War II, or it just might have been the look of pride on their faces. For whatever reason, he felt like he was at home for the first time in his life as he watched them march by in the parade.

But for Janice it had been different. She had not liked Ashford from the first minute she had set foot here. She gamely, he supposed on reflection, tried to make it work during the first couple of years, but soon after Traci was born her hostility was on the front burner. And it was directed not just at Ashford, but at him. He at first was willing to move to a place where she would be happy, but he soon became convinced that she would never be happy with him in any place. He didn't know whether her disdain for him was caused by his having brought her to Ashford, or whether she would have grown to dislike him no matter where they lived. By then it didn't really matter. He had decided that he wasn't too happy living with her either.

When she finally left, it was only watching his children go that hurt.

By then, he had developed many friendships in Ashford and he was aware that a number of the townspeople were going out of their way to help soften his loneliness after Janice moved away.

In particular, several of the men invited Colby to participate in hunting and fishing trips to Canada and out west.

Despite their age differences, he developed close friendships with Claude Murphy and Bud Jakes. He had initially spent quite a bit of time with Edson Drew, who owned the town's lumberyard and was also involved in several timbering ventures around the county, but their relationship soured when Edson began berating the legal profession on almost every occasion they were together. When Colby had finally complained at a dinner party hosted by Bud Jakes and his wife, Edson had reacted strongly. After that evening, Colby and Edson rarely spoke.

He had wondered since whether Edson's badgering behavior had been directed at the legal profession in general or at him personally. Once, while visiting Edson at his house on Clear Lake, he had sensed that Edson was quite defensive about his status in the Ashford community. Edson had conceded that almost everything he owned was directly or indirectly inherited. As the evening wore on and Edson had continued to imbibe, he had for the first time made disparaging comments about the legal profession to Colby. Maybe if he had responded then when they were alone, Colby often thought, Edson's rancorous comments would not have continued to escalate to the point where he had been forced to respond strongly in a semi-public setting.

Also, from the first time Colby met Edson, he sensed an undercurrent between Edson and his mother, which he didn't understand. Once at a V.F.W. social when Edson was on the warpath about lawyers, Colby saw his mother shake her head toward Edson. He didn't say much more after that.

One thing was sure; Colby was saddened by Edson's behavior as their friendship waned.

Colby suddenly realized that it was almost dark and he had another quarter of a mile of tromping through brush in his waders to reach the car. It was remembering that his children were coming next week to stay with him for a month that brought him back to the present. He quickly cleaned the three trout and then headed along the riverbank toward the red glow from the sun, already long set, and his jeep.

Later, as he slowly drove the Wagoneer along the partly sand, partly gravel road toward the main highway, he thought again of watching the parade on his first Memorial Day in Ashford. He wondered briefly if the veterans of the current war in Vietnam would be as well received thirty years from now as Eldon Darwin and his fellow World War II and Korean War veterans were now.

Colby had been deferred from the draft, first because he was a student, and in later years because he was a parent. Now he was too old. I wonder why I don't feel unpatriotic about not wanting to go over there, he thought. I wouldn't run away to Canada like Larry Hollister did, but I never felt compelled to volunteer, either. I don't know how I feel about the anti-war protesters. Is it treasonous to work against the government's policies during a war?

His thoughts were interrupted by the sight of his driveway just ahead. He was home. Now for some fresh trout and fried potatoes.

Colby had become an early riser since Janice left. He liked to work on files brought home over coffee as the sun came up. His routine usually found him at Utt's Cafe having breakfast by 7:30 and in his office by 8:15. He liked to have Rose open up before he arrived.

He hadn't brought any files home last night because of his fishing plans, which allowed him to just sit on his back porch and enjoy the early morning sunlight creep down the trees on the opposite riverbank while he sipped coffee. The porch overlooked the backwaters of the Thunder Bay River dam pond in Ashford. While the same river with its much colder water several miles upstream had provided brook trout the night before, its characteristics behind his house were quite different. He could see the old river channel as a break in the lily pads which otherwise covered the dam pond backwater from bank to bank. The dam had been constructed to provide electricity for Ashford during the 1930's. It was no longer used for that purpose, but still created a pond for nearly two miles upstream from the dam. It had a great warming effect on the water, and the river below the dam could no longer sustain a native brook trout population. However, the Department of Conservation annually planted rainbow and brown trout which created a continuing fishing opportunity on the down-river side of the Ashford dam for many miles.

Colby's modest home was built on an island created in the river by the reservoir of the Ashford dam. Access to the island was by a small causeway. Although much of the reservoir's surface was marked by a heavy cover of lily pads, Colby's view from his porch, looking almost directly upriver at the old river channel winding down toward him through the lily pads, was quite enchanting, especially at sunrise and sunset.

On that morning he looked ahead to his schedule for the day. He remembered his brief conversation with Diane Askew and wondered what records she would be looking for. Had she said her father came here in 1939? If so, he wondered, had the records she was seeking been destroyed by the courthouse and newspaper office fires?

Practicing law in Montgomery County, particularly real estate and probate work, was sometimes made extremely challenging by the lack of historical public records from any time prior to April of 1943. Colby remembered how he had first learned of the courthouse and newspaper office fires.

His stepfather had hosted a welcome party for Colby and Janice on their first weekend in Ashford at his house on Valentine Lake, one of several picturesque lakes nestled in the gentle hills and valleys which surrounded Ashford.

As it turned out, Colby had learned on that Friday that he passed the bar exam from the announcement and list which appeared in the Detroit Free Press. So the welcome party turned into a celebration as well. Not only was the exam result good news for Colby, but he sensed that his stepfather was relieved to know that his investments in Colby's office and books would not be in vain.

The weather on the evening of the party was not as cooperative, however. A brisk northeast wind brought cold, rainy air into the area. Earlier that afternoon, snowflakes had allegedly been seen in town, an occurrence that, while not unknown, was certainly not commonplace during the second week of May.

Nearly every businessman and professional in the county had been invited, and most came in spite of the weather. His stepfather's large, wood-floored living room was crowded with well-wishers and those curious to meet the new lawyer in town. The other three lawyers in the county were there also, Jim French of Hillside, Arthur Green who had offices in both Ashford and Lumberton, and Ivan Henry, the part-time prosecuting attorney who also had a private practice in Ashford. Of the three, only Jim French had been in the county for more than ten years. He had been the prosecuting attorney for sixteen years before Ivan Henry, then fresh out of law school, had challenged and defeated him in the 1960 election.

Mr. Green had retired from a law office in Detroit, moved north to Lumberton in 1964, and was now as active as ever in his 77th year of life.

But it was Claude Murphy, the dean of Ashford real estate brokers, who stood with Colby alongside the raised hearth of the large, rustic fireplace which dominated the east wall of the spacious room, and told him the story of the fires.

"Welcome to Ashford. I'm Claude Murphy," he said as he extended his hand toward Colby. Claude was a fairly short, bald headed man who Colby judged to be in his fifties. His smile was warm and sincere.

"Thanks, Colby Johnson," Colby said as he reached to shake Claude's offered hand.

"Yes, I know. Your mother and Dennis really know how to throw a party. I'm sorta glad you came along to give 'em a reason." They both chuckled.

"How do you fit in the Montgomery County hierarchy, Mr. Murphy?"

"Oh, I'm in the real estate business, Murphy Real Estate. I'm getting to be one of the 'old timers' here, I guess, but please call me Claude."

"Yes, I've noticed your office. Across the street from the Ford Motor Sales, right?"

"That's it. So tell me, Colby, what kind of lawyer do you wanna be? Not that you can specialize here much, but what do you like?"

"I think I like property and business kinds of things best. At least that's where I got my best grades in law school."

"Good, good. Neither Henry nor Green knows real estate law much, and Jimmy French is too much in the bottle to be very reliable any more. I've had to go to Alpena most of the time to get anything done right. I've been using Ben Willard's son Joel since Ben died last year. He's new, but he seems to know what he's doing."

"Oh, I know Joel. He was a senior when I was a freshman in law school, but we were in one class together, Uniform Commercial Code. It was a pretty tough class for a second semester freshman. Joel actually helped me quite a bit, especially when he learned that my mother lived in Ashford. He's a pretty good guy."

Claude smiled. "Well, it'll be good to have someone right here. There's lots of work here on land titles, mostly 'cause of the courthouse fire, or more accurately, fires."

"Yeah, Dennis said something to me about the courthouse having burned when he was talking to me about coming here. What's the story on the fires?"

Claude paused before answering. "Well, to me it's a mystery; didn't seem so at the time, but looking back, three fires within a few months which combined to destroy all the county's records and history is just too much of a coincidence."

"Three fires? I didn't realize that. What all burned?"

"First, the old County Courthouse burned, late in '42 it was. But most of the records were saved on account of being stored in fireproof vaults. A few documents which were left on desks or were stored outside the vaults were burnt, but most survived. They hauled the court files and other documents from the Clerk's office and the Libers and indexes from the Register of Deeds office to the school community building. Within a few days the county offices were up and running out of there.

"In the meantime, a couple of months, or so, later the Montgomery County Gazette building burned to the ground. Most people didn't realize it, but it contained an old newspaper library of both its issues and the old Ashford Herald issues dating back to the 1880's.

"And then in April of '43, the community building burned to the ground, and this time everything in it went up. Nothing was saved. So now we don't have any official or unofficial records of what went on in this county before 1943. Not only land records, but also birth and death records, marriage records, court files, and the list goes on."

Colby was fully intrigued now. "Do they have any ideas about who might have done this, or why?"

"No, none at all. At the time the sheriff thought the first courthouse fire might have been arson, but not much was done about it. Everybody thought the newspaper fire was started by an overloaded coal furnace, and an old drunk was found dead in the community building ashes, so everybody thought he must have dropped a cigarette. But looking back, well, I was at both of the last two fires. They spread awfully fast for being started accidentally. In my own mind now, I believe they were all set to deliberately do away with all our records. And somebody sure succeeded."

"But why, Claude, does anybody have any idea why?"

"Not any good ideas that I know of. I've heard people say that Jimmy French did it on account of how much money he made after the fire reestablishing people's land titles. But I don't put any stock in that theory. Jim probably couldn't have foreseen that he'd have all that work, and he really wasn't that ambitious anyway.

"By the way, there was another fire a couple of years before that. Sam Gassel's law office burned, and they were pretty sure it was arson. But everybody thought at the time ole Hans Kohler and his nephew did it on account of Sam being Jewish and always writing in the paper about how bad Hitler and the Germans were. Nobody else really knew about Hitler then, and Hans Kohler was born in Germany and was real vocal against Sam. But Sam had been the county's only lawyer for nearly 20 years, and you can bet that his files had a lot of interesting documents, too.

"Although I've never said anything about it, I've always been suspicious about Hans and his nephew, Warren, over the courthouse fires, myself. It must be the whiskey making me say it now," Claude chuckled, "but I always thought it was funny that Warren never went away to the war. Just about everybody else in town did, you know. That eliminated a lot of suspects right there. And I'd always heard that there was somebody else's name on their farm deed, some ex-wife of Hans. That would have been one way of clearing it up.

"And I've also heard Edson Drew's name in connection with the fires. That's him standing over there, talking to your mother." Colby looked over to see the man talking to his mother. Edson was of average size and looked to be about his mother's age. He had a fleeting sense of déjà vu as he watched his mother and Edson Drew in conversation. Mr. Drew looked familiar, but he couldn't recall why.

"Edson was in the service at the time of the fires," Claude continued, "but I've heard he was in Ashford on leave when the last fire occurred. He's now a big lumberman in these parts. He inherited a lot of land and has bought even more, most of it since the fires. Some people said he took advantage of the special court procedures after the fire to get title to some property he hadn't owned before. He's cantankerous enough, but who knows. All I know is our history burned up.

"And you know, Colby, in a few years there won't be many of us left who even remember this place in the years before the fires."

Colby had spent quite a bit of time during the weeks following that conversation trying to figure out why anyone might have wanted to destroy all of the county's records and history, and who that person might have been. There were both too many possibilities and too few potential suspects to let him get very far, but he still occasionally found his mind thinking about the mystery of the fires.

By the time he arrived at Gavine's for breakfast Colby had forgotten about Diane Askew—and the fires. He was more interested in reading about the Detroit Tigers' win the night before in the Free Press he had purchased from the stand in front of the restaurant.

CHAPTER 11

Colby returned to his office from lunch, a hamburger and french fries at Utt's Cafe, at 1:15. Diane Askew was already there, seated in his waiting room and looking somewhat tired. He noticed that she was not wearing any make-up—and also that she was nevertheless quite attractive. Her hair was light red and was done up in a bun on top of her head. She looked to be close to his age, thirty-two, and he could tell even while she was seated that she was quite tall. She stood when he introduced himself, and he judged that she was only a few inches shorter than his own 5'11". She was wearing a pale yellow cotton dress with a butterfly pattern. The pattern was the color of her hair. Her eyes were bluish-green. He also noticed her luggage, two large suitcases, on the floor beside her chair.

He showed her back to his office and offered her coffee. She accepted, black with sugar. She assured him when he inquired that she was getting over her jet-lag and was feeling much more rested than when she had talked to him by phone the day before.

After taking a sip of the coffee, she asked, "Shall we discuss your fee or shall I tell you my story first? I must warn you that it may take some time."

Normally he would have said that his clock started after the first half hour, but to her he said, "The rest of today is on the house. You've come a long way and I'll be delighted to help you if I can." And he was delighted. After only a few minutes and some idle chit-chat, he knew that he liked very much being in the same room with Diane Askew.

She began. She first explained that she had never met her father, David Baxter, and in fact had not known who her father was until after years of asking, her mother finally told her the full story.

Her mother had been in love with David for years as a teenager and had finally given herself to him on the night before he left for America, August 1, 1939. She became pregnant that night.

"Mother always told me that my father had been killed in the war, and in fact, before I was born she moved to Sydney with financial help from my grandparents. In those days her predicament must have caused them all great embarrassment in the small village where she was raised. I had always assumed that she had been married to my supposed father, the soldier, but as she later told me, she merely used the name, Askew, of an acquaintance who was a soldier and had been killed during an air raid in London."

"Didn't she try to find David?" Colby asked.

"She told me that he had promised to write but never did. She knew that he was coming to America to find his father, or at least to find out what had become of his father. David told Mother he had recently learned that he was born in Michigan and that his mother had divorced his father when he was just a baby and come back to her native Australia. Apparently they had met and married in France during World War I."

"What was David's father's name?"

"She can't remember. David did show her the divorce decree and she remembers that it took place in Ashford, Michigan. She circled Ashford in an atlas she had at the time. Needless to say, she still has the atlas. But try as she might, she can't remember the surname of David's father. Baxter was from his stepfather in Australia. She does remember that his father's middle name was David. She also remembers David telling her that his father had worked in the timber business. Apparently his mother had given his father some money to get into business and he had done quite well at it."

"When did David's mother tell him all this?"

"She didn't. He found a copy of the divorce papers and his birth certificate in her things after she died. There were also two letters from his father, but Mother was under the impression they were not recent. Apparently their tone was warm. Mother said that David was sure his father would be happy to see him. Of course, David could not know whether his father was still alive."

Colby could see Diane's eyes starting to fill with tears. And all of a sudden he had to turn away to hide his own. It dawned on him that here she was in the same place and for the same reason David Baxter supposedly came to Ashford thirty years before. He also realized how strong Diane was just to undertake her quest. He saw that she didn't try to hide her tears or to seek sympathy with them. They were just there, a fact of her present state of emotion which she did not conceal.

After a moment, he said, "Diane, let's take a walk down to the river. The air will do us good."

She smiled slightly. "Yes." Her hand brushed away the tears. "It would be pleasing." She looked at him for a long moment. "I think you are a nice man. Mr. Willard gave me good advice by sending me to you."

Colby turned to his bookcase as he rose. He did not want her to see that he was blushing. He also was experiencing feelings that a lawyer should not have toward a client.

They walked east from Colby's office toward the three blocks which made up the main business district of Ashford, away from the courthouse. Before they reached the first of those blocks, they turned right, down the street which led to the township park. The park stretched for the length of two blocks along the north bank of the pond created by the old power dam across Thunder Bay River. They walked east through the park to the dam and walked onto the roadway which crossed the dam.

"See those tall, slender trees on the bank of the river," Colby said as he pointed downstream from the dam, "not the pines, but the ones with regular leaves?"

"Yes, I do."

"Those are black ash trees. There used to be more, but people cut a lot of them. The wood is beautiful, dark colored and finishes with a shine. Makes beautiful furniture. The town was named for that grove of trees and the river. Before they built the dam or had any bridges, the early settlers crossed the river at several places where it was shallow and the bottom was gravel or hard. The crossing places were called fords. This place was called the ash ford."

"Hence the name, Ashford," she responded with a smile. "You really know your local history. How long did you say you've lived here?"

"Not that long," he answered, "but it's hard not to listen to all the stories the old-timers tell. Everybody has seemed to want the town's lawyer to know everything about the town, so they tell me."

Between cars, they crossed the road and stood watching the water rush out of the spillway and continue eastward as a river once again. They then went back to the park and sat on a bench watching the ducks feed only a few feet from the youthful swimmers splashing around in the water at the park's small sand beach.

It was a beautiful northern Michigan summer day, no clouds and a temperature in the high 70's. Their bench was in the shade of the park's stately white pines. They had not talked much at first, pausing only when they met the occasional person who was an acquaintance of Colby. In each case he introduced Diane as a friend from Australia. When she asked why he didn't describe her as his client, he said that people would want to know what for, and besides, he already felt she was a friend too. She smiled at that, and he thought he noticed a slight blush creep across her face. On the way from the dam back to the park she reached up and took two pins from her hair and let it fall back down her shoulders. It came nearly a third of the way down her back. Colby thought it was more attractive down and said so. She smiled again. He smiled when she smiled.

When he asked, she told him of her bachelor and master degrees from the University of Melbourne. She had been teaching history at a secondary school in Sydney for five years and was taking this semester off to search for her father. She had thought about waiting for summer break, but realized that Ashford would be in the dead of winter then. She saved for this trip during the two years since her mother told her about David Baxter, and the day before she left her mother had given her a draft for $2,000 U.S. to help pay the expenses of her search. She wanted to talk about fees again, but Colby suggested waiting until they returned to the office.

When she asked why he had come to Ashford, he explained his stepfather's encouragement and told her he liked Ashford. He told her about his passion for trout fishing, but omitted the part about the Memorial Day parade. He did tell her that his father had been killed in the war. This led to Janice and his children and the divorce. He didn't tell her about the few unsatisfactory relationships, one with a married woman, which he had gotten into and out of since Janice left.

When he asked, she told him that she had never been married but had lived with her fiancé for a year while in graduate school. Their engagement had ended when he confessed to her that he liked men better than women. She had been crushed but got over it. She had dated since without becoming too attached to anyone.

Colby looked at his watch and noticed that it was nearly 4:00. "Diane, I've promised you the afternoon of my time, but so far I've not given you much help..."

"Oh, you have been a big help, at least to my morale. I feel like I've found a friend." She glanced down, and he thought he again saw a faint blush spreading up her cheeks.

"Well, me too. But I mean professionally. You came to me for help with searching the records and we haven't done that yet. And the courthouse will be closed in 30 minutes, not really enough time. So I guess I owe you tomorrow morning. You were planning to stay over?"

"Of course. Actually, in addition to the help you might provide, I plan to go to the local newspaper and search through its old editions, at least those from August and September, perhaps October, too, of 1939. There might have been some mention of my father's arrival in Ashford; probably not, but one must not overlook anything."

Colby looked at her warily, not knowing exactly how to explain the fires. Finally, he just told her that the newspaper office had burned in 1943 and that there were no newspaper records or archives from 1939 left. He decided that tomorrow would be soon enough to tell her that the same was true for most of the courthouse records.

CHAPTER 12

"I hope that you can give me a lift to the nearest hotel," Diane said. She and Colby risen from the bench overlooking the river and were walking back toward Main Street. "I don't see much in the way of taxies around town."

"No taxi in Ashford," Colby replied, "but there are three places to stay. The Ashford Hotel, the Ashford Motel and the Mecca Motel. I'd recommend the hotel for dinner, maybe, but not for its rooms. One of the motels would be a wiser choice." He stopped, briefly touching her arm. "Better yet, let me take you to dinner. There's a nice place about six miles out of town called the Stonefront. We can stop at a motel on our way and get you checked in."

"I accept," Diane answered without hesitation, "as long as I'm not taking you from other plans."

"Not at all. On our way back to the office let's stop at the post office. Waldo LaBlanc has been the postmaster since the war. He might have heard of your father."

Waldo LaBlanc greeted Colby warmly and graciously smiled as he was introduced to Diane. They shook hands. He invited them to come around the counter to his office in the corner of a room cluttered with sorting boxes, scales and mailbags. In another corner were several rectangular boxes from which the sounds of young 'chicks' could be heard.

"Baxter, David Baxter you say? It's nobody I know, but yet the name sounds vaguely familiar. It's like I've seen it or heard it somewhere, long time ago. Let me think on it and I'll get back to you, Colby. We have old box rental records, and I used to keep lists of our RFD customers, too. When I get time in the next few days I'll see what I can find. Helen and I are going to the Pettingers' for dinner, and I'm already a little late getting out of here. I'd ask Homer to look, but our counter gets real busy during the last hour."

Colby glanced at Diane and could see that she was excited by the possibility that Waldo might have heard of her father.

After thanking Waldo, Colby led Diane across the street to the bank. The front door was already locked, so they went around to the back and knocked. Shirley Jones, one of the tellers, came to the door, and, recognizing Colby, let them in.

"Thanks, Shirley," Colby said, "This is my friend, Diane Askew. Diane, Shirley Jones. Is Dennis still here?"

"Pleased to meet you," Shirley responded. "No, he left about ten minutes ago."

"Oh well, we'll catch him tomorrow." Colby thought that his stepfather would also be a good source of information about David Baxter. He had been in Ashford in 1939. "Could I use a phone, Shirley?"

"Sure, use mine on that desk." She gestured toward a small wooden desk, its surface clear of paper except for a neat stack of file folders on one corner.

Colby dialed his office. Rose answered on the second ring, "Colby Johnson law office."

"Hi, Rose, it's me. Sorry to have been gone so long. Any messages?"

"Only Mr. Duncan. I told him you were tied up for the afternoon. He said he'd call back tomorrow. Said he was in and out and you'd have a hard time catching him. I finished typing the Walker title opinion, it's on your desk."

"Thanks. Two things, would you call the motels to see if they have a room for Diane for—," he looked at Diane and she was holding up five fingers. "For five nights. Also, call Mr. Kelso and see if we can change his appointment from nine tomorrow morning to two-thirty tomorrow afternoon. Just leave a note on my desk. You'll probably be gone by the time we get back. We're way down at the other end of town."

"Will do. Are you coming in tomorrow morning?"

"I'll be in, but I'm going to spend most of the morning at the courthouse searching records with Diane. And Rose, it's all your fault."

Rose chuckled. "See you tomorrow."

As they walked west along Main Street toward his office, Diane asked, "What did you mean when you told Rose that it was her fault?"

"Oh, yesterday when you called I was trying to get away for the trout stream, but Rose insisted that I talk with you."

"Are you sorry?"

He smiled "Not yet."

After a minute or two of silence, Diane said, "We need to talk about your fee."

"Okay, how much money do you have?"

"Why, do you want it all?"

"No, I just wanted to know your budget."

"Well, I had really not planned to hire anybody, but my mother gave me a $2,000.00 draft and made me promise that I'd get somebody to help me over here. It's yours if you'll give me that much help."

"Hmm, that's a lot of help even at my rates. I usually charge $25.00 an hour, plus expenses. I can't imagine that anything I might do for you would take anywhere near that amount. So I'll start charging after the free morning I've promised you tomorrow—if there's anything more I can do."

"You are indeed a nice and generous person, Colby Johnson, even if you are a lawyer. Thank you."

He smiled at her, and she at him, as they continued walking toward his office.

After a few minutes she asked, "Can you help me cash my mother's draft?"

"Sure. We can either do it through my trust account or you can open an account of your own at the bank."

"Your trust account will do fine."

When they arrived at Colby's office, Rose was already gone. They went back to his desk and Diane sat as he scanned the note left by Rose.

Diane noticed his frown as he read. "What's wrong?" she asked.

"The Mecca is full tonight and booked through the weekend. The Ashford Motel has a room tonight, but it will not be available tomorrow or through the weekend. She even called motels in Lumberton and Hillside. Same story. This is the middle of our tourist season."

"Well, there's always the old hotel we passed. It didn't look like it was full."

"No, Diane, it has a community bathroom and is really pretty rickety." He paused, thinking. "I've got a better idea, if you'd like. I've got an extra bedroom at my house. Of course, this is a small town and people would soon know. It might not be the best way to enhance your reputation around here since everyone would assume the worst regardless of what actually happens. But you're welcome. The room is free until my children arrive next weekend."

"Colby, I'm not worried about my reputation in Ashford, Michigan. There was a time when I didn't even worry about it in the city where I teach. I'd be delighted to stay with you, but how about your reputation? You'll have to live and work here after I'm gone. What will those people think about you having a single woman staying in your house?"

He chuckled. "It's already been done. For some reason nobody gets upset when a man has a guest; double standard, I guess. But thanks for being concerned."

She feigned being upset. "You mean I won't be your first?"

He got up and walked to the waiting room and picked up her bags. "Come on, silly. You'll probably want to shower before we go to dinner."

She did shower while Colby fixed himself a bourbon and opened the beer she had requested. He also sliced some cheese and a ring bologna and put them on a plate with some Ritz crackers, and carried it all to his porch. In another ninety minutes the sun would be setting, but the evening light was already starting to cause the trees and lily pads to change their shades of green.

He heard the shower stop, and a minute later her call came through the door, "Colby, I've got three requests; first, is it okay if we don't go out for dinner? I'm starting to run out of gas. My jet-lag must be lingering on yet."

"Fine with me."

"Good. My next request is to borrow a pair of your pajamas. Mine have all been slept in and I feel too clean right now for a used night gown."

"Okay, I'll get you a pair. What's your third request?"

"I want to wait until I can see your response. I'll need the pajamas first."

He got the pajamas from his drawer, lamenting the fact that they all had long pants, and handed them to her through the door. He then went to the porch and took a sip of bourbon, standing along the porch rail. A minute later she was standing beside him, but had not yet picked up her glass of beer.

"Colby, in my life I have never gone to bed with a man on the first date, much less on the first day of meeting him. But I can't mask the way I feel right now and I'm asking you to love me tonight—for whatever reason you may have—if you can."

At first, Colby thought his daydreaming was affecting his hearing, but when he looked at Diane he knew that he had heard correctly. "Would uncontrollable desire be reason enough?" he asked, trying to hide a grin.

She laughed. "That's the answer I was hoping for." She picked up the bottle of beer and slowly poured it into the glass Colby had placed on the patio table and then sat in one of the lounge chairs. Colby sat in the lounge chair next to her.

She took a sip from her glass and turned toward Colby. "I want to tell you why I've propositioned you so quickly. I really don't want you to think I'm as easy as I clearly am, but I'm only going to be here for five days. I decided while watching you this afternoon that you were a man I could maybe love and I decided that I want to try. Just now in your shower I decided there's no time to waste. I hope you don't mind. Australian girls are known for being forward by American standards."

"I don't mind. I'm attracted to you as well. The only problem is that it's really not ethical for a lawyer to use his position to seduce a client. Am I doing that with you?"

She looked at him and smiled, a smile that made him strangely comfortable. "No. Well, perhaps, who knows? You have made me feel that if there is an answer here about my father, you'll help me find it, and so that's part of my feeling toward you. But I can assure you that my proposition is the result of something quite different. It's your effect on me as a woman, at this point more physical than anything else."

They said little else as they finished their drinks and watched the sun move downward, causing a golden glare to blend the lily pads into the old river channel.

Finally he stood and pulled Diane gently from the chair by her hand. He placed his other hand softly on her cheek and pulled her lips to his. Their first kiss was long, but tender. Afterwards they looked into each other's eyes and smiled. He led her by the hand to his bedroom.

Their love-making started slowly, but quickly progressed as their hunger for each other took control. Her orgasm prompted his, almost simultaneously.

Diane immediately snuggled her head onto Colby's shoulder and fell into a deep sleep. Colby held her and gently caressed her side. Soon he also was asleep.

They made love again in the morning, this time with a tenderness that lasted much longer before they both climaxed in a flurry of passion.

CHAPTER 13

His fear and feeling of approaching panic were not unfamiliar, but it had been twenty-seven years since he had last experienced the near terror that he was feeling this Sunday morning as he watched the sky in the east begin to betray the coming sunrise. Even the V-1 bombs which had come so close to his quarters in London had not caused the anxiety he felt now, an anxiety he had once quenched by destroying the Montgomery County records.

But now David Baxter had reappeared. Not David exactly, but someone claiming to be his daughter; close enough. He had actually talked with her. Colby Johnson brought her to meet him and to ask if he had ever heard of someone named David Baxter. She said she was looking for her father whom she had never met. Maybe she was an impostor. After all, the nephew vividly remembered David saying that he had no family back in Australia, that he had no obligations or kin back there. There was the picture in David's wallet. On the other hand, an impostor might be worse. That would mean someone was wise to David's purpose in coming to Ashford, and probably who his father was.

Either way, the nephew knew his secret was in jeopardy again and that his sleepless nights would continue until he could eliminate all possibility of discovery.

A few miles away, Colby Johnson was lying in bed watching Diane. She had gotten up from the bed and was trying to slip out of the room without making noise. He had awakened anyway but remained quiet while she wrapped herself in a sheer white robe and tip-toed out the bedroom door. A few seconds later he heard the sliding door to the porch open and close.

He reflected on the last few days—and Diane. On Friday they had gone to the courthouse to look for records concerning David Baxter. There were none. His name did not appear in any of the real estate indexes or on any tax record. Colby had the idea of looking at birth records for about the time David would have been born, keeping in mind that Diane thought the surname, Baxter, was from his stepfather back in Australia. There wouldn't have been too many babies born in Montgomery County back then, and the name 'David' would be a strong clue.

But then he remembered that the county birth records from that era were gone. They, too, had been destroyed by the fires. The same for the records of the divorce Diane had mentioned. Nor would he be able to find any newspaper account of either event. That morning for the first time he fleetingly wondered if documents concerning David Baxter might have been the target of the courthouse arsonist.

On Friday afternoon, after he had taken care of some other obligations in his office, they had resumed talking to people who were around Ashford during 1939 and 1940. He introduced Diane to Edson Drew, Bud Jakes and Claude Murphy. They had evening cocktails with his mother and stepfather. All seemed interested in Diane's story, but none indicated any memory of the name David Baxter or of anyone from Australia ever being in Ashford.

They had declined his mother's invitation for dinner, opting instead for the Stonefront. He normally would have stayed, but he wasn't ready to answer all of the questions about Diane which he was sure his mother would have asked during the evening.

Several of his acquaintances were having dinner at the Stonefront, and he and Diane were invited to join a group going to Hunter's Home afterward for dancing. Colby had been about to say "No" when he realized that Diane was saying "Yes." He couldn't remember Janice ever wanting to go out with friends and realized that his initial reaction to the invitation was based on habits formed during his marriage.

They went. Diane seemed to like all of the people and she was an excellent dancer. He had a good time and thought she did too. That night they made love when they went to bed, again when she awakened him during the night, and yet again in the morning.

Afterwards he had fallen back asleep. The next time she awakened him was for breakfast. She had prepared an Australian breakfast: ham, eggs, toast and fried potatoes. She also had mastered his coffee percolator. They were both hungry, but there were two slices of toast and some potatoes left over.

After breakfast, they had gone back to bed, ostensibly to catch up on some of the sleep they had missed during the previous night. They both did sleep, but not until after they made love again.

On Saturday afternoon, Colby had given Diane a sightseeing tour of some of the rest of Montgomery County. They had driven to Lumberton and had burgers and fries and beers at Talley's Log Cabin Bar and Grill. They drove around the Twin Lakes and then back north over the old logging trails of the K-P valley. He wasn't sure if she could actually picture the old steam-engine logging trains passing along the old railroad grades he pointed out, but she said she could.

When they crossed the East Branch at the Shingle Mill Bridge, she agreed to try trout fishing with him the next day. They finally ended up at the county park on the south end of Clear Lake, so named because of its crystal clear, cold waters reflecting its sand bottom and springs. Anticipating that destination when they left, he had suggested they take their bathing suits.

He finished changing first and waited on the lawn for her. She was a stunning sight when she emerged from the bathhouse in an orange checkered two-piece suit. As she walked toward him, he could feel his excitement grow as he remembered their love-making. The orange suit accentuated her light red hair perfectly. The top of her suit showed just enough of her average-sized, but shapely breasts to be enticing, but not enough to be considered risqué. He noticed, not for the first time, how enchanting she was as she seemed to flow over the ground with long, even strides of her slender, slightly muscular legs.

When she had reached him, he touched her hand and kissed her lightly on the lips. They smiled and walked over the lawn to the sand beach. Without speaking they ran across the beach and into the water. When the water was waist deep, they almost simultaneously fell forward in shallow dives.

He was pleased to see that she was every bit as strong a swimmer as him. They swam almost to the middle of the lake and then over to an area of chest-deep water along the undeveloped west shoreline. He remembered his toes digging into the sand as they held hands and laughed. No one else was near them. He pulled her toward him and they kissed passionately. She wrapped her legs around him and they could both feel his hardness pressing to escape his suit. She suddenly released him from the grasp of her legs, reached down and then raised her hand holding the bottom part of her suit. He reached down and slid his suit down to his ankles and then pulled her to him again. She wrapped her legs again around his back and he entered her slowly and tenderly.

Their passion was such that he thought he would drown after they climaxed together. His legs buckled from his momentary weakness, but she kept her legs wrapped around him as they both sank to the bottom. Fortunately, he was able to regain his balance and strength and lift them both back to the surface where they laughed and kissed and laughed some more.

They finally put on their suits and swam slowly back to the park beach. As they walked out of the water, Diane pointed to a large house on a point which jutted north into the lake just east of the park beach. "Who lives there?" she asked, suddenly serious.

"Edson Drew," Colby answered. "You met him the other day. He owns the lumberyard in town, mid-fifties or so, but in great shape, looks younger."

"Oh, indeed, I recall." Diane paused before continuing, "When we were swimming out toward the middle of the lake, I happened to glance toward the house. He, or someone, was standing on the porch watching us with binoculars. It gave me the willies."

"I hope he wasn't still watching when we were tangling ourselves up over by the west shore," Colby said, suddenly a little anxious.

"No, I don't think so. I looked a couple of times while we were tangled up, as you say, and he was nowhere to be seen. I think he must have gone back inside. Besides, we were a long distance away by then," she replied.

"He used to be a pretty good friend of mine until a couple of years ago," Colby said, "but then he started talking about lawyers, really bashing us, almost every time I was around him. I still don't know if he was down on me personally, or on lawyers in general, or was just trying to needle me. In any event, we haven't been very good friends since then, although I don't think of him as an enemy either."

"That sure is some house he's got. It would suit my fancy, all right," Diane said with a smile. "Looks like it would cost a bloody fortune to build today. Do you know how old it is?"

"Not for sure," Colby answered, "but someone told me it was built in the thirties. Edson inherited it, I think, not that he couldn't afford to build it himself. He could, I believe quite easily, but it's hard to find a piece of land like that these days. It does have a spectacular view from that porch."

On the way home from the lake they purchased two steaks at the IGA which they grilled and ate with salad and baked potatoes. At dinner the talk had been light and they laughed about their antics at Clear Lake. Diane noted that they had made love five times within the past twenty-four hours and confessed that it was by far a record for her. He had also said that it was a record for him, which it was—by about two. They talked about making it six, but when he got out of the shower he found her lying naked on the bed, sound asleep. He pulled the sheet and cotton blanket over them as he climbed in beside her. She turned toward him, but he could tell by her breathing that she was in a deep sleep.

Now, he awakened and felt the emptiness of the bed with her gone. He quietly got up and put on his light blue bathrobe. He walked into the living room and looked onto the porch. He could see her standing against the far rail looking out over the river. Her flowing white robe was silhouetted against the water which was now silvery in the early dawn light. He could see the outline of her hair hanging down over her shoulders, but its reddish color was visible only in his imagination. All of a sudden it hit him; she would soon be gone.

He was not prepared for the sensation he was experiencing. It felt like someone had just put a fist in his solar plexus. He could not get his breath, although he knew that he was fine physically. He had only known her for three days, but the thought of not having her here left him feeling completely drained and empty. He was not even sure why she had come to Ashford. She herself had confided to him as they drove through the K-P Valley yesterday that she wondered if her mother had made up the story about David Baxter. And after finding no trace of him, nor anyone who remembered him, Colby was pretty sure that even if he existed, David Baxter had never been in Ashford.

But Diane Askew had come to Ashford and Colby Johnson knew that his life would never be quite the same as before. She turned as he opened the patio door and he could see that she had been crying. But she smiled when she saw him. Her smile caused him to blush; he was glad it was too dark for her to notice.

"Oh Colby, you lovely man. I've just been thinking out here, watching the dawn. I'm going to miss you terribly after I'm gone and it makes me sad. I know we've got two more days, but I'm starting to feel it. I didn't mean to feel this way."

"I'm feeling the same way, Diane," he said as he stepped toward her and lightly wiped her tears with the little finger of his left hand. "I was just thinking about how I'll react when you leave. You could stay, you know."

Diane thought for a full minute and then said, "No, I really have to go back to Australia, and I'm planning to go from here to San Francisco. That's where my father's ship landed in America. There must be immigration records or something there. Maybe my mother just didn't remember the right town. Who knows?

"But I've made a mistake, Colby. I didn't mean to fall in love with you. I just thought it would be nice to be close to you and that I could leave without feeling down. I've almost always grown tired of someone after a few days, not that I've done this very often. But with you I'm going in the other direction. After every day my feelings toward you get stronger."

He kissed her, tenderly. He could see the sun rising over the trees to the east. Holding her face with both hands, he said, "Diane, I've never felt this way before ever, not with Janice or anyone else. I guess I must be in love, too. Why don't you just stay here?"

"Oh, Colby, I can't stay now. I must go to San Francisco, not only for me, but for my mother. And then I have to go back home to see her and tell her what I've found—or not found. You know, he was the love of her life, and she's waited all this time. Can you come with me—at least to San Francisco?"

"Diane, I'd love to, but my children are coming next weekend and I've got a two-day trial starting Wednesday. But we can make a future somehow."

He led her back to the bedroom. This time their love-making was long and tender. Only afterward did he allow himself to think about what being a half-world apart had done to Diane's mother and father, and maybe her grandparents as well. He wondered if the same thing might happen to him and Diane when she returned to Australia. He looked at her and thought that her frown might be caused by the same worry.

It was Diane's first experience with trout fishing, her first time wrestling into waders and her first try at using a fishing pole of any kind, much less a fly rod with a closed face spinning reel. Colby had purchased the waders for Janice during their first year in Ashford, but after one frustrating attempt, he realized that she was not ever going to be a happy fisherman—or anything else which was endemic to northern Michigan life.

He was now glad he had purchased waders a half size larger than Janice needed, a shoe size which Diane barely could get on. He told her they would quit if she felt a blister forming.

The fly rod, spinning reel combination was one he had devised especially for fishing on the East Branch. He carried a fly reel in his shoulder pack which he sometimes used on the small reservoirs of old beaver dams which still could be found along the river. But for most of the stretch he liked to fish, the East Branch had too many overhanging cedars and tamaracks for fly-casting.

They parked on the old B.C.G.& A. railroad grade which they had followed to the river from Sparr. Most of the old cedar cross-ties were still in place, so the two-mile drive along the grade had been slow and bumpy. He turned the Wagoneer around on the narrow grade and pulled it to the side—not that anyone would want to get by. Only a few wooden pilings remained from the old trestle which once carried trains across the river.

He showed Diane the casting technique for the reel-rod combination and was pleasantly surprised at her quick mastery. They entered the river and began fishing side by side, slowly wading upstream. Colby showed her how to cast upstream from the old fallen tree trunks along the riverbank, and how to reel the spinner through the hole created by the current going under the tree. On his second cast he felt the pull of a trout attacking his lure and tugged gently to set the hook. After ninety seconds of applying just enough rod pressure to keep the fish from entangling under one of the logs as it darted from one bank to the other, he finally was able to work a beautiful 11-inch-long brook trout close enough to take in his hand net. As he lifted the fish he glanced at Diane. Her big grin and sparkling eyes revealed her excitement.

After that Colby encouraged Diane to make the first cast over the holes which he pointed out to her. He had caught and creeled two more 'keepers' and one undersized trout on his follow-up casts before Diane got her first strike. She was elated even though she failed to set the hook and the fish got off after only a few seconds. However, on her very next cast she felt another hard tug and this time she did set the hook. It took her three minutes to get the fish near enough for Colby to net. It was to be the largest fish of the day, a 12-incher.

Colby thought to himself as he watched her delight, she's hooked, no pun intended. He said aloud, "Nice fish."

"Thank you," she answered excitedly. "This is fun. Do they always bite like this?"

"I wish they did. Sometimes I only get one or two bites along the stretch we've fished so far."

His caution turned out to be prophetic; they only caught two more keepers, one each, during the next hour. The last of those was a ten-incher Colby hooked in a pool just below two very large parallel tamarack logs spanning a narrow part of the river. When they had landed the trout, Colby helped Diane up to sit on one of the logs and climbed up beside her. Their legs hung in the river on the upstream side of the logs and the current caused a gentle massaging sensation through their waders.

"Can I drink the river water?" Diane asked. "I'm thirsty."

"Probably, but better than that," Colby answered as he unslung and reached into his shoulder pack, "I brought a can of beer and a sandwich for each of us."

"You are a sweetheart. I don't need the sandwich yet, but I'll take the beer. By the way, these logs look like part of an old bridge."

Colby lifted the pull ring from the top of one of the cans and handed it to her. He opened the other for himself. "It is an old bridge. There's an old cabin just over there." He pointed further up the river and to their right.

"I like this trout fishing even though we haven't caught many."

"Oh, we have six nice ones, more than enough for a good mess. We'll have them for dinner, if you'd like."

"I'd like," she answered. "Does that mean we've caught all we need? I don't want to shorten your afternoon, but these wader boots are starting to feel quite tight. And we've got to walk back to the auto yet."

"Oh, I'm ready to quit. We've got enough fish for tonight, and it doesn't look like we'd catch enough to freeze for another meal. Just right. Besides, I'd rather spend the rest of the afternoon looking into your eyes, or something."

She laughed. "What kind of a monster have we created? I want you to do exactly that, especially the 'or something.'"

They both smiled and touched their beer cans. He leaned over and they kissed. For a minute they said nothing as they sipped beer and watched and felt the river current flow under the old logs.

"Colby, I can see why you like it out here. It's beautiful, the river flowing in the sunlight and the shadows, the cedar trees. But I also have this eerie feeling, almost like I've been here before." She paused. "Whose cabin is over there?"

"I don't really know who owns it now. It used to belong to one of the original lumbermen here, Frederick Harkness. He's apparently been dead since long before I came here, but one day when I first discovered this stretch of river, an old lumberjack from Sparr came along, fishing. I was sitting here eating a sandwich. He stopped and I gave him a beer.

"His name was Jack. He probably told me his last name, but I've forgotten and I never saw him out here again. He was pretty old, in his eighties I would guess. He told me he used to work for Harkness, when he lived here and afterwards. He didn't tell me if he knew who owned it now, and I didn't ask. It started to rain and he said he wanted to get back to his car before it stormed too hard."

"Did he tell you anything more about the former owner?"

"No, not really. He said that Harkness had lived here while he worked in a nearby lumber camp, and when the lumber camp moved, he bought this land and lumbered the swamp timber. Later on he apparently bought a lot of marginal land and cut the remaining timber, or so Jack told me that day. Jack said he died in the early forties. A few days later I came across Frederick Harkness' name in an old abstract I was reading for a client, so I've remembered the name."

"Can we go look at the cabin?"

"Sure," he said as he drank the last of his beer. "Are you ready?"

He helped her up and they walked slowly in their waders up the old road, barely discernible because of the young cedar and balsam trees growing along its path.

As they approached the cabin and got the first good view of its front door, Diane suddenly stopped. "Do you believe in déjà vu? I've just experienced it. Not only the cabin, but walking up to it with you. Of course, I'm crazy. You are just so strong in my thoughts and emotions right now, and the cabin looks like one I've seen on a postcard or in a geography book or something. But it did feel very familiar there for a few seconds."

"Well," Colby mused, "it might be worthwhile finding out who owns it now. I can see that someone has been here since I was. That lower window pane to the right of the door was broken when I was here in June. Someone fixed it. Do you want to look in through the windows?"

Weeks later they remembered Diane's déjà vue and wished they had followed up on the cabin's history as they had discussed that day. But the events of the following day put the cabin issue in the back of their minds for a long time.

CHAPTER 14

Colby awakened Monday morning to find that it was already daylight. He looked at his alarm clock and saw that it was five minutes before the alarm would go off at 7:00 a.m. Diane's slow breathing indicated that she was still in a deep sleep. No wonder, he thought, after their trout fishing expedition of the afternoon before and their love-making last night. He quietly turned off the alarm and managed to get up without causing any change in her breathing rhythm. He had to be in circuit court this morning for the monthly motion calendar and Diane was planning to wash some of her clothes and pack. Tomorrow morning he would drive her to Alpena to catch the ten-thirty North Central Airline flight to Detroit, where she would connect for San Francisco. The airline was affectionately known as the 'blue goose.' They were going to meet for lunch after his court obligations and had talked vaguely about trying to find out who owned the old cabin on the East Branch during the afternoon.

"Mr. Johnson, I have to agree with your argument regarding the easement," Judge Glennie pronounced as he sat down in his chair after briefly entering his chambers to get a copy of the Supreme Court case Colby had cited a few minutes before. "I've read only the head notes, but it seems clear the decision supports your position. I'm going to grant a temporary injunction to prohibit the blockage of the road in any manner during the pendency of this litigation. And Mr. Ferguson," he said looking at the defendant's attorney, "you might want to tell your client that he's going to have an uphill battle at the trial. All of the presumptions are with the plaintiff as I see it. A settlement with Mr. Johnson's client would save us all a lot of time, and probably your client some money.

"Mr. Johnson, prepare an order for my decision and send a copy to Mr. Ferguson for his review before I sign it."

"Thank you, your honor. I actually have a proposed order with me. Here, Bob," he said as he handed a copy to the defense counsel and one to the judge.

"Mr. Ferguson, is this okay or do you need time to review it?"

After a few seconds, during which Attorney Ferguson scanned the document, he answered, "No, I don't need any time. Colby has forecast your decision quite well in drafting this and I know him well enough to know that he wouldn't try to slip anything past me or the court. Defendant has no objection to this order in light of the court's decision."

"So be it," the judge said as he signed the order. "Please provide the clerk with copies to certify and get one to Bob, will you, Colby?"

"Of course, your honor, and thank you."

As they walked from the courtroom, Bob Ferguson said to Colby, "I think we can settle this if your client will agree to a 15-foot roadway easement instead of twenty. Hawkins heard the judge in there, and he just got my bill before we went in. My guess is that he'll be reasonable if you can agree to the smaller size."

"Sounds okay to me. Let me talk to my client."

Within fifteen minutes everyone was in agreement. The opposing litigants even shook hands and made subdued comments about letting bygones be bygones.

As Colby walked back across the street to his office he was feeling good about his morning. He had won all three of his motions, and getting the easement case settled was, in his opinion, the way the process was supposed to work; two good lawyers, in this case with a push from the judge, could help their clients find the middle ground.

It wasn't until he was opening the door to his office that he realized that one of the things so very right about his life today, Diane, would be gone tomorrow. But, he thought, he would be seeing her for lunch in a few minutes, and that was good.

"How did it go?" Rose asked as he walked toward her desk.

"Good, we made a triple play, and better, we settled the Anderson case. I've drafted proposed orders on the other two, but didn't want to seem too cocky by having them with me in court. Here, you can type them this afternoon and get them to the opposing lawyers for review," he said as he handed yellow sheets filled with his handwriting to Rose. He also handed her all three of the files he was carrying.

"No problem with that. By the way, Diane called and asked me to tell you that she was ready, whatever that means," Rose said as she raised her eyebrows and chuckled. Colby could feel his famous blush coming on. "And Waldo LaBlanc called. He said for you and Diane to stop by the post office today. He's found something regarding David Baxter."

As Colby sped across the short causeway leading to the island and his house, his mind raced ahead to telling Diane about Waldo's message. He could barely contain his own excitement, but he didn't want to build up her expectations until he knew what Waldo had discovered. For a moment he slowed his car, thinking it might be best if he talked to Waldo before he told Diane. Then he changed his mind and continued on to the house.

Once there, he simply informed Diane about the message and suggested they go right away to the post office, feeling that the action of going would give little time for Diane to get too excited. But his scheme backfired somewhat. When they arrived at the post office, they were told that Waldo had gone home for lunch and would be back at 1:30.

They decided to go to Utt's Cafe for lunch themselves, but the cheeseburgers and fries they ordered were barely touched as they speculated on what Waldo might have found. Maybe it was wishful thinking, but they finally agreed the most likely discovery was an old forwarding address which David Baxter left when he moved on from Ashford. Such a clue would be invaluable to Diane's search. It would not only confirm that he had arrived here, it might, more importantly, lead them to his present whereabouts. At the very least it would lead to a place where he had gone from here.

They were almost giddy with excitement when they paid the bill and left Utt's.

However, a forwarding address record was not what had been found by Waldo. After inviting them back to the seats in his office, he explained. "After you were here last Friday, I couldn't help thinking that I'd seen the name 'David Baxter' somewhere, only not recently. I went through my old forwarding address ledgers, but they only go back ten years and I'm sure I would have remembered everybody in those. I'd almost given up when I remembered an old box in the back of the bottom drawer of that old wooden file cabinet by the sorting table. The old file cabinet was here when I took over as postmaster in 1942 when Gordon Briley died. After I had been here a while, I decided to go through and clean out the old cabinet.

"You'd be surprised what I found. One drawer had over ten thousand one penny stamps, the ones with Wilson's picture. I think they stopped printing those in the mid-twenties. Grove Rouse was probably postmaster back then. I bet he had one heck of an audit problem when he misplaced those stamps," Waldo chuckled. "Well, I turned them back in to the regional office in Bay City. Nobody there knew what to do with them. I got the feeling I should have just kept them. I found out later they were collector items, worth about a dollar apiece."

Colby looked over at Diane and could see she was on pins and needles waiting for Waldo to get to her father. He knew, however, that Waldo would get there in his own sweet time, and that trying to hurry him along would cause him to forget where he was and probably start the whole story over again from the beginning. So he raised his eyebrows toward her and smiled, and then sat back in his chair to listen to Waldo's story.

"At any rate, I also found that old box. It was sort of a dead letter box that Gordon kept. It was full of old letters that couldn't be delivered for one reason or another. Most were to people I knew or remembered. Some had died and some had moved away, I guess without a forwarding address. Most of the letters didn't have a return address. In those days we were supposed to destroy letters after a year, but I guess ole Gordon couldn't bring himself to do it.

"And neither could I. Some of those letters dated back to the early '30s. So I just put the old box in the back of the bottom drawer and forgot about them. In fact, I'm sure I wouldn't have remembered any of the others, but I was sort of puzzled by two of them addressed to David Baxter. Not only was it a name which I had never heard of, but those two letters did have return addresses—in Australia. They couldn't be returned because we didn't have a return mail agreement with Australia at that time. I seem to recall now that I even asked around town to see if anyone had heard of David Baxter.

"So, I finally remembered over the weekend, and this morning I dug out that old box. Sure enough, those two letters were still there. One was postmarked in December, 1939, and the other December, 1940." Waldo pulled open his center desk drawer and pulled out two letters and placed them on the desk-top in front of Diane. "I guess I can turn these over to you, Miss Askew. No, I <u>am</u> giving them to you, forget whatever stupid regulation that might say otherwise. You're the next of kin as far as I'm concerned. They're yours."

Diane sat looking at the two letters as if in shock. Colby could see they were both addressed to 'David Baxter, General Delivery, Ashford,

Michigan, U.S.A.' He couldn't fully make out the return addresses, but could see that they were the same. He also could read the bottom line of each, 'Australia'.

Diane finally broke the silence. "They're from Mother."

She hadn't said another word as Colby had thanked Waldo and led her by the hand out to his car. The only departure from her zombie-like behavior leaving the post office was when she reached over and firmly grasped the two envelopes from the desk before rising from her chair as Colby gently lifted her right arm.

In the car she continued to look straight ahead as if in a trance and continued to clutch the two letters. "Let's skip my office and go over to the house to look at these, okay?"

She didn't answer, but he could see her head nod slightly.

He could also see that she was fighting hard to hold back her emotions. He was surprised that he was close to tears himself. At first he couldn't understand why. If anything, the letters probably proved that David Baxter had never arrived in Ashford. Otherwise he would have picked up the letters, or at least left a forwarding address, in which case the letters would have been forwarded away from this post office.

Then he realized their real significance. The letters were the first tangible evidence that Diane had ever had of her father's existence. They were corroboration of the story which her mother had first related to her only a few years ago. The letters had been posted some thirty years before.

Diane was openly crying by the time they reached his house. He walked around and opened her door and offered his hand. She took it and stepped out of the car. She briefly hugged him and murmured, "I'm sorry to be babbling like a baby."

"It's okay, I'm fighting it myself. How about the porch?"

She nodded and he led her to a chair in the shade of the sugar maple on the south edge of the porch. He then went into the house and returned with a letter opener from his small desk along the living room wall.

She had still not opened either letter when he returned again a few minutes later and placed a tall glass filled with ice and a clear liquid on the small table beside her chair. "Gin and tonic. Do you want me to stay out here with you, or do you want to be alone? Maybe you'd want me to read them first?"

"No, thanks," she said, managing a weak smile through her tears. "I really would like to be alone while I read them. I feel like this might be my only chance in life to be with both my mother and father, at least in a spiritual sense. Do you mind terribly? Why don't you go back to your office and I'll call you in a while."

"Sure, I just want you to know I'm here when you need me."

"I know. I might not have the strength for this if it weren't for knowing you are nearby. How do they say it in your cowboy movies, you're my ace in the hole."

It was almost four o'clock when Diane finally called, over two hours since he left her. He hadn't felt much like working while he waited, but he had busied himself with returning some calls which he knew would not require great concentration, and then he had told Rose the story about the letters and how Waldo had found them.

When the phone finally rang, he didn't wait for Rose. He answered it himself, "Hello, ah, I mean, Johnson Law Office."

He heard her chuckling over the line. "Mr. Johnson, please come home. Your client—no, I mean your lover—no, I'd like to be your love—or whatever I am, anyway, please come home and read the letters."

He was greeted with a warm hug and a kiss, and she lead him to the other chair on the porch. On the small table next to it were the two letters, replaced in their envelopes, and a tall glass filled with ice.

"Gin and tonic?"

"What's your saying over here? If it's good enough for the goose, it's good for her lawyer."

They both laughed. He could see that she had been crying, but her tears were gone now. He pulled the first letter from the envelope. It was dated December 3, 1939. The writing was very fine, clearly feminine, but easily read. He could see the similarity with Diane's. It was one sheet of paper, covered front and back.

> Dearest David,
>
> I had hoped to have heard from you by now and I pray that this letter finds you well and still feeling as you did on the eve of your departure. I have missed you terribly and I reaffirm the pledge of love I made to you then. In fact, our love that night has produced the beginning of our child. Yes, I am going to have a baby, your baby, our baby. The baby is expected in May. I hope and pray that I might be with you by then or soon after. Dr. Rafter has said I shouldn't travel after February, so please let me know your wishes as soon as pos-

> sible by telegram. I can leave as soon as a ship will be sailing. So far I have not had any sickness like many expectant mothers. I hope it continues. At first I was afraid, but then I was happy to be with your child. I love you so very much and do not regret what we did that night. Have you found your father? I want to know everything about America. Do you like it? If not, are you coming back here? I am running out of paper, so please, please let me know you are happy about our baby and tell me what I should do. I know in my heart that this news will make you happy too. I love you, Helen

Colby looked up and saw that Diane was watching him closely. She wasn't crying, but she wasn't laughing any more either. She just looked sad. He felt empty as he thought of her mother writing the letter with so much optimism, but never getting a reply. He picked up the second letter. It was in the same hand, but only covered one side of the page and two lines on the back.

> Dear David,
>
> Since you did not answer my last letter I must conclude that you either did not receive it or have chosen to ignore the fact of our child. I do not know which would make me feel worse. If you did not receive it, or this, I cannot ever reach you for I know of no other way. If you do receive this I must tell you of your daughter. She was born on this May 9th and her name is Diane Helen Askew. I have given her the last name of a friend of my uncle who was killed in the bombing of London in case I never hear from you again. I went to Sydney in March so as to avoid the embarrassment for my family. I move around a lot as I try to make ends meet here for me and Diane. My parent's address is the best way to reach me, although they might hesitate to bring a letter from you just now. I still dream of seeing you. Love, Helen

After Colby had replaced the second letter in its envelope, Diane broke the silence, "I feel like crying one minute and laughing the next, although I am cried out and don't think I will again tonight. To think of the waiting and uncertainty Mother must have gone through, the hope and then gradual realization that my father would not return. She told me that she has never stopped dreaming of seeing him again.

"But the letters have confirmed to me the existence of my father and the feelings of love that my mother felt toward him and how he must have expressed the same to her. Strangely, I felt almost euphoric as I was reading the first letter.

"But I realize that they almost conclusively prove that my father never got here, or that he didn't stay long or leave a forwarding address if he did."

Colby looked at the envelopes again and responded, "The letters certainly have made your father more real to me, but I agree they tend to show that he didn't reach Ashford." After a minute, or so, of silence, he got up and walked toward the sliding door. "I'll fix us another gin and tonic if you want."

"Yes," she said absently.

For whatever reason, they didn't discuss the letters or anything else about David Baxter during the remainder of the evening. Instead they talked about the sunset, Colby's children, who were due to arrive in two days, and their own relationship and when they might see each other again after tomorrow. Colby started some charcoal in the grill beside the porch and cooked hamburgers, which they nibbled at along with some potato chips.

Before the sun had set they had cleaned the kitchen and gone to bed, professing their need to arise early to reach the Alpena airport for Diane's flight. They made love, each reaching a climax much quicker than usual. Afterwards they continued to cling to each other, neither falling asleep. They slowly started again. This time they lasted for a much longer time than usual and afterwards both fell into a deep sleep almost immediately.

Colby awoke to find the other side of the bed empty. It was still dark. He got up and went into the living room. He could see Diane through the patio door sitting in the lounge chair where she had read the letters. She was wearing the thin, white robe which he thought accentuated her beauty. Instead of joining her, he somehow felt like an intruder on her private thoughts, so he quietly returned to the bedroom and lay back on the bed.

But sleep wouldn't come. He thought about Diane's mother waiting for David Baxter's letter, a letter which never arrived. He thought about her loneliness and wondered when she had finally comprehended that David was not going to be part of her life. He realized that Diane was probably reflecting about the same things as she sat on the patio. He heard thunder in the distance and wondered if they would have rain.

He then thought of Diane leaving on the airplane. He already was imagining the deep loneliness he would feel as he watched her walk across the tarmac to the plane. He realized his children would provide some relief, but that they would not fully fill the void he knew he would feel with her absence. Then he tried to suppose how she would feel. She would be going alone to San Francisco. She would have no one to help relieve her burdens. He was sure that she would have the same feeling of loss that he was foreseeing, plus the pain caused by the letters. He also thought of her searching immigration records alone and could picture her returning to her hotel dispirited if she was unable to find information about her father.

He suddenly knew what he had to do. He got up and put on his own light blue bathrobe and walked to the patio door. Diane was still in the lounge chair and he walked over and kissed her forehead. He could see that she had been crying again.

"I'm not usually this much of a crier," she said as he sat in the opposite chair. "It's just that I'll be leaving you at the same time I am trying to deal with the letters and what they mean. I'm a little afraid and ...."

"No," he interrupted. "You don't have to go."

"Yes I do. My mother needs to know and so do I."

"I know. I mean you don't have to go today and you don't have to go alone. I'm going with you to San Francisco."

"But your children?"

"We'll just have to wait until they leave. That'll give me time to get everything caught up or rescheduled at my office. It'll only be two weeks. You can reschedule your flights, can't you? And you have the time, right?"

She thought for a minute, and then replied, "Yes, I do have the time to wait for you." He could sense her relief. "I can stay in one of the motels while your children are here, I guess."

"No, that's not necessary. I'm sure Rose would be happy for your company. She's already let me know that she thinks you're the best thing that's happened to me in a long time. She's got lots of extra room in that old house of hers. She closes off part in the winter to save on fuel oil, but I think she has five bedrooms altogether. I thought about you staying here, you know, you and Traci could sleep in my room and I would sleep in the children's room with Brent. But who knows how Janice would react when they told her about you staying here. She might try to change future visitation, or something. I just don't want to get the kids in the middle of any more of our battles."

"Oh, Rose's place would be nice. I agree about your children. Do you really think Rose wouldn't mind?"

"I'm sure, but we'll ask her this morning. You don't have to move until tomorrow." Signs of the dawn were becoming evident in the east. David added, "I'll fix some coffee. In another hour we can call to change your ticket—and get mine."

CHAPTER 15

By the Monday following the arrival of Colby's children, nearly everyone in Ashford was aware of Diane's quest: the story of her father leaving Australia for Ashford, her journey to search for him, and the old letters found at the post office. From the coffee shop to the barbershop, across the grocery counter and at the afternoon pinochle game in the back of the hardware store, everyone in town was talking about David Baxter. His name was spoken so often that many began to imagine that they had an old familiarity with him.

In fact, of course, one person did. The nephew had only the week before begun to relax as he heard that Diane would be leaving Ashford without finding any record or clue regarding her father. San Francisco might have records of David's arrival in America, but he did not think she would be likely to find anything further. Train tickets were sold over the counter in 1939 without name records, and wartime travel visas for non-citizens had not yet been instituted. No, he was beginning to feel comfortable with her probable failure of finding evidence that David Baxter had ever made it out of San Francisco.

And then the old letters had been found at the Post Office. Not that they proved David Baxter had ever reached Ashford; on the contrary, the unclaimed letters were more likely to mean that he never arrived. But the letters had seemingly provided a new spark to the girl's search. She had stayed on and, he had heard, Colby Johnson was going to San Francisco with her to pursue information about her father. Worse yet, now everybody in town was talking about David Baxter. Who knew what might be found or remembered that could expose his dark secrets? He had already heard speculation that the David Baxter disappearance was related to the courthouse fires. This speculation was apparently fueled by a remark Colby Johnson had made in the Clerk's office after realizing that any documents which might have existed with regard to David Baxter would have been destroyed by the courthouse and newspaper office fires.

Regardless of the source, the rumors were all too true, as he well knew. On that Monday he was fighting hard to keep the near panic he was feeling from showing in his demeanor. After all, it was important that he continue his proper comportment with his employees and customers in Ashford. He fought hard to stay in control, but several persons inquired about his health throughout the morning. His almost total lack of sleep over the weekend must be quite evident, he thought. If only he could divert the girl's search for her father.

On that same Monday morning, Colby Johnson was feeling pleased with how well his children and Diane were getting on. The four of them had spent the weekend together, a picnic and swimming at Clear Lake Saturday and a drive to the old Presque Isle Pointe lighthouse on Lake Huron Sunday afternoon.

Sunday evening after they had dropped Diane at Rose's house, Traci had suggested that she should be staying with them. Brent had also acknowledged Diane was "pretty neat." They both wanted to know if she might someday be their other mother, just like their other father at home. Colby had said "maybe someday." They seemed to like that idea and were delighted that she would be "sitting" with them today while Colby went to his office. They had come into the office last Friday while Colby attended to duties in district court, but had gotten bored quickly and soon were on Rose's nerves. Both Diane and the children seemed happy with the arrangements today, and tomorrow they would be visiting their grandmother at the lake.

Colby was thinking about a conversation he overheard that morning while having coffee at Gavine's Cafe. Two of the other coffee drinkers at the round table seemed to be convinced that the David Baxter matter was related to the courthouse fires. (Nearly everyone in Ashford now referred to the courthouse, newspaper and school fires collectively as the courthouse fires.)

It was certainly true, Colby thought, that the records they had sought regarding David Baxter had all been destroyed by the fires. On the other hand, so were the records about lots of other people. There was no evidence to indicate Baxter even reached Ashford, much less was the reason for arson. But he knew the courthouse fires were viewed by almost everyone in Montgomery County as an unsolved mystery, so he wasn't too surprised that people would be inclined to link the intrigue regarding David Baxter with the fires if the opportunity arose. Apparently his own casual remarks, made without any real basis, had fueled such speculation around town.

Well, it could be. If Baxter had actually reached Ashford and had thereafter been the victim of foul play, someone might have thought it necessary to destroy any records of his existence. Or, if someone had known he was coming and had reason to intercept him, they still might want such records eliminated. But, Colby concluded, such scenarios were conjecture, at best.

Nevertheless, as he was leaving his office to have lunch with Diane and the children, he instructed, "Rose, when you get a chance—probably you'll have time while I'm in San Francisco—see what kind of records you can dig up about the courthouse fires, you know, the courthouse, Montgomery County Gazette and school community building fires. Articles in the Alpena News, police reports, that kind of thing."

"Okay, I can do that. Should I leave the office, if necessary?"

"Sure, just leave a note saying when you'll be back. Go on over to Alpena, if you want. Close the office for the day. Too bad we don't have one of those machines that answer phones. I read about them somewhere; they actually record phone call messages on tape."

"Do you remember when the fires occurred?"

"In 1942 and 1943. I think Ken Chadson can tell you the exact dates off the top of his head." Colby paused. "One more thing, look a few days ahead. See if there were any unusual happenings just before the fires. You know, any strange bodies found or unsolved crimes. I don't know what, but you might see something unusual."

As he walked toward the door, he realized that he was not optimistic that Rose's search would be fruitful. On the other hand, he was not leaving her with a great deal of other work to do while he would be in San Francisco.

His hand was on the doorknob when the phone rang. Rose walked back to her desk to pick it up. Colby could hear only her response, "She is not here right now, but I could take a message, or you could talk to Mr. Johnson. He's her lawyer… hello, hello…"

Rose finally hung up and glanced in the direction of Colby who was still standing by the door.

"What was that all about?" he asked.

"Strange." She was frowning. "Said she was Mrs. Simmons and wanted to speak to the lady from Australia. Then she hung up. It sounded long distance. Maybe she will call back."

When Colby arrived home he found that Diane and the children had prepared a picnic of sorts. Traci proudly led her father around the house and down to the edge of the river. There on the grass a tablecloth had been spread and a plate was placed on each side. In the middle was a pitcher of lemonade and a plate of sandwiches. There was one folding canvas chair. Traci explained that Colby should sit in the chair since he would be going back to work.

"The children made the sandwiches and lemonade," Diane said. "They wanted to surprise their father."

"Ah-huh, we could take care of you, Dad," Brent added. "Sandwiches are easy to make and we could eat them everyday."

Traci looked a little confused. "No, I want Diane to stay and help us take care of Daddy," she pleaded. "This was fun, but we need Diane to help us."

Colby laughed. "Don't worry. Diane's going to be here to help while you're here. Maybe she'll even be here when ...." He stopped, realizing that he was stepping into uncharted waters with regard to his relationship with Diane. "Listen, let's just eat this and worry later about what's to happen after."

As they ate, he could tell the children had made the sandwiches. His baloney sandwich had too much mayonnaise and the peanut butter and jelly sandwich had peanut butter spread on only a portion of the bread slice. But he enjoyed seeing their pride as he smacked his lips and expressed satisfaction with the luncheon fare.

After his second sandwich he put his plate down on the tablecloth and sighed, "Yum. I don't know when I've had a better lunch. I don't even have room for the apple pie."

"We don't have any apple pie, Daddy," Traci announced. "And I don't even know how to make one."

"Well, I do," Diane said, "and if we had some apples I would show you how."

"Really, Diane? Could you show us how to make a pie?" Traci was almost bubbling over at the thought. Even Brent seemed excited at the prospect of making an apple pie.

"And I know where we can find some apples," Colby volunteered.

On the way, Colby remembered the telephone call and asked Diane if she knew a Mrs. Simmons. Diane thought for a moment and then shook her head. She then turned around to continue the counting game with the children in the back seat.

Diane was feeling remarkably serene as she braked Colby's Wagoneer at the intersection of Colby's mother's driveway and the county road. She had just dropped Brent and Traci at their grandmother's house for the afternoon and had nearly four hours before she was scheduled to pick them up and meet Colby at his office after work.

She briefly thought about going straight to his office to see if he would take the afternoon off, but she remembered her pledge to avoid encouraging his future hooky-playing. She smiled as she remembered the previous afternoon. Colby had taken the afternoon off driven her and the children to an old, long-neglected apple orchard, where they had found some early-ripening apples on one of the several old trees which still bore quantities of the red fruit.

The orchard was near the summit of Lone Pine Hill and reachable over an old two-track road which ran north two miles from the nearest county road. The last half-mile consisted of a steep winding grade along the east slope of the hill. The hill itself was an anomaly in northern lower-Michigan, a large deposit of sand and gravel left by the receding glacier some ten thousand years before. The north and east faces of the hill rose abruptly nearly a thousand feet above the Rattlesnake Creek cedar swamp, which formed a semicircle at its base. The road to the orchard approached from the south and then dipped down to the edge of the swamp before beginning its steep and winding ascent to its destination. The road would be a challenge for an ordinary sedan, but the Wagoneer hardly strained as it made the climb to the old abandoned homestead farm.

The apples had been perfect for baking, and the four of them had together made two pies. Nobody had eaten much of the mutton stew Diane had prepared for their supper, but they had completely consumed one of the pies.

Diane thought again of the old orchard. The view from there had been spectacular. Colby had pointed out where they had fished on the East

Branch and the old, now nearly deserted lumbering town of Sparr in the long valley stretching west from the base of the hill. He had said that the next plateau on the western end of the valley was a distant fifteen miles away.

He had also explained that the orchard had been planted by homesteaders sometime during the early part of the century and shown her the crumbling remains of their old log cabin and barn.

She decided to return to the old orchard. She wanted to more closely examine the remains of the old buildings, and she could pick more apples for another pie or two. Besides, just sitting on the ground and taking in the panorama would be a wonderful way to spend the afternoon. And she could dream. For all she knew, the homesteader could have been her grandfather.

The nephew was driving east on M-32 toward Ashford when he recognized the oncoming vehicle as Colby Johnson's Jeep Wagoneer. As they passed, he could see that the Australian girl was its driver and lone occupant. She did not appear to even glance toward him or his car. He slowed without braking and then pulled off the road after she had disappeared from his rear view mirror over a small hill.

He was returning from a meeting in Lumberton that he had originally thought would take the entire day. Nobody was expecting him at his office for several hours yet. He made a U-turn and accelerated. The girl was not driving fast and he soon could see the Wagoneer about a quarter mile ahead. He slowed, trying to stay about the same distance behind her. He could see the Wagoneer most of the time, but would lose sight when the road dipped beyond the rolling peaks scattered along the road's westerly route.

After about five minutes, he saw the Wagoneer's brake lights illuminate and its right turn signal start blinking, just before it went over the hill above the Big Rock Road intersection. He slowed, and when he also came over the small hill's crest, could see that she had turned and was heading north.

He drove on without turning until he was out of sight of the Wagoneer. He then turned around and slowly went back to the Big Rock Road intersection. After looking and not seeing the Wagoneer, he turned north also. He knew that he would be more suspicious on this lightly traveled road, so he stayed well back out of her sight but close enough to see the dust caused by her vehicle. He wondered why he was following her, but could not really establish a reason. He was curious, he supposed, about David Baxter's daughter and where she was going—alone.

He almost missed her. As he came over the rise before the road dipped along the swamp at the base of the west face of Lone Pine Hill, he happened to glance to his right and saw a wisp of dust lift from the side of the hill. He then caught sight of the brown Wagoneer slowly climbing along the trail. He knew she was either lost or heading to the old Bowman homestead. Someone must have told her about the apples.

He stopped his car and turned around and slowly started back south toward M-32. Later he would wish that he had kept going, but now he remembered that one of the last parcels Jack had purchased from him and logged was a forty-acre tract just east of the old Bowman homestead. He had visited Jack at the site and knew that it was accessible over a trail ascending up the far more gradual east slope of Lone Pine Hill. He had easily driven his sedan to the site then and decided to try now.

To reach the east slope trail, he had to go back to M-32 and then east to Kellyville Road. He turned north on Kellyville Road and then nearly missed the trail. He could see that it had not been used much during the past few years, but was not entirely grown over. He turned left on the trail and slowly drove ahead. He expected to see a deep rut or a fallen tree blocking his way at any minute, but to his surprise the road was quite passable over its entire two-mile route to the old logging site.

There was a light breeze from the west, so he felt it unlikely that the girl would have heard him drive to the end of the old logging road, nearly a quarter of a mile from the orchard where he guessed she would be—if she had not just driven up and turned around and gone right back down the hill. But nevertheless he did not risk making more noise by turning his car around. He didn't know what he was going to do, but he knew that he definitely did not want to be discovered by her or anyone else up on this hill.

Diane had been more nervous than she had anticipated driving the Wagoneer up the steep west face of Lone Pine Hill. The trail was narrow and far more steep than it had seemed with Colby driving. Near the bottom it featured a nearly 180-degree turn, the closest thing to a switchback she had seen in Michigan. She felt much better now that she had turned around and parked on the relatively flat south side of the orchard.

She got out of the jeep and folded the paper sack she had brought so it would fit in her back pocket. She decided not to lock the jeep since she had never seen Colby lock a vehicle since she had arrived in Ashford. But she did remove the key and put it in her jeans pocket. Before picking apples, she wanted to inspect the ruins of the old cabin and barn. It was not lost on her that the old barn was much larger, and from a distance appeared to have been much better constructed, than the old family living quarters.

She spent nearly thirty minutes rummaging around the old building foundations, looking for clues as to how the homesteaders had lived. The cabin appeared to have had a main room and two smaller rooms on the back side. The old logs—pine, she guessed, from the bark still remaining on two of them—had long since collapsed on the west side, but the other three sides still stood. The roof had fallen in and was mostly rotten, and she wondered if there had been any floor other than the sand which was visible between the collapsed rafters.

No furniture remained except for parts of the old wood cooking range. It looked as if someone had taken the removable lids from the stovetop and the oven door. She stood for a moment trying to imagine the wife preparing meals for her hard-working husband. Did they have children? "I'll bet a lot of apple pies were baked in that oven," she said aloud.

She left the old cabin and walked over to the barn. Part of its roof was still in place, but looked as if it might collapse any minute. She decided not to go in, peering through the door instead. An old wooden milking stanchion looked to be still workable over in the corner left of the door, its hardwood sides still shiny. Even the leather strap at the top looked to be in good shape.

She walked around the north side of the barn and was again struck by the view of the broad valley stretching for miles westward. An old-single bottom plow, its handles rotted away and its iron share rusty, caught her eye. She decided to sit for a minute on a fallen tree just west of the barn. From there she could enjoy the view and could see most of the old orchard and the field above it on the hillside.

She was now on the north side of the orchard and realized that the Wagoneer was all the way across the orchard on the south side. She looked but couldn't see it. She did see movement, however. Was it a man in a white shirt? She thought so, but didn't see it again. Maybe someone else has come up to pick some apples, she thought. But then she realized that she would have heard a vehicle straining to come up the hill.

She sat on the fallen tree for several more minutes without hearing or seeing any noise or movement and soon was convinced that it had been her imagination.

She remembered the sack in her pocket and started looking more closely at the apple trees, trying to remember the ones Colby had directed them to yesterday and ones with apples that looked the same. After a few minutes she decided to pick from a tree directly in front of her which had a large number of light-red apples on a branch bowed by their weight to within her reach from the ground. She didn't want to climb as she and Colby had done yesterday.

It didn't take her long to fill the sack and walk back to the Wagoneer. She put the apple-filled sack on the floor in front of the back seat and opened the front door. She was glad she had turned the jeep around when she had arrived.

The engine started easily and she moved the gearshift lever from park to drive and pulled onto the trail and turned right to head down the hill. Almost immediately the slope downward increased dramatically. She remembered seeing Colby yesterday shift to the lowest gear and she did the same, feeling a slight slowing of the vehicle by the engine drag. But even with her foot completely off the accelerator pedal she could feel the jeep picking up speed. She put her left foot on the brake pedal and began to push. Nothing happened. She pushed the pedal all the way to the floor. She sensed a brief response, but then it picked up speed again. She pumped the pedal, nothing. She was surprised that she was not feeling any panic even though she was very much aware that the Wagoneer had no brakes as it began the rapid descent down the western slope of the steep hill.

The trees were starting to go by faster. The road was far from straight even up at the top part of the hill, and she remembered the hairpin turn near the bottom—if she got that far. She glanced at the speedometer and saw that she was already going 40, with the steep part of the hill still ahead. Maybe if she switched off the engine—she turned the key off. The Jeep seemed to slow some but kept going. Suddenly she couldn't steer. A small curve was coming up—she saw that she was headed straight for a sizable tree. She turned the key back on. The engine started and she could steer again. She turned to the right and the Wagoneer skidded, but she missed the tree. She turned back and managed to keep it on the trail. But she was gaining speed again.

She looked again at the speedometer. It's needle was passing 50. She could feel the engine drag, but gravity was winning the battle. She turned to the right again and managed to stay on the trail, though all four wheels skidded through the turn.

She was now on a straight stretch of the trail, but it seemed to drop off the side of the hill and go straight down. She thought of the first big drop of the roller coaster back in Sydney as she looked down the hill at the hairpin turn back to the left at the bottom. She knew she could not make that turn. In a matter of seconds she would be off the road, traveling at a high rate of speed down an even steeper decline into a deep gully, that's if she missed the several large pine trees along the road just before the switch-back curve.

It was coming at her. She tried ramming the gearshift into park. For her effort she got only a terrible grinding sound, and the Jeep actually accelerated as the engine was relieved from its drag. She slammed it back down to low, but by now she could see the needle was past 70.

The emergency brake! Where was it? She glanced down. There was a pedal by the door. She put her left foot on it and pushed. Looking up she could see the road already starting to turn. She pushed on the emergency pedal with every ounce of energy she had.

CHAPTER 16

Colby was already upset when the phone rang. It was five-twenty and Diane had said she would pick him up at four-thirty. He had finished some dictation with Rose, but had not wanted to start anything new after she left, a few minutes after five. Even organizing his desktop had only taken five minutes or so.

The phone would be Diane, of course. She would be calling from his mother's where she was picking up the children to tell him she was running late. No big deal. He reached for the phone. "Hello."

"Colby, this is your mother." He could sense her irritation. "Diane was supposed to pick up the children at four. I'll bet she's there sitting on your lap instead."

"No, Mother, she's not here either. I've been sitting here in a stew myself. She was supposed to be here at four-thirty." He felt a slight sense of apprehension. "She had talked about going up on Lone Pine Hill to pick some more apples and to look around the old buildings. She probably got stuck or something."

"Do you want me to bring the children in?"

"It would be easier if you could keep them for a while. Can you feed them if she doesn't show up soon?"

"Sure. I have steaks, but I'll put them back in the fridge and we'll grill some hamburgers instead."

"Where's Dennis?"

"He's not home yet. I think he was going somewhere out of town today, but I can't remember where. I expect him soon, though."

Colby had hoped Dennis would come in his pickup to help him

look for Diane. He thought fast. "Mother, if Diane comes in the next few minutes, call the hotel. I'm going to try and borrow Wally's pickup to go look for her. I'll be there for a few minutes anyway."

"Okay, the hotel—Wally."

"Right, Mom. I've got to run. She's probably up there trying to change a tire or something. 'Bye."

"Call when you find her. Goodbye."

He hung up the phone and headed for the door. After locking it behind him, he turned east and walked briskly toward the old hotel. As he thought of Diane up on the hill and the possibilities that could have delayed her, his level of anxiety increased.

He was relieved to see Wally behind the bar talking with Smitty, the mechanic from the Ford Garage, when he walked through the door.

Wally looked up and hailed Colby, "Well look who's here. We all thought you'd moved to Australia." He and Smitty chuckled. Even Colby smiled.

"No, not yet. But I do hear they've got friendly bartenders over there." Wally feigned hurt. Colby continued, "Seriously, Wally, I need to borrow your pickup. She, Diane I mean, went up on Lone Pine Hill to pick some apples and she's way overdue. I'm afraid she's got a flat tire or some problem with my jeep."

"I'm sorry, Colby," Wally answered. "It's down at the garage. Smitty was just telling me he had to order a new distributor cap. I don't know why the Ford Garage doesn't stock Chevrolet parts."

At the bar, Smitty checked his watch and said, "I'm driving the wrecker home tonight anyway. We can take it out there if you'd like. Just so you fill it with gas when we come back by Reiman's gas station so old man Forrest never knows. He probably wouldn't care anyhow; he likes you, Colby."

"Hey, that would be great." Normally, Colby would have been embarrassed by the remark about being liked, but his worry about Diane was overriding any other emotion.

"Let me call my wife. She never puts on my dinner until she sees the whites of my eyes, but I like to let her know. Helps the mood, you know," Smitty said as he reached for the phone behind the bar.

"Wally, if my mother calls, tell her we've gone to the hill. If Diane has showed up, she can come get us."

"You got it."

They were about halfway to the hill on Big Rock Road when they saw a person walking toward them. Colby noticed a slight limp and wasn't sure at first it was Diane. He recognized the flannel shirt he had loaned her first. "It's Diane. She's been hurt!" As they got closer he could see that her face was streaked with dried blood and dirt.

Smitty braked the tow truck as they approached and Colby jumped out and ran to Diane. "What happened? Are you okay?"

She didn't answer, but instead threw her arms tightly around Colby's neck and seemed to go limp. A second later he felt her body tremble and heard her soft sobs.

"Diane," he whispered. "Honey, are you all right? Are you hurt badly?"

"I'm okay," she said between sobs, continuing to hold him tightly. "I'm sorry to be weeping like a baby. I'm just so glad you got here. Just give me a minute."

"All the time you want," Colby answered as he softly stroked her back.

He continued to hold her and whisper to her until he could feel her sobs gradually ease and then stop altogether. Only then did he gently push her away so he could look at the injury which had caused blood to nearly cover her face. He could see a large abrasion on her forehead. It was an inch or so wide and ran from above her right eye to the hairline on her left temple, but it did not appear to be deep at all. The bleeding had already stopped.

He looked closely at her eyes and was heartened to see that they were focusing in unison and normally. "Where does it hurt?" he asked.

"My forehead is starting to smart a bit," she answered, "but I guess you can see that. I also have a lot of pain in my leg, right here." She pointed to her right thigh, just below her hip. "But I don't think anything is broken."

"Your head looks like only a scrape, a pretty big one, but not too serious. We should look at your leg, though." Oblivious to Smitty, who had gotten out of the truck and was standing by ready to help if asked, Colby kneeled down and began to unbuckle her pants.

As he began to pull her jeans down she noticeably winced and let out a gasp of pain. "Here, let me do it." She slowly slid her jeans down to her knees. Colby could see a large bruise already starting to form, running from just below her panty line to halfway down her leg, but the skin was not broken at all.

He gently pushed his fingers along the bruised area and could feel her flinch each time he applied pressure, but she exhibited no extreme reaction which might indicate a chipped or broken bone.

"Careful, buddy," she said with a slight, almost forced smile. "If you get too fresh down there, I've got a witness."

Both Colby and Smitty, who had been politely looking the other way, at least most of the time, laughed. The tension seemed to ease considerably.

"Oh, this is Smitty. Smitty—Diane." They nodded at each other, Smitty being careful to keep his glance from falling below her eye level. "I don't think anything is broken and there isn't any major swelling," Colby said as he raised himself and stood again. "I think you'll be as good as new in a few days. What happened? Where's the jeep? And, ah, you might want to pull up your pants now before I do get fresh."

Diane reached down and gently pulled her jeans back up, fastening them and her belt. She tried not to show the pain as her pants slid over the bruised area, but it was obvious.

"I ran off the road at the bottom of the hill," she began. Suddenly she was sobbing again, "Oh, Colby. It was awful. I didn't have any brakes and the jeep kept going faster and faster. I could see the trees at the bottom."

"Take it easy, sweetheart." Colby put his arm around her shoulder and pulled her to him. "Let's go have a look." He gently led her toward the truck and helped her climb in the passenger door. He could see her pain as she stepped up to the running board, climbed onto the seat and slid to the middle.

"Can you go back there or should we get you to a doctor first?"

"I'll be okay. I'll show you where it is."

By the time they got to the hill trail and up to the jeep, it was clear to Colby that Diane was in too much pain for them to linger at the site. The Wagoneer was off the trail and amongst several small aspen trees, two of which were bent under the front bumper, almost as if the vehicle had descended on them from above.

"Smitty, I think we had better get Diane to a doctor. I'll get the keys and lock the jeep doors while you turn around," Colby said as he opened the truck's passenger door.

"Okay, but I think it will be easier to back out from here to the road," Smitty replied.

Diane moaned as she tried to shift her sitting position. "Thanks."

The old store at Big Rock had long since been abandoned, but the phone booth outside remained. By the time Smitty pulled the truck up in front of the old store, it was beginning to get dark. The light in the phone booth was an encouraging signal that it might be operable. Colby got out and picked up the receiver. He was relieved to hear a dial tone. He was equally relieved to see that it had a phone directory.

After looking up Dr. Kunkle's home number in Ashford, he inserted a dime and dialed. It rang several times before he finally hung up, the phone unanswered. He then looked up Dr. Rusk's number in Lumberton. It was almost as close and, since he had just done some legal work for Dr. Rusk, he felt more comfortable about calling him at home. He felt in the coin return for his dime and found nothing. He then realized that he was at one of the old pay phones that did not return money and that he should wait until he got an answer before putting in his dime. So he took another dime from his pocket and dialed.

This time a woman answered. He quickly inserted his dime and said, "Hello, Mrs. Rusk, this is Colby Johnson. Is Dr. Rusk home?"

"Oh yes, Mr. Johnson. Charles is here. Just a minute, please."

A few seconds passed before a strong voice came on the line. "Colby, good to hear from you. How can I help you."

Colby explained about the accident and Diane's injuries. Dr. Rusk replied, "Normally I'd say take her right to the hospital emergency room in Gaylord. But it sounds like that might not be necessary. I'll gladly see her. Let's see, you're at the Big Rock corner. That should take you about fifteen minutes to get here. I'll be at my office by the time you arrive. Come on around to the back door."

After saying good-bye and hanging up, Colby got back in the tow truck and told the others about his calls. He ended by apologizing to Smitty for making him even later for his dinner.

"No problem," Smitty replied as he swung the truck across the highway to make a U-turn. "I'm glad to help."

Dr. Rusk had examined Diane thoroughly before concluding that her injuries were indeed only superficial. He had cleaned and applied an ointment to the scrape on her forehead and given her some liniment for the bruise on her leg. He had also given her a tranquilizer after realizing that she was still traumatized somewhat from her experience on the hill. She had fallen asleep almost before Smitty had gotten the truck turned around to head back to Ashford, leaning her head on Colby's shoulder. After a few minutes he had managed to slip his arm from beneath her head and place it around her shoulder while she snuggled her head against his chest.

When Smitty pulled the tow truck in his driveway, Colby had tried to wake Diane with only partial success. He did manage to get her into the house by half carrying and half steering her almost drunken attempt to walk. He thanked Smitty and gave him ten dollars to fill the tow truck with gasoline. With his help Diane managed to get as far as the couch, where she adjusted the pillow and lay down. She was instantly fast asleep.

After seeing that Diane was sleeping, Colby picked up the telephone and dialed. "Hello, Mother."

"Colby, are you okay? Did you find Diane?" He could hear the anxiety in her voice. He realized he should have called from Dr. Rusk's office.

"Yes, Mother, I'm okay and Diane's okay, although she has some scrapes and bruises. She and the Wagoneer took a wrong turn at the bottom of Lone Pine Hill."

"Are you sure she's all right? Are you at home? Do you want me to come in and help her?"

"No thanks, Mom. I took her to Dr. Rusk. He gave her something to help her sleep and she's stretched out on my couch right now. How are the children? I'm sorry I haven't picked them up yet, and I don't have a car at the moment. Can they stay over with you and Dennis?" He knew that Dennis only barely tolerated his children and would consider their staying over to be an imposition.

"Of course, Colby. They are already asleep in the guest room. And don't worry about Dennis. He'll be concerned about Diane's accident, and besides, he actually seemed to enjoy being around Brent and Traci after supper tonight. I saw him showing them how to start a fire in the fireplace, a first, believe me."

"Thanks, Mom, and thank Dennis for me, too. I'm going to keep Diane here tonight, not that I have a choice without a car. But I want to make sure she's not alone when she wakes up. She had a pretty scary experience up on the hill this afternoon. She's tough, but I know this shook her up."

"The children are no trouble at all. I'll keep them until you are ready for them back. Do you need to borrow my car? I could bring it in tomorrow morning and you can drive me back if you want."

"Thanks, Mother, for keeping the kids and offering your car. I think I can get a loaner from the Ford Garage, but if I can't I'll call, okay? I need to go. Diane looks like she's about to turn over and fall off the couch. I'm going to get her into a bed. 'Bye for now."

"Good-bye. Remember to call if you need anything." He heard her phone click and placed the handset back in its cradle.

He looked over at Diane, who had rolled back to be more securely positioned on the couch. He suddenly realized that it was nearly ten-thirty and he had not eaten anything since lunch. A sandwich and a beer would taste real good right now, but first he called Rose to explain why Diane would be staying at his house for the night.

Then, after pulling the covers back on his bed, he walked to the couch and turned Diane toward him so that he could remove her muddy, blood-stained clothes before placing her on the relatively clean sheets. He unbuckled and unsnapped her blue jeans and carefully slid them off her legs. He could fell her muscles tighten as they passed over the bruised area, but she said nothing, did not appear to awaken. He then unbuttoned and removed her shirt. She was not wearing a bra. He briefly wondered whether Dr. Rusk had been offended by her decidedly Australian penchant for going bra-less.

He then gently slid his arms under Diane's back and knees, careful to avoid the area of her bruise. As he lifted, she turned toward him and put her arms around his neck and pulled her head and body up into almost a sitting position. He carried her into his bedroom before realizing that she would be turned around if he laid her on the bed from the side facing the door. He decided the easiest way to solve the problem would be to walk around the bed, even though he would not have much room to maneuver her from the back side. He backed around the foot of the bed and thought he had safely made the maneuver when he brushed her bruised leg against the bedpost. He was startled by her cry of pain and almost dropped her. But he continued to back along the side of the bed and was able to lay her down on the bed without further aggravating her injuries.

He saw that her eyes were open and thought that the bumping of her bruised leg must have awakened her, and indeed her features were grimaced as if in pain. But when her eyes met his her faced relaxed and she attempted a smile. She looked only half-awake and he concluded that she was still under the influence of the tranquilizer.

"Relax, sweetheart, and go back to sleep, you're safe in my bed." He then chuckled and continued, "Of course, if you weren't so banged up you wouldn't be very safe in my bed."

She seemed to almost laugh for a few seconds before her smile faded and was replaced by a frown. "Colby, someone else was up on the hill with me. I just saw him for a second. I really didn't see his face, but I thought it was a man. As I was walking back to the jeep he was going over the ridge. He was wearing a white shirt." He sensed her growing apprehension. "Seeing him up there gave me the willies. Then I didn't have any brakes. Do you think ..."

Colby interrupted, "Shh, Diane. Relax, we'll talk about it in the morning. I want you to go back to sleep now. What you saw might have been a deer's tail. You're safe now, I'm here with you and we'll be all right."

"It wasn't a deer, Colby; it was somebody, a person." There was a touch of anger in her voice. "But you're right, there's no use in worrying about it tonight. Just promise me you'll have someone check it out, or you go with me to look. I'll show you where."

"I promise." He knelt beside the bed and took her hand in both of his. Within what seemed like seconds she was sound asleep again.

He placed her hand back beside her and pulled the sheet and blanket up to cover her arms and shoulders. She seemed to nestle even more into the covers. Thinking she might still be cold, he looked in his hallway closet but there were no more blankets, another household commodity which he had not sufficiently restocked after Janice had departed with almost everything that wasn't nailed down. He remembered the children's beds. He went into their room and retrieved the quilt from each bed. He spread one over Diane and took the other to the couch.

He could hear the thunder while he undressed and before he fell asleep a heavy rain was pounding on the roof. He fell asleep wondering if the rain would wash away any tracks from whatever it was that Diane had seen up on the hill.

Sheriff Wanika had been told about the accident by Colby Johnson, who had telephoned even before the sheriff had arrived in his office. Upon returning the call, Wanika had accepted Colby's invitation to stop by his house for coffee. They drank coffee and talked on the porch. Colby told him about the accident and Diane's belief that she had seen a white-shirted man up on the hill near the jeep. The sheriff was already well aware of Diane's search for her father, as was almost everyone in Ashford.

CHAPTER 17

Colby sensed that the Delta DC-8 jetliner had begun a gradual descent several minutes before he saw any end to the mountain ridges and peaks which dominated the fascinating panorama he had been witnessing from his right side window seat for the past hour. This was his first trip to any place west of the Mississippi River and he was amazed at the span of the western mountain ranges. It seemed as if they had been over mountains for at least half of their flight from Detroit. His fascinated view of the peaks and ridges was only briefly interrupted by a band of clouds somewhere over what he guessed was Colorado. Diane had fallen asleep soon after take-off and was only now beginning to stir as the plane's descent toward a landing at the San Francisco Airport became more pronounced.

It had been ten days since her accident with the Wagoneer and her injuries had all but disappeared. The scrape on her face had been evidenced by a scab for the first few days, but the remaining redness could only be seen by a close examination of her forehead. Her leg injury was still very evident by its discoloration in the area of her upper thigh, but was not visible when she was wearing slacks or a dress. More importantly, the pain was gone.

Of much more significance to Colby was the report that Bill Wanika had filed about the accident which concluded that foul play by a person or persons unknown had likely been the cause. He had decided not to tell Diane about the report, instead hastening their planned departure to San Francisco to look for information about her father's arrival from Australia in 1939. During those ten days, however, he never let her out of his sight.

The children had been delighted that she stayed at the house during the rest of her visit; Brent even offered to sleep on the couch so that his father wouldn't have to, but Colby had declined.

As they neared the ground, Colby could make out the Bay waters ahead and to his right. Just when he thought they were going into the water, the runway appeared and the DC-8 settled down with scarcely a bump. Diane was now fully awake.

After gathering their luggage from the baggage claim area, they boarded a bus for the trip downtown to the King George Hotel, where the travel agency in Alpena had booked their room. The reservation was for one week.

The streets were almost deserted as they stood in front of the Southern Pacific Building looking across Stewart Street at the Port of San Francisco complex. Even the ferry unloaded only a hand full of Sunday morning passengers while they watched at the pier behind the complex. Colby and Diane had awakened early, at least by local time, on this first morning in San Francisco, and both were anxious to explore the city for the sites where David Baxter might have left clues on his arrival thirty years before. They left the hotel just as the sun was beginning to cast its early morning rays around the buildings on either side of Mason Street on which it faced.

"Now where?" Diane asked, standing in the early morning sunlight for warmth.

"I think we go down Geary. The clerk said we could catch a bus or street car at Market."

They walked to Market Street and promptly caught a street car down to the Bay front at its northern end. They interrupted their trek at 3rd Street to catch a bus to the Southern Pacific train station at its eastern end. There they learned from a ticket agent that most railroad passenger and baggage records, if they existed at all, would be stored at the main offices of Southern Pacific at the end of Market Street across from the Port of San Francisco, a mile or so farther on. Of course, those offices would be closed on Sunday. At the agent's suggestion, they had taken another bus from the station.

"It's so beautiful, for a city I mean," Diane said as she slipped her arm around Colby's elbow. "I wonder if my father ever stood here where we are and enjoyed the view of the water and the ships. I guess his ship would have landed just over on that wharf."

"Oh, he probably did," Colby said absentmindedly as he himself surveyed the vista of the Bay and the giant bridge to Oakland.

Neither of them spoke for a few minutes. Colby finally broke the silence. "We'll come back here tomorrow morning to see what records the Southern Pacific might have on its 1939 passengers. I suspect they won't have any, but we'll ask anyway. Let's go over to the Port building. According to the phone book, there should be an immigration office there."

Diane nodded and kept her arm around Colby's as they crossed the street in front of the large Port of San Francisco complex. They entered the main building and looked for a directory. It showed that the Immigration and Naturalization office was on the main floor. There was also a listing for the Matson Navigation Company, the only listing which they determined might represent a passenger shipping line. It indicated a ground floor office.

Since they were on the ground floor, they decided to look for the Matson office first. It was easy to find, but the results were not encouraging. The first door they encountered as they walked down the right-hand hallway had the words "Matson Navigation Company" painted on the top line of the door's opaque glass window and "Matson Lines" on the second. However, a much more prominent "Closed" sign was taped just below and covered any other information which might have been offered by the original sign.

A typewritten sheet of paper was also taped to the upper right-hand portion of the window. It announced that Matson Lines had discontinued passenger service from San Francisco as of May 2, 1969, with the completion of the Matsonia's last voyage to and from Hawaii. It also gave a telephone number and address of a law office where creditors could assert any remaining claims against the company. Colby copied the telephone number on a slip of paper and put it in his shirt pocket. Neither of them had been optimistic about finding ship records anyway.

They retraced their steps to the lobby and then climbed the wide stairway which faced the main entrance to the second level which was listed as the main floor. There they followed the sign to the left and found the door with "Immigration and Naturalization" neatly lettered on the top half of the glass. Smaller letters announced that its occupants' hours were 8:00 a.m to 5:00 p.m., Monday through Friday.

"Well, we've found where we have to come tomorrow, Diane. What say we find us some breakfast and play like tourists the rest of the day?"

Diane put her hand back on his arm and squeezed. "You surely know how to treat a girl. We might even act like it's our honeymoon."

"I'll go for that," he said, and then after looking up and down the hall and seeing no one, he pulled Diane to him and they kissed, their bodies briefly pressing against one another. He pulled his head back and whispered, "How about breakfast in bed, back in the hotel?"

They didn't actually eat breakfast until almost lunchtime.

Colby's first reaction on stepping out the front door of the hotel was how different Monday morning was from Sunday. The nearly deserted streets of yesterday were today clogged with automobiles and the sidewalks were filled with people, men in suits carrying briefcases and women dressed for the office, all scurrying at a fast pace toward their various employment destinations. Even their cable car journey the previous afternoon to the fishermen's wharf area, itself crowded with tourists and Bay area residents enjoying an almost perfect sunny Sunday afternoon, had not prepared him for the hustle and bustle of the city on a workday morning.

Diane appeared to be less awed by the scene than he. He realized that she had spent most of her adult life in a city while he had been seasoned by his years in Ashford where one rarely saw more than five people and two or three cars on the main street at any one time.

Their plan was to walk down to Market Street and catch the street car to Stewart Street where the Southern Pacific Building and Port of San Francisco complex faced each other across Stewart. They had decided to try immigration first because David would have dealt with that office before purchasing railway tickets, if he had indeed taken the train to Ashford. They considered that he might have chosen to travel to Ashford by bus, but it seemed unlikely in light of the vast railroad passenger service network that had existed in 1939 throughout the United States.

Colby realized that he was hungry and Diane quickly assented to his proposal that they have breakfast at the cafe a few doors down from the hotel. At breakfast, they hardly spoke and Colby sensed that Diane was anxious about what they might discover this day. There was little he could do to relieve her tension.

He was a little nervous himself.

Even after breakfast they hardly spoke as they walked north along Geary Street and crossed Market to the cable car stop. The first car that stopped was full and only about four people squeezed themselves on. He and Diane didn't try but they were able to move up to the front of the line. They did get on the next car and stood against each other holding one of the two bars running the length of the car above their heads on either side of the aisle. Their eyes met and they both smiled, somehow seeming to break the tension that had prevailed during breakfast and their walk.

Almost everyone in the cable car seemed to be going to Stewart Street, the last stop on the route. Most waited for the car to clear and the light to change so they could walk back across Market Street to their destinations in the main business district of San Francisco. Diane and Colby, however, crossed Stewart to the front entrance of the Port of San Francisco, went in and up the broad staircase to the first floor, turned left, and walked to the door they had found the previous day. This time a light was shining through the window of the door, accentuating the lettering which identified it as an office of the United States Immigration and Naturalization Service.

They opened the door and walked in. The doorway opened into a small reception area containing a desk, six heavy wooden chairs with armrests for persons waiting, and a small table supporting a Xerox copying machine. The desk had a small typewriter stand attached to the left side, facing the entrance door, which supported an electric typewriter. The room was empty of persons, but the sound of voices could be heard through the open doorway between the desk and copying machine table.

Colby would have closed the door firmly in an attempt to make a sound to announce their arrival but was prevented from doing so by the hydraulic cushion of door closer arms. However, a few seconds after he stopped pushing on the door, the closer accomplished his purposes by pulling the door closed with a short rush, producing an audible click. The voices stopped and they could hear a chair sliding a short distance across the floor, pushing back from a desk or table. Almost immediately a handsome, middle aged woman appeared in the open doorway.

"May I help you?" she asked.

"Yes," Colby answered, "I hope so. My name is Colby Johnson and this is my friend—and client—Diane Askew. We are trying to find out whether any immigration records exist regarding Diane's father, who we believe arrived here from Australia in 1939."

"I'm Marge Poag," she said as she stepped forward and extended her hand, first to Colby and then to Diane. "I'm the administrative assistant to Mr. Carey, the office manager here. Really I'm just his secretary, but after twenty years he got me a fancier title and a raise." She smiled, eyes twinkling. Colby couldn't see Diane's reaction behind him, but he chuckled, taking an immediate liking to Marge Poag.

She continued, "Records from 1939, that's before even my time, hmmm. We do have a records archive over at the old Federal Building, but we don't keep the records from this office here anymore; they go over to the airport office once we finish with them. That's where most of the immigration action is these days." She paused, obviously thinking, before continuing. "You mentioned that Diane is your client. Are you a lawyer?"

"Yes, in Michigan," Colby admitted, "but I'm here mostly as her friend, trying to help her find some information about her father." He could see now that his comment caused Diane to smile. He sensed that she also was at ease with Marge Poag.

"Let's go in and talk with Mr. Carey," Marge invited. It was pretty clear she could make that decision without consulting her boss; Colby couldn't tell whether she had that authority based on their personal relationship or because of her seniority coupled with her readily apparent robust personality. He soon discovered that it was a little of each.

She led Colby and Diane through the door. "Mr. Carey, this is Colby Johnson, and this is Diane Askew. They are trying to find some old immigration records."

"Hello, I'm Ed Carey," he extended his hand across the modest government issue desk to each of them, and then indicated two wooden chairs identical to the ones in the waiting room which faced his desk. "Please have a seat." Without being asked, Marge took a similar chair, but one having a padded seat which was situated at the left side of Ed's desk. Ed looked to be in his late fifties, his full head of brown hair only slightly graying at his temples.

After they were seated, Marge said to Ed, "They are looking for immigration records for Diane's father, who she believes arrived here from Australia in 1939. Colby's a lawyer, but he's here mostly as Diane's friend, he says."

"A lawyer, huh," Ed said in a friendly tone. "Where are you from, Colby?"

Colby answered, "I live and practice in a small town in northern Michigan, Ashford."

"And you, Diane," Ed continued, "are you from Michigan, too?"

Diane blushed perceptibly as she started to answer. "I guess I have lived there for the past month or so, but I'm really from Australia."

"Ah, your accent," Ed interjected. "If you had spoken before, I would never have suggested you might be from Michigan."

They all chuckled. Diane continued, "No, I guess not, but I do not believe it is I who have the accent." They all laughed again.

Marge was the one who directed the conversation toward their business, a role it was apparent Ed expected. "Why don't you start at the beginning so we can get some idea what records might exist about your father's immigration, Diane. First, what is his name?"

"David Baxter," she answered. And then, without further prompting, she recounted the story of what she had been told by her mother and their recent futile efforts in Ashford. She ended with the telling of the discovery of the two old letters from her mother, letters which had added nothing to their search, but which had very much re-energized their campaign.

After she finished, no one spoke for what seemed like minutes. Colby could see that both of the government workers had been moved by Diane's description of finding the letters, during which she had not been entirely successful in masking her own emotion.

Finally Marge Poag broke the silence. "Did I understand correctly that your father was actually born in the United States?"

"Yes," Diane answered. "That is what my mother remembers. She told me that one document he showed her was his birth certificate. It was from Michigan, she was sure."

"Well, I wonder whether he had an American or an Australian passport. If he had been adopted over there as a minor he most likely was considered an Australian citizen by your government and would have remained so unless he chose otherwise. On the other hand, he could have chosen to assert his claim to American citizenship over here had he wished." Marge paused and looked at Mr. Carey.

He picked up her thought, "In which case there would have been a file started by this office upon his arrival. When did you say he arrived here?"

"I believe it would have been in August of 1939, maybe early September," Diane answered. "My mother did not remember the exact date of his departure, but did remember that it was winter, in Australia, of course. I was born May 9, 1940, so the eve of his departure must have been more or less nine months before."

Mrs. Poag smiled and said, "Well, that certainly does define the time period. I'll call the airport today and see if I can arrange an expedited archives search. I believe most of the sections there are categorized by the year the files were closed, but there shouldn't be too many files for U.S. citizens coming in with Australian passports during those days. If we were on the East Coast, I would not be so optimistic. During 1939 and 1940 those offices were swamped with applications by people wanting to get out of Europe, and claims of citizenship by birth were numerous."

"We will be very grateful for anything you can do," Colby said.

"No problem at all," Mrs. Poag responded. "Where are you staying?"

"The King George Hotel," answered Diane.

"We might have something by Wednesday," Mrs. Poag said as she rose from her chair, signaling that their conference was over. "I'll call you either way. If there is no file for David Baxter, per se, we can check the immigration rosters for that time period, but it will take a lot longer. Let's hope to get lucky. I'll talk to you when and if we find something, but no later than Wednesday afternoon."

As Colby and Diane also stood, Ed Carey walked around his desk and extended his hand. "As you can see," he said, "Marge is the person who gets things done around here. I hope that we can find something that will be helpful to you. I will be interested to know the outcome of your search."

Colby and Diane were almost at the door before Colby remembered to ask about the Matson Navigation Company. "We saw yesterday that the Matson Lines have shut down. Are there any other passenger ships still in business here?"

"Not as such," Ed replied. "We get the occasional cruise ship from Vancouver, but it's mostly a sightseeing thing these days. But we have to be here for those. I'm betting this office will be closed soon. As you can see, we don't do too much immigration work from here anymore. Actually we do more intake from private boats than from commercial now. A few freighters carry passengers, but even that is dropping off. They may keep us here until after the Vietnam War is over in case the dependents come by ship—who knows for sure."

"Do you have any idea what ships or company might have been in business from Australia in 1939?" Diane asked. "My mother remembered that David Baxter left in a ship with a name which started with an 'M'."

Ed answered immediately, "It probably was one of the Matson boats. They were by far the most active line between here and Melbourne and carried passengers regularly well into the fifties. I can remember two of their ships, the Monterey and the Mariposa. I believe that the Monterey was refurbished and became the Matsonia. It was making runs to Hawaii until just a few months ago. I think the ship is still somewhere in the bay area."

"Is the Matson company in bankruptcy?" Colby asked.

"Not that I know of," Ed replied. "I think they are trying to liquidate their assets, though. I'll tell you what. I see old Ted Orm every Wednesday at the Rotary Club luncheon. He was in charge of Matson's office downstairs for years. I'll see if he will meet with you later in the week."

A few minutes later, Diane and Colby were standing on the sidewalk at the Southeast corner of Market and Stewart Streets, looking up at the imposing building which for more than three-quarters of a century had been the headquarters of the Southern Pacific Railroad.

"Well, we're on a roll. I say we go in and see what records they might have," Colby said as he gently directed Diane toward the entrance with his hand on her back.

"I'm with you," she responded.

Inside, they found the corridor lined with doors as it led to the two elevators in the center of the building, both on the right hand side. The first door on the left was flanked by a counter and sliding window through which they could see several desks, each occupied by a woman working on a typewriter or talking on a telephone. The closest desk appeared to have a small switchboard and was close enough for its occupant to reach the sliding window above the counter. They approached the counter and tapped lightly on the window to get the attention of the woman at the switchboard desk, who was staring at the paper in her typewriter as if trying to find her place.

At the sound of the tapping she looked up, and upon seeing Colby and Diane, she slid the window open. "May I help you?" she asked politely.

Colby leaned forward on the counter and answered, "We're trying to find some information about a man who we believe many years ago took your train but never arrived at his destination in the Midwest. We thought maybe there might have been an accident or something which caused his death and that maybe the railroad had some record. Would there be a record of accidents or passenger deaths?"

"I'm sure we would have records of passenger deaths if they occurred on one of our trains. How long ago are you talking about?"

"It was in 1939. The man was this lady's father, and we think he might have left here for Chicago, and beyond on the Michigan Central, but it doesn't appear that he reached his destination in northern

Michigan," Colby continued. "We cannot be sure that he took your train, but we're looking for any information we can get."

The woman whistled softly and said, slowly shaking her head, "That's thirty years ago. I don't even know what records they kept back then or where they'd be if they did exist. Today they would be in our insurance bureau, but I don't think they even had an insurance bureau in those days." She paused, staring into the air. Her appearance changed suddenly as a smile spread across her face. "I do know who might be able to help you," she said with an air of triumph. "Doc Egan, he was here in 1939. I just got an invitation to his retirement party and it said he had worked for the Southern Pacific for 45 years. At one time he was the chief detective for the railroad, but now he's called a security consultant, or something like that. I don't really know what he does now, but I see him come by here every day at lunchtime. I'll bet he would know what kind of records we kept back then. Would you like me to see if he's in and has time to talk with you?"

"Of course," Diane responded, her excitement evident.

They could not hear the woman's voice as she spoke into the microphone on the switchboard after dialing a short number. It had taken her nearly a minute to find the number in what appeared to be the building directory. After only a few seconds of talking, she turned away from the switchboard and announced to Diane and Colby, "Doc will be right down to get you. He sounded enthused to have someone ask for him. I can't remember anyone from the outside coming to meet with him for several years, at least. By the way, I'm told he likes to be called 'Doc,' although I'm sure it's not his real name. If I remember the story right, he did an emergency appendectomy on a train once when there wasn't a real doctor to be found; got a big commendation. Seems the patient was the son of one of the company bigwigs."

It seemed like only seconds before the doors of one of the old elevators opened and a medium-sized man with gray hair and a pencil-thin mustache walked out and then briskly down the hall toward the reception counter. He walked up to Colby and extended his hand. "Hello, I'm Emerson Egan." He then turned to Diane, bowing slightly, and said, "Ma'am. My friends call me 'Doc'; I hope you will, too."

Colby answered, "I'm Colby Johnson and this is Diane Askew. We appreciate that you are taking the time to see us."

"No problem at all," Doc replied in a tone which was warm and sincere. "I was told that you were checking into an old murder, or something, on one of our trains back in thirty-nine. I don't remember one right off-hand, but I'm the one who can find out."

Diane interjected, "We don't believe there was a murder—at least I hope not—but my father disappeared, and we think he traveled from here to Chicago on the Southern Pacific Railroad during August or September of 1939. We're just checking out possibilities. We were hoping there might be papers if anything happened. Can we—"

"Come on up to my office," Doc interrupted, "and tell me the whole story. I'll see what we can find out. That's a long time ago, but who knows? We never seem to throw anything out." He turned and directed Diane and Colby to the elevators with his outstretched right arm.

Doc Egan's office was on the fourth floor and might have been missed by anyone searching because its outer door connected to the side of a small foyer extending from the main hall to two other doors behind the elevators. Colby guessed that neither of those offices or rooms had windows, but was not surprised to see that Doc had a northerly view overlooking the Port of San Francisco Building and part of the Bay. The office was small and cluttered with papers and books, but the effect was not entirely chaotic. In fact, it appeared that a mission was underway to organize the diverse documents that were stacked in various places around the office.

"I apologize for the mess," Doc said as he removed piles of files and papers from each of the two chairs facing his old wooden desk across from the window, "but I'm retiring soon and have been asked to get all of my files arranged for the archives. For the past several years I've been the company historian, so to speak. Most of the time I'm trying to explain to some junior executive what or why the company did so and so back in the fifties or forties. I don't much know what they're doing these days, and certainly not why."

After Diane and Colby were seated, he walked around the desk and sat in an old wooden chair with what looked to be homemade back and bottom cushions. Both the chair and the cushions appeared to have seen better days. He continued, "Tell me about your father, Miss Askew, and why you think something might have happened to him on the Southern Pacific."

Diane began again to recount the tale of David Baxter, at least as much as she knew of it. Colby interjected his knowledge a few times when he thought Diane had missed something, but on the whole he was beginning to marvel at how, with the many reiterations he had listened to, the story was beginning to take on a rehearsed quality in his mind. He even sensed ahead of time when Diane would omit a point he thought to be material.

Diane finished by recounting the finding and reading of the old letters from her mother, a narrative which almost always brought her to the verge of tears and had a similar effect on her listeners, including Colby.

After Diane finished, Doc Egan turned his chair so that he faced away from them and looked out the window. It was impossible to see his face or guess what he was thinking. After a minute, or so, he turned back and faced Diane. He had not been crying, but his demeanor was quite solemn nonetheless.

"I'm glad you came when you did," he began. "I doubt that anybody will know about these when I'm gone from here. I was the last in-house Chief Detective, you know. I was replaced by an outside security firm—cheaper, they said. They were probably right, but it isn't as good, at least as I see it. My old employees, good men and a few women, at first were employed by the outside company and as they retired they weren't replaced. Most retired early. I think they were encouraged to.

"I digress too much. What I'm talking about are the records kept by me and my predecessor as Chief of Detectives. I was just a regular detective in 1939; oh, I guess a little more than regular. I was in charge of the Bay area force at that time. I had seven or eight men who helped me police and investigate problems the railroad encountered in the Bay area. Every time we had an incident we had to make a report to the Chief Detective's office. My predecessor, Chief Detective John Schmier, started keeping files of all those reports on a monthly basis and when I took over in 1948 I kept doing the same thing. Not only did I continue his practice of filing everything, but I never discarded any of his old files. His office, and mine in those days, was over at the 3rd Street Station. Unless someone has come along and needed the additional room, which I doubt, those files are still in the old storage room on the third floor of the station."

Doc paused for a moment. Neither Colby nor Diane spoke, neither wanting to interrupt his train of thought. He finally continued, "No, I don't think they have ever been moved or destroyed. You see, I left my name on each file cabinet with instructions saying that I was to be notified if they were to be moved. And a lot of the old-timers still work over at the station, friends of mine. I think someone would have told me if something had happened to the files.

"I'll go over tomorrow and see if I can find the files for August and

September of thirty-nine. If anything happened to your daddy on the Southern Pacific Railroad, there would likely be something in those files.

"Give me a number where I can reach you."

They gave him the numbers of their hotel and room and thanked him enthusiastically.

They hardly talked as they walked back to the King George. Both sensed that they might soon learn something about David Baxter's fate back in 1939, but at the same time they were dreading what the news might be.

They were expecting to hear from both Marge Poag and Doc Egan sometime during the next two days. Doc Egan phoned first.

CHAPTER 18

"Did you really mean what you said last night, about getting married? Maybe it was the wine talking."

"Are you having second thoughts about your answer?" Colby countered. Diane was lying on her side with her head resting on his left shoulder. He was lying on his back, aware of her bare breasts against the side of his chest. The sunlight of Tuesday morning was just beginning to streak through the curtains of their east-facing room in the King George Hotel. They had begun making love almost before he was fully awake and he now lay contentedly with Diane snuggled warmly against his side.

"Yes, I'm sure about my answer. I had already thought about what my answer would be if you asked. On the other hand, no girl ever imagines that her dream proposal will come in the middle of a sexual encounter, though I'm not complaining. But I don't want to hold you to some impulsive decision which you might later regret."

"No, it was not an impulsive proposal, Diane. I'd thought about it as well. When you were preparing to leave Ashford a couple of weeks ago, well, I'd never felt so empty. Not even when Janice left, although I felt pretty bad about the children going.

"Of course I had planned to broach the subject to you differently, but last night I looked down into your eyes and just couldn't wait. I don't know if a man can love a woman more than I did right then—or do now."

"Colby, you sure know how to make a lady feel good. For what it's worth, I feel the same way about you. I never knew before that I could be so intensely in love. It actually scares me some. But it frightens me more to think of not being with you tomorrow, or the day after, and the day after.

"I have always been skeptical about love at first sight, at least until the day I met you in your office. Initially I thought it was just my relief to finally get to Ashford, to be at my journey's end. I had been planning this trip for three years, almost from the time my mother told me about my father. That's why I wanted to make love that first night. I actually thought it might bring me back down to reality—maybe cool my sudden attraction to you." Diane chuckled softly. "It didn't seem to work that way.

"By the way, how many more children do you want?"

Colby had awakened a few seconds before the phone rang. It was 10:25 a.m. He knew because he had already checked his watch on the stand beside their bed. Diane was still sleeping. They had both fallen asleep after their early morning tryst and subsequent confirmation of his marriage proposal from the previous evening.

He answered the phone before the second ring, but not before its bell had awakened Diane. "Hello, this is Colby Johnson."

"Mr. Johnson, this is Doc Egan." Colby could sense the excitement in Doc's voice. "You won't believe this, but I've found some information about David Baxter. I'm sure it must be the same one. And it's not bad news either. I've confirmed that he reached the passenger station in Gaylord, Michigan. Is that where you thought he was going?"

"It sure is."

Diane jumped up from the bed, reacting to Colby's obvious enthusiasm.

"How soon can you get over to my office?" Doc asked.

"It will probably be at least an hour. I, er, I'm waiting for a call," Colby fibbed, not wanting to admit that he and Diane were still in bed at 10:30 in the morning.

"That'd be just fine. Come on over here and I'll show you what I found, and then we'll go to lunch. A celebration is in order and, well, this has got me a little excited."

"If I had started with the regular file cabinet that contained the reports from our train conductors of mishaps and incidents, I'd probably still be reading," Doc explained to Colby and Diane, who were sitting across from him in his small office, each trying to suppress the excitement which had been building since they received Doc's call an hour earlier. "The reports were filed by year so they took up over half a file drawer for 1939. But I saw another cabinet marked 'miscellaneous correspondence' and decided to try it first. The 1939 file was no more than an inch thick. I knew it wouldn't take me long to get through that.

"It contained two telegrams related to David Baxter from the station master of the Michigan Central Railroad Depot in Gaylord, Michigan. Here, I've made copies on our Thermofax machine." He handed two slightly brown copy papers to Diane.

The copies were not very clear, but were recognizable as duplicates of Western Union telegrams. The first was dated September 7, 1939, and was addressed to the Station Master, Southern Pacific Railroad, San Francisco, California. It read:

> RECEIVED TRUNK ON 29 AUGUST 1939 FROM SOUTHERN PACIFIC CHECKED IN SAN FRANCISCO TO GAYLORD ON 25 AUGUST STOP NAME ON TRUNK IS DAVID BAXTER SIDNEY AUSTRALIA STOP INFORMATION REQUESTED ON WHETHER TRUNK WAS MISADDRESSED OR OTHER REGARDING DAVID BAXTER STOP
>
> DAVID DRESSBACK STATION MASTER
> MICHIGAN CENTRAL DEPOT
> GAYLORD MICHIGAN

Beneath the text was a handwritten note directed to the Chief of Detectives inquiring as to whether his office had received any reports involving one David Baxter.

The second page was also a copy of a telegram, this one dated September 8, 1939, and addressed like the first. It read:

> DISREGARD MY TELEGRAM OF 7 SEPTEMBER 1939 STOP DAVID BAXTER ARRIVED GAYLORD THIS DATE AND CLAIMED TRUNK STOP
>
> DAVID DRESSBACK STATION MASTER
> MICHIGAN CENTRAL DEPOT
> GAYLORD MICHIGAN

After reading each, Diane passed it to Colby. After reading the second telegram, Colby looked up to see Diane staring into space with no expression on her face. After a few seconds he noticed that tears were forming in her eyes. He stood and walked over to her chair and put his arm around her shoulder. She leaned her head into his side and began sobbing quietly. Doc Egan sat across the desk and said nothing. Colby realized that

Diane had just read one of the very few tangible references to her father that she had ever seen.

Diane regained her composure in only a minute or two and said as she wiped away her tears, "I'm sorry. I just couldn't help myself. Suddenly knowing that he did reach Gaylord is a great relief in a way, but it doesn't answer the basic question of what happened to him. It is even more of a mystery that there is no trace of him to be found in Ashford."

Colby continued to stand beside Diane with his hand now resting on her shoulder, but he didn't respond because he didn't have anything to add. Diane had said exactly what he was thinking.

Finally Doc Egan interjected, "I don't know about either of you, but I'm hungry. Why don't we all go to lunch? I know just the place, only a block or two up Market Street, the Tadich Grill. What do you say?"

Colby, glad of the chance to direct Diane's thoughts away from the conclusions to be drawn from the telegrams, answered for them. "Sounds like a splendid idea, but just so we don't have an argument when we get there, I'm buying lunch for all of us. We are very grateful for your help, Doc."

"I accept," Doc answered.

Diane was nearly back to being her cheerful self as they left Doc's office and walked toward the elevators.

They did not discuss the telegrams during their short walk up Market Street or during their lunch at the Tadich Grill, where they all had the Dungeness crab salad recommended by Doc. Instead, Diane and Colby mostly listened to Doc's interesting anecdotes about his long career as a railroad detective for the Southern Pacific.

After lunch Diane and Colby walked back to the Southern Pacific Building with Doc and bade him farewell on the sidewalk in front of the main entrance. Only then did they bring up the telegrams, profusely thanking him for his efforts in locating them. Diane gave him a hug and a kiss on his cheek. Colby warmly shook his hand. As he finally left to enter the building, he reminded them that they were welcome to call on him again if they thought he could be of any further assistance.

After Doc walked through the door, Diane and Colby continued to stand in front of the Southern Pacific Building. Both were looking across toward the bay and the Port of San Francisco Building.

Colby spoke first. "Are you thinking what I'm thinking?"

"They said they would get back to us on Wednesday, but it couldn't hurt to check in with them a day early, I wouldn't think," Diane answered.

"I agree. We're right across the street. Let's go over and see if they've found anything," Colby said, still not bringing up the telegrams and what they must mean.

So they walked across Stewart Street to the Immigration and Naturalization Service office. They walked in and found that Marge Poag's desk was unoccupied and looked to have been that way for the day. They heard someone coming from the hallway behind her desk and recognized Ed Carey as he walked out to see who had entered the waiting room.

"Oh, hello," he said as he recognized Diane and Colby. "Marge is out at the airport now, trying to track down the location of our 1939 archive files."

"I hope we are not being too meddlesome by stopping by today, but we were right across the street and decided to come over. We've got some news, if you're interested," Colby said.

"I'm glad to see you," Ed responded, "and of course I'm interested in anything new you have. Marge and I both were very taken with your search."

They continued to stand in the waiting room while Colby described the discovery of the telegrams from the Gaylord station master and their contents.

After Colby had finished, Ed Carey mused aloud, "Well, that seems to remove any doubt about whether he arrived in the country and got up to Michigan. But I wonder why it took him so long to get there. It took him nearly two weeks for what should have been a three-day trip. Maybe he waited here in San Francisco trying to get approved for a United States passport. In those days passports could be processed fairly quickly. Of course he would have needed both a birth certificate and somebody to verify that he was one and the same person."

"That might have been a problem for him. Who in the United States could have verified his identity?" Diane interjected.

"His father in Ashford, Michigan, maybe," Colby answered.

Ed listened and then said, "I'm going to phone the airport office and leave a message for Marge to call me. I'll tell her what you've found and of the apparent delay in Baxter's leaving San Francisco. It might help her in her search."

Just then the door opened and an older couple walked in. They appeared to be Asian and it was soon apparent that neither could speak English. Ed Carey was able, however, to communicate with them, showing why he and the Port of San Francisco office were still valuable for the service.

After a short discussion with the new couple, Ed turned to Diane and Colby and said, "These people are going to take some time. As soon as Marge learns something, one of us will call you at your hotel. I would think tomorrow afternoon at the earliest. She should find out today where the 1939 archives are stored, and tomorrow morning get a chance to start looking for a file on David Baxter."

Diane and Colby thanked Ed and left.

Wednesday morning was cold and damp as a dense fog seemed to literally roll in from the Pacific Ocean through the Golden Gate, covering the bay. It became less dense over land, but when Diane and Colby walked out of their hotel at 7:45 they could barely make out the sign for the Francisco Cafe, their breakfast destination, less than half a block away across Mason Street.

After they ordered, neither spoke for a moment, as both seemed focused on some distant image. Finally Diane interrupted the silence. "A penny for your thoughts."

"We haven't really discussed your father since we learned that he arrived in Gaylord," Colby responded. "I was just trying to figure out what might have happened from there."

"I know," Diane said. "I've been thinking about it, too. Last night I was more interested in the crabbing boats down at the wharf, or at least I didn't want to really think about David Baxter, my father. It still is strange for me to refer to anyone as my father. I spent so many years thinking that my father had been killed in the war. However, each time I learn something about him, he becomes even more elusive. Do you know what I mean?"

"Yes, I've been having the same feeling. When we discovered the letters from your mother, it felt good but it didn't help us at all. It only meant that he wasn't in Ashford when the letters came. Now we find that he actually arrived there, at least he got as far as Gaylord, but we already know that he didn't stay around Ashford long enough for anybody to remember. What happened to him? It's still a dead end."

"What do you think could have happened to him?" Diane asked.

"I think the most likely explanation is that he arrived in Ashford and learned that his father had moved to someplace else. In that case, he probably followed and might be anywhere now. It would help if we knew his father's name. You're sure that Baxter was his stepfather's name rather than his birth surname?"

"Yes, my mother was very positive about that. She had known David's parents while she and David were growing up. She had been very surprised to learn after his mother died that Mr. Baxter was not David's real father. She told me David had been unaware as well."

Their breakfast plates were placed on their table by a tall, slender blond waiter. He quickly returned with a glass coffeepot and refilled both of their cups.

They ate in silence, each seemingly lost in thought.

Colby finished before Diane and sipped coffee as he watched her spread orange marmalade on her last piece of toast. He finally said, "That is most likely what happened, but I still think about what the fires destroyed. I'm sure other people's documents were important to them, too, but this is the first time I've ever been really stymied by the lack of those courthouse records. Maybe we wouldn't have found anything about him anyway without knowing the name of his real father, but odds are there weren't that many divorces in 1919 or 1920. And we know his mother's first name, and of course, his. It's probably just a coincidence, but ever since I realized that the lack of records was blocking our search, I've had a feeling that the courthouse fires were somehow involved with David Baxter's disappearance. I know there are more rational explanations. It does seem probable that he got to Ashford and found someone who knew where his father had gone to and that he just followed on. We may never find out where that was."

Diane finished her last bite of toast, took a sip of coffee, and mused aloud, "There is no reason that I can think of to worry anymore about the steamship records, since we know now that he arrived in San Francisco. The lack of records or anyone who can remember him in Ashford is not encouraging, to say the least. It seems that our best hope is that there are some sort of immigration records. If he received an American passport, there must be some sort of information, an address at least.

"I guess we pin our hopes on Marge Poag."

"Let's go back to the hotel and wait for her call," Colby said as he reached for the bill on the table. He looked at Diane and smiled. "I guess we'll just have to find something to do with our time."

"I swear, you are about as randy as any man I've ever known," she said, smiling back.

"Are you complaining?"

"Not in the least. I encourage it."

They were actually reading, Colby the morning paper and Diane a novel, when the phone in their room rang at 11:45.

Colby answered, "Hello, this is Colby Johnson."

"This is Ed Carey." Colby could sense excitement in his voice. "Marge just called from the airport. She has found an index of an archived file for one David Baxter. It's a 1939 file so it's probably the right one. She called the manager of the archive where it's stored and the manager found it right off. Marge is going by to pick it up and will be back here by one-thirty. Can you be here by then?"

"We'll be there, and thank you."

They went back to the Francisco Cafe for lunch, not wanting to try any place new for fear that it might be slow and cause them to be late. They hardly spoke while eating hamburgers and french fries. Each seemed to be afraid to expect a real breakthrough since their previous discoveries of information about David Baxter had actually led nowhere. Their conversation avoided any speculation as to what might be contained in the old immigration file they were about to see.

After lunch they walked the block east to Union Square, where they boarded a northbound cable car. They transferred to the eastbound car at California Street, getting off at its terminus. From there it was less than two blocks to the Port of San Francisco Building. At 1:20 they were standing outside the INS office. Not being able to think of anything to do during the ten minutes remaining before their appointment, they went in, expecting to sit in the waiting room until 1:30.

Before they could sit down, Marge Poag walked into the room from the direction of Mr. Carey's office. "Hi," she said, smiling. "I thought you might be early. I know I would in your shoes. Come right on into Mr. Carey's office. He and I were just going through the file."

"Thank you," Colby replied, ushering Diane ahead of him as they followed Marge Poag around her desk and into the office where Ed Carey sat behind his desk with a manila file open before him. They could see that the file contained only three sheets of paper, two of which were forms.

"Sit down, sit down," Ed said without getting up, gesturing toward the two chairs facing his desk.

They did so and Marge walked over and sat in the same chair as before, to his left beside the desk.

Without any further pleasantries, Ed continued, "There's not too much here. His immigration record shows that he arrived in San Francisco

August 23, 1939, aboard the SS Monterey, which as I mentioned before was renamed the Matsonia and was sailing between here and Hawaii until just a few months ago. I think the ship is dry docked over in Oakland right now. He came here with an Australian passport.

"There is also a copy of his application for an American passport. It shows that he claimed to be born in Montgomery County, Michigan, on August 2, 1919, and that he had a birth certificate with him and that a photograph was taken of the certificate. The photocopy is not in the file, but that's not unusual. In those days they actually used photographic film to make copies and often the film was stored as negatives in the photo developing lab. I doubt we'll be able to find it now.

"What is a little strange from my experience with files from that era is that there is no form on which the birth certificate information has been copied. Usually all of the information from a birth certificate was typed on a form and it was attached to one's passport application."

"So there is no information about his mother and father in the file?" Diane asked.

"Actually there is," Ed answered. "On his immigration form it shows that he is the son of Donna W. Baxter and Donald M. Baxter of Sydney, Australia. In parentheses after Donald's name it says 'adopted.' It also notes his claim that he was born in the United States, but it doesn't indicate who his birth father was over here."

"It doesn't sound like the file contains anything new," Diane said, dejection obvious in her voice.

"There is one item which might be helpful. There is a note in the file showing that David could be reached at an address in Seattle."

"Seattle?" Diane and Colby said almost simultaneously as they both leaned forward in their chairs.

"Yes, Seattle, Washington. It gives a name, Jonathon Baxter, 26 South Mead Street, Seattle, Washington."

CHAPTER 19

Colby awoke to see sunlight streaming into the room on both sides of the heavy curtain covering the window of their ground floor room in the Holiday Inn. Aware of the city's reputation, he was surprised that it wasn't raining on this Friday morning, their first in Seattle.

After learning that David Baxter had intended to visit one Jonathon Baxter in Seattle, Colby and Diane had tried to find the telephone number through long distance, but were informed that there was no listing for a Jonathon Baxter in Seattle. So they decided to fly there to look for him or someone who knew him. Their plane landed at 9:15 p.m. It was 10:30 by the time they had rented a car and found a room at the Seattle–Tacoma Holiday Inn, just south of the airport on Highway 99. They were thankful they had been served dinner during the flight from San Francisco.

Before going to bed, Diane had looked in the Seattle phone book and counted sixty-two listings under "Baxter." As the long distance operator had said, none were for a Jonathon or John.

Now Colby lay awake listening contentedly to Diane's slow breathing and feeling the warmth of her body lightly touching his as she lay beside him, still very much asleep. He continued to be amazed at just how deeply he felt about her. He had never been this close to his first wife, even after seven years of marriage. He smiled, thinking of how he had already relegated Janice to first-wife status in his mind, confident now that Diane would soon be his second, and last, legal mate. Every day he was with her was like a miracle; he couldn't imagine how he had ever lived happily without her by his side.

His thoughts shifted to the day ahead. He had picked up a Seattle map at the car rental office and had already discovered that South Mead Street was only a few miles north of the airport and that it intersected with Highway 99. It looked as if it would be easy to find.

He wondered again about Jonathon Baxter. The immigration form had stated that David's adoptive father was named Donald Baxter, a statement consistent with Diane's recollection from her childhood. Who was Jonathon? They had both seemed sure that he must be related to Donald, but they had no clue as to how. Today they would try to find the answer to that question.

South Mead Street was easy to find. It was not easy to find the address of 26 South Mead Street. In fact, after they turned right on Mead from Highway 99, the first house number they were able to find was on the second block east of the highway. It was number 122. The numbers went up from there.

The first block off the highway was occupied entirely by a relatively new warehouse. It seemed clear that the house which must have been at number 26 had been razed some time since 1939 to make room for the warehouse.

"What do we do now?" Diane asked.

"Well, we've got several choices, none of which promise an easy, quick or certain solution. If Jonathon was David's grandfather by adoption, or even his uncle, it is very possible that he has died since 1939. Or he could have just moved to another place. If he owned a house here, it would appear in the real estate records at the county courthouse, although depending on the type of indexes here in Washington, it might be very difficult to find without knowing what year he purchased the property and what year he sold. And of course, he might have been just a renter.

"If he died here owning property, the court records of his probate administration would provide all kinds of information, including who his next of kin were. Again, those records would be easy to find if we knew when he died. But, of course, we don't.

"We might ask the owner of this warehouse when it was built and whether they have any of the old abstracts of title for the land. If so, that might make our search easier. The last way I can think of is to call all of the Baxters in the phone book. If he was here for a long time it is likely that some other Baxter in town is related to him or knew him."

"No easy way at that," Diane replied.

"Might as well give the easiest idea a shot," Colby said as he drove the rental car down to the highway intersection and turned right and then right again into the parking area in front of the warehouse office. The sign in front of the warehouse said "Crosley Auto Parts Distributors—Wholesale Only."

"Wait here," Colby said. "I'll be right back. It'll only take me a second to find out if there is anyone here who has the abstracts. I doubt it, really." Before Diane could respond, he was out of the car and walking toward the entrance door.

Inside, Colby was faced with two offices on either side of a short hallway with an open door at the end which led to the main warehouse. A small sign over the second door on the left said, "Customer Pick-up." The door was open.

As Colby peered in, the gray-haired man behind the desk asked, "May I help you?"

"I'm not sure," Colby answered. "I'm looking for a house at twenty-six South Mead Street, but it looks as if it's been replaced by your warehouse."

"It probably has been. When we built this place six or seven years ago, we had to tear down about a dozen old houses on Mead and on First Avenue. I was with the company at the time, but I don't remember which one was number twenty-six. Most of them had been vacant for years before we built. Was it your old family home or something?"

"No," Colby responded. "I'm trying to track down someone who lived there a number of years ago. I was hoping that your company might have the old abstracts or property title work to show who owned that property in 1939 and since."

The old man seemed to ponder for a few seconds, and then said, "I don't know for sure, but we might have something to help you. The boss, Mr. Milstep, has just retired. He started this company over on Ohio Avenue back in fifty-two and then built this building when we got too big for the Ohio place. I remember it took him a couple of years to buy all the land he needed here.

"Like I said, he's retired now, his son runs the place. We call him Junior. But every Friday afternoon at three o'clock old man Milstep personally brings the payroll checks by and hands them out. He spends the rest of the afternoon just chatting with each of us. It's pretty nice. They must have some understanding because Junior plays golf every Friday afternoon, and he's never here when his father comes by with the checks."

"Do you think Mr. Milstep would have time to talk with me if I came back while he's here?" Colby asked.

"Oh, sure. He usually brings my check last, about three-thirty. I'll tell him about you and introduce you if you can come back about then."

"I'll do it. By the way, have you ever heard of Jonathon Baxter?"

"No, I don't believe so."

Back in the rental car, a 1969 dark blue Chevrolet Impala, Colby related to Diane his conversation with the old man.

When he had finished, she asked, "What are we going to do until three-thirty? That's nearly five hours from now."

"Well, since it's Friday, we should go to the courthouse and look at probate records. Otherwise, we won't be able to until Monday. On the other hand, I've got a hunch that we'll hit pay dirt with Mr. Milstep this afternoon. Besides, we would spend most of the time today just finding out where the probate records are kept. And if we don't get anything this afternoon, we can always start calling the Baxters in the phone book tomorrow.

"So, I say we do a little sightseeing, have a nice lunch at a Seattle cafe overlooking the water, and if we've still got time, we could go back to the motel and pretend like we're honeymooners."

Diane smiled. "I like all your ideas, but not necessarily in the same order as you suggest."

They arrived back at Crosley Auto Parts a few minutes before 3:30. This time Diane accompanied Colby into the warehouse. A man was standing in the doorway under the "Customer Pick-up" sign talking to someone on the other side of the doorway. He was of medium height and looked to be in his sixties. He was wearing a light blue suit and a navy blue and yellow striped tie.

As they closed the main door behind them, the man stepped back into the hall and turned to face them. "Hello, I'm Bill Milstep. You must be the gentleman who Jerry was just telling me about."

Colby reached for Bill's outstretched hand. "Yes, I'm Colby Johnson and this is Diane Askew. Thank you for seeing us. We appreciate Jerry suggesting that we come back this afternoon to catch you."

"Good afternoon," Diane said as she too shook hands with Bill Milstep.

"Let's go into my off…, I mean my son's office." Bill directed them to the doorway across the hall from Jerry's door. "I called it mine for so long that I can't break the habit. I am finally getting used to getting up every morning without worrying about the store. That took a while, believe me. I do enjoy coming down here every Friday to give out the checks. As I grew older and started looking back, I realized that the most important thing I'd done with this business was to build a family of our employees and help provide their livelihood, as they have mine."

By then Bill had directed them to chairs facing a modest size, mahogany colored desk. He went around and sat in the high-backed chair behind the desk. The desk itself was remarkable for its orderliness. Other than the phone and a pen set, its top was completely bare.

"Can't get used to this big chair and clean desk. Bill Junior didn't like the old wooden chair I'd used for thirty years. I guess that's okay. I've got it at home and can sit in it whenever I want. How he runs this place without invoices and correspondence stacked six inches high on the desk, I'll never know, but the business is doing great. I guess he must know what he's doing." Bill grinned, showing his fatherly pride.

Colby and Diane were immediately at ease with the friendly chatter of Bill Milstep and both returned his smile.

He continued, "Jerry told me you were interested in finding someone who used to live on Mead Street where the warehouse is. He couldn't remember the name. I talked with most of the owners at one time or the other. Who was it you were looking for?"

"A Mr. Baxter," Colby replied, "Jonathon Baxter. He lived at 26 South Mead Street in 1939. We don't know much more than that."

Bill looked puzzled. "That's not a familiar name. I'm sure I would recognize the names of everybody we bought out to build this place. Baxter isn't one of them."

"How about abstracts of title?" Colby asked. "Do you have any of the old abstracts you might have used to research title for the various lots you bought?"

"I don't," Bill answered, "but our attorneys probably do. Snider and Burkett, they're downtown. I believe the lawyer who handled the land purchases was Tom Ryan, a good ole University of Michigan man like myself."

Colby laughed. "I was wondering about your tie, familiar colors. I spent 1961–64 living in the Law Quad. Did my under grad at State, though. Sort of divided loyalties at the big game each year."

"L, S & A, 1932, major in economics, minor in history," Bill replied. "Never used it professionally, or at least as a credential. But it was always useful. When I graduated it was the height of the great depression.

My uncle had a Crosley automobile dealership here in Seattle and offered me a job as his accountant. It was the only offer I had, so I came west. Other than a visit now and then, I never went back. I grew up in Saginaw.

"When my uncle died in 1948, I bought the business from his widow. When Crosley stopped making cars a few years later, all I had was a large parts inventory my uncle had accumulated, so I started selling them all over the country. Soon I was dealing in parts for all makes of cars. I kept the Crosley name. Nobody ever objected."

"I graduated from the University of Michigan Law School in 1964," Colby related. "I'm now a lawyer in a small town in northern Michigan, Ashford, about 130 miles north of Saginaw."

Diane, who had been silent since they had arrived, interposed, "You Yanks and your school ties. I think you are almost as bad as the Brits."

Bill laughed and turned to Diane. "Miss Askew, with that accent you're certainly not from Michigan. Where are you from and how do you fit in the picture? In fact, I'm not sure why you are looking for Mr. Baxter, not that I need to know for that matter. But I would like to help."

So Diane repeated her story about coming from Australia to search for David Baxter and described their reason for being in Seattle.

When she had finished, Bill looked at his watch. "It's after four on a Friday afternoon, but who knows? Stranger things have happened than finding a Seattle lawyer still in his office at this time."

He picked up the phone and dialed from memory. "Hello, is Tom Ryan still in? … He is? Tell him it's Bill Milstep calling."

Twenty seconds later, Bill continued, "Tom, do you still have the abstracts and closing files from my purchase of the property for the warehouse? … Will they be hard to get? …

"I know it's late Friday, but this is very important to me. It's for one of your fellow alums of the Michigan Law School, if that's any consolation. I'd like to come by and pick them up about five if I can. … His name's Colby Johnson, but he only graduated five years ago, so I doubt … Yeah, I'll owe you one. We actually only need one file and abstract. Just a second."

He looked up at Colby. "What was the address?"

"Twenty-six South Mead Street."

Bill repeated the address into the phone and then arranged to meet Tom Ryan in the parking garage by his office.

After hanging up he said to Colby and Diane, "My wife and I always eat out on Friday nights. Where are you staying?"

"The Holiday Inn by the airport," Colby answered.

"There is a wonderful Chinese restaurant about two blocks south of your motel on ninety-nine, it's on the right. Do you like Chinese and would you care to meet us for dinner?"

Diane responded, "We would be quite delighted. What time?"

"How about seven-thirty? I'll phone Helen and ask her to arrange for a reservation. With any luck, I'll have the information for Twenty-six South Mead with me. The restaurant's name is Leo Ping's."

Diane and Colby easily found Leo Ping's and were there a few minutes before seven-thirty. Just as they were getting out of the rental car, the gray Buick which had been parked in front of Crosley Auto Parts when they were there earlier pulled into the parking lot beside them. Bill Milstep was the driver.

Colby was standing beside the Buick's passenger door after it stopped, so he opened it just as it appeared Mrs. Milstep was preparing to.

"Why, thank you. You must be Colby. I'm Helen Milstep." She offered her hand as she stepped from the car. She was still a lovely lady at, Colby guessed, sixty, tall and thin with dark brown hair. The hair was just beginning to show some gray. Her eyes sparkled as she smiled.

"And you must be Diane. Bill has told me all about you and your search for your father. I hope he can help you, but I'm selfish. I have always been interested in Australia and I've so many questions I want to ask you."

Colby and Diane each started to reply with a greeting but were interrupted by Bill, who was coming around the car carrying a big cardboard box. "I've got all of the abstracts and copies of the deeds for the warehouse property. Tom expressed his apology for not sorting through these for number 26, but he didn't see that address on any of the deeds so he sent them all."

"Oh, that's fine," Colby said. "Somewhere in that stuff should be a plat map which will help me figure it out. I really appreciate this, Bill."

He opened the back door of the Impala and took the box from Bill. He slid the box into the back seat and closed the door. "These documents will keep until tomorrow. I want to toast our good fortune in meeting Bill, and through him, you, Helen."

They all laughed and walked toward the entrance to Leo Ping's.

The evening was, in fact, delightful for all. Diane and Helen engaged in a long conversation about Australia while Colby and Bill recounted highlights of their respective college days in Ann Arbor to each other.

Their only disagreement came when the check was delivered by the waiter. Colby insisted on paying to show his and Diane's gratitude for all Bill had done for them. Bill insisted even more ardently, explaining that he was the host and would feel bad if not allowed to treat Colby and Diane as his guests for dinner. Bill finally won the argument, but not before consenting to have dinner again on Sunday evening as Colby's guest.

After leaving the restaurant, Colby and Diane were in such good spirits that they forgot about the box in the back seat of the Impala when they reached the Holiday Inn. There was something else on their minds as they went straight to their room.

CHAPTER 20

The nephew sat on the screened porch overlooking the lake and sipped his morning coffee. He hadn't been able to sleep much lately. He, along with almost everyone in Ashford, knew that Colby Johnson and the Australian girl were out west trying to find David Baxter's trail from when he arrived in the United States, and then follow it. It wouldn't be hard to follow if they discovered who David's father was.

He thought back to that morning thirty years ago when David Baxter's letter had arrived. Oh, how he wished that he had immediately shown it to his uncle, or that he hadn't taken David hunting, or that he would have continued on to get Doc Lister right after the accident.

Why hadn't he done one or all of those things? Even if David had died from the gunshot, he would have lived long enough to tell Doc, and maybe others, that he was shot by accident. The nephew had not known one day of real peace since receiving that letter.

And now what little harmony he had managed to make for himself over the years had been shattered by the arrival of a young lady claiming to be David Baxter's daughter. His attempt to scare her off by cutting the brake line on the jeep had been clumsy and had an opposite effect to that which he had intended.

He now realized that his next step must be more decisive. This time there must be no error in judgment or execution.

He would continue to monitor their progress on the West Coast through Rose, who was keeping all of Ashford informed, apparently with Colby's blessing. He wished it would end soon, for he was finding it harder to be patient. And he was becoming more run down each day from lack of sleep.

Yes, he thought, if they discover who David Baxter was coming here to see, it won't take long for them to connect me. If they find out Uncle was David's father, I'll have to act.

Diane was still sleeping when Colby slipped out of their room to get the box of documents Bill had given them the night before. He lifted the box from the back seat of the rental car and carried it with him to the motel's coffee shop. He placed the box on a chair at an empty table and sat on an adjacent chair.

The waitress looked at the box curiously, but said nothing as she took his order for a donut and black coffee. He looked into the box.

The top file was labeled "Deeds—Milstep Purchases." He picked it up and looked inside. He saw about a dozen documents which he recognized to be warranty deeds. He shuffled through them and saw that each conveyed land to William and Helen Milstep, husband and wife.

Smart, he thought. They own the land and lease it to their business corporation. Their lawyer gave them good advice on that one.

He started looking at the grantor names, those who sold to the Milsteps. He soon verified, as Bill had told him yesterday, that none of the sellers was named Baxter.

He went through the deeds again, this time examining them more closely. Most of the grantors' addresses were either South Mead Street or 1st Avenue South; two of the deeds were neither. None listed the address of 26 South Mead Street, although one showed the grantor's address as 24 South Mead and another as 28 South Mead. He pulled those two deeds from the file and laid them on the cafe table, taking care to place them where he would not drip coffee.

He noted that all the deeds were for property in Block 2 of Smith's Addition to Seattle. He paused to sip his coffee and take a bite of the donut the waitress had placed on the table. He looked again at the two deeds he had taken from the file. One had been executed by Mr. and Mrs. Michael Kelly of 24 South Mead Street. The land description was Lot 5 of Block 2 of Smith's Addition to Seattle. The other deed had been executed by Mr. and Mrs. John Eckstein who lived at 28 South Mead Street. The land conveyed by the Ecksteins was Lot 7 of Block 2.

Colby felt a tinge of excitement. The land at 26 South Mead would be Lot 6 of Block 2, of that he was certain. He purposely paused to take another drink of his coffee and another bite of the donut. He wiped the donut glaze from his fingers with the napkin in his lap and reached for the file containing the remaining deeds.

He looked again at each deed, this time looking only at the land descriptions. The deed for Lot 6 was the last one. As he had already anticipated, the grantor of Lot 6 was one of the two not showing an address of either South Mead Street or 1st Avenue South. Those two had apparently not lived in the houses when they sold them to Bill and Helen Milstep.

The person who had sold Lot 6 to the Milsteps was Sharon B. Domke of 3520 South 198th Street, Seattle, Washington. Colby immediately wondered if the initial stood for Baxter.

He would soon know the answer, he hoped. He put the deeds back in the file folder, placing the Domke deed on top, and laid the folder on the table. He then lifted about half of the abstracts of title from the box and placed them on his knees and began sorting through them.

The abstract for Lot 6 was the third one down. He pulled it from the stack and placed it on the table and put the rest of them back in the box.

He could barely contain his anxiety as he began to look at the entries in the abstract. He knew that this was probably the moment of truth in their search for Jonathon Baxter, and perhaps for David Baxter as well. He decided to work his way from the last entry of the abstract back toward the beginning. His efforts were rewarded almost immediately. The next-to-last entry was for an Order of the Probate Court Assigning the Residue of the Estate of Jonathon S. Baxter, deceased, to his daughter, Sharon Baxter Domke.

He didn't mean to, but his reaction to the discovery included a verbal shout of some sort and he was immediately aware of the other restaurant customers staring at him. He looked around at them, smiling sheepishly, and shrugged his shoulders. He was, after all, an experienced lawyer and fully capable of masking his emotions in public.

But he definitely wanted to share the discovery with Diane right away, so he gathered the file folder of deeds from the table and placed them back in the box, put the abstract for Lot 6 on top and headed for the door. He was nearly there when he realized that he hadn't paid for his donut and coffee. His smallest bill was a five, but he was in too much of a hurry to wait for change. He placed the five under the coffee cup and rushed out, chuckling to himself as he walked again toward the door. Leaving a four-dollar tip for a coffee and donut was quite out of character for him.

Diane was just coming out of the shower, drying her hair with a towel but wearing nothing else, when he burst into the room, still carrying the box. "Colby, you scared me. I was just coming to find you, but please shut the door." And then she noticed his elation. "What has happened? Care to share it with me?"

"We've found Jonathon Baxter, or rather, his daughter. Here in Seattle, at least she was eight years ago." He sat on the bed and picked up the phone directory from the night table and begin looking through it. "Domke, Domke … here it is, Domke, Harold, 3520 South 198th Street. That's it!"

"What's it? Colby tell me what, how. Please calm down," she said with some exasperation as she began to dress.

"I found the records of the administration of the estate of Jonathon Baxter. He died in 1960. He had a daughter whose name is Sharon B. Domke, her married name presumably. There is still a telephone listing for a Harold Domke at the address she used on the deed when she sold her father's old house to Bill and Helen. Chances are Harold is her husband. Chances are even better we've found someone who knows about Jonathon, and maybe David."

"What if she's passed on or something since the deed?" Diane asked.

"Don't even think that, Diane. I know you've been disappointed before when we thought we'd found a clue, but each time we've found something it's helped us to get here. This could be the final answer."

"Oh, I know, Colby. It's just that I don't want to be disappointed anymore. Shall we call or just go there?"

"Let's settle this quickly," Colby said. He too felt some anxiety. "I'll call the number in the book and ask for Sharon Domke, or do you want to?"

"No, Colby my love, you find out."

Colby looked again in the phone book and dialed the number. The motel operator came on to say that he had to dial "9" first.

He redialed.

After the third ring, a woman answered, "Hello."

"Is this Sharon Domke?"

"This is she."

"My name is Colby Johnson, Mrs. Domke. I am with a lady named Diane Askew whose father was a man from Australia named David Baxter who we are looking for. We believe that he once came to visit your father here in Seattle. Jonathon Baxter was your father, am I right on that?"

"Oh my … oh my." Sharon Domke seemed unable to respond for a period of time which seemed to Colby like minutes, but was only a few seconds. "Yes, oh yes. I remember David very well. He was my cousin, at least by adoption. I didn't know he had children. I didn't know he was even married. Where is she?"

"We are here in Seattle, at the Holiday Inn by the airport."

"Please come here, to my house. I want so to meet David's daughter. Can you come right over? I'm not far from the airport."

"Yes, we can come right away, in a few minutes."

"Let me give you directions."

David glanced over at Diane as he prepared to turn right from the Holiday Inn parking lot on to Highway 99. She was pale and visibly shaking.

"Are you okay?" he asked.

"No, I'm not. Can we talk for a minute before we go to her house? I need just a few minutes to get used to this. It happened so fast. All of a sudden we have found someone who knows, or knew, my father. Other than my mother, I have never talked to anyone who knew him."

"I noticed a donut shop down the street the other day. I don't especially want to go back in the motel restaurant this morning. I'm afraid I made quite a scene there when I discovered the estate records for Jonathon Baxter. You'll feel better after a donut and coffee."

A few minutes later Colby and Diane were sitting at a small table in the Sea-Tac Donut Shop on the west side of Highway 99, a few blocks south of their motel. By the time she had finished the second glazed donut, Diane had stopped shaking and much of the color had returned to her face.

She smiled at Colby and said, "You're a prince. Thanks for understanding. It's been months and we've gotten nowhere. I find myself unable to imagine success at this point."

"There's no guarantee that Sharon Domke can even help us," Colby replied. "All we know is that she knew your father, and apparently liked him very much. She was ecstatic about seeing you. After all, she is legally your cousin since apparently David was adopted by his stepfather, her uncle. Let's look at it as a reunion of sorts and not expect too much else. She may never have seen David again, assuming he did come here after San Francisco. We'll just have to see. At least we will know if there's a trail to follow from Seattle."

Diane looked out the window and said, almost to herself, "Yes, this is what we came for."

The house was easy to find. It was only four blocks from the donut shop. As they drove down the driveway, they could see that it was on the small lake they had seen across the highway just before they had turned east on 200th Street.

Sharon Domke was waiting for them at the end of the driveway. "I was beginning to worry that my directions weren't right," she said to them even before the car had come to a complete stop. She then ignored Colby and walked around to the passenger door and opened it. "You must be Diane." She took Diane's hand and almost pulled her bodily from her seat, but then held her at arm's length. "Oh, I can see that you are David's daughter, even though I last saw him when he was younger than you are now. Your smile and your hair…

"Please do come in. We've so much to talk about."

They went in and sat on the deck overlooking the small lake. Sharon had made coffee and tea and had some cookies on a side tray near the three chairs she had arranged on the deck. After a minute or two of Sharon, Colby and Diane all trying to ask and answer questions simultaneously, Colby stood up and raised his hand. The two ladies stopped talking.

"Ladies of the jury, metaphorically speaking, of course. If I may suggest, a lot of Sharon's questions may be answered if Diane tells her story first, and then Diane and I can learn what Sharon knows of David afterwards. Does that sound like a reasonable plan of procedure here?" Colby said after he had their attention. He smiled and they smiled back.

"Makes sense to me," Sharon said as she nodded. "Please tell me everything, Diane."

Diane did, starting with the disclosure by her mother that David Baxter was her father and ending with the information that brought them to Seattle. She even told about Bill Milstep and his help in getting the abstracts for them.

When she finally finished, Sharon had tears in her eyes. "You mean you never saw your father?" she asked, rhetorically. "It must have been horrible growing up without knowing your father." She was gazing out over the lake. "I had such a wonderful father, and so too did David. Adopted father, I later learned, my Uncle Don."

"Tell us," Colby said softly.

"I don't quite know where to begin," she said, "but maybe you should know what I know about the Baxter family. After all, you are one of only three of us left. My son Danny, named after our grandfather Baxter, lives in Vancouver.

"David's father, Donald, and my father, Jonathon, were born and raised on a small farm in British Colombia. I believe their parents, Daniel and Claudia, had immigrated from England and were given the small farm as an incentive.

"During World War I, Donald went to fight in Europe, but my father was exempted under Canada's second son rule. Donald was two years the older. My father stayed and worked on the farm. In fact, I was born there.

"When Donald came back after the war, he tried to work on the farm with his father and brother, but he was apparently too restless. Of course, what I know I heard from my father's point of view. I only saw Uncle Donald during one brief period in my life. Anyway, Donald answered an advertisement in the Vancouver paper for work in Australia. I believe he went over in 1920.

"I think he married David's mother a year or two later. Apparently David was a couple of years old at the time, but I didn't learn that he was not Donald's birth son until 1939 when we last saw David. Donald died in 1937. My father might have known that David was adopted before then, but I don't think so.

"The first time I saw David was in 1933. Uncle Donald, who had become a successful sugar cane farmer in Australia, paid for Dad, Mom and me to go to Australia. I think the original idea was for Dad to work on Uncle Donald's farm. Their mother had died a few years before and I don't believe my father cared for his new stepmother. I also believe my mother was tired of being the second family on a small farm, especially during the Depression.

"David was fourteen and I was thirteen then. It was summer there, winter here. He was my immediate hero. He took me everywhere and let me do everything with him. I was sort of a tomboy then and we got along like two peas in a pod. Truth is, I had my first romantic urges as a young girl toward your father. Of course I had to hide them. After all, he was my first cousin."

She paused for a few seconds, looking abstractedly out over the lake. "I think I met your mother that summer, Diane. I remember another girl who was with us a lot of the time. He told me in 1939 that he was going to bring her over here after he was settled and marry her. I remembered her then as that girl, but I can't remember her name now."

"Helen," Diane interjected.

"Yes," Sharon exclaimed. "Helen, I remember now. We had such fun, the three of us. I believe you indicated that she is still alive." Diane nodded. "Wouldn't it be wonderful to see her again! I wonder if she remembers that summer?"

It was not the kind of question for which an answer was expected, and nobody gave one. After a brief pause, Sharon continued, "We didn't stay in Australia. My mother got sick on the trip over and couldn't get well. I think she had tuberculosis. Dad decided he should bring her back to British Colombia. She died in the ship's infirmary on the way back.

"When we got back, Dad was able to get a job in a cannery. He first rented and then bought the house on South Mead Street. I lived there through my high school years, but never really thought of it as home. He lived there until he died in 1960.

"After Grandfather died in 1935, Uncle Donald came back to British Colombia to settle some issues relating to the old family farm. Dad met him up there. From what I know, they had a very hard time of it dealing with their stepmother."

Colby thought of his own stepfather and their sometimes cool relationship. He noticed two canoes crossing the lake in front of them. Sharon poured more coffee into his cup. Diane's was still full.

Sharon continued, "Uncle Donald had brought David with him to British Columbia, and Dad brought him home one week when he had to report for work at the cannery, and then took him back up the next weekend.

"I don't mind telling you that it was one of the best weeks of my life. It was during summer vacation and we went all over Seattle. Wherever the street cars went, we went. We even caught the steam local down to Tacoma. Oh, how I wished then that we weren't cousins. I think he wished so, too."

She paused, her eyes glassy and unfocused as she looked out at the lake. "The last time I saw David was in September, 1939. I remember that the Germans invaded Poland while he was here. We argued over whether Hitler would stop there. I thought he would. David insisted that it was just the beginning. He was right, of course.

"I remember that David was pretty restless while he was here. He had just learned that he was adopted and was bound and determined to find his real father, or at least what had happened to him. He talked a lot about it with Dad and some with me.

"I remember being happy to learn that he wasn't really my cousin so I could openly think about him and me, you know. At the same time he was pretty emphatic about his commitment to your mother. I'm sure he didn't know she was pregnant, though.

"I remember asking him, pretending to be joking, of course, if he couldn't have two wives—you know, like the Mormons used to. He just smiled and said if he could have a second one it would be me."

Sharon paused again, and then seemed to be slightly embarrassed. "Please don't think that I was not in love with my husband. We married in 1942 just before he left for Africa to fight and had twenty-six wonderful years before he was taken by lung cancer. We have a son I wouldn't trade for anything in the world. But I still get starry eyed thinking about David Baxter. He was just … just my first love, I guess."

She seemed to have finished her story, so Colby asked, "Did David ever tell you his real father's name?"

Sharon thought for a moment before answering. "I'm sure he did, but I won't be able to remember it after all these years. It didn't mean anything to me at the time so I didn't make any effort to remember it."

"Did he leave an address where he could be reached in Michigan or the name of who he was going to look for?" asked Diane.

"Not with me that I can recall, although I don't know why I didn't ask for one. I guess I thought he would be getting in touch with me when he got there. He had promised to invite me to the wedding." Her eyes were looking into space in the general direction of the lake.

"Now that I think about it, I do recall that he was expecting something from the immigration service. Something to do with an American passport, I think. I heard him talking about it with my father, reminding him to send it on to Michigan in care of David's real father. I remember them talking about it on our way to take David to the train station. I remember that night very well. I was hoping to take the train myself sometime soon to visit him when he got established in Michigan. He took the electric train to go to Tacoma, and then east over the mountains and on to Chicago, the Milwaukee Road.

"I'm sure that David left his real father's name and address with Dad. And Dad never would have thrown that address away. He was a real stickler for keeping things like that, anything having to do with family history. My son, Danny, takes after my father that way."

CHAPTER 21

"Are you sure this is okay with you?" Colby asked.

"Quite," Diane answered, squeezing his left hand, which she held in both of hers. "But I'll be counting the hours till I'm able to join you again."

They were in the gate waiting area for the American Airlines flight from Seattle to Chicago scheduled to leave at 8:10 a.m. that Monday morning. It was 7:35.

A lot had happened since they had discovered and visited Sharon Domke. They ended up spending all of Saturday at her house and she had joined them Sunday evening at dinner with the Milsteps. Colby liked her a lot, but it was clear from the start that she and Diane were developing an extremely close relationship. Even though Sharon was nearly fifty and the same age as Diane's mother, Colby sensed that they were becoming more like the sisters that neither had in childhood.

During their discussions on Saturday, Sharon became more and more certain that her father would have saved the information about David's father in Michigan. She had removed all of her father's notes, diaries and documents from the house on South Mead Street when she had sold it to the Milsteps. The papers had filled her father's old steamer trunk. The trunk had been stored in her downstairs family room for years, where it had served as the base of a table in one of the room corners. She mentioned that her husband had not been happy that she had saved all that "junk," so she had covered the trunk with a cloth until after his death.

Her son Danny had discovered the trunk and its contents one day the previous summer while visiting. He was a graduate student of anthropology at the University of Vancouver. He had asked to take the trunk back with him so that he could examine its contents, and Sharon had consented. The trunk, still unperused, Sharon thought, was now serving as the base of a living room table in his apartment.

Danny was presently on a "dig" somewhere up in the Northwest Territory, but was expected back Thursday or Friday. Sharon did not feel comfortable going into his apartment while he was gone, no doubt fearful of what she might find that she didn't want to know about.

After much discussion, they decided that Colby would return to Michigan to take care of some matters in his law office that Rose kept reminding him of every time he called, and Diane would stay in Seattle with Sharon. They would drive to Vancouver to search through the trunk as soon as Danny returned.

That decision had been reached Saturday evening after they had finished a dinner of planked salmon at Sharon's home. She explained that she had been preparing salmon in every conceivable manner since her mother had died and her father had brought home a fish nearly every night from his job at the cannery. Colby and Diane thought it would be hard to top her "planked" recipe and told her so.

Sharon had met Colby and Diane this morning at the car rental lot, where they had transferred Diane's luggage to Sharon's automobile and returned the Impala. Now it was only minutes before Colby would be boarding a jet for the first leg of his trip back to Ashford. This would be the first time since he had met her that he would be apart from Diane for more than a few hours. He was already experiencing an uncomfortable emptiness which he knew would become even more intense when he boarded the aircraft.

"Colby and Diane." Sharon was calling them as she walked from the other side of the waiting area, where she had stood while they were saying their good-byes. "I just remembered something as I watched you two looking so forlorn. That day when we brought David to the train station, he was trying to reassure me that we would see each other again. He showed me a letter which his father had sent to his mother many years before. As I remember, he wrote about a piece of land they had bought together, or something like that. But the important thing to David was that his father said that he had put David's name on the title with his own for that land, so that if something happened to him the land would belong to David. I remember David saying, 'See I'm a landholder over here. Even if I don't find my father, I'll have that land.'"

"You saw that letter?" Colby asked. "Did it have his father's name on it?"

"I did see the letter and seem to remember somehow that it was dated sometime in the early twenties, but I wasn't looking at it very close. I was more concerned about David's leaving. Fact is, I'd totally forgotten about it until now." A crease marked her brow as she thought for a few seconds, then continued, "I think he only signed it with his first name, but I seem to remember that it was a formal name rather than a nickname, something like Ferdinand or Nicholas, something royal-sounding. But I don't think I would have remembered it when I left the train station that day, even if I had thought about it."

"Not important. We are going to find it this week in that old trunk anyway," Diane reminded them.

At that moment Colby's flight was called. "Thanks for everything, and please take good care of our girl," he said to Sharon as she turned to walk away.

"It has been and will be my pleasure. Have a safe trip, Colby."

He could feel Diane's arms tightening around his waist and he bent slightly to kiss her. "I love you so very much. I won't be content until we are together again," he whispered to her. "It won't be long."

She was trying to hold back tears as she whispered back, "I will always find my way to get back to you. Words can't express how deeply I love you. I'll be on the first plane after I find what we're looking for." She was no longer able to hold back her tears.

"We'll have to stay together always when I get back because I don't know if I can go through this again," she said with a smile through her tears.

They kissed again and then Colby turned and walked down the ramp to the airplane.

His feeling of emptiness intensified as he waited for the airplane crew to close its doors and take off. He finally forced himself to focus ahead to the time when he would be meeting Diane at the Alpena Airport, no more than a week from now, he was sure. By then they would maybe be able to put Diane's search behind them, one way or the other, and be able to focus on their own plans with each other. It was a comforting train of thought. The plane had barely lifted off the ground when he fell asleep.

He awoke and looked at his watch. He had been sleeping for almost two hours. Something was gnawing at his mind. The fact that Diane was not with him was part of it for sure, but something else was bothering him. It was there in the depths of his consciousness begging for his attention. He started thinking back to the airport, and then he remembered what Sharon had told him about the letter David had showed her. His mind told him he was getting warm.

But he couldn't think of anyone in Ashford that he had known or heard of named Ferdinand or Nicholas. Then he remembered the land title in David's name. That's what had been bothering him. David's name had been on the deed for a parcel of land in Montgomery County. For sure, then, his name would have appeared in the grantor-grantee index in the Register of Deeds office.

Colby thought about it some more and realized that the name on the deed would probably not be Baxter. He couldn't be certain, but it was unlikely that David's father knew of his adoption in Australia and change of surname.

He thought some more and began to believe that he still might be able to locate the deed by tracing through the grantee index for the time period of the early twenties. There wouldn't be many deeds to two males, one named David and the other with a royal-sounding name. It just might work.

And then it hit him like a ton of bricks. The records he had been thinking about, those which might well lead him to David Baxter, no longer existed. They had been destroyed by the courthouse fires!

Colby sat for a minute listening to the soft whine of the airplane's jet engines. It had occurred to him when he had first gone to help Diane look for some evidence of her father at the Montgomery County Courthouse, that many of the records they might have found, his birth certificate and his parents' divorce proceeding file and tax records before 1943, had been destroyed by the fires. He had wondered before if the fires were in any way connected to David Baxter.

But now the idea was taking a more viable form in his mind. The existence of a recorded deed might have been a much greater reason to destroy the public records than would have other documents. David's birth certificate and his parent's divorce file would remain unseen in old file cabinets unless someone was specifically looking for those documents. On the other hand, the deed would become evident whenever a title search was done for the sale of that land. The title to that land could never have been marketable without David, as an adult, joining in the sale. Of course there could have been a forgery, or as Colby suddenly realized, a proceeding after the fires under the Burnt Records Act where someone in possession of the property could have easily reestablished title without anyone else ever knowing that David had been a co-owner.

We now know that David did make it as far as Gaylord, Colby thought. What if someone who knew about the deed and wanted the land met David at the train station? He could think of several scenarios that might explain why David never got to Ashford, most involving foul play.

And he began to realize that if someone had caused David Baxter's disappearance, that person would have had to destroy the public records of Montgomery County in order to protect his or her secret. He shivered as this observation sank in.

"Good morning."

"Rose, what in the world are you doing here at seven in the morning?" Colby had hoped to get into the office early enough to leaf through the mail and messages before having to face anyone on his first day back, but he found Rose at her desk when he attempted to unlock the front door.

"I just figured that the stacks were too high and you would be wasting a lot of time this morning without me to guide you through the maze," Rose answered as she stepped from behind her desk to receive the hug and kiss on the cheek she expected from Colby. She was not disappointed. "I tried to put some order into this mess last night, but finally decided that being here when you arrived this morning would be the smart play. There's coffee, and I even stopped at Goldie's Bakery for some donuts."

"Well, aren't you sweet!" Colby said as he gave her a second long hug. "I knew I came home early for some good reason."

"You call being home two weeks later, early?" Rose said as she pulled away from Colby playfully and went back to her desk. "Any longer and I would have had to start a search for you. Speaking of searches, how's Diane?"

"She's fine," Colby replied as he poured coffee for himself and topped off the cup on Rose's desk. "She stayed to search through some records at a cousin's place in Vancouver. They think David Baxter left his father's name with his uncle whom he visited before leaving for Ashford in 1939. We tracked him that far.

"By the way, in one of my weaker moments I proposed to Diane."

"Well, I'll be danged," Rose responded, her face and smile reflecting her approval. "I had this feeling from the minute she walked in this office. I could tell how taken you were with each other, even though I got the feeling you and she were both trying to hide it. I never got those kind of vibes from you and Janice together, even during your early days here.

"Wow, I'm excited. This is neat. When's the wedding?"

Colby was pleased that Rose obviously approved of Diane and their relationship. "We don't have a date yet, but I think we'll probably go back to Australia, though we did think we'd ask her mother if she might want to come here instead. But don't worry, you'll be among the first to know."

They both sat for a few minutes sipping their coffee, each immersed in their own thoughts. Colby ate a donut and then picked up another.

Finally Rose broke the silence, "The stack of 'can't be delayed much longer' stuff is on your chair. I'm sorry that I didn't leave a very big space on the desk for you to work. But you should try to look at most of the rest as soon as possible. Almost all of those things require attention within a day or so. I've got my dictating pad and I'm ready to go when you are."

They worked at it for almost three hours without a break, the pile of file folders, letters and documents on Colby's desk getting smaller while the stacks on Rose's side table grew, one with dictation notes for correspondence and simple documents, another for filing, and a third of files for which Colby wanted additional information. She would be busy for a week just catching up; yet, she had expected as much.

Colby had also set aside on his desk several files which required additional research or more detailed drafting than he was willing to trust to dictation.

Finally he said to Rose, "Let's take a break. If you get the letters out to Beardsley, Jakes and Fryman and I call Attorney Lewis on the Sherwood case, I think we will have taken care of the emergencies. Is there any more coffee?"

"I'll make another pot," Rose replied as she carried the last of the papers to her desk area. "By the way, almost everyone in town has taken an interest in Diane's search. People have been stopping me on the street to ask if I've heard anything and a few have even called, some several times, to hear the latest. I hope you don't mind that I've kept everybody informed."

"No, not at all. Part of our strategy is to have as many people as possible thinking about it. Maybe someone will remember something or talk to someone who remembers David Baxter being here." Colby paused and then asked, "Out of curiosity, who's called about this?"

"Actually several have," she answered, her eyes looking upward as she sought to remember. "Edson Drew, Waldo LaBlanc and your stepfather have each called more than once. You sure must have struck a nerve with them. I think they're as anxious as Diane is to find out what happened to her father."

"Huh," Colby grunted, but otherwise didn't respond. Rose excused herself. Colby was thinking again about the fires. A lot of people still living in Ashford were here back in 1942 and 1943. He thought that probably one of them knew more about the fires than had been revealed.

His thoughts were interrupted by Rose returning with a fresh cup of coffee, which she set on his desk. "By the way, that Mrs. Simmons called again, just a couple of days ago, actually."

"Did she hang up again?" Colby asked.

"No, this time she said goodbye, but she didn't leave a message. Said she would call back."

"Did she ask for the lady from Australia again?"

"Well, this time she said she would talk to the lawyer if the lady was out. I told her you were both gone for a few days and asked if I could have one of you return her call. She said she would call again and thanked me."

Colby gazed out the window, shrugged his shoulders and went back to the files on his desk.

Rose watched him for a few seconds and then said, "Do you need anything else? I'd better get started on those letters."

She had reached his office door when Colby looked up. "Just one more thing, Rose. Did you ever try to find the police reports about the fires?"

"Yes," she replied as she turned back toward Colby. "I called the State Police Post in Alpena. They ship all of their old files to the state archives after eight years so they didn't have anything here locally. You could go to Lansing to search the archives, but they thought that the sheriff here would have copies of any reports they might have done.

"So I called the sheriff's office. Charlotte, the day dispatcher, office manager and everything else, as you know, promised to search. She could only find records dating back to 1946, when the new courthouse was finished.

"As a last resort, I called Charles Green. He was the sheriff during all of the forties. He told me that he operated out of his home after the first fire destroyed the old courthouse in 1942 until he moved to the new courthouse in '46. All of the closed files for that period were in file cabinets down in his basement. He laughed because he had apparently forgotten about them until I called. He sent Stella downstairs to make sure they were still there. I heard from someone that his arthritis has gotten so bad now that he can hardly get out of his chair.

"At any rate, he said you were welcome to stop by anytime to search through them if you'd like."

"Super," Colby exclaimed, "you have been busy. I think I'll go over to Charlie's this afternoon. Thank you for your efforts here."

Charles, or Charlie as everyone called him, Green had been the Montgomery County Sheriff for thirty-six years, finally retiring in 1966 when his arthritis had first become a problem for him. He had still been the sheriff when Colby first came to Ashford fresh out of law school. Rather than having an adversarial relationship, which Colby as a young defense and civil lawyer might have anticipated, they had quickly become friends. Charlie often stopped by Colby's office during the afternoon for a cup of coffee and a chat. Colby came to believe that Charlie viewed him as part of the future for the county and wanted to make sure he had a feeling and some knowledge about the past.

When Diane had first come to Colby, he had called Charlie about David Baxter. Charlie had never heard the name that he could recall. Now Colby was looking forward to going to his house, both to see Charlie, although he had been saddened by his arthritis during his last visit, and to search through the old files.

It took Colby most of the afternoon to determine how everything was organized and stored in the old sheriff's files. He must have climbed the stairs from the basement a dozen times to ask Charlie about the various drawer headings and file groupings. Each time they spent several minutes shooting the breeze, so to speak. Charlie had news about what had happened locally while Colby had been in San Francisco and Seattle. And of course he wanted to hear all about what they had found out west and how.

Finally Colby began to figure out the filing organization. The system was that there was no system. There were two file cabinets, each with four legal size drawers. The first contained records of everything that ended up in court. It included both speeding ticket duplicates and indictments for murder trials. The matters which went before the Justice of the Peace were interspersed with Circuit Court jury trial folders.

The only order was a chronological one: the files were arranged by date. The critical date was the day the subject matter became a proceeding in a court of law.

The second file cabinet contained files of investigations, complaints, and other matters which were never prosecuted, which never became a court case of any kind. These too appeared to be in chronological order, the pertinent date being the date the file was opened. Colby noted that none of them contained file codes or other indexing information commonly used by modern law enforcement agencies, including the present-day Montgomery County Sheriff's Department. He wondered whether the current sheriff's office organization and filing systems had been implemented before Charlie retired or after.

Once he got the hang of it, he easily found the three files for the respective fires. Charlie had already said that he could borrow them, so he extracted each carefully from the drawer and placed them in his briefcase. The third file, the one for the school's community building, was by far the largest, but it was contained in an accordion file folder and was easy to carry separately, so he did.

At the top of the basement stairway he paused to turn off the light and close the stairway door, setting his briefcase on the floor to free up a hand. He then walked into the living room and thanked Charlie for letting him look through the files and told him that he was taking three of them.

"You're welcome to use the dining room table if you want, Colby, to read the files," Charlie offered from the pillow chair he had been sitting in since Colby arrived.

"Thanks, Charlie, but I've got to run. Mother and Dennis have invited me to the lake for dinner, and I haven't even had time to unpack from my trip. I'll probably be calling you after I've gone through these files."

He was almost out the door before he remembered his brief case, which was still sitting on the floor by the basement door. He went back and picked it up, thanking Charlie again as he did so.

Later in the week he was to wish that he had taken advantage of Charlie's offer to read the files at his table, especially since Charlie could have quickly answered a question about a family relationship which it took him critical hours to discover later on.

At the very least, he was to afterward lament to himself, he should have gone through the files the next morning. As it was, he didn't get to them for three days.

That evening, as he'd promised, he drove to the lake for dinner with Dennis Mays and his mother.

CHAPTER 22

Colby returned to the office a few minutes before 5:00 p.m. Rose was in his office with a half-finished note on his legal pad when he walked in.

"Oh, I'm glad you got back before I left," she said with obvious relief. "Elmer Lewis called and asked to meet with you tomorrow morning. I told him your calendar was clear, but that you were involved in another project and might not be available. He wouldn't take 'no' for an answer. Said his client was leaving Friday for a vacation and he wants to try and settle before she goes. Unless you call him at home tonight and tell him otherwise, he'll be here at nine in the morning."

"That's okay," Colby said, recognizing for the second time in one day that he had responsibilities other than Diane's search for David Baxter. "Might as well face the music. I'll be happy to settle that one, too, if we can."

"He did say he'd bring the donuts but that we had to provide the coffee," Rose commented with a chuckle, relieved that Colby would be able to keep the appointment.

Colby grinned and then changed the subject. "Would you put this file in the safe, please?" he asked as he handed the accordion file to Rose. "There are also a couple of files in my briefcase that go in, too. For some reason I don't want to be responsible for losing them again now that I've found them. These are the sheriff's files on the three fires."

"I'll treat them carefully," Rose answered as she accepted the file from Colby.

Colby was twenty-five minutes late by the time he arrived at the house his mother shared with his stepfather on Valentine Lake. He knew that his mother valued punctuality, but by the time he had unpacked his bags from his late arrival the night before and showered and dressed, the time had just slipped away.

She didn't seem to notice his tardiness, though, as she gave him a kiss at the door. "Colby, my dear, you look like the trip was good for your health. Come on in."

He did so and shook hands with Dennis, who was standing behind her.

"Hello, Mom, hello, Dennis, nice to see you both. Thanks for inviting me."

"You go sit on the porch with Dennis. I'm going to put the potatoes in now to bake and I'll come join you. He fixed a pitcher of martinis. Is that all right, or do you want bourbon?"

"A martini is fine," he said as he followed Dennis to the screened porch overlooking the lake. He noticed that as usual his mother was ill at ease in his company when Dennis was also present. He wondered why.

Colby sat in the chair Dennis directed him to, which had the nicest view of the lake. "What a view! Do you ever tire of it, Dennis?"

"No, I never have in over forty years," Dennis answered as he handed a martini to Colby. "Well, tell me about your trip. Did you ever find any clues about this David Baxter?"

"Yes, some. We're pretty sure that he arrived in Gaylord, on September 8, 1939."

Dennis' eyebrows rose enough to be noticed by Colby. "How can you know that? I didn't know trains kept passenger lists back then."

Colby momentarily wondered how Dennis would have known David had traveled by train, but decided it was just good deduction on his part, given the available modes of travel in 1939. He explained to Dennis and his mother, who had just come from the kitchen and, he noticed, poured her own martini, about meeting Doc Egan and his discovery of the telegrams from the Gaylord station master.

"That's quite lucky for you," Dennis observed.

"Not luck, dear. Colby and Diane obviously worked quite diligently to uncover that information."

Colby replied, "Not much luck, if that's what it was. We still don't have any evidence that he ever reached Ashford."

He again sensed some friction between his host and hostess and changed the subject. "Mother and Dennis, I have some very good news. I asked Diane to marry me and she said 'yes.' I love her very much and I think she feels the same about me." He noticed that Dennis seemed to be frowning as he told them about the engagement.

His mother, however, broke into a big smile and rose to come over to his chair. "Oh Colby, I'm so very happy for you. I could see that you two were very fond of each other before you left." She leaned down and gave him a kiss on his cheek. "Congratulations."

Dennis also rose from his chair and walked over to Colby. He offered his hand and said, "Yes, congratulations," but with considerably less enthusiasm. "Do you have a date set yet?"

"No, we may go over to Australia to see her mother and might get married there. Would that bother you too much, Mother?"

"Not as long as I can go along. That would be a good way to spend some of that money you're always talking about, Dennis. What do you say, shall we go to Australia for the wedding?" Colby realized that the martini his mother was holding was not her first.

Dennis answered in a tone which belied the cold look in his eyes, "If that is what you would like, my dear." He looked at his watch and continued, "Isn't it about time the potatoes should be done?"

"Oh dear, yes," she said as she hurried back into the kitchen.

A few minutes later she called them in to sit down for dinner.

There was little conversation as they began eating. The main course was a brook trout for each of them which Dennis acknowledged catching that morning in nearby Packer Creek. "Not much sport," he said; "creek's too small. A lot like catching 'em in a barrel."

By the time dinner was finished, everyone, including Colby, was in a lighter mood. After his mother had cleared the table and brought in dessert, fresh apple pie with ice cream, Dennis asked Colby, "Why did Diane stay in Seattle?"

Between bites of apple pie and ice cream, Colby told them about how they found Jonathon Baxter's name and were finally able to track down his daughter, Sharon Domke. He explained that Jonathon had been David Baxter's uncle through the adoption of David by his stepfather, and of David's visit there in 1939.

"Sharon is pretty sure that David left his real father's name, the person he was coming to find here in Ashford, with her father. She believes the name is among a bunch of her father's papers which are in a trunk at her son's apartment. But they can't look through the trunk until later this week because her son is away on a trip.

"Diane and Sharon really hit it off and are acting just like the cousins they are. I expect they'll either find the name or not find the name by this weekend. One way or another, we hope to put this search behind us by then. We're running out of clues. If we don't find out who David Baxter's real father was and who David came to find here in Ashford, I don't know where else to look." Colby noticed that his stepfather was frowning again.

With that, his mother stood and began clearing the dessert plates. Colby offered to help with the dishes.

"You used to help me all the time when we were living in that apartment in Ypsilanti. I washed and you dried," she reminisced with a smile. "But not tonight—Dennis just bought me an automatic dish washing machine, and I love to use it. Thanks anyway."

While she carried the plates to the kitchen, Dennis said nothing. His mind, Colby thought, seemed to be dwelling on another time and place.

Finally Colby stood and said, "Dennis, I apologize for eating and running, but I'm beginning to feel the effects of what they now call 'jet lag.' Only yesterday I was in Seattle."

"Oh, sure. Glad you could come, Colby."

"Thank you for going to the effort of catching the brook trout. That's one thing you taught me, how to love catching and eating trout."

For the first time that evening Dennis smiled. "I hope you and Diane find what you're looking for."

"Thanks, Dennis."

His mother came out of the kitchen as he walked around to the front doorway and said, "You don't have to leave just when you've finished eating. That's what you used to do when you were a teenager."

"I'm sorry, Mom. I'm about to fall asleep. I'm really tired from my trip. Dinner was delicious, as usual. Thank you."

"Here," she said as she held out a pie dish wrapped in foil. "I made an extra apple pie for you. Dennis can eat the rest of the one we had tonight while I'm gone."

"I didn't know you were going away. Where to?" Colby asked.

"Your Aunt Marjorie is going into the hospital for surgery, and I said I'd come down to be with her."

"Aunt Marjorie? She was always so good to me when I was a kid. Is it anything serious?"

"She says not, but with her, who knows? I'm taking clothes for a week, just in case."

"Give her my love, please. And you drive carefully. Are you going to call Dennis when you get there?"

"Of course. And Colby, I am happy about Diane. I liked her very much when she was here."

They hugged and he turned and walked to his Wagoneer.

It was almost nine-thirty by the time Colby had finished unpacking and stowing his clothes. Most went into the dirty clothes hamper. He vowed to do the wash as soon as he was sure he would be awake long enough to put the clothes in the dryer.

He walked over to the phone and placed his hand on the receiver. A quick calculation told him that it was only six-thirty in Seattle, so he reached in his shirt pocket and extracted the number Sharon had given him, making a mental note to be sure and get it in his phone directories, here and at work. He decided to direct dial, a service only recently available in Ashford. He reasoned that Diane would be there if Sharon was.

After three rings Sharon answered, "Hello." It sounded like she had been laughing.

"Hello, Sharon. This is Colby."

"Oh, hi, Colby. We were just talking about you. You have one very fine fiancé. I love her just like I did her father."

"Have you and she been drinking?" Colby asked, already knowing the answer from the slight slur in Sharon's speech.

"Well, happy hour in Seattle starts promptly at five. It is now six-thirty. What are two lonely women supposed to do? All Diane wants to talk about is you." Sharon laughed. "I had to have a drink. Hold on, here's Diane."

"It's not true that you are all I talk about, but I might have mentioned your name once or twice." Colby was relieved that Diane's speech wasn't slurred the way Sharon's had been.

"I don't care if I am all you've talked about," he said, "because you're all I've thought about since I got on that airplane. I miss you. When are you going to get a look in that trunk?"

"I've missed you, Colby darling, so much. As soon as we go through the trunk I'm coming ho… I mean to Ashford."

"No, you had it right the first time—this is home, yours and mine. Wherever I am, that's your home for as long as you want it to be."

"Oh, Colby, I'll be there as soon as we get through with the trunk. After that, unless we find something, I'm going to call it quits on my search. I'm going to concentrate on being your wife. I've found you and Sharon, so the search has been worth it already. I may never find my father, and I'll always wonder. But I've learned a lot about him from Sharon."

"Listen, Diane, I had dinner with Mother and Dennis this evening and told them of our engagement. Mother was absolutely ecstatic. She really likes you. Not that it matters, but I never saw her get this excited about Janice, other than when the babies were born. She also said that if we decided to get married in Australia, she might come over for the wedding. Wouldn't that be grand?"

"It would indeed. I can't wait to get back there, but I might have to bring Sharon. We have had a marvelous time."

"When do you get to look in the trunk?"

"Danny called Sharon last night. He and his crew were going to start the drive home this morning and expect to arrive tomorrow evening. Sharon and I plan to be at his apartment first thing Thursday morning. She said it might take us a couple of days to get through everything."

"Diane, call me collect the minute you find anything, and then get on a flight home, and I mean home, yours and mine, here. You have both my home number and this one. Also, let me give you Mother's number. There is somebody on my home party line who sometimes leaves the receiver off the hook. It happened last winter and nobody could call here for a week, so just in case. Have you got a pen?"

"Just a second." Colby could hear her asking Sharon for something to write with. "Okay, give me her number."

"It's 785-3309."

"Okay, I've got it."

"And Diane, call me any time for any reason, collect. I love you."

"And I love you, Colby."

"I guess we'll have to end this call sometime."

"I'm afraid so."

"Oh, I almost forgot to tell you. After hearing about your father being the owner of land here from Sharon at the airport, I started thinking more and more about my hunch that your father's disappearance was related to the fires. So this afternoon I dug up the old sheriff's investigation files for all three fires that I told you about. Probably nothing there, but I'm going to go through them tomorrow or Thursday. Who knows. If there is anything in them that might be a clue, I'll know by the time you get here this weekend."

"I love you, Colby, and not just because of romance. You are truly a good person. I will be counting every minute until I get there."

"I love you too, Diane, and for all of the same reasons. Take care of yourself. Tell Sharon thanks for me. Good-bye until this weekend."

"Good-bye, my love."

After hanging up the phone, Colby sat there for several minutes, amazed at how deep his feelings of love and camaraderie were toward Diane, and how intensely he missed her, and how very much he was looking forward to meeting her at the airport in Alpena.

CHAPTER 23

On his second full day back, Colby concentrated on his office responsibilities and hardly thought about the old courthouse fire files locked in his safe. His settlement negotiations with Elmer Lewis occupied most of the morning, and during the afternoon he drafted pleadings for a half dozen files and two fairly complex lease agreements for Bud Jakes, the local oil and gasoline distributor.

It was nearly 7:00 p.m. when he finished the last pleading file, a response to a motion for summary judgment and an affidavit, which he placed on Rose's desk with a note for her to have the client sign the affidavit after it was typed.

He started to pick up the last file he had set aside the previous day but realized that he was too weary at the moment to do it justice. Besides, the deadline for the answer it required was not for another ten days and he probably should consult with the client first anyway. He made a note to Rose, asking her to set up an appointment with the client, and put the file on her desk.

He was almost out the door before he remembered the fire records. He went back and opened the safe and pulled out the files. He placed the two smaller folders again in his briefcase and carried them all to his car. He started to turn right toward his house as he exited the parking lot. He hesitated and turned left instead. He was too fatigued to cook; he would have dinner at the Ashford Hotel.

He ordered the roast pork special and was thinking to himself that a piece of Mrs. Downing's apple pie would be good for dessert. Then he remembered the pie which his mother had given him the night before and realized that it would go to waste if he didn't start eating it soon. So he resigned himself to having his dessert at home; not a bad choice either, he mused. The only problem would be that at home his constant loneliness for Diane would become more acute.

He had almost finished as much of the roast pork, dressing, mashed potatoes and corn on the cob as he could eat when he heard someone say, "I heard you were back in town. Mind if I join you?"

He turned around to see Edson Drew walking in from the lounge doorway. Colby could see that he had been drinking in the bar, probably for quite a while. "Not at all, Edson, but I'm just about ready to leave."

Edson sat down opposite Colby and offered, "May I buy you a drink?"

"No, thanks, I've got some files in the car which I'm planning to work on yet. I'm a little behind because of my trip."

"How was the trip? Did you and that Australian girl find out anything about this David Baxter character?"

Colby had not spent much time with Edson Drew during the past two years or so, and was now somewhat annoyed that he had interrupted his dinner and, worse, was asking questions in a half-intoxicated and demeaning manner. Rose had said that Edson called more than once inquiring about the David Baxter search while he and Diane had been out west. As he looked now at Edson sitting across from him, he was reminded of the first time he had seen him, at a party at his mother's house on Valentine Lake a few days after Colby had arrived in Ashford. He remembered that Claude Murphy had identified Edson as one who might have benefited from the fires and a suspect in the eyes of some.

Suddenly Colby became more interested in the conversation. "Oh, we didn't find much, but we may know soon who David Baxter was looking for when he came here."

"I thought you already knew that. Wasn't it his father?" Edson asked.

"Well, yes, but we don't know his father's name. Baxter was his stepfather's name, the man who adopted David over in Australia." Colby paused momentarily, watching Edson closely. "I'm curious, Edson. Why all the interest in our search for David Baxter? Rose told me that you called the office a couple of times to find out whether we had found any clues out west."

Edson looked down at the table and then looked up at Colby with a strange look on his face, one that Colby likened to that of a young boy who has just been caught with his hand in the cookie jar. "Everyone in Ashford is interested in this thing. It's the closest thing we've ever had to a real mystery around here in my lifetime. I'm no different than half the town." Edson sounded almost apologetic.

"Yeah, I guess you're right," Colby said. He paused and then continued, "We think we'll know the answer soon. We've discovered where we can find the name of David's father and Diane is on her way to get it right now." He had decided to stir the pot. If Edson was the arsonist, he might show his hand.

He responded by asking, "Who is she going to see?"

"I'm afraid I can't tell you that," Colby answered, wondering as he did so if it was wise to offend Edson.

Edson appeared slightly irritated, but merely shrugged his shoulders and stood up. "I hope you find what you're looking for and not something else," he said and walked away.

When he got home, Colby didn't even eat a piece of the pie his mother had sent home with him the night before. He just set the files on his dining nook table and went straight to bed. He dreamed about Edson Drew in the Memorial Day parade. Instead of a rifle, Edson was carrying a torch.

Colby awoke on Thursday morning aware that he hadn't yet opened the files which he brought from Charlie's basement. He determined to do so this morning. He filled his percolator and plugged it in, and while it perked, took a shower. Afterwards he put on an old sweatshirt and jeans and walked back into the kitchen just as the percolator produced its last perk before shutting down. He poured coffee into his favorite mug, took a sip, and then set it on the counter while he opened the refrigerator and extracted the uncut pie given to him by his mother two nights before.

He took the coffee and the generous piece of pie he had cut for himself over to the table where he put the files last night.

He decided to start with the first fire. There was not much in that folder. It contained only clippings from the Montgomery County Gazette and Alpena News about the fire and a four-page report from the state police post in Alpena. The clippings indicated that arson was originally suspected. The police report, however, did not find conclusive evidence one way or the other. It did not rule out the possibility that a chimney fire might have been the cause. There was no report from the sheriff.

It was 9:40 by the time Colby finished reading the newspaper clippings and the state police report. He called his office.

"Hello, Johnson Law Office," Rose answered.

"Hi, did you find the stuff I left?"

"Oh, hi. Yes I did. You must have worked late last night."

"Yeah. Is anybody looking for me this morning?"

"Only one call so far, Edson Drew. He said it wasn't important and that he'd call back this afternoon," Rose reported.

"If he calls again, just tell him I'll get back to him tomorrow or maybe late this afternoon. I'm at home going through these files I got from Charlie. You can call me if you need me, but please don't tell anyone else where I am—except Diane, if she calls, or my mother."

"Okay. I will need you to sign these pleadings so they can go out in today's mail. Do you want me to bring them by when I finish typing?"

"No," Colby said, "I'll come by the office later. Call me when everything is typed and proofed."

"Will do. Talk to you later." Without waiting for a reply, Rose hung up.

Colby poured another cup of coffee and carried it back over to the dining nook table. He picked up the file for the newspaper fire and began to read. There were two newspaper clippings from the Alpena News, a report from a Frankenmuth Mutual Insurance Company adjuster, a two page report from the Riley Township Volunteer Fire Chief, and several pages of notes and two pages from the daily log of the Montgomery County Sheriff. There was no report from the state police arson investigator.

He read the newspaper clippings with interest. There was no mention of suspected arson. The second clipping, dated several days after the fire, concerned the vow of Frank West, the Gazette publisher, to be back in business without delay. Colby noted with interest that the publisher had already secured a location to continue his paper, the basement of Drew's Lumber Store.

Colby could see nothing of interest in the insurance report after reading it carefully. The fire chief's report was mostly about the effort to extinguish the blaze and an assessment of the damage. It also contained a list of the volunteer firemen who responded to the fire call. All but the chief were paid two dollars each; the chief was paid five dollars. It contained one entry which seemed to indicate the chief had believed the fire was started by an overloaded coal furnace.

The notes from the sheriff indicated he had talked with the state police and that neither he nor they thought an arson investigation was necessary.

The entries in the log also appeared to be fairly routine. It was included in the file apparently because it contained an entry noting that someone called in to report the fire at 5:35 a.m. on February 28, 1943.

The first entry on the page reported that a Deputy Rock saw a strange automobile parked on Rouse Road at the driveway of the Harkness place at Valentine Lake on his way into work at 4:00 p.m. on the 27th. Apparently no one was with the car. The deputy had also noted its license number, probably, Colby reasoned, in case any thefts were reported in the area.

There were only three houses on Valentine Lake which had their access from Rouse Road. He was not familiar with the Harkness place, even though he had heard the Harkness name somewhere since he had come to Ashford. He might have read it in an abstract or old contract or something, he couldn't be sure. It didn't ring any bells in the context of Valentine Lake, though. He made a mental note to ask Dennis Mays or Charlie Green about the Harkness place when he got a chance. There was still a lot about old Ashford families which he had yet to learn, he realized.

Colby put all of the papers on the table back into the Gazette file folder and reached for the large accordion file. He knew that it was more extensive in part because a body had been found in the ruins. He also suspected that by now the sheriff, state police and everyone else were wondering if the fires were related.

This time an extensive report from the state police arson investigator as well as one from the homicide investigator were in the file. Also, Deputy Sam Rock had made a report about his questioning of persons who lived in the vicinity of the school building. It showed that the fire was discovered just after dawn on April 15, 1943, by George Stevens, who lived across from the school. There was also a report from the township fire chief similar to the one in the Gazette file folder. It noted that the fire apparently started in the area near the back entrance to the building where the body had been found.

The file also contained what appeared to be a complete copy of the April 19, 1943, edition of the Montgomery County Gazette, as well as several clippings from the Alpena News and later editions of the Gazette. Colby noted with some surprise that the Gazette was apparently back in business less than two months from the date its own building was destroyed by fire.

Colby first read the homicide report. He had known that someone died in the fire, but none of the details. The victim was one Johnny Burger, described in the report as an alcoholic, semi-vagrant individual who did odd jobs around Ashford. His current address was unknown. The report stated that until two months before he had lived in a small house trailer a mile east of Ashford. That trailer had burned and the victim at that time had told the fire chief he set fire to the trailer because he was out of fuel oil and was cold.

A partial autopsy was done which showed the victim died of asphyxiation, probably by inhaling smoke. The report concluded that the victim died in the school community building fire, a conflagration probably ignited by himself.

The arson report was detailed in that it measured charred logs to determine that the fire had burned longest in the area near the back door where the body was found. It included a detailed report about the fire at Mr. Burger's trailer house and his confession that he had set that fire himself to get warm. It pointed out that the night of April 14th had been unusually cold, in the low 20's.

It also included findings that Mr. Burger was a heavy smoker and often passed out after drinking heavily. It reported that he had been asked to leave the Ashford Hotel bar earlier that evening because he had fallen asleep at the bar and was snoring. Colby pictured the old man snoring at the bar and getting the heave-ho because of it.

The report also stated that the fire started in an area where the Register of Deeds kept stacks of loose papers which would ignite quickly. The investigator concluded that the fire had been started by Mr. Burger, either by accidentally dropping his cigarette while passed out, or, as had been the case with his trailer, by intentionally setting fire to a stack of papers because he was cold.

If it wasn't so serious, it would be funny, Colby thought as he closed the file.

He next read the two articles in the Gazette about the fire, one of which pointed out that the three fires within the previous year and a half had destroyed almost all organized records of Montgomery County's history. The article did not, however, suggest that the fires were linked in any way. He also read the other clippings in the file, none of which offered anything new.

Then, more out of curiosity than anything, he again picked up the old edition of the Gazette and started glancing at the other stories. He read one with more than idle interest; the story was about Montgomery County soldiers who had received orders for overseas and had come home for their final stateside leave before departing. He recognized three names in the story: Bud Jakes, Edson Drew and Dennis Mays. Dennis Mays left on the 5:00 a.m. train from Gaylord on April 15th, the morning of the fire, and Bud Jakes and Edson Drew were on the same train two days later.

So, he thought, Edson Drew was here at the time of the last fire. Since he made arrangements with Frank West to rent space in his retail store after the Gazette fire, he must have been in Ashford then, too. I'll ask him when I return his call.

Diane was feeling restless. She had enjoyed her time with Sharon and was growing very fond of her; she could tell the feeling was mutual. Except for her mother, she felt as close to Sharon as she had ever been to an adult who was not her lover. It had been an interesting and exciting week, but now she was ready to end her search, one way or the other, and get back to Colby.

She reflected on the past three days and realized that Sharon had done everything she could to make them entertaining and eventful. After Colby's plane left Monday, they had driven around Seattle and had even gone up in the new space needle, a tower left over from the world's fair. On Tuesday they had explored more of the eastern shore of Puget Sound, finally ending up in Tacoma at the southern end of the sound. Yesterday, Wednesday, they had driven up to Anacordes, caught the ferry to Orcas Island, walked over to the Orcas Hotel and had lunch, and then taken the afternoon ferry back to the mainland.

All in all it had been an eventful week and she had seen a lot of interesting and picturesque places which she had not previously known to exist. And Sharon's company was wonderful. Diane was completely comfortable with her and they talked and laughed together easily. But as the week dragged on, she became more and more anxious about what they would find in the old trunk. Was her grandfather's name recorded on some paper stashed away by Jonathon Baxter and now stored in Danny's apartment in Vancouver?

She was almost at the point of not caring whether they found it or not; she just wanted to get it over with and get back to Colby. When she allowed herself to think about it, she realized that she had given up hope of finding her father alive. Now it was just a matter of trying to find out what happened to him. And she understood that their chances of doing even that were not very good.

Sharon came into the room where Diane was sitting and gazing out over the small lake. "How about spaghetti tonight? I've got some good Italian wine. We'll make a feast of it."

"Sounds splendid to me," Diane replied, conscious that Sharon's appearance had caused her spirits to rise. "What time are we leaving in the morning?"

"If we leave at six, we'll have plenty of time to stop for breakfast along the way and still be at Danny's apartment before ten. If we get there any earlier, we'll probably have to shake him out of bed anyway. I'll set my alarm for five and call you. Can you get ready in an hour?"

"Without any effort at all," Diane answered.

Thursday afternoon, after stopping by his office to sign the documents Rose had typed, Colby decided to return the fire files to Charlie Green.

After being beckoned to come in by Charlie, again sitting in his living room chair, Colby brought the files in and took them downstairs and placed them in the filing cabinet where he had found them. As he was walking back up the stairs, he remembered the notation regarding the Harkness place on Valentine Lake.

As he came into the sitting room he asked Charlie, "Have you ever heard of the Harkness place on Valentine Lake? I've seen the name a couple of times in old abstracts, and I ran across an old trout fisherman a few years ago who told me about his old cabin on the East Branch, but I didn't know he had a place on Valentine Lake."

He was surprised when Charlie's response was deep laughter. "What's so funny, Charlie?"

"I can see that you don't know, but I am surprised," Charlie answered. "Frederick Harkness was Dennis Mays' uncle. The old Harkness place is where your mother and stepfather live."

Colby hadn't known.

Before he left Charlie's house, Colby made one more trip to the basement. He again pulled out the Gazette fire file and found the log entry regarding the automobile seen at the old Harkness place driveway on the night before the newspaper fire. He jotted down the car's license number which Deputy Rock had entered in the log.

"By the way," Charlie said as Colby entered the living room again, closing the basement stairway door behind him, "I'm pretty sure Dennis still owns that old cabin."

The drive to Vancouver Friday morning took almost three hours, one of which was spent just getting from Sharon's house to the highway north of Seattle. They left at 5:00 a.m. By the time they had reached the north side of Seattle, Diane had fallen asleep. She slept until she was awakened by Sharon with the news they had arrived at Danny's apartment.

"I drove straight through since you were sleeping. I'll fix breakfast for all of us here."

Their knock on the apartment door was answered after a half minute or so by a disheveled young man who had obviously been awakened by their arrival. It was Danny. After hugging her son, Sharon introduced Diane as their cousin from Australia.

An hour later, after they had all eaten a breakfast of bacon and eggs brought and prepared by Sharon, Danny excused himself to get ready for his day at the university. He had earlier helped Diane move the trunk to the middle of the small living room and had cleared his books and papers from the coffee table and room so that Diane and Sharon could spread out the contents of the trunk.

As Sharon cleaned up the breakfast dishes, Diane opened the trunk. It was completely filled with papers, account books, diaries and the like, the records of Jonathon Baxter's lifetime.

Diane took a deep breath and then removed the first handful, several account books which had been placed in the front left hand corner.

"George Johnson, please," Colby said in reply to the receptionist who answered the phone at the Secretary of State's office.

"May I tell him who's calling?"

"This is his cousin, Colby."

"One moment, please."

Colby had spent Thursday evening mulling over the implications of the car being seen at Dennis Mays' gate on the night of the newspaper office fire. It was probably of no consequence, maybe just a call of nature by someone riding by. On the other hand, he had just learned that Dennis was home on leave at about the time of the last fire, and someone at his driveway gate the night of the earlier newspaper office fire seemed to be a coincidence worth exploring.

It was also puzzling to Colby that he had never known the name of his stepfather's uncle. He had heard the name Harkness before in some context, but had never made the connection. Why had Dennis never mentioned his uncle, he wondered.

Colby's thoughts were interrupted by his cousin's voice through the phone. "Colby, how in the hell are you? I haven't heard from you in over a year. When are we going trout fishing again?"

George was the oldest son of his father's older brother, Peter, and Colby was always amazed at his cousin's gregarious personality. George had done very well in the political world of Lansing and was currently a Deputy Secretary of State and in charge of the Motor Vehicle Division, although only seven years older than Colby.

"I'm doing quite well," Colby answered. "I guess you heard about Janice and the children. I can't remember if I've talked to you since then."

"Yeah, you did, but I think it was more in passing when I called you about Father's heart attack."

"Mother told me that Uncle Peter has recovered pretty well, is that so?" Colby asked.

"Yes, he's back almost to his old self. He and I play golf out at Walnut Hills almost every Saturday during the summer. Of course, he rides a cart now. Before, we walked," George answered. "I'm sorry that I don't have a lot of time right now to chat, Colby, but I am coming up to fish in your river sometime soon and hope we can get together then. Tell me what's on your mind, or is this just a social call? We certainly need to talk more."

"No, I do have a favor I'd like to ask. Can you trace a license plate from 1943?"

There was a pause on the other end before George said, "You've come up with a doozy of a question. I really don't know. We're putting the information these days on a computer mainframe storage device, making it easier to keep and retrieve. But I have no idea as to what 1943 registration information still exits or where it would be. Is it important, Colby?"

"It might be. It might help me marry a pretty Australian girl. Would it take much for someone in your office to check to see if it's available without tearing down the Capitol?"

"You'll have to tell me about the Australian girl when I have more time to talk. Give me the plate number and I'll have someone take a look. 1943, you say?"

Colby recited the license number which Deputy Rock had noted in the sheriff's log the night of the Gazette fire. Then he and George said their good-bye's, promising to get together soon.

CHAPTER 24

Rose walked into Colby's office carrying a manila file folder thick with various documents. "Don't forget the Brandt hearing at ten-thirty. Here's the file. Is that thing ever going to be finalized?"

Colby reached for the file and answered, "I don't know. I thought this might be the last hearing, but Mack told me yesterday that he has one more motion to file. I asked him if we could delay this and consolidate the hearings, but he insisted upon going ahead today. Well, he has to drive over from Alpena each time while I walk across the street, so I really can't complain too much.

"What time is it, anyway?"

"It's nine-thirty," Rose answered. "You have plenty of time. What are you looking so down in the dumps about?"

Colby looked up at Rose and smiled sheepishly. "I didn't know it showed. I just talked with my cousin George down in Lansing. I don't think much will come out of one of my courthouse fire clues. I guess I'm really not a very good detective, but I do have an idea who may be responsible. I just can't seem to find anything to support my suspicions.

"I really would like to help Diane, and I feel more and more that the fires and her father's disappearance are related. I'm afraid she may not come up with anything in Vancouver and I know she really would like to finalize this thing before we get married. I have this premonition that we'll never get married unless she finds out what happened to David Baxter, although she says otherwise."

"Why don't you confront your suspect?" Rose asked. "Maybe you can get him to admit it. That's the way Perry Mason always does it."

Colby laughed. "Well, if Perry Mason can do it maybe I should," he said, still smiling. "Who knows, it might work. I could do that after my hearing. I'll think about it.

"In the meantime, I'd better review the file again before I have to argue the thing."

It was 11:30. Colby was pretty sure that Edson Drew was in his office. He could see Edson's car parked in front of the store just two spaces in front of his own. What he wasn't sure of was why he was about to confront Edson with respect to the fires and David Baxter.

He really didn't have very much to go on other than his intuition. He remembered that Claude Murphy had originally mentioned Edson Drew as a suspect in the fires at his stepfather's party when he first came to Ashford. Since then he had seen evidence in several abstracts of title he had reviewed that Edson had indeed been able to acquire title to land which he might not have owned prior to the fires. It looked that way, anyway, but neither Colby nor anyone else could prove it unless a former owner of one of the parcels was found or came forward.

And Edson had shown an unusual interest in the search he and Diane were conducting. Rose said he called her several times while they were out west, wanting to know if they had discovered anything. Why was Edson so curious? Colby believed that the reason given by Edson at the hotel restaurant Tuesday night was an unlikely explanation.

Also, as Colby had discovered from the old Montgomery County Gazette found in Charlie's files, Edson had been home on leave and in Ashford at the time of the last fire. Colby had also discovered that Edson did not enlist until a few days after the original courthouse fire, so he was probably here then.

Not much to go on, but enough to support Colby's suspicion. He opened his car door and walked toward the front door of Drew Lumber Company.

When Diane saw it, she almost didn't recognize it. It was an old, battered address book. The entries were in what she now recognized as Jonathon Baxter's handwriting. She first looked under "Baxter." There were several listings there, one for David's father in Australia, two others in Pennsylvania, and even one for Sharon, apparently for the period of time before she married. But none for David Baxter.

Disappointed, she paged through the remainder of the book, not really expecting to find anything helpful. She had actually turned the page before it registered; she had seen the name David in parentheses beside one of the listings.

She quickly turned back to the page and there it was. Beside the name was a notation, "(David's father)." And the address was stated as Ashford, Michigan.

"I've got it," Diane exclaimed, handing the book over to Sharon who was also sitting on the floor looking through a stack of letters addressed to Jonathon Baxter.

Sharon took the book and stared at the name Diane was pointing to. She looked away and closed her eyes. "Yes," she said, "that's the name. I didn't remember the last name, but the first name I do recall. As I mentioned, it sounds like royalty."

"Funny," Diane said as she reached for the address book, "but this name was never mentioned that I recall during the time we were inquiring of nearly everyone Colby could think of in Ashford. I should call Colby. May I use Danny's phone? I'll reverse the charges, of course."

"Of course you may," Sharon answered. "It's over by the refrigerator on the wall."

"Let's see," Diane mused. "It's daylight savings time here, but not in Michigan. Two hours difference, so they shouldn't be at lunch yet."

She dialed '0' for the operator and gave her the number of Colby's office with instructions to reverse the charges. Rose answered on the second ring. Diane started talking immediately but was interrupted by the operator asking Rose if she would accept the collect call.

Finally Diane was able to speak, barely able to mask her excitement. "Hello, Rose, how are you? Is Colby in?"

"No," Rose answered, "he's out. He went to District Court and was planning to meet with someone afterward." She didn't tell Diane that it was about her father, not wanting to build up false hopes. "Can I have him call you?"

"No, Rose. I'm in Vancouver, but Sharon and I are going to be leaving to drive back to Seattle in a few minutes. Just tell him that I found my grandfather's name and that I'll call him again from Seattle when I get there. I'm going to try to catch a flight back to Alpena tomorrow."

Edson Drew didn't have an office as such. His desk was in the far left corner as you walked in, set off by a rack of roofing and siding samples standing along the front and part of one side of his space. It afforded him some privacy for conversations, but he could see and be seen from nearly every place in the store.

He did not look up as Colby walked into the store. Only when Colby rounded the rack shingle samples did Edson appear to notice him. Edson pointed to a chair facing his desk, inviting Colby to sit. "To what do I owe this pleasure?" he asked. Colby thought he detected a hint of sarcasm in Edson's voice.

"I was in the neighborhood and thought maybe you could help me with some information," Colby answered.

"Sure, if I can." Colby continued to sense mockery in Edson's reply.

"I'm trying to find out as much as I can about the courthouse and newspaper fires," Colby began. He watched Edson's face closely as he continued, "I'm beginning to think they were in some way connected to David Baxter's disappearance."

Colby did indeed elicit a reaction as Edson nearly came out of his seat, shouting in a voice loud enough for everyone in the store to hear, "Damn it to hell, I'm sick and tired of hearing about the fires. Don't you think I know that people have been saying I'm the one that set 'em, only behind my back all the time. Let 'em say it to my face if they've got the guts." Apparently realizing that he had been shouting, Edson lowered his voice and continued, the sarcasm gone, "I wasn't even in town when the Gazette office burned. I was in Detroit on a twenty-four hour pass.

"And I never even heard of David Baxter until that Australian dame came to town. Like I told you the other night, I'm curious like everyone else in Ashford, but don't go trying to make something out of it."

After Edson had stopped, Colby sat for several seconds, saying nothing. Finally he said, "I don't remember accusing you of anything, Edson, although the thought has crossed my mind. But I really only wanted to talk to someone who was here at the time of the fires."

Edson still looked angry, but before he could respond, the phone rang. Edson picked it up and listened briefly before handing the handset across the desk to Colby. "It's for you."

It was Rose. She told Colby about the call from Diane. "Did she leave a number?" he asked.

"No, she said that she was leaving right away to drive back to Seattle—said she'd call you from there after she had purchased her ticket to fly back here. She thought maybe you could meet her at the airport if she told you when."

"Did she tell you her grandfather's name?"

"No, Colby, she didn't, and I didn't think to ask until after she hung up."

After he ended the conversation with Rose, he looked up at Edson and said, "Well, the mystery may be getting closer to being solved. Diane has found the name of her grandfather."

Edson no longer appeared angry, but his eyes were anything but warm as he asked, "Who is it?"

"I don't know yet. She didn't tell Rose, so I'll have to wait until she calls tonight to find out. I'll let you know when I hear."

"You do that," said Edson coolly.

After his meeting with Edson Drew, Colby returned immediately to his office, skipping lunch. He wanted to be there when Diane called again, even though he didn't know when to expect her call.

He had forgotten to ask Edson a couple of the questions he had earlier thought of, such as what kind of automobile he owned in 1943, and about one of the questionable land acquisitions Colby had come across. He had been taken aback by the shouting episode, and the news about Diane had further diverted his attention. But why had Edson reacted so strongly to the questions about the fires? On the other hand, he had been cool, but not visibly fazed, when informed that Diane had discovered her father's name.

Of course, Edson had tacitly admitted to being in Ashford at the time of the original courthouse fire and at the time of the last, when the school community building burned. Why didn't I ask him about his car, and maybe about the Harkness place, Colby thought.

Colby had been back at his office about five minutes when the phone rang. His initial disappointment that it was not Diane was replaced with anticipation when Rose announced that the call was from George Johnson's office in Lansing.

"This is Colby Johnson."

"Mr. Johnson, this is Evelyn White from George Johnson's office. How are you today?"

"I'm fine, thank you. And you?"

"Fine, thanks," Evelyn answered. "Mr. Johnson asked me to search for a vehicle record from 1943 for you and I have it. You are in luck because the records were slated to be destroyed soon. They are only supposed to be kept for twenty-one years, but nobody has been culling them for the past ten years, or so. At any rate, I found the card for the license number you gave Mr. Johnson, er, George. Have you got a pencil?"

"Yes, I do," Colby said, his pulse quickening.

"The automobile was registered to Edward Hausler, 1255 Ford Road, Wayne, Michigan. It was a 1937 Chevrolet Coupe. Would you like me to make a Xerox of the card and send it to you?"

"Er, yes, please," Colby said, his mind on the information. He realized that he was disappointed it hadn't belonged to Edson Drew. It was the same make and model that Deputy Rock had described in the log.

"Your address, Mr. Johnson?"

Colby gave her the address, thanked her and said good-bye.

Edward Hausler was an unfamiliar name to Colby. He knew that the automobile seen on the eve of the Gazette fire by Deputy Rock was likely to have been an unrelated event, but he had found no other clues at all in the old sheriff files. Still, at that time of the year, especially back then, why would someone from Wayne be parked at a Valentine Lake driveway on Rouse Road?

He was familiar with the city of Wayne, having grown up in Ypsilanti, practically next door. Wayne was considered a suburb of Detroit, but was only a few miles east of Ypsilanti, a city which did not consider itself a suburb.

On impulse, Colby picked up the phone and dialed information for the Detroit area. "May I help you?" an operator asked.

"The number for Edward Hausler, please, I think in Wayne," Colby replied.

After a brief pause, the operator said, "The number is 772-4171. Do you need any other numbers?"

"No, thank you very much."

Well, he thought after hanging up from the operator, I'm on a roll. He dialed '0' and instructed the long-distance operator to place a person-to-person call for Edward Hausler at the number he had just been given.

On the third ring the phone was answered by a woman.

"This is long distance, person-to-person for Edward Hausler. Is he available?" said the operator.

The woman answered, "No, he just left for work. He's on the evening shift, you know, and won't be home until late tonight."

"Would you like to leave a message, sir?" the operator asked, speaking to Colby.

"No, thank you," Colby replied and started to hang up, but changed his mind. "Operator, I would like to leave a message. Operator."

"Yes, sir, I heard you. What is the message?"

Colby gave her his office and home numbers and asked that a message be left for Edward Hausler to call, reversing the charges.

Probably a dead end anyway, he thought to himself, but it was still the only clue he had uncovered about the fires. He knew that Diane's discovery of her grandfather's name would be much more likely to lead them to a solution of David Baxter's fate, and he was beginning to have second thoughts about a connection between David and the fires.

On the other hand, he reasoned, his investigation was far from exhaustive. If he really wanted to solve the mystery of the fires, he would need to talk with everyone he could find who had been in and near Ashford when the fires had occurred. He wondered if anyone ever delved into the fires that deeply. Probably not, since apparently no one else had even examined the old sheriff files.

And was any of it related to the disappearance of David Baxter? Was he, Colby, more interested in Diane's quest to find her father, or in his own long-standing curiosity about the fires?

His reflections were interrupted by Rose appearing in his office doorway. "You have a call from Attorney Kelly from Alpena," she said. "He wants to talk to you about Edson Drew. Do you want to take it?"

Colby momentarily wondered if he had gone too far toward accusing Edson of being the arsonist this morning, but decided not. "Sure, which line?"

A rhetorical question, Colby realized, since only one of the two lines on his phone was blinking. He picked up the handset and pushed the blinking button, realizing as he did so that he couldn't recall Kelly's first name. "Hello, this is Colby Johnson."

"Colby, this is John Kelly. How are you today?"

"Fine, thanks, and you?"

"Oh, I'm doing okay for a Friday afternoon." Kelly paused and then continued, "Colby, I've been counseling Edson Drew for the past several weeks and negotiating with your prosecutor over there, Joel Henry, about the role Edson played in the fire at the old Montgomery County Courthouse in 1942."

Colby could hardly believe what he was hearing. He didn't know what to say, so he said nothing. Was the mystery going to solve itself just this easily?

Kelly kept talking. "Edson has told me of your interest in the fires and about your meeting earlier today. He wants to apologize for his behavior and he also wishes to tell you all about the fire, but he wants me present. Is that okay with you?"

"Er, sure," Colby stammered, still not fully believing what he was hearing. "When and where, John?"

"Could you come over to Alpena this afternoon? I'd be happy to come to Ashford, but I'm expecting a phone call which would be rather awkward for me to miss."

Colby too was expecting a call, but he realized that Rose could take the message. After all, he would be seeing Diane sometime tomorrow. "Yes," he answered, "I can drive over. What time?"

"Well, it's just after two now, how about three-thirty?"

Colby looked at his watch and then replied, "I can make it. Are you still in the old highway department building across from the courthouse?"

"Yes, I'm still here. Edson and I will see you at three-thirty."

After what seemed like the twentieth ring, Diane hung up. She could see Sharon standing outside the phone booth checking her watch. They only had twenty minutes before her plane was scheduled to leave. She had been able to get a flight which would get her into Alpena at nine tomorrow morning, but she had to fly from Seattle to St. Louis to New York to Detroit and then to Alpena. She could take a more direct route through Chicago, but that flight wouldn't leave until tomorrow morning and wouldn't arrive in Alpena until tomorrow evening at six. She wanted to get there, to see and be with Colby, as soon as she possibly could.

She had tried both numbers at the office and also his home telephone. No answer at any of them. She remembered one more number she could try. She searched for it in her address book and found it.

Colby arrived at John Kelly's office at 3:20 and recognized Edson Drew's car as one of four parked in the lot behind the old highway building. Once inside he was ushered directly into John Kelly's office by the middle-aged, dark-haired secretary whom he met once at a bar association picnic. He couldn't remember her name, but his impression then of an officious demeanor was reinforced by her conduct now.

John Kelly was in his chair behind the desk and Edson Drew was sitting in one of two plush chairs facing the desk. The men rose as Colby entered the office. Edson was closer and extended his hand to Colby.

"Thanks for coming over. I'm sorry for my outburst this morning,"

Edson said in greeting.

"Don't worry about it. Thank you for asking me here," Colby said to Edson and then reached across the desk and shook hands with Kelly. "Good to see you again, John."

"Same here, have a seat. Would you like coffee or anything?"

"No, thanks," answered Colby, "I'm fine."

"Colby," Kelly began, "let's get right to business. It's Friday afternoon, and as you can see by our parking lot, most of my partners have already left. I'm sure you've things to do also. The call I was expecting came a few minutes ago, so we shouldn't be interrupted. I appreciate that you could come over."

"No problem," said Colby.

Kelly nodded and continued, "Edson came to see me first about a month ago, partly because of your inquiries made on behalf of your client—an Australian lady, I believe—and partly, as he explained, because he had lived with this secret for a long time and wanted to rid his conscience of it.

"Because what happened might or might not have been considered a crime by the authorities, my first activity after Edson told me the story was to contact Joel Henry and tell him the story, not using names of course. I believe he met with Sheriff Wanika and they both decided that the crime, if any, was minor and occurred so long ago that it would be not worth pursuing. They agreed to give my client a letter of immunity in exchange for his statement which I had already proffered, without revealing his identity, of course.

"We had originally asked that the statement be kept confidential, but they refused to do that. I can see their point. The origin of that fire is too big an issue to keep from the public. Edson knows this may hurt his business, but he is willing to go ahead anyway. The statement is in this envelope," John said, as he pointed to a manila envelope on his desk.

"I just talked with Joel, and he would appreciate your taking it back to Ashford with you. He said he would track you down this evening to get it from you."

"I will be happy to do that," Colby replied. "Do I get to read it first? And did you say that we are only talking about one fire here? What about the others?"

Edson responded softly, "I only started one of the fires."

"Edson, why don't you tell Colby the story just the way you first told me"' Kelly said. "I have a copy of the report for you, Colby, but I wanted you to be able to ask Edson about anything of which you are unsure."

"Sounds fine."

Edson took a deep breath and started, "This has been bothering me ever since it happened. It was an accident, but we should have come forward and reported it at the time. After a while it became too late to do without looking real bad. And then when you and your client started asking questions, and someone told me that you thought her father's disappearance might be related to the fires, I decided I had to do it anyway. That's when I came to see Mr. Kelly.

"It was after an ice skating party, you know, down on Kuala Bay on the river. The bay ran up to right behind the old courthouse. It was a good place to skate, the snow didn't drift too much there and was easy to shovel off. There were probably about fifteen people skating early in the evening, a lot of them school kids. I was twenty-two at the time and so was Clyde Green. It was a Sunday night in January, 1942, just over a month after Pearl Harbor. We both had decided to enlist and were leaving the next week.

"Anyway, they had a big fire down on the ice, and after everyone else had gone, Clyde went back to his car and got a bottle of bourbon. We sat by the fire and drank from his bottle and talked about everything, girls, the war, where we wanted to be stationed, everything.

"But after a while it started getting cold, the wind was blowing hard out of the northeast. We decided to move up to an alcove behind the courthouse basement stairs to get out of the wind. Clyde suggested we move the fire with us."

Edson was staring out the window as he talked, almost like he was seeing the long ago events unfolding again. "There were two logs sticking out from the fire with ends that hadn't started to burn yet, so he grabbed one and I grabbed the other. We ran up the hill, still in our skates, so the fires wouldn't go out. He threw his log down in a safe enough place, but as I got close I tripped. My log sort of pushed his up against the building and they both blazed up. Next thing we knew, the old siding had started to burn.

"We shoveled snow with our hands on the fire, but it just kept burning. It only took us a few minutes to realize that we weren't going to get it out that way. We were both volunteer firemen, so we ran to his car and drove over to the fire station. We had to change out of our skates and by the time we went in and turned on the siren, we could see a glow in the sky from over by the courthouse.

"Neither one of us knew how to work the fire engine, so he wrote

'Courthouse' on the chalk board and we headed back over to the courthouse. When we got back there, the whole back side was in flames. By the time the fire engine got there, it was too late to stop it.

"Nobody asked us anything about the fire and we didn't say anything to anybody. The next Thursday we both took the bus to Bay City to enlist."

"What happened to Clyde Green?" Colby asked.

"He was killed in the war, North Africa. I never saw him after our Army training camp. He was shipped over there almost right away. I was stationed at Ft. Wayne near Detroit for almost a year before I was sent. As I told you before, Colby, I was here on leave when the school building burned, just before I was sent to England. It was eerie. Fortunately, I wasn't drinking much that night or I might not have been so sure I didn't start it too."

"That's about the whole story, isn't it Edson," Kelly asked, his desire to get started on the weekend apparent.

"Yes, sir, it is."

"Colby, is there anything you want to ask Edson?"

"Yeah. Edson, do you know anything at all about either of the other fires?"

"Well, I was here when the school burned and went to the fire to help if I could, but it was so hot nobody could get near it—tamarack logs, I heard. But other than that, I don't know any more than you do," Edson replied.

"How about Diane's father, David Baxter?" asked Colby.

"No, nothing that I haven't learned from what you two have dug up." Edson paused and then said, "But I've got the same feeling you have. I think the other two fires are related to him."

Colby thanked them both and left, taking the envelope for Joel Henry with him. As he drove he thought about the story he had just heard from Edson. He was pretty sure it was the truth.

He stopped at a gasoline station on the edge of Alpena and walked to the phone booth out front and placed a collect call to his office. Rose had not received a call from Diane, but informed Colby that she had been out of the office for about thirty minutes to file some documents at the courthouse and take the mail to the post office.

By the time he reached Ashford it was nearly five-thirty. Rose had gone. There was a message on his desk in her handwriting. It said, "That Mrs. Simmons called again, said she would call back. No call from Diane."

Colby fell asleep at just after 10:30 that evening. He had not heard from Diane nor had he been able to reach anyone at Sharon's house in Seattle even though he had tried her number every hour since 6:00 p.m. Michigan time.

He was somewhere between worried and angry; worried that something might have happened to them on the drive down from Vancouver, and angry that they didn't call because he was sure they were okay. He had his first drink of bourbon at about eight and his fourth glass was only half finished when he conked out at ten-thirty. He didn't wake up to call again at eleven as he had planned.

Throughout the evening he had reflected on the chronicle which he heard that afternoon from Edson Drew. Somehow things were more complicated now than they'd been before.

CHAPTER 25

Colby awoke with a moderate headache, which became more severe when he sat up, and soreness in his back. He was fully clothed and had been sleeping curled up on the sofa in his living room, which explained the sore back. The lights were on and he noticed the half-full glass of bourbon on the coffee table next to the sofa. That and the memory of the three before it explained the headache.

He looked at his watch, which told him it was 4:30. Diane had not called, or at least he thought he would have been awakened by the phone ringing. It was on the table at the end of the sofa next to where his head had lain.

It was too late to call Sharon's house again so he went to the kitchen and took two aspirin, turned out the living room lights and went into his bedroom and to bed.

When he again awoke, sunlight was streaming in through his bedroom window. He looked at his watch. It was 8:10. When he sat up he was relieved to find that the aspirin had worked pretty well to relieve his headache. His sore back was also only a memory.

His first thought was to call Sharon, but he realized it was only five-ten in Seattle. He decided to wait until it was at least six-thirty there. He remembered that Sharon had said she was usually up by six-thirty or seven.

He filled the percolator with water and coffee and plugged it in. While it was perking he went in and turned on the shower, adjusted the water temperature and stepped under the spray. The warm water was soothing and he could sense that his mood was becoming more upbeat as his body relaxed under the pulsating stream. He stayed in the shower a long time.

When he finally turned off the water, he could hear the phone ringing. He hurriedly stepped out on the bathroom tile floor and nearly fell as his wet foot slid until it came against the cabinet of the washbasin. As it was, he winced in pain as his toe caught the corner of the cabinet. He somehow was able to maintain his balance and rush out the door, dripping water profusely as he ran toward the phone.

He was too late. It had stopped ringing at about the same time his foot hit the washstand cabinet. By the time he picked it up, all he heard was a dial tone.

Diane heard the Detroit Metropolitan Airport public address system announce her North Central Airlines flight to Alpena as she stood at a pay phone listening to the phone ring at Colby's house. She really didn't expect an answer anyway. If he had gotten her message from yesterday, he would be on the way to Alpena to meet her at the airport. She hung up after one more ring and walked toward her gate. In a little over an hour she expected to be with Colby. The thought made her warm and tingly all over. She laughed out loud, oblivious to several people staring at her as she rushed by.

The nephew glanced at his watch and closed the Zephyr's front door. It started easily, as he knew it would. He had allowed a little extra driving time because he liked to keep the Zephyr's speed under 50 miles per hour, even on the highway. It would take him almost an hour to reach the Alpena airport.

The feeling that he had missed an important opportunity continued to pervade Colby's thoughts as he sipped his coffee and ate a second slice of toast. He was sure the phone call he didn't answer in time was from Diane, so he had immediately tried to call Sharon's house after he had dried himself from the shower. The operator was not able to get through. After his third try, he prevailed on the operator to investigate the problem and she reported to him that there were overloaded circuits along the way.

As much as he had been hoping for it to happen, he was still startled when the phone rang next to him. He practically pounced on it. "Hello," he said expectantly.

"This is the operator. I have a person-to-person collect call for Mr.

Colby Johnson from Mr. Edward Hausler. Are you Colby Johnson?"

"Yes," he answered, momentarily wondering who Edward Hausler was.

"Will you accept charges for this call from Mr. Hausler?"

He remembered. "Yes, I will."

After the operator had disconnected herself, Colby said, "Hello, Mr. Hausler. I very much appreciate your returning my call."

"No problem, Mr. Johnson. It's your dime. How can I help you?"

"I'm a lawyer in Ashford, Michigan, and I'm trying to help a client track down her father. Way back in March of 1943 a 1937 Chevrolet registered to you was seen up here. It's probably just a coincidence, but I am trying to find out what you were doing up here at that time, if I'm not being too nosy by asking."

"Mr. Johnson, I don't mind you asking because I've nothing to hide. But the truth is that I've never been to Ashford in my life. I did own a 1937 Chevrolet at that time, though."

"Are you sure you've never been here?" Colby asked. "Do you remember where you were and what you were doing in the spring of 1943?"

"Oh, I'm sure I've never been there. I know where it is because I knew another officer in the Army who came from there." There was a short pause and then Edward began again, "Wait a minute. I know how that car got up to Ashford and was seen there."

"How?" Colby asked.

"I traded cars with that guy one weekend. It was about then, too. He wanted to take a trip somewhere and needed a car that could get there and back on a ration card. His wouldn't. It was a big old luxury thing. I remember I took his car to Belle Isle that weekend. It had just opened for the spring."

"Do you remember his name?"

"No, I can't say as I do. I think it was a simple name, but I don't know as I would recognize it if I heard it. I've never been very good at remembering names, especially after time has passed."

Colby could feel his mood sinking again after feeling optimistic only seconds before, but he decided to explore Mr. Hausler's memory anyway. "Could his name have been Edson Drew?"

"No, I'm pretty sure that wasn't it."

"Are you sure he was an officer?"

"Yes, I'm very sure of that. He was one rank over me."

Colby knew that Edson Drew had not been an officer during the war. "Is there anything that you can remember about the guy?" he asked.

"Well there is one thing, not about him exactly, but about his car. It was the only one like it I've ever seen. We sure had a good time taking it to Belle Isle. I think we had seven people in it and it didn't seem too crowded. It was a Lincoln Zephyr."

Colby could not remember afterward if he had properly thanked Mr. Hausler as he hung up, but he had learned who was seen that night on Rouse Road. It was Dennis Mays. The Lincoln Zephyr was still in a garage out at his house on Valentine Lake. He had shown it to Colby several times and proudly told him that it had been purchased new by his uncle. He still drove it to town on occasion.

It made sense, too. Of course Dennis would be seen at the Harkness place on Valentine Lake; it was his home.

One thing that did puzzle Colby, though, was why his stepfather had never talked about his uncle, Frederick Harkness, in Colby's presence. Dennis had often told Colby tales about the old lumbering days, but Colby had never heard him mention his uncle's name, not once. The first he knew about Frederick Harkness was when he came across the name in that old police log and asked Charlie Green about him. He wondered if Dennis had intentionally avoided mentioning his uncle's name, and if so for what reason.

Diane clutched the arms of her seat as the Convair 570 began its descent toward the Alpena airport. She could see out her window that the sky, which had been cloudless for most of the way from Detroit, was now becoming dark and overcast. The airplane was starting to bounce quite a bit as it descended, but it was soon on the ground without incident.

Only a few seconds now, she thought as she climbed down the stairway from the airplane and walked along the tarmac toward the small terminal building. She knew she would cry as soon as Colby took her in his arms.

She walked in the doorway behind only a few of the other passengers and ahead of most and quickly scanned the crowd. Colby was not there. She looked more closely. He wasn't to be seen. Someone was calling her name. She turned toward the voice. It was not Colby; it was his stepfather, Dennis Mays.

"Diane, Diane, over here," he said loudly, waving one of his hands.

She tried not to show her disappointment as she walked toward him. "I had thought Colby would be here. You did tell him I was coming on this flight?" she asked.

"Yes, of course I did," Dennis lied. "He was very busy and asked me if I would pick you up and bring you to him."

She didn't know whether to be hurt by Colby's absence or curious about what he was doing that was so important. She said to Dennis, "I am sorry to have had to call you yesterday, but nobody answered at Colby's office or his home. I hope I am not imposing on you."

"Not at all," he said. "I'm rather glad you did."

After picking up Diane's luggage, they walked out of the terminal to the small parking lot. The sky had grown dark, and a few drops of rain began to fall. Dennis stopped beside a long, black automobile of a type which Diane had never seen before. It was very old, but elegant nevertheless.

"Is this yours?" Diane asked.

"Yes," he said. "It's a 1938 Lincoln Zephyr. My uncle bought it brand new from the Ford dealership in Ashford. There weren't very many of them made. It's a collector's item. I've kept it up and only drive it now and then, mostly for special occasions."

"It's beautiful," Diane said as Dennis opened the passenger door for her. "I'm honored that picking me up is a special occasion."

As Dennis walked around the car to the driver's side, he said aloud, but out of Diane's hearing range, "It's a special occasion, all right, very special."

Colby decided to go downtown and wait for Diane's call at his office. That way he could make some calls on his second line without tying up the phone line Diane would hopefully be calling in on. She would know that he was likely to be in his office on a Saturday morning and would try there if no one answered at his home number.

The first call was to Dennis Mays. The Saturday teller at the bank said that he was not expected and almost never came in on Saturday. There was no answer at the Mays home. Colby remembered that his mother was in Ypsilanti taking care of his aunt.

His second call was to Charlie Green. After Colby identified himself, Charlie laughed and said, "I thought I'd be hearing from you again soon. I think you might have missed your calling. You've got some bloodhound in you."

"Well, this thing gets more interesting all the time," Colby said, and then told him about his meeting with Edson Drew and John Kelly.

When he had finished, Charlie said, "Sounds like the truth to me. I always believed that the original courthouse fire might be unrelated to the newspaper and school fires because of the timing. There was more than a year between that first fire and when the Gazette burned. But after that, it was only a few months before the school building burned.

"And Edson Drew was always a hellion of sorts, played everything to the edge, but deep down I think he is basically an honest person."

"Another question, Charlie, why doesn't my stepfather ever talk about Frederick Harkness? Didn't he inherit most of what he has from his uncle, that uncle?"

"Yes, he did inherit a lot of land from Frederick, most of which he later sold. Dennis was Frederick's only living relative as far as I know. He was no one to be ashamed of. He came to these parts after World War I, as I recall. For many years he lived alone in an old cabin on the East Branch over near Sparr."

Colby interrupted, "I do know of an old cabin over by Sparr on the East Branch, but I never associated it with Dennis. I think he did say that his uncle had once lived in an old cabin in the swamp. I wonder if it's the same one. Actually, now that I think about it, I recall meeting an old fisherman once near the cabin. I think he mentioned that it had once belonged to Frederick Harkness.

"Dennis never told me his uncle's name that I can recall, then or since. Old Frederick never married?"

"I never met a wife or ever saw him with a woman. But I have heard several times that he came here with a wife who supposedly left him soon after they arrived. He was a pretty good man; I mean he built up a pretty good business by the time he died and had a reputation for being honest and fair, but he wasn't very sociable. I don't think I talked to him more than a half-dozen times in my life even though I'd been sheriff for six or eight years when he died."

"One more thing you might find interesting, Charlie, is that I found out who was in the car Deputy Rock had reported out on Rouse Road the night of the Gazette fire."

"Who was it?" Charlie asked.

"It was Dennis Mays. He had traded cars with an army buddy that weekend. Sort of explains why it was in the old Harkness place driveway, doesn't it?"

There was a long pause before Charlie said, "That's funny. Your stepfather always used to say after he got a few drinks that he was the only person in town who wasn't a suspect for setting the fires because he was out of town every time."

"That is very puzzling because your file for the school fire had a newspaper in it with a story about soldiers home on leave. Dennis was here on the day before the fire, although he was scheduled to take the early morning train from Gaylord that day. He would have been at the train station about the time the fire was discovered. The police report of the car on Rouse Road the night of the Gazette fire and the newspaper article about soldiers on leave indicate that Dennis was here at the times of both of the last two fires."

"I wonder why he would keep saying that he wasn't here," Charlie mused. "I always thought that it was his own private joke. Maybe it was something more."

By the time they reached the highway to Ashford, Diane had fallen asleep. She hadn't slept much on the airplanes because she was so focused on seeing Colby at the airport. Now that she was on the ground and being safely driven to where he was, she sensed seeing him would be anticlimactic and her exhaustion overcame her anticipation.

She was finally awakened by a truck horn. She looked out of the car window and recognized the turnoff at Big Rock Road. They had gone through Ashford and were still going west!

"Dennis, where are we going?" she asked, suddenly alarmed.

He didn't answer the question, but instead said, "I'm glad you are awake. There are some things I must tell you and show you. This was his car, you know."

"Whose car?" she asked, her alarm slowly turning to fear.

"Your grandfather's," he answered.

Colby answered the ringing phone, silently praying that it would be Diane. It wasn't, but it was the next best thing, the operator announcing that she had gotten through to his party in Seattle.

"Hello, Sharon, this is Colby."

"Hi, Colby, did Diane get there okay?"

Colby felt the bottom drop out, but he managed to answer, "I haven't heard from Diane. When did she leave?"

"She left yesterday afternoon. Had to fly all over the country, but she should have arrived at the airport in Alpena this morning, I think she said about nine. What time is it there now?"

"Just after ten," Colby answered, trying to keep his feeling of panic from being reflected in his voice. "Why didn't she call before she left?"

"She did. I guess she couldn't get through to you, so she called your mother. I think it was actually your stepfather she talked to, but he said he would let you know and that regardless, someone would be there to meet her at the airport this morning. She felt pretty sure the message would get to you. She was also going to call you this morning from Detroit."

The call while he was in the shower, Colby knew. He forced himself to ask, "Sharon, you did find David's father's name, didn't you?"

"Yes, his name was Frederick Harkness."

"That's what I was afraid of."

"Colby, is something wrong? You sound, I don't know, frightened or something. Is Diane all right? Surely if your stepfather couldn't reach you, he would have picked her up at the airport himself, wouldn't he?"

"I'm pretty sure he did, Sharon, only not because he couldn't find me. I was at home all of last evening," Colby explained, suddenly free of the panic he had been feeling moments earlier, his mind clear and functioning. He felt the way he did when one of his high school football games had finally started, or when he rose to begin his opening arguments at a trial—the panic or butterflies or whatever were gone. He knew the answers. "My stepfather was David's cousin. I think that he probably was responsible for David's disappearance."

"Oh my God," Sharon exclaimed. "And he has Diane with him now?"

"I think so. But I'm going to find them. I'll let you know as soon as I can."

"Please God hurry, Colby, and call me as soon as Diane is safe."

"I will. Good-bye."

After he hung up, Colby reached for the phone book and called the Alpena Airport number. The woman who answered confirmed that the Detroit flight had landed on time this morning, but could not verify that Diane Askew was one of the passengers. The North Central ticket agent had just left on his morning break and was not expected back for another half-hour, or so.

Certainly Diane would have called if no one had been at the airport to meet her. Colby was sure that someone had been, and that the someone was Dennis Mays.

Colby didn't own a handgun, but he did have a hunting rifle, a

30-30 Winchester carbine. He got it out of his closet, along with a box of cartridges, grabbed his binoculars off the shelf, and walked quickly out to his Wagoneer. He thought about calling Dennis' house at Valentine Lake, but then decided that it might give warning that he would be coming.

He backed out of his driveway, drove to highway M-33, and then turned north toward Valentine Lake.

"It was the only extravagant thing he ever did, buying this automobile, and maybe the electric range, but the range was really for Mrs. Simmons. This car was for himself."

Diane had not said anything for several minutes while Dennis had rambled on, partly because she was terrified and partly because she didn't want to encourage Dennis with his bizarre rambling and behavior. But the more he talked about her grandfather, the more her curiosity grew.

Finally she asked, "When you speak of my grandfather, are you talking about Frederick Harkness?"

"One and the same," answered Dennis, seemingly pleased that Diane had joined the conversation.

"How did you know him so well?"

He looked over at her with a stunned expression and said, "You didn't know? Frederick was my uncle. You and I are cousins. I'm going to give you a complete family history lesson before this day is over." He reached down and turned on the windshield wipers as the first large drops of rain splattered on the windshield.

"Did you know my father?" she asked.

"Briefly," he said as he slowed the car and turned right on the old K&P Camp Road. He drove slowly until he rounded the first curve and was out of sight from the highway and then stopped the car. Diane thought that she might have an opportunity to jump out the door until she saw that Dennis was holding a gun and pointing it at her.

"Give me your hands, please."

She did so and he grabbed both of her wrists with his right hand and then laid the gun on the dashboard over by his door. She tried to pull her wrists away, but was surprised by his strength. He reached down with his left hand and pulled two pairs of handcuffs from under his seat. He placed one pair on her wrists and locked them snugly, but not tight. With the other pair, he secured the chain of the handcuffs on her wrists to the hand strap of the car door on her side.

"I am sorry that I have to do this, cousin, but the circumstances of the first two lives I have taken, the circumstances were more accidental than intentional. What I'm going to do today I've planned very carefully and I don't want you jumping the gun by making a dash for it before I'm ready," he said as he snapped the cuff closed around the door strap. "That strap will hold, don't you worry. This baby was made in 1938, not like they make 'em today."

Diane's terror was complete, but strangely her feeling of panic subsided dramatically as she stopped thinking about the possibility of escape. She became almost calm.

Then she thought of Colby. "Please God let me see him one more time," she said softly to herself.

Dennis looked at her but said nothing.

CHAPTER 26

From the bottom of the hill behind the lake house where he had parked his jeep, Colby could see Dennis' salmon-colored Cadillac in its usual spot in front of the garage. He listened carefully but could hear nothing above the soft clatter made by the raindrops hitting the oak trees beside the driveway.

After some hesitation, he decided to leave the gun in the vehicle, at least while he tried to determine what was happening in the house. He knew that his jeep was parked in a blind spot from every room in the house except the back bedroom. Colby doubted they would be there. He walked slowly on the same line toward the house, thankful for the steady rain which muffled the sounds of his approach.

He first looked into the bedroom window, and, as he expected, saw nothing. He did notice that the door was open between the bedroom and the living room. He looked at the part of the living room that he could see through the doorway for several minutes, but neither saw nor heard anything.

He walked around to the front of the house. It looked deserted. There were no lights inside even though the day was darkened by the overcast and rain. He walked to the front door and knocked. No answer. He yelled. No answer. He tried the front door. It was locked.

Dennis had kept a spare key down in the old garage which Colby had sometimes used during the latter stages of his divorce from Janice. That was when he had moved out of his house and stayed with Dennis and his mother for a few weeks. No longer attempting to hide or be quiet, he ran down the hill and opened the back door of the old garage. He forgot about the key. The Zephyr was gone.

The nephew, Dennis Mays, had finished telling Diane the story his uncle, Frederick Harkness, had told him many years before about how he and Donna had met in France and married and had finally arrived in northern Michigan. And about how they had a son and were soon divorced because Donna wanted desperately to go back to Australia.

"This is the cabin where your father was born," he said as he stopped the Zephyr just short of the bridge. He might have also told her that it was where her father died, but he chose not to do that just yet. "We'll have to walk from here, the bridge won't take the weight of the car anymore. I'm sorry about the rain."

Diane recognized the old logs of the bridge as the place where she and Colby had rested during their day of trout fishing. The awareness caught her off guard and accentuated her pain as she realized that she might never see Colby again.

Dennis took the pistol off the dashboard, opened his door and walked around to the passenger door. "You'll have to get out as I open the door," he told her. "I'll open it slowly so you won't fall."

She did as he directed. He handed her the key and instructed her to unlock the cuff on the door handle. When she had done so, he reached over and took the key. He also clutched the open cuff, the other end of which held the short chain between the cuffs on each of her wrists, and led her across the bridge and to the cabin.

When he reached the cabin door, he placed the gun on a window ledge beside the door and reached over the window and groped until he found the key. After unlocking the door, he put the key back.

"Now that you know where the key is, you can always come here without me," he said with a smile that was somewhere between leering and maniacal.

She wondered, not for the first time, if he was insane. He had seemed lucid, and even kind, while describing how her grandmother and grandfather had married and come to this place and of David's birth. But he had kidnapped her and she felt sure that he might shoot her at any minute.

Inside the cabin he moved a chair away from the round oak table to a place next to the wall where an iron ring protruded from one of the logs, still holding the open cuff and leading Diane with his other hand. He then retrieved a short length of chain hanging from a rafter and put it through the iron ring, locking the open cuff through the links on both ends of the chain, and instructed Diane to sit in the chair.

"I have never figured out why that iron ring was built into the wall, but I've finally found a use for it," he said.

Next, he pushed the table over to where she was sitting and then placed a kerosene lamp on it close to the wall. "It's pretty dark in here, but this will help you read what I'm going to show you," he said as he lit the lamp.

He then picked up a shovel from beside the door and walked out of the cabin. She could see him as he walked past the windows around to the back of the cabin. She stood up. The length of the chain gave her some freedom of movement. She could probably push over the table, and certainly her chair and the lamp, but she couldn't think of how it would help her.

Colby found the house key, still on the nail behind the door. He took it and walked quickly toward the house. He realized that he needed help. He had wanted to 'save' Diane himself, until this moment not really thinking that she might be in real danger. But now he was not so sure and realized that he wanted her back from any possibility of danger, safe and sound by any achievable means.

He let himself into the house with the key and went directly to the telephone. On the stand was a note from Dennis to his mother. It said that he was going to the old cabin for the weekend and might not be home by the time she returned.

After reading the note, Colby picked up the handset and dialed the sheriff's office, a number he knew by heart, courtesy of a few of his clients who sometimes ended up in jail and were reached by the same number.

He recognized the voice of Charlotte Jones, the weekend dispatcher, as she said, "Montgomery County Sheriff's Department, may I help you?"

"Charlotte, this is Colby Johnson, is Bill there?"

"No, he's not."

"How about a deputy?"

"Actually I'm here all alone right now. Everybody on duty, including Bill, went to an accident scene on M-33 south. I can get him on the radio if you'd like."

"I would like that very much. Charlotte tell him it's an emergency. If he is near a phone, ask him to call me at 785-3309. If not, you call me back, but I'd really like to talk to him about this without people listening in. This may literally be a matter of life or death. I can only wait by this phone for a few minutes."

"I understand. I'll call him right now. If he can't call you within the next five minutes, I'll call you back. Better yet, you hang on until I've reached him."

Colby could hear Charlotte calling on the radio in the background. As he waited, he thought about where Dennis might have taken Diane. He kept coming back to the same conclusion. It must be the old cabin on the East Branch once owned by Frederick Harkness. He couldn't think of any other place. He hoped that it was the same one he had often seen while fishing. He then remembered his encounter with the old fisherman, Jack. That would be the place, he thought with more confidence.

His thoughts were interrupted by Charlotte's voice on the phone. "Colby, are you still there?"

"Yes."

"Bill is going to a house near the accident scene to call you as we speak, so I'll hang up."

"Thanks, Charlotte."

As he waited the two minutes before the sheriff called, Colby realized that it was helpful to them that Dennis had taken the Zephyr. It would be easily recognized and likely remembered by anyone who saw it.

He practically pounced on the phone when it rang. "Hello, Bill?"

"Yes, is this Colby? What's the emergency?"

"I'll try to tell you as briefly as I can. I believe that Dennis Mays has kidnapped Diane Askew, you know, the Australian girl who has been here looking for her father, and is holding her against her will."

"Yes, I remember Diane and the story about her father from the time you brought her in to meet me. But Dennis Mays, your own stepfather, you must be joking."

"No, I'm not joking. The person who Diane's father, David Baxter, was coming out here to see was Frederick Harkness, Dennis' uncle. Harkness was Baxter's father. Dennis would not have inherited a dime if David Baxter had been alive at the time old Frederick died, just a year or two after David would have arrived here.

"And I'm pretty sure that he met Diane at the airport this morning, himself, instead of giving me the message last night as he was asked to.

"Also, I just talked with Charlie Green this morning. Dennis lied to him about his whereabouts at the time of the last two fires. He was here both times, once in a borrowed car, we think to be secretive."

"I guess it's better to be safe than sorry," the sheriff said. "And he's your stepfather, who also happens to be the bank president. Oh, my! Where do you think they are?"

"The only place I can think of is the old Frederick Harkness cabin on the East Branch. Do you know where that is?"

"Yes, I do. Dennis took me there fishing a few times. It will take me at least a half hour to get there. Where are you now, Colby?"

"I'm at his house at Valentine Lake. I can take the old Shingle Mill Bridge Road and be there in fifteen minutes. I'll get there and probably wait for you unless I think she's in immediate danger."

"Good idea."

"Bill, I almost forgot—he's got the old Zephyr. Maybe you can ask your people to be on the lookout for it."

"Colby, it hadn't registered, but now that you mention the Zephyr, I saw it about an hour ago heading west out of Ashford. The sun was reflecting off the windshield and I couldn't see who was driving, but I could see a lady in the passenger seat, looked like she was sleeping. I thought at the time it was your mother.

"Sounds like your idea of the cabin is probably right. I'm heading that way with full sirens. See you there. And Colby, be careful."

Colby slammed down the phone without saying good-bye and ran down the driveway to the Wagoneer.

Dennis suddenly stopped talking. He had told her of meeting David at the train station in Gaylord and of having lunch. He told her about stopping at the cabin and the shooting at the beaver dam. He pleaded with her to believe it was an accident, although he told her that had he taken more decisive action after the shooting, David might have lived.

He opened the old coffee can which he had dug up behind the cabin and removed an old leather satchel. Remarkably, the papers inside were still dry and legible. David Baxter's Australian passport and a picture of her mother were on top. Dennis insisted that she read the letters from Frederick to Donna and the divorce decree under the caption of Frederick Harkness vs. Donna Harkness. She did, and also noted the birth certificate of David Alexander Harkness.

And finally he told her where David was buried, across the river under the cedar tree with the axe blade embedded in the trunk. The grave, he told her, was about three feet from the tree, fronting the axe blade. It was in a sand hill about 300 feet downstream from the bridge and about 50 feet north of the river. He told her that he once came and put flowers on the grave, about fifteen years ago, he thought.

He also told her that her father's coming here had ruined his life, but he didn't seem to acknowledge his own role in his misfortune. And then he stopped talking. She didn't say anything, either, but she wondered why he had bothered to give her such explicit directions to her father's grave.

Suddenly Dennis looked out the window. "Colby's down by the car," he half shouted as he lunged for his gun, which was on the opposite side of the table from Diane's chair. "I'm going to have to do this before I'm ready!"

Just as he turned from the table with his gun, Diane reached under the table top and lifted on her side with all of her might and energy. The table came up and toppled over on Dennis, the top edge catching him in the back just above his buttocks. The table accelerated his momentum away from Diane, causing him to fall forward. His forehead hit the top edge of the raised stone hearth in front of the fireplace, making a pop which to Diane sounded like a cracking stick.

Diane fell back, startled by a second sound, the noise of an explosion. It took her several seconds to realize that his gun had fired. After listening and hearing nothing more, she slowly raised her head to look over the table at Dennis. He was lying on his stomach, very still. She could see blood under his forehead slowly spreading on the floor.

And then she saw the fire. The kerosene lamp had gone over with the table and had smashed against the floor near where Dennis lay. Kerosene had splashed over a wide area of the floor and part of his back. Already his shirt was on fire. Flames were also shooting up the side of the stack of firewood beside the fireplace.

She had turned to run out the door before she realized that she was still chained to the wall. She screamed.

Colby was peering around the Zephyr at the old cabin, this time with the 30-30 in hand, when he heard the gun go off in the cabin. He started running. He tripped over a loose board on the bridge, but jumped up and kept running. He heard Diane scream and then shout his name. He slammed into the door which opened without resistance, sending him tumbling into the room. He saw Dennis lying on the floor and Diane huddled behind the overturned table, the wall behind her covered with flames. The cabin was already filling with smoke.

"Get down on the floor and crawl toward me," he shouted.

"I can't," she screamed. "I'm handcuffed and chained to the wall."

"Get on the floor anyway so you can breath. Where's the key?"

"It's in his pocket, but he's on fire."

Colby started crawling toward Dennis, but saw that he would be unable to get close enough to retrieve the key, even if he knew which pocket to search. He told Diane again to stay down, jumped up and bolted out the door, holding his breath until he was outside.

He could hear Diane screaming behind him in the cabin. He grabbed the pail from atop the barrel outside the door and ran toward the river. The spring was closer, but he had dropped his gun when he tripped on the bridge and picked it up as he ran back toward the burning cabin carrying the pail of water and the 30-30.

He stopped just outside the door and stripped off his shirt. He pushed it down in the pail of water and then, on his hands and knees, crawled into the cabin and toward Diane, pushing the pail and dragging the gun.

Diane had stopped screaming and had laid herself face down on the floor, as far away from the burning wall as the chain would allow. Already the smoke had filled her eyes, causing unbearable pain, and was affecting her breathing. Even worse than her physical pain was her last image of Colby running out the cabin door. Was he saving himself while she was left to die?

And then she felt him against her and the wet cloth being pressed on her face and over her nostrils and mouth. He was pulling her hands away from her body causing pain as the hot metal of the cuffs burned into her wrists. And then she heard an explosion, much louder than the first, and then another.

She realized that her hands were no longer attached to the wall. She was free. She was going to make it. But something was wrong. Where was Colby? He wasn't coming out with her.

She turned back and crawled until she came to his prone body. She clutched his belt and braced her legs against the edge of the overturned table and pulled as hard as she could. She fell backwards on the floor, but he was moving with her now. She pulled again and realized that he was helping this time.

She kept pulling and he kept coming. A minute later they were both lying on the ground a few yards from the door of the cabin, both gasping for and getting lungs full of fresh air.

"All gone now," Diane half shouted in a voice hoarse from smoke. She was staring back toward the burning cabin.

"What's gone?" Colby asked.

"The papers—the letters from old Frederick, the divorce decree, Father's birth certificate. Dennis still had the old documents my father brought from Australia. He showed them to me. But they were on the table when I pushed it over. I think those old papers were the first things to burn from the overturned lamp. They started the fire," Diane answered, the timbre of her voice more subdued.

Soon the heat from the fire, now shooting from the cabin's roof, caused them to crawl farther away. By the time they heard Sheriff Wanika's siren, they were standing, though still very much holding on to each other.

EPILOGUE

At 2:00 p.m. on the Wednesday after he died, a funeral service was held for Dennis Mays at the Ashford Congregational Church. Most of the 200 plus persons who attended thought the heavily bandaged hands and arms of his stepson and his fiancé were for burns they sustained while trying to rescue Dennis from the burning cabin.

That was the story Sheriff Wanika had told those who asked, although no official report was ever filed with regard to any of the events that occurred the day of the cabin fire. But had someone chosen to look closely, they would have been able to find some rather interesting entries in the dispatcher's log put there by Charlotte Jones in the course of her duties. It is not known if anyone has ever asked to see the dispatcher's log for that day.

Two days after the funeral, his widow entertained her son and future daughter-in-law for dinner in her house at Valentine Lake. She shared with them several documents which had been left behind by Dennis. One of them was a copy of a deed he had executed and recorded the day before his death, transferring title to the 80 acres and old cabin on the East Branch to Diane Askew, citing as its consideration: "to right a great injustice done to the grantee and her forebears."

Another was a letter to his widow apologizing for taking his own life and explaining that he had deeded the 80 acres to Diane because it was in his name alone and he could do so, and asking her to deed any remaining property that Diane might want which they jointly owned. He explained that she, not he, was the rightful heir to everything he had inherited from Uncle Frederick.

He also left a savings account passbook in Diane's name which showed a deposit entry of $75,000.00, also made the day before he died.

The last document was an affidavit signed by Dennis Mays and notarized in which he set out the relationships as he knew them among Frederick and Donna Harkness, David Baxter, a/k/a David Harkness, and on information and belief, Diane Askew.

After a very brief discussion between Diane and Colby, with Diane being the dominant party, Diane announced that she would not be requesting any further conveyances as suggested in the letter from Dennis to his widow. In fact, she said, she would refuse to accept same. It would all be in the family anyway, she explained.

Diane told them that she had been very frightened, but began to expect toward the end of her ordeal that Dennis intended to kill himself rather than her. She only lashed out at him when she thought he was going to fire at Colby. In retrospect, she believed that he was only going to shoot himself earlier than planned.

On another note, Diane announced that her mother had told her in a phone conversation the previous evening that she would prefer to come to America for the wedding if it could be timed to coincide with the memorial service planned for David Baxter's exhumed remains to be reburied in the Ashford cemetery next to his father.

She and Colby set the dates, November 5th for the memorial service and November 8th for the wedding. That left her less than a month to find a wedding dress.

The official cause of the original courthouse fire was changed as the result of Edson Drew's statement, but no official changes have ever been made with regard to the newspaper office and school building fires. After some pillow talk, Colby Johnson stopped searching for the answers.

The day before her mother was to arrive for the memorial service and wedding, Colby awoke to find Diane already up and sitting at the table in the breakfast nook. A half-filled coffee cup and one of his legal pads were on the table in front of her. She held up the pen and looked at him as he walked toward her.

"Just in time," she said. "I'm finished."

"Finished with what?" he asked.

"I've just written my family history, at least on my father's side. I couldn't sleep so I got up just after midnight. I've spent so much time lately thinking about what might have been had David reached Ashford. Every time I think of how close he was to reuniting with his father, I realize how much happiness was foreclosed for so many people by his death. Frederick never saw his son or even knew how close he came. My mother's life was ruined in many ways, and I think of how much more my childhood would have been if my father had been part of it. And even Dennis—his life must have been filled with both fear and misery.

"But mostly I've been thinking about my father lying alone out in that swamp, at some point realizing he was going to die without ever seeing his father. Every time I picture him there I can't hold back my tears.

"The letters and everything else that burned up in the cabin, they were the last of the records about him and my grandparents that existed. I read them, though, and I've written it all down, what I can remember, and everything Dennis told me, too. It's all here on this pad. Somehow it's made me feel better, just putting it on paper. I get a good sense of who I am—as if I'm part of them, even if they never knew it."

Colby looked at her, seriously for a few seconds, and then with a smile. He said, "We may want to add some more to your journal sometime, about our search for him and everything. Maybe we'll write about all of this for our children and grandchildren. It might make a good book. It could be a tribute to David and Frederick—and your mother.

"But in the meantime, I'm putting your notes in my fireproof safe. No sense in doing any of this again."

"I was there the night he was born, you know," said the gray-haired lady who had slowly shuffled, with the help of a cane, to stand beside Diane as the casket containing the bones of David Baxter was lowered into the freshly dug grave. "In fact, I helped deliver him, he was breached. Your grandmother, herself, told me what I had to do before she passed out. I was just a camp cook then, didn't know anything about babies. A wonder, after that experience, that I ever married."

Diane, not sure she had heard correctly, turned toward the woman. "Wh...what did you say?"

"His name was Harkness then, they named him David, David Harkness. I realized that it must be that same baby when I read you were from Australia. His mother took him back to Australia, left poor Frederick heart-broken. I worked for Mr. Harkness years later, after my husband died. My name is Simmons, Mrs. Simmons."

THE END

ACKNOWLEDGMENTS

I would have never begun or completed this project without the help and encouragement of my former wife, Karen Stevens, who, I am happy to say, remains a wonderful friend. Her critiques had a much greater effect on the final product than she realizes.

Karen's aunt, Marjorie Burns, was kind enough to read and edit my first draft and direct me toward a much better story. My friends, John Armstrong and Bob Fitzke were readers of early drafts whose criticisms and encouragements were important to this project. Darrell Briley and Rowena Garon helped me learn enough about Seattle and San Francisco, respectively, to describe places and events there with reasonable accuracy. And John Weber, former publisher of the Montmorency County Tribune, was my source of much information about the real courthouse fires as well as the ships that sailed between Australia and San Francisco during the 30's and 40's.

Joe, Gloria, Ben, Lana and Babe Peterson all contributed to my well-being and survival on Summer Island during the months I worked on this project.

My wife, Sarah, my father-in-law, Jon Stapleton, and my children, Joe Stevens and Kirsten Brown, have all helped and encouraged me to go forward with BURNT RECORDS.

There are many more who have added in lots of different ways to this effort. All are remembered and appreciated.